MAYDAY! MAYDAY!

The most exciting missions of rescue, interdiction and combat in the 200-year annals of the U.S. Coast Guard

Samuel A. Schreiner, Jr.

Foreword by Admiral Paul A. Yost, Jr.,
COMMANDANT, U.S. COAST GUARD

DHF

DONALD I. FINE, INC.
New York

Library of Congress Cataloging-in-Publication Data
Schreiner, Samuel Agnew.
Mayday! Mayday! : the most exciting missions of rescue,
interdiction, and combat in the 200-year annals of the U.S. Coast
Guard / by Samuel A. Schreiner.
p.   cm.
Includes index.
ISBN 1–55611–195–9
1. United States.   Coast Guard—History.   2. Coastal surveillance—
United States—History.   3. Life-saving—United States—History.
I. Title.
VG53.S47   1990
359.9'7'0973—dc20   90–55085
CIP

Manufactured in the United States of America

10 9 8 7 6 5 4 3 2 1

Designed by Irving Perkins Associates

Foreword

by Adm. PAUL A. YOST, JR.
Commandant, U.S. Coast Guard

When Mr. Sam Schreiner first told me of his plans to write a book on Coast Guard heroes, I was delighted. Although it is the nation's smallest armed service, the United States Coast Guard has had its fair share of heroes. The stories told here cover the breadth of our missions from search and rescue to protecting the environment. They also span much of our 200-year history.

The stories are true and thoroughly researched. They are recreated with a novelist's style. The U.S. Coast Guard provided historical data and interviews with service members for this book. The author's opinions are his own.

Some of these cases occurred during my watch as commandant. I remember reading official message traffic, award citations and newspaper stories. None of those accounts depicted the drama and courage involved as well as this book does. The author has certainly captured the spirit of the men and women of the U.S. Coast Guard.

SEMPER PARATUS

Contents

For Dorrie,
who went sailing with me.

Introduction

The Making of Heroes

I N the beginning was the Coast Guard. Leery of power and weary of war, the founders of the new republic called the United States of America did not have a Navy, and the Army consisted of 627 men and officers left over from the Revolution. Military emergencies, if any, could be dealt with by the militia of the uniting states. But foreign commerce was another matter. The revenue it generated through customs duties was a vital source of income for the federal government, and the nation's first secretary of the treasury, Alexander Hamilton, was not willing to see it eroded by nature or by man. In 1789, the first year of the republic, the federal government created the Lighthouse Service to maintain the beacons needed to lead vessels safely into America's ports. Although he proposed it in that same year, it wasn't until 1790 that Hamilton, with the approval of President George Washington, finally persuaded Congress to authorize a Revenue Cutter Service to build and man ten ships for the purpose of curtailing smuggling the length of the country's coast from Maine to Georgia. It wasn't until 1848 that the federal government got into the business of saving lives as well as property by establishing a chain of shore-based lifesaving stations under the Revenue Cutter Service. By 1915, all three functions were combined into today's Coast Guard.

The missions assigned to the Revenue Cutter Service were as ambiguous, difficult and begrudgingly funded as those given the Coast Guard 200 years later. Unfortunately, the smugglers of 1790 were, like too many of the drug dealers of 1990, U.S.

1

citizens. There was some small excuse for the smugglers, however; they had gotten into the habit of doing it during colonial
years when evading British taxes was considered patriotic in
many quarters. Hamilton's instructions to the first officers and
men chosen to man his revenue cutters took this circumstance
into consideration. They are worth recalling in part since they
remain the ideal for current Coast Guard behavior:

"While I recommend in the strongest terms to the respective
officers, activity, vigilance and firmness, I feel no less solicitude
that their deportment may be marked with prudence, moderation and good temper. Upon these last qualities, not less than
the former, must depend the success, usefulness and consequently continuance of the establishment in which they are
included. They cannot be insensible that there are some pre-
possessions against it, that the charge with which they are en-
trusted is a delicate one, and that it is easy by mismanagement,
to produce serious and extensive clamour, disgust and alarm.
They will always keep in mind that their countrymen are free-
men, and, as such, are impatient of everything that bears the
least mark of a domineering spirit. They will, therefore, refrain,
with the most guarded circumspection, from whatever has the
semblance of haughtiness, rudeness or insult."

From the beginning, the cutters and their crews were armed
to provide them with the means to be firm—and to make them
instantly available as a naval force in time of war, another mission that has been carried down through the years. The extent
to which the service has lived up to Hamilton's call for "prudence, moderation and good temper" has, of course, depended
upon the vagaries of human nature. This has been true too of
another problem that Hamilton foresaw when he warned his
crews to be "on guard against those sallies to which even good
and prudent men are occasionally subject." Considering the
enormous profits and temptations involved in illegal trade of all
kinds, the instances of Coast Guard corruption such as one that
came to light in Florida just days before the writing of these
words are very few. Admiral Paul Yost, the commandant, called
this latest defection from duty a case of a few "bad apples in the
barrel."

Hamilton's prescience as to the attitudes and problems his

new service would encounter was amazing. Resentment on the part of rumrunners, drug dealers and customs cheats is understandable. But when I first started to write this book, I was surprised at the feedback from some elements of the pleasure boat fraternity. They found Coast Guard inspections of their craft for required registration and safety equipment annoying and intrusive, as they surely will the new tests for boating while intoxicated. They were incensed by accounts of damage to, or seizure of, private yachts in the search for, and confiscation of, what they considered to be trifling amounts of narcotics. They delighted in tales of ineptitude and faulty seamanship on the part of young Coast Guardsmen still in training. But none of these critical "Sunday sailors"—a small minority of those I know—had yet had the kind of personal experience that first interested me in the Coast Guard. Twice during long-distance sailing races, the yacht on which I was crewing ran into difficulties and we were forced to send out the distress call, "Mayday! Mayday!" Having a white-hulled Coast Guard cutter materialize out of the night sooner than seems humanly possible creates an unforgettable moment of relief and gratitude.

These experiences led me to pay more attention to the kind of sacrifices Coast Guard people make to help "those in peril on the sea"—a peril all too often caused by inexperience, ignorance, indiscretion, inebriation. Having developed the hard way a sense of awe and respect for the forces of wind, water and weather on earth or above it, I had to hold in admiration men and women who daily wrestle with these forces on behalf of others whose only claim upon such service is a shared humanity. What the 38,000 people on active duty with the Coast Guard are doing with their lives was expressed simply at the 1990 graduation exercises of the Coast Guard Academy in New London, Connecticut. Samuel B. Skinner, Secretary of Transportation, to whose department the service has been shifted from treasury, told the class: "By your choice of profession, you have expressed your willingness to put others ahead of yourself." Bad apples there might be, but I couldn't agree more in the light of my research into the Coast Guard's history and present practices.

By both the commission it has been given and the commitment of its people, the Coast Guard is a maker of heroes rather than millionaires. After a decade of greed triumphant that has seen the flowering of the graduate school of business as the mecca for supposedly the best and brightest of our society, it is a refreshing corrective to visit New London and watch some 800 young men and women literally marching toward a career of service. It is even more reassuring to go aboard a cutter and have a young sailor without benefit of college education tell you with believable sincerity that he's where he is to "save lives by stopping drugs going in."

Coast Guard heroes are being created continuously and out of all proportion to their numbers by reason of the challenges confronting them. When I finally decided to write a book dramatizing episodes in which Coast Guardsmen displayed the courage and skill we associate with heroism, my major problem was picking a manageable few to stand for the many. It was clearly impossible to arrive at a chronological or all-inclusive selection. Instead, with the advice and aid of Admiral Yost and his staff, including Dr. Robert L. Scheina, Coast Guard historian, I opted for an eclectic collection that would give a sense of the scope of the Coast Guard's 200-year mission, demonstrate the techniques and training upon which Coast Guard personnel rely, and reflect the thoughts and feelings of these very human people in difficult situations.

While I was at work on the book, Coast Guard headquarters in Washington kept sending me briefs of their nominations for Secretary Skinner's "Way-to-Go" awards. I quote three of these as hard evidence of the exceptional acts that are being performed nearly every day by the service and as witness to the difficulties of making choices for this book:

—Case of Machinery Technician Second Class Greg Miller, crew member of the 110-foot patrol boat *Edisto* out of Crescent City, California: "On December 3, 1989, the cutter *Edisto* was returning from a search and rescue case and received a radio call of a man trapped on a jetty by a fifteen-to-eighteen-foot surf. A small boat was launched, but could not reach the jetty in the surf. MK2 (Machinery Technician Second Class) Miller dove into the cold water and swam to the jetty. He found the man on the jetty suffering from an ankle injury and hypothermia (body temperature was down to eighty-six degrees). Miller re-entered the water and towed the victim to the waiting boat. The man was later taken by ambulance to a local hospital where he recovered."

—Case of Boatswains Mate First Class Charles Bowen and Subsistence Specialist Third Class Jason Leonard, crewmen on U.S. Coast Guard cutter *Point Arena* out of Norfolk, Virginia: "On December 24, 1989, the cutter *Point Arena* responded to a distress call from the grounded sailing vessel *Struttaway* off the Little Creek, Virginia, jetties. The weather was below freezing with ten-foot seas and forty-five-knot winds. The fifty-eight-year-old man and fifty-four-year-old woman aboard the sailboat were unable to handle a towline in the heavy weather. The cutter *Point Arena* launched a small boat, but its engine failed. The small boat grounded, tossing one of its two crewmen into the icy pounding surf. After swimming ashore, BM1 Bowen and SS3 Leonard carried the man and woman ashore, where they were taken to a local hospital and treated for exposure. Two lives were saved by the efforts of BM1 Bowen, SS3 Leonard and the crew of the cutter *Point Arena.*"

—Case of Health Services Technician Second Class Tracy Wingate, member of U.S. Coast Guard Air Station at Houston, Texas: "On January 6, 1990, an air station Houston HH-65 Dolphin helicopter responded to a distress call from the fishing vessel *Joanne B*. The master had suffered a severe head injury. The Coast Guard helicopter flew a hundred miles offshore in rain and low visibility to the vessel. HS2 Wingate, the duty corpsman, was lowered by rescue basket. He applied first aid to stabilize the victim. It took forty-five minutes to strap the victim into a back board and maneuver him from his bunk out on deck. The master and Petty Officer Wingate were hoisted into the helicopter. The helo was low on fuel and flew to an oil rig to refuel. Petty Officer Wingate continued to treat the victim, who was disoriented and had rising blood pressure (a bad sign for a head injury). The victim was flown ashore and taken to a local hospital, where he was found to be in critical condition. Petty Officer Wingate's actions saved the life of the *Joanne B*'s master."

Undoubtedly, each of these incidents involved as much fear

and pain—and as much gratification in the outcome—as any of those more fully developed in this book. But it would take a work of encyclopedic dimensions to give due credit to all hands. For instance, it may seem that too little attention is being paid to the Coast Guard's wartime services in view of the fact that they have been made part of the Navy in every conflict in the nation's history. Because of this circumstance, the experiences and even the records of Coast Guardsmen have been merged and blended with those of people in all of the other services. The effort here has been to concentrate on the distinctive nature of Coast Guard service, and the few wartime episodes were picked for the way they seem to reflect the Coast Guard's special skills and mission. Although it has become part of Navy rather than Coast Guard history, no book about Coast Guard heroism would be complete without reporting on the feat of Signalman First Class Douglas Albert Munro, USCG, the service's only Congressional Medal of Honor winner.

In the fierce battles of World War II such as those that raged on Pacific beaches where U.S. Marines stormed heavily fortified Japanese positions, people weren't often seen standing around taking notes. Stories were reconstructed from debriefings of participants and often passed along in bare-bones form. There isn't much in the archives about Douglas Munro except that he was born in Vancouver, British Columbia, Canada, on October 11, 1919, attended high school in Cle Elum, Washington, and finished freshman year at Central Washington College of Education before enlisting in the Coast Guard on September 18, 1939. The rest is contained in the citation that went along with his medal: "For extraordinary heroism and conspicuous gallantry in action above and beyond the call of duty as petty officer in charge of a group of twenty-four Higgins boats, engaged in the evacuation of a battalion of Marines trapped by enemy Japanese forces at Point Cruz, Guadalcanal, on 27 September 1942. After making preliminary plans for the evacuation of nearly 500 beleaguered Marines, Munro, under constant strafing by enemy machine guns on the island, and at great risk of his life, daringly led five of his small craft toward the shore. As he closed the beach, he signaled the others to land, and then in order to draw the enemy's fire and protect the heavily loaded boats, he valiantly placed his craft with its two small guns as a shield between the beachhead and the Japanese. When the perilous task of evacuation was nearly completed, Munro was instantly killed by enemy fire, but his crew, two of whom were wounded, carried on until the last boat had loaded and cleared the beach. By his outstanding leadership, expert planning and dauntless devotion to duty, he and his courageous comrades undoubtedly saved the lives of many who otherwise would have perished. He gallantly gave his life for his country."

In light of the nature of the Coast Guard's long service, it is exasperating to read through the correspondence between the otherwise farsighted Hamilton and his customs collectors, who were charged with supervising the construction and manning of the first ten cutters. Almost all of it consisted of complaints by Hamilton about overruns on the budgeted $1,000 per vessel and the stipends he deemed adequate for the crews. This quibbling over costs turned out to be as persistent a theme throughout the Coast Guard's history as Hamilton's call for firmness and courtesy. The Coast Guard, shunted from Treasury to Navy to Treasury to Transportation, has ever had to beg for funds. At the 1990 academy graduation, Secretary Skinner felt obliged to go out of his way to assure cadets that, despite defense cuts brought on by the apparent outbreak of international peace, the Coast Guard's civilian service would justify a 1991 budget that "we can live with."

My conclusion is that the Coast Guard will go on living, whatever the budget. Perhaps budget battles toughen the spirit. In any case, survival under difficult circumstances is the essence of the Coast Guard's mission. The truth is that the nation needs the Coast Guard today as never before. There are now more than fifty million boaters—a quarter of the population—who venture out on the water in 16.4 million boats, and all of these are in need of Coast Guard discipline and protection. Water pollution from spills of oil and other hazardous wastes have become increasingly frequent and devastating occurrences in our technologically advanced society, and the Coast Guard stands as the first line of defense against these calamities. Regardless of relations between nations, there is a deadly war in progress—the war against drugs—in which the

Coast Guard plays an essential role. If in the past, the Coast Guard's heroes have too often been unsung, the future promises a different kind of history for this unique and useful body of men and women.

—Samuel A. Schreiner, Jr.
Darien, Connecticut
May 28, 1990

Chapter 1

The *Eagle* Flies

HE shipyards of America were busy places in the late 1790s. As a neutral, the very young United States was caught in the middle of war between the revolutionary republic of France and the monarchy of England. Both of these powers preyed upon neutral commerce on the high seas, and the U.S. merchant fleet was losing ships, men and revenue at an alarming rate. Despite a sharp division in American public sentiment between Jeffersonian Republicans who favored France and Hamiltonian Federalists who favored England, enough consensus existed with regard to the need for a Navy that Congress authorized the construction of six warships and the enlistment of fifty-four officers and 2,000 enlisted men in 1794. In that same year a treaty between the United States and England, tying up some of the loose ends from the American Revolution, eased the British depredations, but those by the French increased. By 1797, the French had seized 300 U.S. vessels, and the small beginnings of three years before turned into a frenzy of shipbuilding.

Unwillingly and almost unwittingly, the United States was entering into its first international conflict. It wasn't called war. With deft political maneuvering, President John Adams managed to keep the country technically neutral, as his predecessor, George Washington, had decreed. Thus, historians were forced to invent a suitable term for several years of serious shooting, and they came up with "the quasi-war with France." In those years, sea battles were not limited to navies. Nations in

conflict officially granted letters of marque to private citizens
authorizing seizure of foreign persons and property, and these
citizens became privateers. The French were liberal in handing
out letters of marque, and the United States permitted its merchant vessels to sail "in an armed condition."

It would be a strange struggle during which cool, commercial
heads would prevail over politically passionate hearts. Dependent on foreign trade for many manufactured goods and most
luxuries, on the employment this trade provided and on customs duties for federal revenue, the nation's urban and monied
interests, represented by the Federalists, kept the brakes on
anything that could be called an all-out effort to win. When it
came to using force against England or France, they chose
France because the English eventually paid for the ships and
cargoes they seized, whereas the French never did. Even so,
they managed to have the language of authorization limit the
action of American ships—government or private—to attacks
on "French armed vessels" with the result that business as usual
continued, with unarmed French merchantmen going in and
out of U.S. ports. Just to make sure that matters didn't get out
of hand, Congress instructed the Treasury Department to have
its Revenue Cutter Service police the coastline to keep American citizens from privateering against the ships of nations with
which the country was at peace.

Ambiguous as these instructions seem in view of the fact that
the United States was supposed to be at peace with the same
France it was fighting at sea—indeed, a trio of special envoys
from President Adams to the Directory, which was the French
revolutionary government, was engaged in prolonged negotia-
tions in Paris at the time—they were all too typical of assignments that the Revenue Cutter Service and its successor, the
U.S. Coast Guard, would receive down through the years. But
orders were orders, then as now. Although it was only eight
years old, the service's ten original cutters, built to a budget and
kept in constant use, were not adequate to the task. Alexander
Hamilton's replacement at the Treasury, Secretary Oliver Wolcott, ordered the construction of eight larger, more heavily
armed ships. One of these would be called *Eagle II* to distinguish her from the cutter *Eagle* then on service on the Georgia

coast. It was already an honored name; the bald eagle, the national emblem, adorned the Revenue Cutter Service's ensign. The new bearer of the name was destined to add to its glory.

What these Treasury orders did to—or for—the shipyards already inundated with crash construction orders from the fledgling Navy isn't hard to imagine. Three heavy-duty frigates—*United States, Constitution* and *Constellation*—were being rushed to completion. A clue as to the fuss and bustle involved is offered in accounts of the launchings. The *United States* was sent down the ways in such a rush in Philadelphia that it went aground on the opposite shore; in Boston, the *Constitution* couldn't be slid off the ways. A clue to the temper of the times is that Philip Freneau, the nearest thing America had to a poet laureate of the Revolution and a Francophile Republican, wrote: "O frigate *Constitution!* Stay on shore!"

Perhaps because it was an older hand at the business than the Navy, the Treasury didn't seem to have the same trouble with its new ships. They were designed and built by different people in different places, but the *Eagle*'s story was typical. Her plans were drawn up by one of the nation's best naval architects, Josiah Fox, and she was built by William and Abra Brown in Philadelphia. Half the new cutters were rigged as double topsail schooners; the *Eagle* and three others were what was called "jackass brigs"—that is, they carried square topsails on the fore and main masts. She was fifty-eight feet long, twenty feet in beam and had a nine-foot depth of hold. Although listed as a ten-gun vessel, the *Eagle* mounted sixteen nine-pounders, and her small arms probably equaled those listed for a comparable cutter—ten muskets, ten pistols, ten cutlasses and twenty boarding pikes. Considering her performance, her sailing qualities must certainly have matched those of her sister ship *Pickering,* which was described in a newspaper of the time as "a fine sail boat," able to make headway against a tide in a light breeze. She carried seventy in crew.

Whatever other dangers these men might face, none of them stood in danger of getting rich. The captain's wages were $50 a month; the three mates received $35, $30 and $25 respectively; petty officers were paid $20; and seamen between $12 and $17. Their provisions for twelve months at sea evoke a shudder in the age of cholesterol. The only meat consisted of fifty-four barrels of beef and fifty-four barrels of pork. Mainstays of the diet are glaringly evident in listed quantities: twenty-five hundred weight of rice, 180 hundred weight of bread, 2,625 pounds of cheese, 125 bushels of potatoes. With respect to the quality of provisions, there is an interesting entry in the journal of the frigate *Constellation*'s captain for July 14, 1798: "Condemned a Number of Potatoes, that proved unfit for Men to eat, and hove the same into the Sea." The eighteenth-century cutter crew did have recourse to a balm not available on any military vessels these days—their share of 1,515 gallons of rum.

Launched in the late summer of 1798, the *Eagle* went to sea under the command of Captain Hugh Campbell. However "quasi" the war, she, like the other cutters, was ordered into the Navy. It was Secretary of the Navy Benjamin Stoddert's strategy to assign the small cutters to a flotilla headed, protected and, of course, commanded by a large naval vessel. Unfortunately, a fire in 1833 destroyed detailed records of the Revenue Cutter Service in the preceding years, but there is in the National Archives a handwritten log reconstructed from newspapers and other sources that provides an outline of the cutters' campaigns. The earliest entries with respect to the *Eagle* read:

—"*August 20, 1798.* You will prepare the brig cutter *Eagle* for sea immediately. Secretary of the Navy to Capt. Campbell."

—"*September 21, 1798.* The *Eagle,* presumed to be ready for sea is ordered to cruise between the capes of Delaware and Virginia under Captain Murray, USN, of the *Montezuma.* Secretary of the Navy to Captain Campbell."

—"*September 25, 1798.* Captain Murray, USN, with the *Montezuma, Retaliation, Norfolk,* all naval, and *Eagle* to make a cruise to the West Indies, to consume about three months. Secretary of the Navy to Captain Murray."

—"*October 13, 1798.* If Murray has left Norfolk before your arrival, proceed to Savannah and cruise from Savannah to St. Marys. Secretary of the Navy to Captain Campbell."

It's known that Captain Campbell never did catch up with Murray. Whether he was held up by some natural circumstance like weather or chose to disregard orders from distant headquarters, as sometimes happened in those days of slow communication, Captain Campbell gave himself an opportunity to become one of the early heroes of the quasi-war. Sailing along the coast of Georgia, he spied the French privateer *Bon Pere,* overpowered her six guns with his sixteen and took her into port as a prize. Because the contest was so uneven, the *Eagle* evidently wasn't forced to do much damage to the *Bon Pere.* A handy schooner, she was in good enough shape to be converted into a U.S. cutter and rechristened *Bee* in honor of a judge by the name of Thomas Bee.

No American ship could dodge West Indian duty for long. An agreement had been reached whereby the British would convoy U.S. vessels across the Atlantic in return for American protection of British vessels in the Caribbean. This represented quite a vote of confidence from the English regarding the capability of America's brand new naval forces. So important and lucrative was the trade in sugar, rum and slaves through the West Indies that Britain, according to some historians, lost the war with her colonies on the northern continent by keeping her fleet in the Caribbean. The terse notes in the Archives recounting the *Eagle*'s southern cruise to the West Indies are enough to show that Britain's faith was not misplaced:

—*"December 11, 1798.* Captain Campbell ordered to prepare the *Eagle* for a cruise to the West Indies. Secretary Navy to Capt. Campbell."

—*"January 8, 1799.* The *Eagle* to proceed immediately to Prince Rupert's Bay and join Capt. Barry, U.S.N., of the Frigate *United States.* Secretary Navy to Capt. Campbell."

—*"May 20, 1799.* The *Eagle,* cutter, is a very proper vessel to retain in the Navy service, and you may if you please consider her as belonging to that Establishment. Secretary of the Navy to the secretary of the treasury."

—*"May 25, 1799.* The *Eagle,* Campbell, remains near Guadeloupe. Campbell has captured one privateer and recaptured an American vessel. Secretary of the Navy to the president."

—*"June 22, 1799.* The ship *Nancy* from the Island of Desolation with $50,000 in oil, on the 9th of May, 1799, was captured by the French privateer *Revenge,* and with the brig *Mehitable* was recaptured by the U.S. brig *Eagle* and carried into St. Kitts."

Of the four captures she's credited with, the action in which the *Eagle* not only repossessed the *Nancy* but seized the *Mehitable* must have been the most exciting and gratifying. The other cutters also acquitted themselves well. Over the course of approximately four years, the forty-five military vessels employed by the United States in the quasi-war captured ninety-five armed French vessels. The eight revenue cutters are credited with thirteen of these victories. If, as it would seem, the underlying cause of the struggle was commercial, nobody could doubt that the American effort was worth it, even with its sacrifices. The cutter *Pickering,* for example, sank with all hands during a gale she encountered on one of her voyages to the West Indies.

In this instance, there was a very exact measurement for success—insurance rates. Just before the French launched their attacks on U.S. shipping in 1776 the going rate for covering a West Indian voyage was 6 percent of the cargo's value. By 1798 when the newly built American vessels of war were just getting into action, rates had shot up to between 30 and 33 percent. The $50,000 cargo of the *Nancy*—a large amount in today's values— suggests the kind of losses being covered. By 1799, the rate had fallen to between 15 and 20 percent; by 1800 with hostilities still in progress it was down to 10 percent.

It is fascinating to discover how themes sounded in those earliest years of what became the Coast Guard echo down through history. Because of the diversion of cutters to naval service in the Caribbean in 1798, smuggling along the continental coasts increased. In 1989 when the Coast Guard was diverted from policing by a natural disaster—hurricane Hugo—rather than a man-made crisis, there was a similar increase in cocaine running. Treasury Secretary Wolcott tried to solve his problem by asking Navy Secretary Stoddert for the return of his ships, and another repeated them as heard. This time it was a certain scorn on the part of a "naval person," as Winston Churchill used to style himself, for those charged with the mundane tasks of protecting life and property.

In an interservice letter probably not meant for other eyes, Stoddert discussed the Wolcott request with one of his officers, Thomas Truxton, Captain of the *Constellation:* "Our revenue

Cutters are too small to be of the smallest use on our Coasts—I doubt whether they are much better in the Islands.—By a Law of last Session, the President may add as many of them as he thinks proper to the Navy Establishment, the rest will be reduced to mere revenue Cutters." That this attitude spread outside the service and beyond its times is reflected in an account of this conflict by another naval person, historian Samuel Eliot Morison, in the *Oxford History of the American People.* He states that there were fourteen American men-of-war at sea by the end of 1798 and reports on a few of their battles, particularly those of the *Constellation.* There is no mention of participation by the Revenue Cutter Service, although a careful reader is left to wonder how fourteen men-of-war multiplied into Morison's "four task forces of three to ten ships each" in the Caribbean.

Truxton, the man on the scene, seems to have been more generously aware of the contributions of his Treasury counterparts. Probably because of his response to the secretary, we observe this entry in the Archives' summary: *"August 17, 1799. The Revenue Brig is added to the Navy and Captain Campbell, her commander, is promoted to the rank of Master and Commandant in the Navy."* Two other cutters—*Scammel II* and the ill-fated *Pickering*—were also retained by the Navy. But after the war ended in early 1801, the Navy showed no sentiment or lasting appreciation for the services of these tough little seagoing terriers. The two remaining cutters were sailed up to Baltimore, where they were sold off as surplus—*Eagle II* for $10,-585.73 on June 17, 1801, and the *Scammel II* in December for $8,001.87.

The Coast Guard took a different view of *Eagle*—of all of its *Eagles.* More than in memories, mentions in books, pictures on walls, the *Eagle* lives on in the shape of a sailing ship berthed in the Thames River in New London, Connecticut, on the waterfront of the U.S. Coast Guard Academy. She is a handsome square-rigger, one of the few remaining "tall ships" in the world, and aboard her Coast Guard cadets learn what it was like to go aloft and handle sail in a gale just as their predecessors did in the Revenue Cutter Service.

Visitors to the academy can have a look at today's *Eagle* when she is in port. Standing on her deck and listening to *her* history they might also hear another of those fascinating echoes of the past. The *Eagle* that Coast Guarders sail today was once a training ship in the German Navy—a prize of World War II just like the *Bee,* that prize-turned-cutter after *Eagle II* took her in the quasi-war with France so long ago.

Chapter 2

The Testing of Kelly Mogk

"Mother nature and the sea take their toll. You just can't rescue everyone. Something doesn't have to go wrong that you don't rescue everybody. But this mission was hard for Bill Harper, who's young in the Coast Guard and hasn't been on many rescues. It was also hard for Kelly Mogk, who was on her first rescue. But I could remember that somebody died on my first seven flights after I became a Coast Guard pilot. I thought: 'Am I in the wrong profession?' I began to wonder: 'Am I a jinx?' But in the twelve years since, I've saved many people on hundreds of search and rescue cases, and it's been very fulfilling. These were the worst conditions under which I've ever put a rescue swimmer down, and the effort Kelly Mogk made is what makes our work worthwhile."

> —Lieutenant Commander William Peterson,
> Aircraft Commander, U.S. Coast Guard,
> in an interview with the author.

THE mission that Commander Peterson was describing was one of the most celebrated rescues in the Coast Guard's recent history. For her part in saving the life of a downed Air National Guard jet pilot, Aviation Survivalman Third Class Kelly Mogk, the rescue swimmer, was awarded the Air Medal and congratulated in person by President George Bush. The entire crew of CG 6516, an H-65 helicopter out of Air Station Astoria, received Oregon National Guard awards. Guard com-

17

mander Major General Charles Sams said this of the mission: "I
felt the Coast Guard operation was well done under some very
difficult conditions."

Running against this chorus of praise in the days and weeks
immediately following the event that took place on the morning of January 3, 1989, was an offbeat countermelody in the local
press. For example, two typical headlines read: JET FALLS, ORE-
GON FLIER DIES and COAST GUARD–RESCUE CREWS WEREN'T
READY. The sad fact was that one of the two fliers who ejected
over the Pacific Ocean from an F-4 on training exercises died.
It was death rather than life that captured the attention of the
press with this reasoning: if one man lived, why not the other?
The reporting effort thus went into digging out details of per-
ceived errors and mistakes such as equipment failure and mis-
use of personnel. Implied was a charge that the Coast Guard had
sent a woman to do a man's work since this was the first actual
mission of the first woman ever to qualify as a rescue swimmer
in the Coast Guard or any other branch of the armed services.
The press critique culminated in a picture of a Coast Guard
officer at his desk in a pensive mood with the caption: "Captain
Hamilton, commander of Coast Guard Group Astoria, ponders
what went wrong."

If he was thinking about this mission at all, it's probable that
the captain was shaking his head over *what went right,* given
all the circumstances. Few search-and-rescue—SAR, in Coast
Guard language—cases are more illustrative of the problems,
perils and providential happenings that are the stuff of the Coast
Guard's daily life. The sheer magnitude of the SAR effort suggests what Coast Guardsmen are up against. Statistics compiled
for the year 1987 showed that on an average day that year the
Coast Guard completed 154 SAR cases, saving sixteen lives—or
one life every ninety-one minutes—in the process. Since achieving perfection in either men or machines remains an elusive
goal of human endeavor, it is inevitable that Coast Guardsmen
must do their best with what's at hand under the stress of inces-
sant demands for their services.

This was precisely the situation in which the crew of CG
6516—Commander Peterson; Lieutenant Junior Grade William
L. Harper, copilot; Aviation Electronicsman Second Class James

Reese, flight mechanic; and Petty Officer Mogk—found themselves on that January Tuesday morning. In the wake of critical press accounts, including letters from aggrieved friends and relatives of the airman who died, this crew told the story of their day to 350 people jammed into a 150-seat auditorium at the Oregon National Guard headquarters. For two and a half hours they fielded questions from the floor. They were sent away with a standing ovation from people who had come to complain. A year later, Peterson, Harper and Mogk told the same story individually to me, and it speaks not only for itself but for the whole SAR operation. In my talk with him, Admiral Paul A. Yost, Jr., commandant of the Coast Guard, cited the Kelly Mogk story as one of the most deserving of a place in any account of outstanding achievements during the service's 200-year history.

It began, as do most such cases, with the SAR alarm sounding throughout the Coast Guard's Astoria Air Station about midmorning. Neither Peterson nor Harper were members of the day's duty crew. When not flying, Peterson was the station's assistant operations officer and Harper acted as flight services officer. Nobody was flying that morning. There was a low cloud cover running up to 1,500 feet, mist and rain, winds of fifteen to twenty miles an hour—"a regular West Coast winter day," according to Peterson. The two officers were sitting across a desk from each other shuffling papers. But when it was announced following the alarm that there had been an F-4 crash, Peterson and Harper both jumped up and headed down for the SAR center. The situation was very unusual; most SAR cases in that area involved fishing or pleasure boats that got themselves into trouble.

The duty crew was already outfitted in the insulated orange flight suits that "coasties" call Mustangs. They're worn for visibility and protection against hypothermia if crew members have to ditch in water. Peterson listened in on the SARTEL, which is the Coast Guard's 24-hour-a-day instantaneous search-and-rescue phone line, to the information being relayed by the Coast Guard Search and Rescue Center in Seattle, Washington, from Big Foot, the code name for North American Air Defense

Command. In essence, one of two Coast Guard F-4s going through high-G maneuvers had malfunctioned and spun out of control; the other F-4 had seen its pilot and weapons officer eject and disappear with parachutes into the overcast. Their position was estimated at thirty-five miles due west of Tillamook Bay, about the same distance south of Astoria, but the F-4 reporting couldn't see them in the water because of the clouds. Airmen are particularly sensitive to the plight of other airmen. Although a helicopter had already been rolled out for the duty crew, the station's engineering officer rushed into the SAR center and said, "I've got another helicopter if you want it." The operations officer just looked at Peterson, who looked, in turn, at Harper. No words were needed. "I'll take it," Peterson said, "and I'll take Harper. Pipe another crew." Over the loudspeaker, the operations officer said, "Put another helo on the line. Provide rescue swimmer."

With notes on the probable position in hand, Peterson and Harper jumped into their Mustangs and headed for the flight line. There they discovered that their crew would be Petty Officers Reese and Mogk. The selection and composition of a crew for CG 6516 was characteristic of an emergency service. Although rated as an air commander himself, Harper was more than willing to fly copilot to a more senior officer in this instance. In fact, it's not uncommon in the Coast Guard for officers to fill in as needed under the command of enlisted personnel. Reese and Mogk were next in line to the duty personnel for their respective jobs. A swimmer was specified on the basis of the apparent nature of the emergency since the H-65 is only rated for one crewman. Having rescue swimmers available at all was relatively new to the Coast Guard as a whole and to the Astoria Station in particular, not to mention having a woman swimmer.

There was no time for talk as the crew took positions in the small helicopter—Harper in the left and Peterson in the right forward seats, Reese and Mogk in jump seats behind. Although it would be a relatively short flight, Peterson was happy to learn from the engineering officer that the fuel tanks were topped off. Since the location of the downed fliers hadn't been pinpointed, nor their survival actually assured, it could be a long search. While Peterson warmed up the engines and prepared to taxi out as soon as the duty helo got off the runway, Harper, who would be acting as navigator, entered the position data into the flight computer, and a position index was printed on the cockpit's screen. If all went well, the plane's electronic sensors would feed information from the various aids to navigation into the computer, which would keep them on course.

As CG 6516 started to move into position, the crew heard over the radio of a second unanticipated development. In an exchange with operations, the duty helo reported a fuel control malfunction with the anticipator on one of its two engines. Takeoff had been aborted but there was a request for permission to continue with the fuel control in manual position. "Negative," operations responded. "You could turn into a SAR case yourself. CG 6516 is on the line." Peterson and Harper looked at each other; instead of being backup, they were quite literally on the line. They took off. It was 1059, only nine minutes later than the duty helo could have made it into the air. It had seemed like a lot longer.

At least they wouldn't be all alone out there. Following standard operating procedure, Air Station Astoria's Falcon jet would take off immediately after them and be on station before they arrived. Flying high, the jet couldn't do anything about plucking survivors out of the water, but, given a break in the clouds, it might be able to spot them and drop what's known as a datum marker buoy that would lead CG 6516 right to the site. The radio told them too that a helo would be coming in from the Coast Guard's Group North Bend down the coast to the south. But the weather being what it was, Peterson and Harper couldn't anticipate much help from the Falcon other than a boost in communications, and they knew that the North Bend helo would come in behind them. Rather than try to penetrate the overcast at sea, Peterson elected to stay low—between fifty and a hundred feet—and pushed his bird as fast as she would go. With maximum gross weight and a little extra in the form of a hundred-plus-pound swimmer, CG 6516 made about 140 knots, giving it an estimated time of arrival in one half an hour.

Over the intercom, Peterson started briefing the crew. He felt that it was imperative to give Kelly what might be bad news as soon as possible so that she could brace herself for it. "I hope we don't have to deploy you," he told her, "but the chances are very good that we will. Depending on what we run into out there we might have to leave you for the North Bend helo to pick up. We'd be pretty crowded in the cabin with two more bodies that could be in bad shape. Of course you know that it's your decision whether you are willing to go."

"No problem. I'm ready," Kelly said. Nevertheless, the thought that she could be left in the hands of strangers was a new and disturbing one.

Once they crossed the coastline, Harper was even more disturbed. "Our navigation computer had lost its lock," he recalled later. "Because the loran signal is weak in that area, the number on the position index began to grow. The way it works is if the index shows, say, .1 or .2 we understand in the cockpit that the internal tests of the navigation computer tell it that it is accurate within one tenth or two tenths of a mile. That number grows as the computer loses its cross-reference checks with different navigational aids until, at 9.9, it's telling you that it has no idea of the position." In addition, the low level flight kept CG 6516 from getting good reception from the airport VOR signals, the standard inland navigational aid. Flying blind above the overcast, the jets—their own Falcon; "Harry Two," the wingman of the downed F-4; and another with the call sign "Hit Man Two"—could still provide only the rough latitude and longitude. Down where they were, CG 6516 was equally blind. Often the ceiling dropped right to the water with visibility as low as a quarter of a mile; there were no visual points of reference. Fortunately, Big Foot was equipped with radar that could pick up low flying objects, among them the outbound CG 6516. With its electronic eye on them, Big Foot could give them their own position and a heading toward the general search area, but it couldn't find anything for them.

Just as Big Foot was squawking through the radio, "You are approaching last known position," CG 6516 broke out of the mist into an eerie clearing. Like some huge, squat tank the clearing had a circular wall of dense fog and a roof of low clouds. The sea was in an angry state—sixteen-foot waves with a six-foot, wind-driven chop on top of that. At the low altitude they had to maintain to stay under the ceiling, their chances of seeing any object on the surface were minimal since it would keep disappearing in the troughs of the waves. But almost immediately after his craft entered the clearing, out of the corner of his right eye Commander Peterson caught a white flash out the right window. It could have been a smoke flare from a survivor who had seen the chopper. He wheeled his bird in a sharp bank to the right and within seconds found himself looking through the nose screen at a pod of spouting whales. The diversion took him off course, and he banked left in a sharp 180-degree turn to go back to the datum position and at least drop a datum marker for future reference. Suddenly and without any warning, CG 6516 was directly over two small black rafts. The time was 1127. "It was really almost pure luck," says Commander Peterson. But thinking back on all the navigational problems, Lieutenant Harper takes a stronger view: "Finding them was almost divine intervention, I'd say."

In Peterson's view the luck factor in the discovery was geometrically increased by the size and color of the rafts. They were small, and they were solid black. Black is hard to distinguish against a dark sea, which, of course, is why the Coast Guard itself uses highly visible colors like the orange of the Mustangs and the red of its life jackets. "They don't use color in military jets because in time of war they don't want to be seen by the enemy, no matter what, and they do a pretty good job of that," Peterson says wryly.

Passing over the rafts downwind, Peterson again wheeled sharply to head into the wind and go into a low hover. One raft was empty, but the helmeted head and shoulder of a man— Second Lieutenant Mike Markstaller, the pilot—could be seen draped over the rim of the other. The helicopter crew thought that they detected a motion of the man's head that indicated some life, some perception of their arrival. But his position alone showed that he was in very bad shape. He hadn't been able to drag himself up onto the raft, and his hold on it was precarious. Something under water was pulling his body down, and every cresting wave was breaking over his lolling head. If he was actually surviving, it was due to the fact that he had managed to inflate his LPU life vest, his "water wings," which provided a little buoyancy and, at close range, a small spot of visible orange. Peterson dropped low enough to have a look at the man's face and eyes. His skin was dark, his stare vacant. Having seen too many people die before his eyes, Peterson told the rest of the crew, "He's dying. We've got to be quick."

This close to the water, they were all conscious of the terrible conditions facing the rescue swimmer. But the need for a swimmer's services was too clear for discussion. The fastest method of deployment for swimmers is a free fall, and Kelly elected to go that way. This requires hovering the helicopter close enough to the water to prevent the swimmer from being injured in the impact, a hazardous procedure above unpredictable high seas in the H-65. "This helo does not, repeat not, get its feet wet," says an official Coast Guard publication. "A water landing with power on is pretty well guaranteed to destroy the aircraft in a dramatic way; when the tail fan—rotating at about 3,600 RPM—hits the water, parts will fly." Commander Peterson was well aware of this, but he brought CG 6516 to within five to ten feet of the wave crests, and Kelly, looking like a small figure from another planet in her dry suit, flippers, mask and snorkel, dropped into the sea.

All the way out, Kelly had tried to keep her mind off the prospect ahead by rehearsing the past, going through all the procedures taught in training that might apply to this case. From the moment she hit the water, she had to act quickly and continuously, relying more on instinct and training than on conscious thought. As soon as she reached Markstaller, she knew that Commander Peterson had been right in his assessment of the man's condition. He was severely hypothermic, barely conscious. Obeying the first commandment in the rescue swimmer's bible, Kelly tried to maintain that consciousness by talking to him.

"Hang on. You'll be all right. We're here. The chopper's right up there," she said.

He tried to speak, but all that came out was a strangulated sound that Kelly couldn't understand. Still, he seemed to be following her with his eyes. She took his hand and squeezed it. He squeezed back. She knew than she was dealing with a very live person inside a frozen shell. She *had* to save him somehow.

Despite the weather, the water was clear as green glass when she looked down below the raft through her mask. The sight she saw was almost beautiful in a horrible way. Still attached to him was the pilot's parachute. Moving lazily in the currents twenty feet down· it was as fully ballooned with water dragging him down as it had been with air holding him up. The first order of business was to get that off, and it was fortunately a business that had been taught in the Navy's swim school at Pensacola, Florida, under the heading "parachute disentanglement."

Chattering away when she didn't have to close her mouth to keep from swallowing the water washed over them by nearly every wave—"Don't worry . . . We'll get you out of this. . . ." –Kelly studied the harness that held the parachute's backpack onto Markstaller's body. She had a moment of panic: *My God, what's this?* The harness had a different configuration from the one she had trained with, and it took her eternal seconds to figure it out. When she did, she found that she couldn't work the fittings with the gloves she was wearing to protect her hands from fifty-six-degree water. She tore a glove off, and let it float away. With a hand free, she unbuckled the chest straps, the leg straps. The parachute should have fallen away, but it didn't. Ducking under water again, Kelly saw that the shrouds were tangled around Markstaller's legs in a mess worse than anything her instructors had ever conjured up.

By now, Kelly knew that she could get no help from Markstaller. Even if he could be made to understand what she wanted, his injuries were crippling. There was no way that she could assess precisely what they were, but his left arm and leg waved as limply as seaweed under the water; his right arm, locked in a death grip on the raft, looked disjointed at the shoulder. She would have to cut the shrouds. Getting her knife out and taking a deep breath, she hauled herself down on Markstaller's dangling body so as not to expend energy diving. She slashed at a line. The knife didn't cut. She realized at once that even if she could manage to saw through the rope, it would take too much time. And then a lesson from school popped into her head: "If you cut one line, you've got two. Use cutting only as a last resort. If one line is tangled up and you cut it you have two separate lines that can get tangled up." She would have to do it the hard way—pull each line off his legs herself.

Kelly popped to the surface for a breath and another encouraging word to Markstaller. She was talking as much to herself as to him. She could soon be in trouble too. Water was seeping in around the cuffs at her neck and wrists, oozing into her clothes and around her body with every movement. No time to think about that. Another breath and she pulled herself down again to begin unraveling the lines.

Above the scene in CG 6516, the crew could see every move Kelly was making. Ordinarily, a helicopter can't hover too close to a rescue in progress because the downward wash of cold air from the rotor will add to the hypothermic effect. On this day, however, the stiff breeze nullified the rotor wash, and Peterson hovered as close as he dared. "I could see them totally," he says. "I could see Markstaller's eyes. I could see the chute down there. I could see her working. It's a team effort going into these things. I felt personally that we weren't doing enough because it was only Kelly down there trying. She was repeatedly diving and coming back up and trying to hold him up because he was getting pulled under. I sort of felt useless." Harper's recollection is the same: "Both of them were taking quite a beating from sea and wind. The survivor was looking around sort of dazed. He was moving real slowly. Bill Peterson voiced a couple of times a concern that he might die while we sat there and watched."

Fortunately for their nerves there was a little something they could do when the H-65 from North Bend arrived on the scene. Harper, manning the radio, vectored them to the other raft on Peterson's instructions. He kept tabs on the fruitless search they were making while Kelly kept diving. Harper also maintained contact with the Falcon overhead and gave a running account of the action to be forwarded to base. For twenty minutes or more nobody knew how it would come out, least of all Kelly Mogk.

Even after Kelly got the last line off Markstaller's legs, and the chute slowly sank away, the fight wasn't over. She had to get him up to the helo. There are three methods of hoisting a person into a helicopter—by basket, by a sling that is graphically called a "horse collar" and by bare hook. Just before Kelly jumped, it had been decided in a quick cockpit conference to use either the sling or hook. A survivor either has to climb into a basket or be stuffed into it. Even from above, they guessed that Markstaller would be incapable of getting in himself and that he might be further injured by being womanhandled into a basket. Besides, the harness or hook were much quicker. Kelly was glad that that basic decision had been made, and the next one was automatically taken out of her hands. There was no lifting ring on Markstaller's harness, so she would call for the horse collar as soon as she got him away from the raft.

"OK, I've got you free now. Let go of the raft so we can haul you up," she told him. He made no move to obey. Kelly could hardly blame him. Even with the chute gone, the seas were still washing over him—over both of them. Kelly could duck and hold her breath, but water washed into Markstaller's half-open mouth, and he had to choke and spit it back up. He was a man slowly drowning, and the raft must have seemed to him a last hope. She tried to pry him loose. No good. Maybe he couldn't hear her over the shriek of wind and loud clatter of the chopper. "Let go of the raft! Let go of the raft! Let go of the raft!" she yelled over and over while she reached for her knife. Her thought was to slice through the rubber, but before she could try that a kind of miracle occurred. He let go. She didn't know whether he had suddenly heard her or had drifted further away from consciousness. She didn't care; he was free. Kelly sent the thumbs-up hand signal to drop the sling.

Beyond making sure that they had seen her, Kelly was too intent on keeping Markstaller afloat until she could get him into the sling to notice what was happening in the sky. Having thoroughly searched around the second raft without seeing any signs of life, the North Bend helo had pulled into a hover behind CG 6516. Watching Kelly get the horse collar under the survivor's armpits, Peterson was alarmed by the man's blue skin and nearly black lips. He made a hard decision. He had to make it without knowing how Kelly felt, beyond the fact that he had seen her function heroically. Minutes lost could mean losing the survivor's life. Since the Coast Guard's rescue swimmer program wasn't due to arrive at North Bend for another six months, they would have only a flight mechanic aboard. They would have plenty of room and a possible use for Kelly. Peterson got on the radio to them: "I think this guy we're bringing up is very,

very close to being dead. I want you to be able to come in and pick up my rescue swimmer. You can ferry her to the other raft, and she can search around there."

Although she had been warned, it was one of the worst moments of the whole experience for Kelly when Peterson passed his decision down to her with hand signals. She could hardly believe it was actually happening. But it was. She watched Markstaller's body hauled aboard, watched the door close, watched the plane wheel away. She felt very much alone. Now that the action was over, she was aware of her own exhaustion and, especially, of her chill. Trained as an emergency medical technician as well as a swimmer, she knew that, with her dry suit turned into a squishing wet suit, she was already in the first stages of hypothermia. She was fast becoming a SAR case herself. It didn't help that she knew as well as Commander Peterson did that the people from North Bend had as yet no experience with swimmers. They wouldn't, for instance, understand her hand signals, and in seas like this hoisting would be tricky with nobody in the water to ease it as she had with Markstaller.

It only took about five minutes for the North Bend helicopter to position itself in a hover over Kelly, but five minutes is a long time when you are freezing to death. They sent down a bare hook, and Kelly attached it to her lifting ring. There was a hard jerk as the winchman put strain on the hoist and a wave fell away under her. But she was swinging up to safety—and to warmth. . . .

As harrowing as those first minutes after Markstaller was hoisted out of the water were for Kelly Mogk, they were worse for her crewmates on CH 6516. In anticipation of major problems, Peterson instructed Reese to get out the hypothermal rewarming bag and cranked up the heat to full blast in the cabin. Warming would be the only response to lethal hypothermia within their power. But an unanticipated problem arose as Reese, a husky man himself, was wrestling Markstaller aboard. Over the intercom, he said, "Hey, this guy is really big. I don't think I can handle him. I need some help back here. He's badly hurt, too. . . ." The pilots could hear Markstaller groan in pain as Reese tried to move him around.

"Better crawl back there and see if you can help, Bill," Peterson said to Harper.

Peterson had used the right verb. The H-65 is not designed for movement between cockpit and cargo space. Harper unbuckled, unstrapped and unplugged. While Peterson banked sharply to come to a course for Astoria, Harper moved gingerly over the central instrument panel, making sure his head didn't accidentally bump one of the overhead fuel control quadrants or emergency cutoff levers. Peterson took over communications and navigation. He noted that the time was 1152, exactly twenty-five minutes after they had spotted the rafts. With less fuel, he could push the bird to 150 knots. He radioed base that he wanted to land at the hospital in Astoria and gave them an estimated flight time of twenty minutes.

While Harper was still inching his way aft, Reese came on with a new problem: "This guy's really cold. Somebody's going to have to get in that bag with him. I'm too big. We both won't fit."

"I guess it's gotta be you, Bill," Peterson said. "Strip down and get in with him. And listen: Keep talking to him. Be specific. Tell him he's not saved yet. I've seen too many people on other rescues who relaxed once we got them aboard and died. Keep telling him he's not saved—all the time."

Harper was having a duty thrust upon him that he hadn't bargained for. Squeamish about things like displaced bones and blood, he wondered how he could function. But one look at Markstaller, and the man's desperate need for instant action caused Harper to forget his own feelings. Markstaller was lying on his back, but it was stiffened into a rigid arch by the cold. His broken left arm was useless; his right tortured by dislocation at the shoulder. When he started to ease Markstaller's legs into the warming bag, Harper noted that the left leg had a ninety-degree bend between knee and ankle. The shoe, still fully laced, was dangling half off the left foot and was full of blood. Harper took off the shoe and pulled on the leg to keep the bones from crunching on each other as he put it into the bag. Then he pulled the leg out the other end, fearing that it would bring a rush of blood to the wounds if it warmed first and cause fatal bleeding. When he got the right leg into the bag, Harper stripped to his underwear, put his left arm under Markstaller's back to keep his weight off the injured man, wrapped his legs around Markstaller's good right one, and, in his words, "snuggled up to him—the best way to put it. He felt just real, real cold."

Harper followed Peterson's advice and started talking to Markstaller. "I tried to break it down to basic military communication," he says. "I told him, 'Your job, your mission, is to stay awake and stay alert. Do you understand me?' I'd make him answer me. His speech was very affected like it was when you played in the snow as a kid and your tongue wouldn't work. I asked his name and he knew and said, 'Mahk Mmahmmahr.' I asked where he was from, and he was able to say something like Portland. He couldn't answer other questions like what's your unit, how long were you in the water, did you see another chute. But he did understand that his job was to stay awake. He warmed slowly, stopped arching and moved his right leg a little. He moved his right arm up and started to grasp me. He got a hand full of my undershirt in back and started squeezing me close."

While this was going on in back, Peterson was dealing with a call from the North Bend helicopter: "Listen, your rescue swimmer just collapsed back here. She looks hypothermic. She's draining water. I don't see anything at the other raft. I don't recommend she go back down."

"If she's hypothermic and exhausted, I agree you don't want to put her back down," Peterson said. "But let her call the shots."

There was no landing pad at the hospital in Astoria. It was a case of "elevator in and elevator out, down into a parking lot between parked cars and light poles," according to Peterson, who fortunately had negotiated it successfully on other occasions. Hospital authorities had not wasted the short warning time Peterson had given them. Not only had they moved cars to make room for his landing, but they had had special blood-warming equipment flown in from Portland. This foresight turned out to be another factor in the miracle that saved Markstaller. His body's craving for heat was still so strong when they landed that he didn't want to release Harper. The only way they could get Markstaller on a stretcher was for Harper to wriggle out of the undershirt that Markstaller clutched all the way into the hospital. There it was determined that his core temperature was only eighty-four degrees, the turning point between con-sciousness and unconsciousness.

Having delivered Markstaller's nearly dead body, Com-mander Peterson took the elevator up and hopped over to the Coast Guard air base while Harper got back into his Mustang. CG 6516 was in need of refueling, but the morning's work wasn't finished as far as Peterson was concerned. The empty raft out there presented a mystery demanding solution. While he was refueling, Peterson called for a new crew, including a fresh swimmer. His people on the first flight had been through enough emotional and physical experiences for one day. The North Bend helicopter had delivered Petty Officer Mogk to the sick bay at Astoria, where she was being treated for a wrenched back from the hoist in addition to hypothermia. She had sensibly ruled herself unfit for another dive that day.

By the time Peterson got back on scene, homing in on the datum marker he had dropped, there were rescue craft en route from points all along the coast. Much better equipped than the rest for both search and rescue was an Air Force H-3, a helicopter large enough to have both a medical unit and two rescue swimmers who, unlike Coast Guard swimmers, were equipped with oxygen tanks for staying down in dives. But Peterson's reappearance was providential since the H-3 was groping through the murk with an inoperative direction-finding system and couldn't locate the datum marker. Peterson vec-tored the H-3 to the raft. The rescue swimmers located First Lieutenant Mark Baker in a tangle underneath his raft. When they got Baker aboard the H-3, the flight surgeon performed a minor miracle by rewarming him and restarting his stopped heart, but he couldn't restore life. He was pronounced dead by drowning after a negative brain wave examination in a Portland hospital. Baker had two broken arms, and there was doubt whether he had even been conscious when he hit the water. Baker and Markstaller's injuries were caused by ejecting at 600 miles an hour, a speed far outside what is considered the "safe envelope of ejection" for their type of aircraft.

As this is being written, Markstaller is gradually mending after numerous operations and is eager to get back into the cockpit again. One of the more unusual aspects of an unusual

SAR case and a most heartwarming one for the crew of CG 6516 in view of the bad press is that Markstaller and Harper have become personal friends. Generally, rescuers never see the rescued after the event. "Markstaller and I found we have a common interest," says Harper. "He's a little bit younger but we both like sports cars and talk back and forth about those. He's been to my house and brought dates by and met my wife."

Looking back on a hard mission, Harper sees it as fulfillment of his purpose in transferring three years ago from the Army, where he was an aviator with the rank of warrant officer. "I wanted to get into an ongoing peacetime mission where you save lives," he says. Kelly Mogk, who was transferred to Air Station Sitka in Alaska in the course of normal rotation, views it in much the same way. Although her citation reads that she "demonstrated exceptional fortitude and daring despite extreme conditions that tested the limits of her endurance," she says that she was just doing the job she was trained to do. Kelly didn't particularly want to be a swimmer, but she did want to be in the Coast Guard, and she did want to be an Aviation Survivalman. By the time she enlisted, the Coast Guard had made it mandatory to graduate from the Navy swim school before graduating from its own ASM school.

One of the reasons Kelly Mogk chose the Coast Guard is that, in her words, "there are no restrictions saying a woman can't do something." Kelly is only one of many Coast Guard women proving that. Already at least four other women have followed her pioneering lead to become rescue swimmers. "I don't know if a lot of women are having success in the Coast Guard, but it is their own fault if they are not," Kelly says. "The Coast Guard is not going to give you anything, but the opportunity is there. I think the Coast Guard is a real class service, and it appealed to me more than the others. I wanted to do something that helps people."

The final word on the testing of Kelly Mogk came quite rightly from the man whose background and point of observation put him in the best position to pass judgment on her performance. "She's a super gal—a real hard worker, a credit to the Coast Guard and to the rescue swimmers," says Commander Peterson. Although nobody with whom I discussed the case seems to have thought of it, the praise for Petty Officer Mogk suggests that she has inadvertently created a slight problem for the Coast Guard. She has made the title of her rank—aviation survival*man*—obsolete.

Chapter 3

The Hanging of Horace Alderman

T was a tragedy played out in times of greed, not unlike the times in which this book is being written. America was riding high that year. A complacent Republican president sat in the White House, and the rich were getting richer in the markets. A gratifying show of American might was in progress in Nicaragua, where U.S. marines were keeping a U.S.-supported government in power. Although space seemed still unreachable, an American by the name of Charles Lindbergh astonished the world by flying the Atlantic alone, and a new wonder called television was first demonstrated in the United States. Some citizens of the southern states and Florida were still suffering from the ravages of a hurricane that had killed 372 people the previous September, injured 6,000 and destroyed $80 million in property. For most Americans, however, it was a year to enjoy the star turns of entertainment celebrities—Babe Ruth swatting his sixtieth home run, the movies reproducing sound in Al Jolson's *Jazz Singer*, two heavy sluggers named Tunney and Dempsey creating controversy with a "long count" fight. The year 1927 was also a year in which the nation's losing battle against the smuggling of an illegal drug—alcohol—was reaching new heights of strong determination and deadly encounter.

The government then viewed the struggle to uphold the laws against liquor as a war in the same way the government views the current contest with dealers in other substances. The assistant secretary of the treasury in charge of Prohibition enforcement was, in fact, an army general—Lincoln C. Andrews. With inflation in mind, General Andrews's testimony before a Senate committee that bootleggers were hauling in an estimated $3 billion a year indicated that the enemy had as much incentive to stay in business then as now. His admission in the same testimony that the government was succeeding in confiscating only 5 percent of the illegal alcohol serving the cravings of the country has a familiar ring. Stirred by this bad news, if not by other ills of the nation, President Calvin Coolidge committed $30 million in 1927 dollars to stopping the trade, and a Prohibition Reorganization Act created a special Prohibition Bureau within the Treasury Department.

One significant difference as of this writing between the war of 1927 and the current conflict has to do with the use of the Coast Guard. Then, as now, the Coast Guard was the service charged with keeping contraband from entering through America's 6,000 miles of coastline. Indeed, the Coast Guard's beginning in 1790—"a system of revenue cutters"—was the founding fathers' answer to the problem of suppressing smuggling along the shores of the new nation. To carry out its mission during Prohibition, the Coast Guard was granted the largest increase in funds and personnel in its 200-year history. A $14-million dollar budget empowered the service to acquire its first aircraft, renovate twenty World War I destroyers, build 203 new cabin cruiser–type cutters and one hundred smaller boats, and enlarge its force from 5,982 men to 10,009. By contrast, on the very day that I interviewed him for this book, Admiral Paul A. Yost, Jr., commandant of the Coast Guard, was darting in and out of budget meetings in which his staff members were trying to cut down on services to meet the demands of the Graham-Rudman bill, which required automatic across-the-board cuts in federal spending as part of the government's attempt to balance the budget. Yet, across Washington from the Coast Guard's riverfront headquarters, the administration was sounding an uncertain trumpet call for its reduced forces to march forward in "the war on drugs." It has to be assumed that this difference in commitment to the fight has nothing to do with the fact that the Coast Guard is currently under the Department of Transportation instead of the Treasury.

True, back in 1927 when the airplane was still in its infancy and contraband came in the form of kegs and bottles instead of powders, the sea was a more likely avenue of choice for bringing the "good stuff" from abroad. Over the horizon from major centers of import and consumption like Boston, New York and Miami the ships of smugglers anchored or drifted in what were known as rum rows. Safe beyond the three-mile and later twelve-mile limit of territorial waters established by international agreement, the crews of those "mother ships" peddled their wares openly to contact boats that shuttled the goods to the thirsty on shore. Contact boats were usually small, fast craft that operated at night or in bad weather to elude the Coast Guard. In dealing with this system, the Coast Guard used its destroyers and larger cutters to cordon off the mother ships on rum row, and its smaller vessels to chase the contact boats that slipped through the net.

The most useful war-horse of the Coast Guard fleet, as judged by its order for 203 of them, was the "six-bitter." Seventy-five feet long, the boat took its name from the slang word of the day for a quarter—"two bits." It was not designed for beauty but for "seaworthiness, habitability and speed." It had an open deck mounting a one-pounder cannon and a .30-caliber Lewis machine gun forward, a square pilothouse with windows on all sides amidships and two trunk cabins over the crew quarters and engine compartments aft. The six-bitter was powered by two six-cylinder gasoline engines that turned twin screws, and she could make seventeen to eighteen knots. One of the war-horses was patrol boat CG-249, the stage on which the most dramatic incident of the twelve-year Prohibition battle took place.

CG-249 was a part of the Coast Guard fleet at Section Base Six, Fort Lauderdale, Florida. Then, as now, the waters between Florida and the Bahamas and the islands curving away to the south and east from Cuba through Hispaniola, Puerto Rico and the West Indies were infested with smugglers. Any sortie out to sea could turn into an exciting adventure for any Coast Guard boat. But the crew of CG-249 had no such anticipation on August 7, 1927. Their assignment on that pleasant summer day was a "milk run" to take a passenger over to Bimini in the British Bahamas, some thirty-eight miles across the Straits of Florida.

CG-249's skipper, Boatswain Sidney C. Sanderlin, was so sure that they were embarked on nothing more serious than a day's outing that he agreed to leave one crew member—Motor Machinist's Mate Morris Ginsberg—ashore to play on the Coast Guard baseball team. It would be the kind of close contest with a team of farmers from Pompano that could end up in a fistfight, and a man of Ginsberg's grit was needed. Sanderlin had no way of knowing that he could have put that fighting spirit to better use. In any case he was left with six good men—Boatswains Mate First Class Frank L. Tuten, Boatswains Mate Second Class John A. Robinson, Seaman First Class Hal M. Caudle, Seaman Second Class Jodie L. Hollingsworth, Motor Machinist Mate First Class Victor A. Lamby and Motor Machinist Mate Second Class Frank Lehman. Hollingsworth, acting as cook, was making his first trip on CG-249, but the rest had shaken down into a compatible team.

Even the nature and mission of their guest did not alert the Coast Guard crew to trouble. He was Robert K. Webster, an agent of the U.S. Secret Service, and he was being given a free ride by CG-249 only because his service, like the Coast Guard, was part of the Treasury Department. His work would be ashore in Bimini, a small slice of tropical paradise that had been so overrun by gangsters and bootleggers from the states that it was being called "Chicago on the Gulf Stream." Not content with the enormous markups they were getting on the booze from England and Europe that they managed to smuggle into the states, some of the Bimini operators were buying their supplies with counterfeit U.S. currency. This was too much for the British authorities, who had been turning a blind eye to the lucrative trade, and Webster was being sent over to cooperate with them in running the counterfeiters to ground. Although his sturdy body was turning a little jowly and paunchy, Webster had the unmistakable look of a law enforcement officer who had learned how to handle hoodlums.

CG-249 cast off docking lines at 0900—9 A.M.—and headed east at a comfortable cruising speed. So lulling was the voyage through calm water that Lehman turned into his bunk for an after-lunch nap when Lamby relieved him from his watch in the engine room. He never got to sleep. Sensitive to the sound of the ship's engines, he couldn't contain his curiosity when he heard them being revved up to full speed. He pulled on his dungarees, stepped into his shoes and went up on deck. Seaman Caudle, minding the helm, was alone in the pilothouse. The windows were open to take advantage of the breeze that the ship's speed was creating.

"What's up?" Lehman shouted through the window.

"Skipper wants to close with that boat up ahead," Caudle said. "Here, have a look."

Caudle handed the binoculars out through the window. When he brought her into focus, Lehman saw a speedboat about forty feet long with an open cockpit and trunk cabin forward. She had the lines of a boat that the rummies might use for contact work with mother ships or for runs to close-lying islands like Bimini. She was holding a proper course from Bimini to the Florida coast, but she was riding too high to be carrying much of a load. As he passed the glasses back to Caudle, Lehman wondered why Sanderlin would waste time chasing her down. Perhaps the skipper just wanted to show Webster, who was standing out on the foredeck with him, how the Coast Guard operated.

The men on the speedboat could have had no doubt about the identity and intentions of the cutter. By this time, the distinctive silhouette of the six-bitter was a familiar sight everywhere along the coast and throughout the Bahamas. But the speedboat showed no signs of slowing down as CG-249 approached. Sanderlin called to Tuten, his second in command, "Hey, Frank, bring me that rifle hanging in the pilothouse."

Sanderlin's choice of a rifle—instead of having the cannon or the machine gun on deck manned—indicated that he probably agreed with Lehman that the speedboat wasn't a promising catch. Or it may have been because the rifle was loaded with tracer bullets that would leave a visible trail of smoke on a bright day. Whatever, Sanderlin's aim was good, and he laid three ribbons of smoke across the other boat's bow. The speedboat stopped dead in the water. Sanderlin ordered the cutter's engines down to an idle and crept to within speaking distance. There were two men aboard the speedboat, one perched on a high stool at the wheel mounted on the aft bulkhead of the cabin and another half sitting against a small raised deck in the stern.

"Come alongside," Sanderlin yelled.

"Can't," the man at the wheel said. "Engine won't start."

"Well, we can sure come alongside you," Sanderlin said.

CG-249 had drifted beyond the speedboat's bow. Sanderlin motioned to Caudle to bring the cutter around, and he steered her alongside the forty-footer, starboard to starboard. Using the speedboat's lines, the crew tied her off to CG-249 with the bow line of the speedboat secured to a cleat opposite the cutter's pilothouse and her stern line secured at the cutter's bow. There was no identification on the forty-footer other than a number on the bow, V13997. The men on board looked like down-on-their-luck bums. The man behind the wheel—the spokesman and evidently the skipper—was lean, sunburned, middle-aged, dressed in dirty brown trousers and a dirty white shirt with the sleeves rolled up. His gray-haired crewman wore similar attire. Both men were barefoot. Except for an oil drum and the other clutter of a boat as messy as the men who manned her, the cockpit was empty.

"Where are you from?" Sanderlin asked.

"Miami."

"What are you doing out here?"

"Fishing."

"Your names?"

"I'm Horace Alderman," the man at the wheel said. "This here's Robert Weech."

"Any liquor aboard?"

"No."

During this brief interchange, John Robinson jumped over to the cabin top of the V13997. The sliding hatch was open, and Robinson could see suspicious sacks stashed around the engine. "Don't believe him, it's a rummy, Mr. Sanderlin," Robinson said.

"All right, you're under arrest. Come aboard the patrol boat," Sanderlin ordered.

Weech spoke for the first time. Sanderlin was known throughout the service for his amiability. It came through in his expression and tone of voice, and Weech was evidently encouraged to make a preposterous plea: "Have a heart, Captain. We got practically nothing—just twenty and a half cases, forty-one sacks. We couldn't afford more. You can count 'em. It's our first time, honest, but we need money to get shoes for the kids, and the fishing's been lousy. Let us go, and you'll never see us again."

Sanderlin couldn't blame Weech for giving his plea a try. Prohibition was a very unpopular law with millions of Americans, and coasties were often ambivalent about having to enforce it. Trying to live on servicemen's pay when they were constantly coming in contact with men making fortunes by catering to the tastes of the nation's best citizens made it difficult for some coasties to resist bribes. It could be so easy. Stories of tempting situations were always circulating through the service. There was one, for instance, about a chief boatswains mate in New York. As commander of a six-bitter, he was assigned to use his craft as part of the cordon the Coast Guard had established around the rum row off Gardiner's Island. While the chief was enjoying an off-duty night in a noisy, crowded speakeasy, a thousand-dollar bill appeared as if by magic beside the glass delivered from the bar. No words were spoken. If the chief pocketed the bill, all he had to do was steer off course for an hour or so while the contact boat made its lucrative passage to the mother ships. The story was a true one and one that could be told because the chief left the thousand dollars on the table, kept a sharper watch than usual and rather reluctantly made a big bust. Under certain circumstances appeals such as Weech's could be more effective than a bribe, since letting the culprit go "just this once" involved a redeeming element of selfless human sympathy. But, whatever his feelings, Sanderlin had no choice but to go by the book with a Secret Service agent looking over his shoulder.

"Sorry, fellows," he said. "You know the law. Hop up here."

Sanderlin frisked the men when they came aboard the cutter. They had no weapons and looked as harmless as they claimed to be. There wouldn't be any trouble; there seldom was. For most rummies a temporary rest in jail was just a part of doing business. Sanderlin had a .45 automatic tucked in his hip pocket just in case, but he told the crew to get rid of theirs and get busy transferring the contraband from the speedboat to the patrol boat. The men put their guns on either side of the wheel in the pilothouse and went to work. Webster opened the first sack that came aboard and read out the label on a bottle—"Four Roses." At one point, one of the sailors heaving sacks let Alderman go back into the speedboat's cabin to retrieve his coat, but for the most part Alderman and Weech slouched against the rail opposite the CG-249's pilothouse door and looked on morosely as the "money to get shoes for the kids" became federal property.

During this process, Robinson was still on the cabin top of the rum boat; Tuten, Caudle and Lehman were in the cockpit passing the sacks over to Lamby, Webster and Hollingsworth on the patrol boat's forward deck. When the last sack had been transferred, Sanderlin announced his intention of radioing back to base for instructions. Ordinarily he would have turned around and either towed or escorted his "prize" back to Ft. Lauderdale, but his primary mission of delivering Webster to Bimini complicated matters. His thought was to leave Robinson and Lehman or Lamby as a prize crew on V13997 to try to take her to Florida since he couldn't bring her back into British waters. He would keep the prisoners and contraband aboard while he went on to Bimini seventeen miles ahead. He wanted to make sure that he was doing the right thing and also to check out the names Alderman and Weech against the wanted lists.

The radio could have provided the amiable Mr. Sanderlin with a lifesaving lesson about deceptive appearances. Alderman—full name James Horace Alderman—was down in the books as "a bad actor." He was sometimes called "the Gulf Stream pirate" because he was known to hijack booze from others of his kind when he couldn't afford his own. At forty-four, he was in midcareer as a professional smuggler. In between booze runs from the Bahamas, he would ferry Chinese coolies from Cuba. He was, in fact, out on bond awaiting trial on charges of alien smuggling on that fateful day, August 7. Previously, he had spent a year and a day in the federal penitentiary for making the mistake of hiring an undercover U.S. Customs agent as cook on one of his rum-running voyages. He had developed an abiding hatred of law enforcement officers and a wild man's fear of being caged behind bars.

Getting to the radio aboard CG-249 was an awkward business.

The radio was at the back of the pilothouse; between it and the doors opening onto the deck on the side, a two-foot-wide chart board was stretched from window ledge to window ledge. It could be removed, but it was easier just to duck under it. Sanderlin brushed past Alderman lounging at the rail, entered the pilothouse and started to stoop under the board. A pistol he had evidently conjured up out of the coat he had retrieved appeared in Alderman's hand. He shot the stooping boatswain in his broad back. The bullet went through Sanderlin's body, came out the top of his chest and embedded itself in the door of the radio cabinet. Sanderlin slumped forward to the deck, oozing blood.

Lamby, still on the foredeck where he had been stowing the liquor sacks, was the first to react. He ran down the port deck past the pilothouse and across from Alderman. He was headed for the magazine under the after deck where there were more firearms. Alderman started to go through the pilothouse to cut him off, changed his mind and ran back to the starboard deck, from which point he could get a clear shot at Lamby. Lamby was lowering himself into the engine- room hatch when Alderman's bullet, fired from above, caught him in the chest and sliced down across the lower part of his spinal column. Instantly paralyzed from the waist down, Lamby tumbled to the engine room deck and crawled on his elbows up between the engines in search of some shelter.

At about the same moment, Robinson, still on the cabin top of the speedboat, saw a small wrench he could reach through the hatch, grabbed it and threw it at Alderman. Alderman spun around and covered him with the gun. By now, Alderman, the only man on either boat with a gun in hand, didn't have to threaten to shoot. He had already put two men out of commission, each with a single shot. Robinson, a man of quick reflexes, saw that the stern line between the rum boat and the cutter had come loose, leaving a small gap between the vessels. He dove into that gap and swam under the patrol boat to surface on the other side where Alderman couldn't see him. Tuten, Caudle and Lehman literally dove for cover in the speedboat's cabin. They looked wildly around for a weapon. Caudle picked up a small screwdriver. Lehman told him to drop it; brandishing it would only cause the trigger-happy Alderman to start shooting again.

Standing by the patrol boat's pilothouse and waving his gun, Alderman started giving orders. He told Webster and Hollingsworth to jump over into the cockpit of the rum boat. He told the others cowering in the cabin to get out and join them. "Out or I'll shoot through the roof," he said, and they believed him. He directed them to put their arms up and lock their hands over their heads. They were in no position to disobey. He saw Robinson's head in the water near the bow of the patrol boat and told him to climb out and join the rest of the crew. Robinson hauled himself onto the stern of the speedboat.

Once he had them all assembled, hands up, Alderman turned to Weech, who had watched the murderous performance in a state of silent shock. "Get that liquor back on our boat, Weech," he said. Weech hesitated, and Alderman asked, "You are with me, aren't you, Weech?"

"Sure. Sure thing. All the way, Horace," Weech said and started putting his back into the work.

While the miserable Weech hauled and heaved the sacks between the boats, Alderman launched into a monologue to his captive audience: "I've had it with you Coast Guard bastards. You've screwed me long enough, and you're not going to make me do time again. I'm going to kill you all, one at a time. I'm going to make you jump into the water and wing you. You'll make good shark bait. And I'm going to do it with your own guns. . . ." Alderman paused long enough to reach into the pilothouse through the open window and take one of the .45s from beside the wheel. He fired into the deck with it and grinned. "Just wanted to make sure it works. You got such lousy equipment. Yeah, this'll do fine. . . ."

Webster, much older than the Coast Guard crew and equipped with much more experience in dealing with crazed criminals, tried talking soothingly to Alderman: "Why do you want to hurt these young fellows? They haven't done anything to you. . . ."

"Well, I'm going to see that they never have a chance to," Alderman said. Seeing that Weech had finished his job, he told him, "Get down there in the cutter's engine room and yank the gas lines off, Weech. And tell that fellow hiding down there to get out here with the others because I want you to throw a lighted match down that hatch once you get the gas line off."

Alderman wasn't mad after all—just diabolical. His fevered mind had concocted an almost perfect plan. He would kill them all and blow up the patrol boat. Explosions aboard gasoline-powered craft were common enough that the disappearance of CG-249 with all hands would be accepted as a tragic accident. But to have the story stick, he had to be sure that there would be no survivors. It was a very bad moment for the men listening to him.

Nevertheless, Webster wouldn't give up. If Alderman could reason that well, he might also listen to reason.

"Do yourself a favor, Alderman—and us, too," he said. "Put us off in the dinghy and give us a crack at reaching Bimini. Even if we make it through the Gulf Stream, which is doubtful, you'll have plenty of time to get lost. That way you won't face a lot more murder charges. In fact, the boys here and me might see our way to saying the boat blew up and took the others with it and we were just lucky."

"I don't trust any of you chickenshit bastards. And if you want to know, you are going to be the first to go, you pot-bellied son of a bitch. . . ."

In a momentary lull, they could all hear Lamby's voice crying out from the engine room, "I can't move . . . I can't move . . . I tell you I can't move. . . ."

In a pleading voice, Weech said, "But you've got to. You'll be burned alive."

"I can't . . . I tell you I can't. . . ."

Weech emerged from the hatch to pass on the unnecessary information about Lamby's condition, and Alderman said, "Well, shoot him."

"I don't have a gun," Weech said.

Alderman stuck his own pistol in his belt while he kept the .45 pointed at the captive crew. With a hand free, he reached through the pilothouse window, took another .45 and tossed it to Weech: "There, you've got a gun, and I know it works. Now shoot him."

"I can't shoot a wounded man."

"Well, forget it. We can't waste time. Let him burn to death; they're all going to die anyway. Did you get the lines off?"

Evidently ashamed of his softness or afraid that it would irritate Alderman, Weech said, "Yeah. I had to kick that fella a little to get him to show me where to find a wrench, but I got 'em broken. There's gas all over the bilge."

Alderman hopped over to the cabin top of his own boat and said to Weech, "OK, drop a match down there."

While the rest watched in horrified fascination, Weech peered over the hatch, struck a match and let it drop. Then he jumped back to the rail, ready to go overboard if need be. But nothing happened. He tried it again . . . and again . . . and again. He ran out of matches. "They just fizzle out in the bilge water or something," he shouted over to Alderman.

"If you got them lines off like you said, it'll go soon enough. Come on over here and get more matches, Weech."

Weech meekly followed instructions and was starting back to the patrolboat when Frank Tuten broke the strained silence. His thought was evidently to try anything that might buy time. Alderman was squatting by the sliding hatch on the cabin top. He had retrieved his own pistol from his belt and had a gun in each hand. Hollingsworth, Caudle and Robinson were standing on the small raised afterdeck; Lehman, Webster and Tuten were standing on the cockpit floor in front of a fifty-five-gallon oil drum. Their hands were still on their heads. "You'd better start your engine, Alderman, or you're going to go with us when he sets that patrol boat afire," Tuten said.

Alderman glared at Tuten, but he followed his advice. "Get back here and watch these bastards while I start the engine," he told Weech. "I'm going to give you another gun and let 'em all have it if one of them moves."

Alderman handed Weech his pistol. Then he dropped down into the cabin. The engine sputtered into life. When Alderman came back up, he took his gun from Weech. Once more Weech started for the patrol boat and once more Alderman called him back since the engine seemed to be stalling. "Get down there and give it more juice," he ordered.

Weech vanished below, but the engine still faltered. Alderman took his eyes off his captives to look down and see what Weech was doing. Webster, ever quietly watchful, started to take his hands down and move forward. Alderman caught the movement in his peripheral vision, looked up and fired. The .45

slug killed Webster instantly, although the thrust of his strong body carried him forward and down into the engine compartment.

The others were aware of Webster's movement too. It was as if he had given them a prearranged signal, although there had been no such understanding. Caudle leaped clear over Lehman to grab for one of Alderman's hands, and Tuten lunged for the other. Hollingsworth jumped onto the oil drum, and Alderman spun him off into the water with the impact of another bullet from the .45. Lehman stooped to pick up a boat scraper he had seen on the cockpit deck as he rushed forward. He reached over Tuten and Caudle, who were struggling with Alderman's arms, and hit Alderman on the head. The blow knocked Alderman back, but he kept firing even with Tuten and Caudle on his arms. Lehman struck again and again until Alderman lay spread-eagled, and the guns fell from his limp hands. The clips were empty.

Weech dropped his .45 by the engine and tried to escape through the speedboat's forward hatch. Robinson wrestled with him and threw him overboard. Weech swam for the patrol boat. With Alderman either unconscious or dead, Tuten and Robinson jumped aboard their own boat to fend Weech off. Tuten used a dinghy oar to bat him away. Lehman climbed on the stool by the speedboat's wheel to board the cutter and get his hands on the last .45 on the pilothouse shelf. He saw Alderman make a movement and hit him twice again on the head. The .45 jammed as Lehman tried to put a shell in the chamber, and he threw it down in disgust. Hearing a noise in the water near the bow, Lehman ran to the rail. Hollingsworth, a good swimmer, was thrashing around and calling for help.

"What's wrong?" Lehman asked.

"I'm shot in the head," Hollingsworth said.

Lehman saw a rope dangling over the side of the rum boat. "Grab that rope, Jodie, and we'll get you out in a minute," he said.

The action was too fast for thought. The engine on the speedboat was still running. Caudle paid no attention to it when he went below to check Webster for signs of life and picked up the gun Weech had dropped. Coming back up to the cockpit he stumbled against a lever near the wheel. The boat started moving in reverse. The bow line lashing it to the patrol boat parted. Caudle yelled at Lehman, "What'll I do? What'll I do?"

"Push that big lever forward and come alongside again," Lehman yelled.

Caudle either couldn't hear or didn't understand. The speedboat backed away. Hollingsworth was still clinging to the line and being tumbled in a propeller wash. A frantic Caudle yanked the wires off the spark plugs, and the engine died. In the sudden silence, Caudle heard Hollingsworth and pulled the bleeding man aboard. He saw a large shark swoop through the spot where Hollingsworth had been and under the boat. Caudle was marooned on a powerless boat with a wounded man and a murderer who might regain consciousness at any time. The hundred yards between him and the patrol boat, also powerless with its gas lines broken, might as well have been a mile.

Aboard the patrol boat Robinson came forward and said to Lehman, "Watch that man overboard, Frank. I'm going down and look for some handcuffs."

"Well, give me a gun," Lehman said.

"Here, take mine," Robinson said, tossing him the .45 he had recovered when he checked Sanderlin and found him dead as soon as he boarded the CG-249.

Lehman went to the stern where Tuten stood, oar still in hand, watching over Weech, who was clutching a rope. Lehman pointed his gun at Weech and said, "You son of a bitch, I'm going to kill you." Caudle was covering the prostrate Alderman with his .45. Across the water separating them, he heard Lehman and yelled, "You shoot that son of a bitch, and I'll shoot this one."

Weech started to beg in the same whining voice he had used before: "I'm fifty-two years old and never been in trouble. I got a wife and two kids who will starve if you kill me. . . ."

"So's our skipper got a wife and two kids and you didn't think of that," Lehman said.

"I didn't kill your skipper. That other fellow did," Weech said.

Tuten, a middle-aged seaman of long experience who was now in command of CG-249, said, "Don't kill him, Lehman. Let's help him aboard when Robinson gets back with the cuffs."

Then he called over to Caudle, "Don't do anything you'll be sorry for, Hal." Tuten's calm voice and sane advice brought the excited sailors back to their senses. They put their guns away.

After they hauled a shaking Weech aboard and handcuffed him, they launched the dinghy, and Tuten rowed over to tow the speedboat back alongside. Robinson went below to see what he could do about Lamby, still lying between the engines and groaning with pain. Lehman went into the pilothouse to call the base on the radio. In his death throes, Sanderlin had flipped over on his back and drawn up one knee. Lehman had to straddle his skipper's chest and face and try to avoid the staring eyes while he chanted, "NAMJ calling NEFX . . . NAMJ calling NEFX . . ." When base responded, he said, "We had a fight with rum runners and have two dead and two wounded. Send the old man's speedboat out on the double. We're four hours southeast of Lauderdale and dead in the water. . . ."

As an engine man, Lehman guessed that whatever Weech had done to the gas lines on CG-249 would be hard to undo, especially without help from the paralyzed Lamby, who was moved gently up to the foredeck. He was right. He found that Weech had twisted hunks out of the two copper tubes that fed each engine directly from a gravity tank. Scrounging around through junk boxes, Lehman found a length of hose that he could cut in half to join the tubes. The diameter of the hose was larger than that of the tubes, but he tightened the hose down by twisting wire around it. With full carburetors the engines started right up. They hadn't run minutes before Lehman knew that he had created a lethal bomb. The patches weren't tight enough, and gas was dripping into the bilges. With the carburetors starving for the gas they should have been getting, the engines started backfiring and shooting eighteen-inch flames across the narrow walk between them. Lehman could smell the fumes that could blow any second. He was lucky, plain lucky. He got the engines shut down again before the gas reached an explosive concentration. But he didn't give up. He started looking for another solution and finally found some clamps that would be more effective than the wire. He was still working at installing the clamps when the fast boat from base arrived bearing the commandant, Lieutenant Junior Grade Beckwith Jordan; the executive officer, Ensign E.E. Hahn; and an armed complement of men.

Jordan realized that the need of the moment was to get the wounded to a hospital as quickly as possible. Lamby seemed to be near death, and the bullet that had hit Hollingsworth had entered his left cheek and exited his right eye to cause undetermined damage. The physically unharmed men of CG-249 were psychologically shattered by their experience. Jordan took them aboard his boat with the wounded and replaced them with a relief crew under Hahn. Since there was nothing more to be done for the dead—Sanderlin and Webster—and the prisoners had at last been rendered harmless in handcuffs and chains, Jordan left them aboard CG-249 too. Lehman stayed behind to help the new machinists get the engines going. When CG-249 was under way toward home, Lehman went back to the stern to sit alone and try to come to grips with the horror he had seen. His last memory of that day would be watching the fins of sharks slicing through the water just beyond the propeller's turbulence as they followed CG-249 with its bloody cargo of murderer and murdered.

Lamby died four days later; Hollingsworth recovered except for the loss of an eye. Alderman was charged with three murders and piracy on the high seas. In addition to his rampage with CG-249, there was evidence that his contraband cargo had been hijacked. Nobody in Bimini could recall that Alderman had bought any booze, but two men in a Chris-Craft that disappeared on that same August 7 had purchased twenty and a half cases that included some bottles marked "Four Roses." A conviction bringing a mandatory sentence of death by hanging was not hard for the prosecutors to get. In support of the Coast Guard testimony, Weech turned state's witness and was rewarded with a light sentence of a year and a day.

Once sentenced, however, Alderman, with the aid of his lawyers, put up as fierce a fight against death as he had on the cabin top of his speedboat. Incredibly, the sentiment of the drinking public was on his side. To this, Alderman cleverly added some sentiment from the nondrinking public by converting to Christianity in his cell. President Hoover was petitioned to pardon the repentent sinner soon after he came into office. When that tactic failed, Alderman's lawyers continued to delay execution with legal wrangling over the site. Since Alderman had been convicted of federal crimes, it was decreed that he should be executed on federal territory. The first choice of a proper place was the roof of the federal courthouse in Miami, but the Alderman attorneys did some digging and discovered that the courthouse was built on land leased from the state of Florida. Looking for a way out of this impasse, the authorities did some research too. They found an old federal statute still on the books to the effect that murderers and pirates were to be hanged at the port where they were first brought ashore. In this light, the logical site became the roof of the Broward County Jail, where Alderman was being held. County officials were not happy. There had never been an execution in Broward County, and the now religious Alderman was being viewed as a martyr by many of their constituents. Somebody came up with the idea of having an engineer survey the roof of the county jail, and he declared it structurally unsound for the weight of a gallows and the necessary accompaniment of witnesses to a proper hanging. An exasperated judge finally ruled that Alderman be executed, as prescribed, on the nearest federal post, which was U.S. Coast Guard Base Six, Fort Lauderdale.

The Coast Guard wasn't any happier than the county. Already on the wrong side of misguided public opinion, they didn't want the added publicity of hanging a martyr. But they couldn't argue that the big corrugated-iron airplane hangar at the base wasn't adequate to the occasion. Their task was eased somewhat by the appointment of a U.S. marshal as hangman and a court order prohibiting the press from being present at the event. But some newsmen did get wind of it and were standing outside the gate of the base when a hearse and two automobiles filled with marshals, police and the prisoner drove by at 6 A.M. on August 17, 1929, almost exactly two years after the shoot-out on CG-249.

Alderman, wearing white shirt and pants, was led up the steps of a temporary ten-foot wooden platform overhung by a rope noose. He was silent and seemingly composed until a black hood was fitted over his head, and the rope was drawn snug to his neck. Then in a breaking voice he started to sing, "God be with you till we meet again . . ." At 6:03 A.M., the song was ended by the sharp crack of the trapdoor being sprung. The hooded figure dropped out of sight, and at 6:19 A.M. the rope was cut. A U.S. Public Health Service doctor pronounced Alderman dead while a Coast Guardsman who had seen too much of death—Chief Boatswains Mate Frank Tuten—stood by as witness on behalf of his comrades.

Tuten was not only bearing witness to an act of justice but to an event of historic proportions. It was the first and only hanging in the long annals of the U.S. Coast Guard. But in the year 1929 it was only a drop in a sea of crime. Crime was making daily headlines, what with gangster Al Capone getting a year in jail for pleading guilty to packing a concealed weapon, former Interior Secretary Albert Fall going on trial for taking a $100,-000 bribe, and prisoners rioting and killing each other in New York and Kansas jails. Calling crime the nation's greatest concern, President Hoover appointed the Wickersham Commission to look into the connection between Prohibition and crime. But history took the matter out of their hands that same year with the great stock market crash. It brought on the Great Depression, which would lead to the New Deal and repeal of the unenforceable laws that resulted in the tragedy of CG-249.

Chapter 4

The Half-Billion-Dollar Drug Bust

I T had been an unusually uncomfortable and boring patrol, and on that dawn of Sunday, October 1, 1989, the fourteen men aboard the 110-foot U.S. Coast Guard cutter *Cushing* were glad to be heading back to their home port, Mobile, Alabama. For most of ten days they had been running in and out of gales that roiled the waters and swept the Gulf of Mexico clean of its normal traffic of fishing boats and pleasure craft. Whether she was encountering the fringes of hurricane Hugo, which was literally tearing through the Caribbean islands and along the southeast coast of the United States or an entirely different storm, the *Cushing* was vaulting high waves and being lashed by driving rain and salt spray blowing off the white-capped wave crests for ten hours at a stretch.

Since missions of rescue require Coast Guardsmen to go out regularly into the worst kind of weather, a description of what they were up against in this particular patrol by the *Cushing*'s skipper, Lieutenant Mark Sikorski, a graduate of the Coast Guard Academy with eleven years of sea duty under his belt, is the best measure of how bad it was. "The weather was really spooky because the barometer was just plummeting," Lieutenant Sikorski recalls. "On September twenty-fourth, our first gale, it dropped to twenty-nine point six. On our radar screen, I could see these counterclockwise clouds spiraling all around us and I kept thinking, 'My gosh, we're in the middle of something, and I don't want to be here.'"

52

It's not that the captain was afraid his ship couldn't stand up to the storm. Only a year old, the *Cushing* was one of the fleet of swift, sturdy patrol boats that are bearing the brunt of America's drug war at sea. Powered by two V-16 Packsman engines built in Britain, each of which delivers 4,000 horsepower governed down to 3,000, she can make more than twenty-six knots at full speed and accelerate from zero to top speed in thirty seconds. Her power is such that controlling her under certain conditions, such as docking, requires great finesse and expert seamanship; the slowest she will go with engines engaged is twelve knots. Her cruising range on a single load of fuel is 2,000 miles. Apart from personal weapons for the crew, she mounts a twenty-millimeter deck gun and two M-60 machine guns. Equipped with the latest in electronic navigational and operational gear, she is altogether a ship to inspire confidence.

In the equation they used to create a vessel with maximum efficiency and capability for her size, the designers of the 110 footer didn't factor in comfort. Quarters are cramped for the full complement of sixteen men and women. Women, in fact, can only serve on a 110 as commanding officer or executive officer—there are some—the two ranks assigned cubbyhole private cabins. Anyone taller than six feet has to duck at doorways and scrunch into the fixed seats at galley tables that are reminiscent of a grade-school cafeteria. Ladders leading from deck to deck are pinched and perpendicular. There are grab rails everywhere for a very good reason; under way in nasty weather, the 110 does her best to knock sailors off their pins. The old adage in sailing days for men who had to go aloft to work on the yardarms was "one hand for the ship and one hand for me," and it could apply to crewing the 110 in rough seas. Thus, the men of the *Cushing* were sleepless and muscle sore that Sunday morning.

This discomfort was as much a part of their job as the weather and could have been taken in stride but for the boredom. The *Cushing* is one of two cutters on regular patrol out of Coast Guard District Eight, headquartered in New Orleans. Berthed in Mobile 150 miles away, they cover an unusually large operational area—the entire Gulf of Mexico, which includes the Mexican coast and the coasts of Texas, Louisiana, Mississippi, Alabama and part of Florida. Their mission is primarily law enforcement—that is, interdiction of illegal traffic, whether in drugs or other substances or in people, and maintenance of marine safety laws and regulations. In addition, of course, they have to be alert to environmental abuses and ready to participate in any rescue efforts within their range. Given all this responsibility, action is normally the antidote to any miseries encountered on patrol. In the active sea lanes, the *Cushing* would often average several boardings a day, but in the whole ten days of this patrol she had been involved in only one, which turned out to be routine and unproductive.

It was mostly the frustration of having gone through a brutal buffeting for nothing that prompted Lieutenant Sikorski to linger one more day off the tip of the Yucatán Peninsula some 450 miles south of Galveston, Texas, before turning north toward home. The area could be productive since many ships transiting the Yucatán Channel from Colombia to reach Mexican or U.S. ports pass through it. But on this trip the *Cushing*'s crew had come to believe that the weather had left them alone out there, and they could hardly wait for the skipper's order to come to a course for Mobile. Then, in the dark hours of the morning of October 1, the watch on the bridge had a radar contact and summoned Sikorski from his bunk. Some fifteen miles away and moving steadily, the blip had to be another vessel. "Let's kind of follow it and see where it goes and maybe in the morning we'll check it out," the skipper told the watch.

For some nine hours, the *Cushing* followed a phantom blip that was moving west toward Mexico. Finally, they brought their quarry into view, and Sikorski could see through his glasses that they were closing with a small ship—about 185 feet long— with a familiar configuration. It had a pilothouse up forward and a long, flat afterdeck like one of the supply vessels that work the oil rigs off Louisiana. But this one had evidently been converted to serve as a freighter; there were clearly visible container trailers lined up on the deck. As common in these waters, the ship flew the Panamanian flag. There was nothing at all suspicious about the freighter, but, eager for some kind of action, Sikorski decided to check it out.

Ever since its founding in 1790 as the Revenue Marine under the Department of the Treasury, the Coast Guard has had a broad mandate to enforce smuggling laws with respect to U.S. vessels or to any vessels within U.S. waters. Title 14 of the U.S. Code states that the Coast Guard "may make inquiries, examinations, inspections, searches and arrests upon the high seas and water over which the United States has jurisdiction for the prevention, detection and suppression of violations of the laws of the United States." It's a slightly different matter, however, in the case of a foreign vessel encountered in foreign waters, the situation which now confronted the *Cushing*. Elaborate international protocol must be followed before a boarding and inspection. But there's no law against asking questions, nor any law requiring answers. Sikorski raised the ship they were pursuing on the radio and queried the captain through his Spanish-speaking petty officer, Machinery Technician Second Class Octavio Garza.

The captain's responses were willing and open, an indication that all was in as good order as it appeared to be. The vessel was the *Zedom Sea*, bound from Barranquilla, Colombia, for Tampico, Mexico, a port about 200 miles south of the U.S. border. This tallied well with her course. Her cargo, according to her captain, was gelatin and cement—an odd but not incredible combination. The *Zedom Sea* was registered in Panama but owned by the Sultan Navigation Co. of Maracaibo, Venezuela. While Garza was talking with the captain, Lieutenant Sikorski checked his name and that of the ship against his current information lists of suspected traffickers in illegal cargo and found nothing. Nevertheless, he requested permission to board to check the ship's documentation papers, a first step in that international protocol. The captain's response was disarming: "OK, sure. Come aboard."

"Ask him how many in crew," Sikorski told Garza.

"Nine," was the answer. "Garza, you take command of the boarding party," said Sikorski. "Musgrave, you go as assistant. Take seven men with you; I don't like to be outnumbered."

Both ships came dead in the water while preparations for boarding went forward on the *Cushing*. Cutters never go alongside another vessel for purposes of boarding. Quite apart from exposing themselves to counterattack in a worst-case scenario, there's more than a probability of damage in the grinding of steel against steel if there is any kind of a sea running. Lashed aft on the 110's deck is an all-purpose boarding and landing craft called a RHIB—rigid-hull inflatable boat. It's five meters long, has a fiberglass hull ringed with rubber pontoons, and is powered by a sixty-five-hp outboard. Kept always inflated for action, the RHIB is picked up on a boom and swung overside, where the men get aboard. Launching and managing the RHIB can be a tricky and dangerous business in rough weather, but luckily for the crew of the *Cushing* the weather had finally cleared and the seas had calmed.

A boarding is always an experience to raise the adrenaline. It's impossible to know just what might happen. Unless resistance or threats have been encountered in advance, Coast Guardsmen are charged with being courteous, with boarding in a friendly manner. No long arms are carried, and the boarding party's nine-millimeter sidearms are holstered. To be sure, precaution is always taken to prevent surprise from turning into disaster and to make possible instant retaliation. On this morning, for instance, the nine-man boarding team wore bullet-proof vests under their life jackets, and Lieutenant Sikorski had an M-60 mounted and manned on the bridge wing of the *Cushing* to give them cover. A request was radioed ahead to the *Zedom Sea* to have the entire crew assembled on the bridge.

Both Garza and his assistant, Boatswains Mate First Class Jack Musgrave, had experience in the techniques of boarding and searching. Although neither had yet been involved in a cocaine bust, they had participated in marijuana seizures when that was the most common contraband. Garza's action was quite a while in the past. It had happened during a first enlistment, and he had since spent some time as a civilian as well as completing a tour of duty with the Coast Guard's environmental strike team before coming aboard the *Cushing*. Musgrave, a twelve-year career man who had at one point been detached to serve as law enforcement officer on a Navy ship, had been through many marijuana busts and one weapons seizure. Nevertheless, riding over to the *Zedom Sea* in the RHIB, they could feel the butterflies that feed on high adrenaline stir in their stomachs.

The ship's master, Arsenio Marin Pineda, had eight crew members with him on the bridge when the Coast Guardsmen came aboard. Going by the book, Garza immediately sent his people fanning out into every corner of the ship to check on whether there was anyone in hiding. They came back empty-handed. The only initial surprise was to find a twenty-six-year-old woman serving as cook. "Everything looked routine to us at first," Musgrave says. "Pineda had his whole crew with him, and he was cooperative. He was more than willing to let us look around the ship, and nobody seemed to be nervous. The only unusual thing I noticed was that a couple of the containers were padlocked."

Since he doubted that they would lock containers of cement and gelatin, Musgrave asked Garza to ask the master for a manifest showing the contents of each container. Studying it, Musgrave grew "curiouser and curiouser." For starters, the manifest gave the destination of the cargo as Veracruz, 300 miles south of Tampico. Some of the ten containers were described as being topped off with 130-pound bags of gelatin while others, including the two with locks, contained a minimum amount of cement—about two tons per container. The manifest said that the cargo came from the Medellin Company. Having another look around, Musgrave noted that one trailer had fiberglass walls, which is quite unusual. He also saw a lot of cement spilled near the doors of the locked containers. Rusty and dented and crewed by a motley group of Colombians, the *Zedom Sea* was a vessel on which a little sloppy cargo handling might be expected. But the Coast Guardsmen knew that cement dust could prevent narc dogs from catching the scent of drugs.

Garza felt that there was enough accumulating evidence to warrant asking the master's permission to look inside the trailers. Pineda threw up his hands and said, "I don't know what's in there. We loaded in Colombia. It could be anything. I'm not responsible. I don't even have a key. I would have to get permission."

Garza thought it was time to harden up a little. "Well, get it," he said.

The captain picked up the radio mike and started talking. Garza could tell from listening to one side of the conversation that the party at the other end was adamant about not permitting the U.S. Coast Guard to inspect the containers. Pineda

signed off and shrugged an apology of helplessness. Leaving
their seven companions aboard the *Zedom Sea,* Garza and Musgrave zipped back to the *Cushing* in the RHIB to confer with
Lieutenant Sikorski out of earshot of the Colombians. A detailed
report by his petty officers left no doubt in Sikorski's mind that
they would have to take a look inside those trailers. But they
couldn't do it without going through the whole protocol dance
of getting permission from the government of registry—in this
case, Panama—through the State Department in Washington.
The timing for this could hardly have been worse. Not only was
it a Sunday morning, which meant dealing with skeleton crews
that might have little authority, but U.S. relations with Manuel
Noriega's Panama were a confused mess. As if this were not
enough, nature once more conspired to frustrate the tired and
testy *Cushing* crew.

The cutter couldn't raise the Eighth District in New Orleans
on the radio. "We were 500 miles out, and we use high frequency when we are that far away," said Sikorski. "It is very
susceptible to atmosphere. The weather happened to be beautiful where we were, but we couldn't get the atmospherics right
for the right signal path. "I was trying to call everybody I could
think of—every single Coast Guard group in the Gulf Coast and
Key West and other ships I knew were in the area. It was like
something in the atmosphere was zapping our signal. After
about an hour of not reaching anybody, I recalled my boarding
party, but I told *Zedom Sea*'s master that we would be back as
soon as we got permission."

The *Zedom Sea* got under way again about noon, October 1,
and the *Cushing* began shadowing her while working with the
radio. If nothing else, the *Cushing*'s people were gaining experience in a kind of seamanship that would soon prove useful.
Because of the *Cushing*'s jackrabbit speed, they had to run on
one engine and often idle to keep *down* to *Zedom Sea*'s eleven-
knot pace. At four P.M., they finally made radio contact with
New Orleans and requested a "statement of no objection" to
boarding and searching against the master's will. It would take
an untold number of hours to obtain that statement, if ever they
did. By following the *Zedom Sea* they were increasing hourly
their distance from the home base to which they had been so

gratefully headed before that radar blip popped up on the screen. Lieutenant Sikorski couldn't help wondering whether he was right in putting his weary men through this experience in view of the fact that the *Zedom Sea*'s skipper had been so cooperative and confident, her crew so relaxed and nonresistant. He summoned Garza and Musgrave for a serious sharing of minds. Garza recalls the conference in these words, "Our captain asked me and Musgrave if we thought we should continue to follow that boat. We discussed it and decided we should keep going. We just had a feeling that something was wrong."

It was 11 P.M. before the *Cushing* received the desired permission. Under the circumstances it was swift action, and it might not have come through at all if the U.S. State Department hadn't been still recognizing the authority of the ex-Panamanian president Eric Delvalle because of the "stolen" election that gave Noriega power. Delvalle had granted blanket permission for U.S. ships to search suspicious Panamanian vessels before his term expired on September 1, and Washington considered this adequate for the *Cushing*'s purposes. By then, Sikorski decided that it would be the better part of valor to wait until morning before attempting a boarding. There was no chance that the slow *Zedom Sea* could elude them, but there was always a chance that something could go wrong or be overlooked in the dark. Besides, the whole crew would have to be employed in the operation, and this leisurely passage through calm seas would give most of them a chance for some sleep before the call to action.

At 8 A.M. on Monday, October 2, Lieutenant Sikorski called the *Zedom Sea* on the radio and informed Master Pineda that he had received Panamanian permission to board and search. Once again, Pineda appeared to be cooperative. The *Zedom Sea* slowed to a stop. This time Sikorski detailed ten men to the boarding party with Garza again in command. Going along as assistant was the *Cushing*'s executive officer, Lieutenant Junior Grade Tom Meyers; Musgrave would be in charge of the search party aboard the *Zedom Sea*. Having an officer serve under an enlisted man is not uncommon in the Coast Guard and reflects the service's flexibility in using people to the best advantage in a given situation. Garza's command of Spanish meant that he was better equipped than anyone else to understand what was going on and control the action. A 1986 graduate of the Coast Guard Academy, Lieutenant Meyers had participated in two marijuana busts while he was on summer cruises as an under-graduate, but he wasn't averse to learning from the more experienced petty officers. It was a morning with a sun of brass and a sea of glass. By 8:15 the *Cushing*'s boarding party, guns still holstered, had scrambled up to the deck of *Zedom Sea*, ready to go to work.

This time there was a subtle difference in the way they were received. Although there was no open hostility, the *Zedom Sea* crew, including the master, appeared to be nervous. There was no meeting of eyes, and the freighter's crew did not turn around to watch them—a very unusual lack of curiosity in Musgrave's experience. After satisfying themselves once more that there were no hidden persons or weapons, the Coast Guardsmen started on the containers. Skipper Pineda still maintained stoutly that he had no key to the two padlocks on the cement containers on the after part of the deck. Anticipating this bit of resistance, Musgrave had brought along bolt cutters, and he handed them to the three men he assigned to the aft containers. He and two others would check out the forward ones. Garza would stay with two companions on the bridge to keep watch over the *Zedom Sea* crew while Lt. Meyers would be free to roam the ship, camcorder in hand, to make a film record of any evidence that might be found. The Coast Guard has learned that videos of law enforcement action in progress can be power-fully persuasive in court, and the lieutenant's assignment as photographer was vital to the mission.

Electricians Mate Second Class David Holland and Quarter-master Michael Spencer, working on the aft detail, clipped the lock on one of the containers and found themselves looking at a raised floor of cement bags, as proclaimed in the manifest. They took one out, ripped it open, and assured themselves that the content was actually cement. So far so good, but it was strange that there was so much waste space in the partially filled container. They climbed into the container to check the walls, a common hiding place for contraband. They were looking for signs of recent welding, fiberglass patches—anything irregular.

They started shifting bags to get at the walls. When Holland lifted a cement bag from the second layer, he saw a very different kind of package. It was a bale of white burlap material marked "30." He plucked it out, ripped it open and found thirty smaller bundles in green plastic tape. He tore one of them apart and found a styrofoam container like the kind in which electronics are shipped. Inside this container was a white powder that could only be cocaine—a kilo of the substance.

All the while he was making these discoveries, Holland was yelling, "Hey, look at this! Come here! Look what I've found!" to Spencer and Boatswains Mate R. E. Smith, who had just started looking around inside the other locked container nearby. When the powder appeared, the three of them started whooping with excitement, and Lieutenant Meyers came running with his camera. There was a moment or two, as Meyers confesses, of very unprofessional conduct as pent-up frustration was released by sudden elation. "They said I let out a couple of yells. My heart skipped a couple of beats," Holland said. And no wonder. Quickly flinging more cement bags aside, they realized that the whole trailer—and probably the other one too—was floored with bales of cocaine. They were onto something really big.

But professionalism quickly took hold again. They had to be sure that the substance was cocaine. Not that they had any real doubts from the look and feel of it. It was very white, like baking soda, and taken in hand and squeezed would pack a little. They had with them a narcotics identification kit, designed to make a quick test of the nature and strength of an illegal substance. The kit consists of a plastic pouch in which there are small tubes of chemicals. The test involves putting some of the substance in the pouch, breaking the tubes and reading a change in colors against a scale. On the third test of the powder Holland found, it not only proved to be cocaine but was so pure that it "knocked the kit right off the scale," according to Musgrave.

It was 8:50 A.M. when Lieutenant Sikorski, waiting impatiently aboard the *Cushing,* got a call from Garza reporting the find and the fact that the substance had tested positive. The excitement that they all were feeling came through in Garza's voice, and Sikorski had a little trouble in sounding professional himself. "OK, let's take control of the situation," he told Garza.

This meant taking the *Zedom Sea*'s crew into custody. They kept the master, engineer and cook aboard the *Zedom Sea*—the master and engineer because if they had any plans to scuttle her they would have to go down with the ship, the cook because dealing with a woman aboard the 110 would be awkward—and sent the other six over to the *Cushing* in the RHIB. All of the prisoners were ordered to change from their own clothes into Coast Guard coveralls. Their personal belongings, including anything that could be used as a weapon right down to belts, were bagged and tagged. As an extra precaution, the six men brought over to the *Cushing* were chained to the rails.

Once the bust had been made, Sikorski wanted to waste no time getting under way for home port. He appointed Executive Officer Meyers as commander of a prize crew to sail the *Zedom Sea* with Garza, Musgrave and Seaman Alton McVey as his complement. But for the time being he left the other six men from the *Cushing* with them to help with the heavy labor of moving cement sacks to get at the cocaine and make an estimate of how much they had found. They only had access to five of the containers because of the way in which the others were positioned. Only two of the five—the two with locks—contained cocaine. Uncovering it all took some six hours of grueling work. Cement dust turned the men's dark blue coveralls so white that they looked as if they had been rolling around in cocaine. There was certainly enough of it to make that possible, and the mounting count made the work a kind of joy. When they finally got all the cocaine moved into one trailer it turned out to be a little more than 200 bales of thirty kilos each, which would weigh out at 12,000 pounds, or six tons. They were flabbergasted. Most cocaine smuggling is done in quantities of ten or twenty or thirty kilos.

District headquarters in New Orleans was only a little less excited than the men on the scene. A quick rundown of the records convinced them that the *Cushing* had in hand the biggest maritime drug seizure in history, even if no more were to be found in the five untapped containers. The timing of this bust was perfect. The *Cushing* was about 700 miles, or two and a half days, out of New Orleans, traveling at the eleven-knot pace of her prize. Coast Guard Commandant Paul Yost was already scheduled to be in New Orleans on October 5 for a Naval Institute affair, and Secretary of Transportation Samuel Skinner, under whose department the Coast Guard falls, was available to come down on that day too. The brass from Washington would add glitter to what promised to be a media event. If so, it could be the most important result of the whole affair.

As the fifth branch of the military which is tucked away in a civilian agency, the Coast Guard has fed on a lean budget for two centuries. Even multiplied by dependents and retirees, its 38,000 active-duty personnel spread thin across a continent constitute no effective voting power. Nor do they have the public relations and political clout of the billion-dollar suppliers of the Pentagon that is wielded on behalf of military appropriations. In addition, there is healthy competition within the Coast Guard itself among districts, units, ships, aircraft. The Eighth District had been overshadowed in the drug war headlines by its neighboring Seventh District, which covers the Caribbean out of Miami. If Sikorski could make it to New Orleans on time, October 5 could be a banner day for the district, the service and the nation. Through the air crackled the command: "Forget Mobile. Come right in here and be prepared for a big show."

Sikorski wasn't averse to having his ship star in such a media event, but he was relieved when New Orleans agreed not to release the story until they pulled into port. Sikorski knew that they would be transiting some lonely territory and negotiating the narrow canal from the Gulf up to New Orleans at a snail's pace. Even rich drug lords weren't likely to take kindly to the loss of so much revenue, and the *Cushing,* limping along on one engine to stick with the *Zedom Sea,* would be vulnerable to ambush. The passage over open water went without incident, but it wasn't a relaxed time for the four Coast Guardsmen aboard the prize. For the most part, Lieutenant Meyers restricted the three prisoners to their quarters and the galley. But he did let the master come up to the bridge every four hours to check on the automatic pilot and take his own navigational fixes. He also encouraged the engineer to make rounds every four hours with one of the *Cushing*'s people accompanying him. They did not use the cook's services; instead, they had the makings for sandwiches ferried over from the *Cushing* by the RHIB. There wasn't much sleep to be had, because Meyers felt it wise to have at least two Coast Guardsmen, preferrably three, awake and alert at all times.

Sleep was in short supply aboard the *Cushing* too. With four less in crew and six prisoners who had to be fed, watched, shackled and unshackled, normal watches went by the boards. When the *Cushing* was approaching the mouth of the Mississippi late on the fourth, Sikorski had an unpleasant surprise. Fortunately, New Orleans warned him by radio that there had been a leak to the press before three helicopters appeared over them, fluttering down to close range to take pictures. They arrived at the canal leading into the New Orleans harbor about 1 A.M. on the fifth. What with oil rigs and other shipping, it would be like threading a needle in the dark. Putting either the *Cushing* or her prize aground or causing a collision in the glare of publicity would be unthinkable. Since they were all tired and more than usually subject to human error, Lieutenant Sikorski had a professional pilot sent aboard the *Zedom Sea* and a fleet of small Coast Guard utility boats dispatched to shepherd them through the passage. He personally held the bridge of the *Cushing* all night long.

The two ships arrived safely at the Coast Guard support center in New Orleans at 9 A.M. on October 5, 1989. After turning over the prisoners on the *Cushing* and the *Zedom Sea,* with its containers of contraband, to agents of the Drug Enforcement Administration, the Coast Guardsmen were whirled off into a kaleidoscopic two days of greetings, congratulations, luncheons, posing for pictures and TV appearances. At Sikorski's request family members had been driven over from Mobile for the arrival, and on October 6 the *Cushing* sailed to Mobile to continue the round of honors. The accolades were well deserved. No more cocaine was found in the other containers, but the haul finally came to 12,208 pounds with a street value of $554.9 million. Two other recent seizures—twenty tons in a Los Angeles warehouse and nine tons in a Harlingen, Texas, house— were larger, but as of this writing the *Cushing*'s remains the record drug bust on the high seas.

Aside from the quantity of contraband involved, the action in the Gulf of Mexico was a textbook case of how the Coast Guard regularly goes about the business of interdicting illegal drug shipments. But, as Lieutenant Sikorski is the first to admit, luck—or a fairy godmother—had nearly as much to do with his operation as skill. He calls it "a Cinderella story." The sad fact is that the *Cushing*'s single bust exceeded the total amount of cocaine confiscated by the Coast Guard in all of the previous year. The huge warehouse seizures only hint at how much gets through. Interdiction is a chancy and difficult business, as further illustrated by a fascinating footnote to the *Cushing* case that has yet to make the papers.

The storms that swept through the Gulf of Mexico and the Caribbean that fall of 1989 seem to have activated smugglers as much as they did Coast Guardsmen. Almost on the heels of the *Zedom Sea* seizure, the *Cushing*'s sister 110s of Patrol Boat Squadron Two at Roosevelt Roads, Puerto Rico, found themselves involved in more drug busts than they had had in years. They had barely got their base back in working order and themselves recovered from around-the-clock coping with the ravages of hurricane Hugo when the action began. The timing of this upsurge in smuggling has produced at least two theories. One is that smugglers use storms and the resulting life-threatening devastation that necessarily deflects Coast Guard attention from law enforcement as an opportunity to engage in more open trafficking; the other is that a government crackdown in Colombia at this particular period made drug dealers desperate to get their goods out of that country at any risk. Whatever the reason, the smugglers were certainly using any means. Although all of the cutters out of Puerto Rico were scoring hits, the experiences of USCG *Vashon* are sufficient to show what the Coast Guard faces in its battle. Lieutenant Junior Grade Mark S. Ogle, executive officer of the *Vashon,* wrote this typically spare but effective report about those days:

"On twenty-second October, while patroling south of Vieques Island, Puerto Rico, *Vashon* observed a twenty-two-foot sport fishing vessel running at high speed toward Puerto Rico. *Vashon* decided to intercept but could only close to a hundred yards due to the proximity of reefs and speed of the pursued vessel. The two men on board ignored hailings, blue light and siren. When they were almost to shoal water, they turned due north and ran their boat completely out of the water on a beach on Vieques Island. The men jumped from the boat with the engine still running and fled into the wooded mountains. *Vashon*'s landing party was not far behind and spent the next four hours in the rain in pursuit of the suspects. Soon after, a Puerto Rican police helicopter and Navy K-9 units joined the search. *Vashon* crew members who stayed with the boat located 495 pounds of cocaine in a secret compartment under the center console. The shoreside search located stenciled diver gear and a duffel bag that would prove to be incriminating evidence against the two fugitives.

"On December eighteen, while in the Mona Passage on a four-day patrol, *Vashon* diverted to intercept a 150-foot freighter, the *Vita Nova*. Coast Guard and Customs aircraft kept surveillance until *Vashon* was on the scene just after dusk. When hailed, the vessel shut off its lights and began erratic course changes. The vessel did not respond to the radio, loud hailer, blue light or siren. *Vashon* launched its small boat to attempt to communicate alongside the vessel, but the crew members ignored all requests to stop or allow a boarding. Shortly thereafter smoke came from the pilothouse and it appeared the crew could be burning evidence. The small boat retrieved a torn Colombian passport thrown over the side by one of the crewmen. The vessel also appeared to be sitting lower in the water as it continued heading south. Water could be seen rising in the engine room through open portholes. Finally, the engine died. All seven crew members proceeded to the bow and waited in a standoff as their ship sank and the Coast Guard rushed for a 'statement of no objection' to board from Malta, the claimed country of registry. The small boat personnel convinced the crew members to wear life jackets and rig a life raft. Operational Control's order was not to board without consent or a statement of no objection or until the Colombians abandoned ship. Despite a request for next-of-kin information in case of fatalities, the Colombian crew stuck it out until the stern was under. When they finally abandoned ship, the small boat quickly towed the raft with the crewmen to *Vashon*. Then three members from the small boat jumped aboard in waist deep water and cut the *Vita Nova*'s cargo hold straps free. Much to the Colombians' displeasure, duffel bags and bales containing 735 pounds of cocaine floated to the surface when their freighter sank.

"Two days later, while returning to home port at night, *Vashon* received information concerning an air drop that was to transpire near Ponce, Puerto Rico. The cutter proceeded to the drop site. Two sailboats were anchored 300 yards west of Isla de la Muertos Island, south of Ponce. As *Vashon* approached the sailing vessels, six chem-lights were observed in the water near the vessels. The cutter's small boat with boarding team waited until a Puerto Rican police helo illuminated the area. The boarding team sprung on the sailboats and detained three Germans and one Canadian, as the small boat retrieved 520 pounds of cocaine.

"While, in the end, no convictions were made, the obvious Coast Guard interest in the suspects has seriously curtailed their activities.

"Needless to say, it was a white Christmas for *Vashon.*"

Even if their efforts to stem the flood tide of drugs make for another boy-with-his-finger-in-the-dike story, the Coast Guardsmen aren't discouraged. Seaman Brandon Spies of the *Vashon* joined the Coast Guard for the sole purpose of helping to wage the drug war, and he was elated at being coxswain of the small boat involved in the air drop incident. "I don't know whether I'm saving any lives by stopping drugs going in, but I like to think so," Spies said. For Lieutenant Sikorski, an invitation for him and his crew to tour Mobile schools in a "Say No to Drugs!" campaign immediately after their experience was more rewarding than the ultimate conviction of the *Zedom Sea*'s nine crew members on a charge of possession with intent to distribute a drug that calls for a life sentence. The aura of heroism surrounding the men of the *Cushing* held the children's attention when Sikorski, himself a father of three, told them: "The cutter *Cushing* is proud to have made the seizure. It's our contribution to stamping out drugs in our society. We're really dedicating it to you. You're the people that we're most aware of and hopefully we're doing our part to stop it from affecting your lives."

But when you talk to Coast Guardsmen, it is easy to detect another motive that underlies a decision like the *Cushing*'s to wait out just one more trying day on the off chance that it will bring action. They are, after all, people who joined the service because it offers the stimulation of risk and action in a good cause. Coast Guardsmen share with members of the other armed services the knowledge that they might at any time be required to put their own lives on the line in order to protect their society. In a very real sense, doing this with grace and effectiveness is the ultimate aim of their chosen way of life. Although they don't articulate this feeling in these terms, it reveals itself in indirect ways, as in Lt. Sikorski's favorite remembrance of his experience.

Coming into Mobile, *Cushing* hoisted a broom. A few days later there appeared in the Mobile *Press and Register* the following letter: "It was with a thrill that I noticed that object flying from the outboard starboard halyard in the picture of the USCG *Cushing* as it arrived in its home port of Mobile after that exciting two and a half–week patrol in the Gulf. The object is without doubt an almost brand-new broom, signifying to all a 'clean sweep!' The last time I saw one of those it was lashed to the periscope of a submarine returning from a patrol in the Pacific in 1944. As an old Navy type to some fine new 'coasties,' I signal you 'Tare Victor George!' Well done, and we are all proud of you.—Chester Hall, 3815 Claridge Road, Mobile." After telling me about this, Lt. Sikorski said, "That letter was the thing that touched me most. It made me feel really neat because it is the type of thing that links us from service to service, from generation to generation."

Chapter 5

The Anatomy of an Oil Spill

ON that hot and hazy June Friday in 1989, Captain Eric J. Williams, III, commanding officer of the U.S. Coast Guard's Marine Safety Office at Providence, Rhode Island, enjoyed a pleasant break in routine. Duty called for his participation in a late-morning change-of-command ceremony at the Coast Guard's Station Castle Hill just minutes away from his home in Newport. With no pressing business on his office calendar, Williams saw no reason to drive all the way back to Providence after the event ended in early afternoon. He went home, shucked his uniform and began preparations for a backyard barbecue, the perfect prelude to a relaxing summer weekend in one of America's most spectacular resort areas.

A chance to experience life in Newport was a compensation for the Williams family, which had put up with the peripatetic existence of a "coastie" for twenty-three years. Already centuries old before there was a United States, Newport proper is a tidy cluster of expensively refurbished colonial houses and public buildings surrounded by the dazzling turn-of-the-century mansions and estates of America's first industrial barons. It is the center of a lively summer festival featuring internationally famed jazz concerts, tennis matches and yacht races. Graced with parks, nature preserves and beaches, the Newport area is the glistening star among the advertised attractions of the "Ocean State," as Rhode Island calls itself. For the Williamses this promised to be the kind of weekend for which the delights of Newport were designed.

Williams was just rounding out the first of three years at a post that is considered comparatively soft in a service with frigid outposts in Alaska, where loneliness or exposure are constant threats, and steamy tropical stations, where the order of the day can be chasing armed drug runners or dealing with hurricane devastation. In fact, a colleague congratulating Williams on his assignment said, "So you're going to sleepy old Providence? Nothing ever happens there. You ought to have plenty of time for fun." Although Williams so far found even the routine responsibilities of his first full command challenging enough to stave off drowsiness, there had been no dramatic crisis to test his mettle nor any indication that one would ever develop.

Just as he was laying the charcoal for his fire that afternoon, his wife called from the house, "The office is on the phone, Eric. They say it's an emergency."

On the way to the phone, Williams glanced at his watch— 1650, ten minutes to five. If it turned out to be a real emergency, the timing was miraculous. The Providence office would have been closed by five. The word that came over the wire was rather vague but alarming: tanker aground on Brenton Reef and spilling oil.

"How bad is it?" Williams asked.

"Nobody knows," said the officer on duty. "He slid back off the reef into deep water, and Group Woods Hole told the fellow to anchor. They're sending out boats from Castle Hill and Point Judith with boom."

"Good," Williams said and, with the time still in mind, added, "I'll head for Castle Hill and get back to you from there. But meanwhile start calling contractors before they get away for the weekend and tell them to stand by."

Dashing upstairs to change back into his uniform, Williams began rehearsing the organizational structure and procedures for dealing with environmental problems. If that tanker were leaking oil near Brenton Reef, whatever happened next in terms of governmental action would depend on him. Being a military organization—the fifth service—despite being also part of the civilian Department of Transportation, the Coast Guard has a well-defined hierarchy with preestablished lines of authority that are automatically triggered by any crisis. Starting with

Washington at the top, the Coast Guard is divided into Atlantic and Pacific Commands, each of which is broken down into districts. Reporting to the districts are groups, comprised of stations such as Castle Hill, which are equipped with small boats for use primarily in rescue work; air stations, with helicopters, small jets and seagoing cutters; and Marine Safety Offices. The MSO is charged with—in the words of Captain Williams—"anything that goes wrong in the port area—fires, explosions, pollution problems, terrorism, national defense matters, law enforcement including drug smuggling." Brenton Reef, lying just a mile off the tip of the Newport peninsula and at the mouth of Narragansett Bay, the waterway to the large commercial port of Providence, was clearly within the bounds of Williams's command.

From training and past experience in ports like New York and Baltimore, Williams knew that he could find himself handling almost awesome power. The district would "flush"—an expressive Coast Guard word for transferring command downward—full authority to him as CO of MSO Providence and make him on-scene coordinator. Other units such as groups and air stations would "chop" their "assets" to him in his capacity as OSC. Chop is another blunt Coast Guard word that means cutting something away or turning it loose; asset is a term for everything from man power to aircraft to boats to equipment. In addition, Williams would be able to call upon Atlantic Command for its Atlantic Area Strike Team, a cadre of highly trained and well-equipped pollution specialists stationed in Mobile, Alabama. It was both reassuring and sobering to contemplate having all these resources under his command as he hastily dressed, but he might well discover that the alarm was false or exaggerated when he reached Castle Hill.

Captain Williams didn't have to wait out the frustrating minutes of negotiating Newport's narrow labyrinth of one-way streets at rush hour to learn for sure that he was confronting a real disaster. As soon as he stepped out the door of his house, he caught the unmistakable smell of oil drifting through town on the light southerly breeze. The strength of the smell increased by the second as he approached Station Castle Hill near Brenton Point. Only a massive spill would give off such an odor. He pulled up in front of the station with a screech of brakes. This wasn't the time to appreciate Castle Hill's handsome brick Georgian building surrounded by acres of lawn, although there had been much talk during the ceremonies that morning of the fact that it was larger and more comfortable than the vast majority of rescue stations. When its predecessor had been wiped out in the hurricane of 1938, local citizens had lobbied the government and raised private funds to see that the new Castle Hill installation would be in keeping with the elegance of surrounding estates. Unanticipated at the time, this form of snobbery would turn into a form of serendipity a half century later.

What his nose had told him was confirmed by the frantic activity Williams encountered inside the station. Like Williams, the new commanding officer, Chief Warrant Officer Fourth Class Al Beal, had left for his Cape Cod home and a long weekend after the ceremonies. Beal's executive officer, Boatswains Mate Chief Jim Annis—the man "on deck"—was leaning over a console in the communications center with a phone to one ear, radios crackling in the other and station personnel crowding in for orders. Nobody on duty had awaited Captain Williams's arrival to start dealing with the emergency. The commanding officer of Group Woods Hole, Captain Fred Hamilton, had set boats and planes in motion. Castle Hill's outboard was already circling the tanker, radioing reports. A forty-one-footer was casting off with a load of the emergency containment boom that is always kept on hand in a trailer parked at every rescue station, and another cutter was bringing more boom from Station Point Judith on the western rim of Narragansett Bay. An H-3 helicopter from Air Station Cape Cod was hovering over the scene.

With information coming into his communications center faster than he could digest it, Chief Annis had to give Captain Williams an alarming briefing, beginning with the first distress call at 1639 hours: "Coast Guard, this is *World Prodigy*. We just made aground, I repeat, we just made aground at Number Two buoy. Number Two buoy. And we have a heavy spillage. Heavy spillage." It had already been established that the *World Prodigy* was a 532-foot vessel owned by the Ballard Shipping Company, headquartered in Athens, Greece, and was bound from Bulgaria to Providence with a load of approximately eight million gallons of number two fuel oil. The potential for an environmental disaster of epic proportions was evident. The words "heavy spillage" sounded like an understatement in view of the Coast Guard helicopter's estimate that the oil slick was spread over an area of one by one and a half nautical miles as early as 1720 hours, less than an hour after the grounding.

Number Two buoy was in line of sight from the third story at Station Castle Hill and only a mile off the rim of scenic Brenton Point. Captain Williams ran up the fire escape on the outside of the building to a landing where the station's "big eye" binoculars were set up. Through the powerful glasses, he could bring the ship close enough to see details like flakes of rust on the black topsides. But it was the overall view that conveyed the news he dreaded. She was five degrees down by the bow; she was sinking. There was absolutely no time to lose.

Captain Williams ran back downstairs and into the empty corner office of the station's commanding officer. While he waited for his first call—to his Providence office—to go through, he noted that the desk was still bare; Warrant Officer Beal hadn't yet had time to unpack the nameplate and personal pictures that would establish his presence. This little detail somehow made easier what Williams knew would have to be his preemptive act of assuming command. His instructions to Providence were brief but urgent: Get the civilian pollution contractors already on standby started toward Newport; issue a recall for MSO personnel and send a contingent to Castle Hill; notify the state's Department of Environmental Management and Coast Guard headquarters in Boston and Washington of the situation as far as it was known. Williams wanted Providence to handle as many phone calls as possible because the two lines into Castle Hill were inundated, and he needed what he could commandeer of them for the most critical communications.

One of these was his next call—to an attorney named Thomas Walsh. Williams had been encouraged to learn that Walsh had called Castle Hill before he arrived to identify himself as representing the shipping company. Under the laws pertaining to oil spills, the responsible party is the spiller, who, as such, is charged with taking action to mitigate the spill, clean it up and pay for it. If Walsh's call meant that his clients would assume responsibility, Captain Williams still stood a chance of getting home in time for a late-night barbecue. "What are you going to do about this?" he asked when Walsh got on the line.

"I don't know," Walsh said. "I haven't been able to get through to my people for any authorization. They're in Athens, you know, and it's night and going into the weekend over there. I'll get back to you. . . ."

The question left hanging as the phone went dead was: When? Lieutenant Paul Cromier, the first Coast Guard officer aboard the *World Prodigy,* confirmed what Williams had observed through "big eye." The ship was down by the bow and sinking at the rate of about a foot an hour. Captain Hamilton arrived at Castle Hill, and Williams was able to catch up on the resources that Hamilton had summoned before he took over command from Group Woods Hole. He was grateful to learn that Hamilton had alerted the Atlantic Strike Force and that there was a ninety-five-foot cutter on the scene to oversee the booming operations. Williams asked Hamilton to investigate the options for beaching the *World Prodigy* if she couldn't be kept afloat—a worst-scene scenario in an area like Newport and at a time like Friday, June 23, 1989.

As a Newport resident, Williams was acutely conscious of what a runaway spill or a sinking or a beaching could do to the community. Fourth of July, the unofficial start of a season that would generate most of Newport's annual $300 million in tourist revenue, was little over a week away. With no end of the leakage in sight, the odor of oil was pervasive and nauseating. Once oil reached the beaches, the water and sand would be dangerous for swimming and sunning, and there was a distinct possibility of contamination of the drinking water supply. Damage to wildlife would cause more than disappointment for bird-watchers and sport fishermen; commercial fishing provides some 9,000 jobs in Rhode Island with sales of tautogs, or black-fish, alone bringing in upwards of $15 million a year. If it came to rest in the wrong place, the hulk of the *World Prodigy* itself could become a menace to navigation in waters that were crowded with both commercial and recreational marine traffic.

As a career Coast Guard officer who had made marine safety his area of expertise, Williams was also acutely conscious of the ecological drama in Alaska that had held America and much of the rest of the world in thrall all through the spring of 1989. The news of the grounding of the *World Prodigy* would be a disturbing echo of the grounding of the *Exxon Valdez* in the ears of an aroused public. Although the Exxon Corporation had assumed responsibility in Alaska as prescribed by law, the fine points of legality could get lost in the confusion surrounding a disaster. Much of the outrage over the damage in the Valdez accident was directed at federal authorities, and the Coast Guard in particular. Nerves in Washington were still rubbed raw by the Alaskan fiasco, and Williams could anticipate instant and intense reaction to this new threat. In addition to undergoing official scrutiny, Williams's every act would be taken in the full glare of publicity from the media. It was not likely that either a concerned administration or a concerned citizenry would be forgiving of mistakes.

With all this in mind, how long could Williams dare to wait for Walsh's call? And, if mighty Exxon had been slow in responding in Alaska, what could be expected of Greek owners awakened in the middle of the night in Athens? When no call came by 1830—6:30 P.M.—Newport time, Williams took it upon himself to "federalize" the case. Although the repercussions of federalizing can be complicated and far-reaching, the authority vested in a man in Williams's position made the process so simple as to be virtually nonexistent. "I just grabbed my chest and said, 'Here we go,' and then started announcing it to anyone who cared to listen," he says.

Williams had instantly put himself in a position to coordinate and direct the activities of federal, state and local governmental agencies; to make decisions as to the disposition of the *World Prodigy* and its cargo; to enter into contracts with private pollution-control companies and shipowners. He had also turned his borrowed desk at Castle Hill into the place where—as Harry Truman would put it—"the buck stops." It was a decision that would prove to be a major determining factor in the outcome of the crisis, and it was a decision that took both courage and confidence.

A measure of the courage involved can be taken from the result of one of Williams's first acts after having assumed his new powers. Some entrepreneurial divers were circling the *World Prodigy* and proposing that they take underwater film of her hull. Williams hired them on the spot. Reviewed almost immediately on the Coast Guard cutter *Cape Horn*, which was standing by the tanker, and later in the projection room at Castle Hill, their videotapes showed indentations of 150 feet on both sides with at least one hole large enough for a diver to enter. Four tanks with more than 30,000 barrels—a million-plus gallons—of oil had been holed. Coast Guardsmen aboard the *World Prodigy* reported an increasing list and gradual sinking. By 7:50 P.M., the draft at the bow had increased from a normal thirty-three feet to thirty-nine feet. Williams was doctor to a very sick ship, and its condition worried him more than the still spreading sheen of oil.

Williams's confidence came from training and experience. The command role he was stepping into was new to him, but he had been rehearsing for it all of his professional life. A graduate of Beloit College in Wisconsin, Williams enlisted in the Coast Guard in 1966 when he got his draft notice. After going through officer candidate school, he was commissioned an ensign a year later and opted for sea duty on a buoy tender in Hawaii. If that was a season in paradise for a young man from the Midwest, a combat tour in the Delta area of Vietnam was its reverse. From there he went to Group New York, where he served again on a buoy tender as executive officer and developed enough interest in marine safety to make it his career path. But there would be many detours en route to an MSO command since Coast Guard policy is to keep its officers qualified for as many different kinds of duty as possible through rotating assignments.

Typically, Captain Williams was taken off his boat and out of his specialty to work in the public affairs office in New York for three years, and there he learned the ropes of dealing with the media. After that he went through port safety training and industry training in Baltimore. Among other things, the latter experience gives Coast Guard officers an inside view of how business is affected when they take action against commercial vessels. There followed three years of duty in Baltimore and four years of administrative work in Washington headquarters before Williams was sent back to New York as deputy commander and then on to Providence as CO.

In the course of this broad-based service, Williams was in on the ground floor of the Coast Guard's mission on environmental protection that began with the 1970 Clean Water Act and the Federal Water Pollution Control Act. He was involved in writing the contingency plans for action on a local level when he was in New York and in handling spills of up to 100,000 gallons in Baltimore. He hadn't encountered anything of the magnitude of the *World Prodigy*'s rapid leakage, but he didn't have to thumb through a manual to get started on establishing control. Instead, he picked up the phone and began giving orders. If he had a regret at the moment, it was that he couldn't go to sea in one of the cutters or hop in a helicopter to provide "hands on" aid to the ailing ship. He couldn't even risk the time to run up for another look through "big eyes"; he'd have to rely on others to be his hands and eyes. To that end, one of his first calls was to the man whose chair he occupied—Warrant Officer Beal.

The ceremonies at Station Castle Hill that Friday morning had had the relaxed feel of a homecoming for the new CO, CWO4 Al Beal, a career "coastie" with a chest full of ribbons to testify to varied and distinguished services. He had put in a tour of duty at Castle Hill in the seventies, and knew the facility and the local waters well; he had just come from a stint as assistant operations officer at Group Woods Hole on Cape Cod, the overseer of Station Castle Hill, and was on familiar terms with the personalities and capabilities of the personnel that would be under his new command. To make the occasion even more like home, Beal's wife, children and in-laws were present at the brief formal part of the change-of-command ritual and the lunch that followed. The new CO's brother and sister-in-law led the way when the whole family started back to the Beal home on Cape Cod to continue the celebration.

Beal's sister-in-law was standing in the driveway when he reached home. "Hurry, get to the phone!" she yelled at him. "A Greek tanker ran aground right in front of your station!"

Beal laughed as he got out of the car. "Come on," he said, "you can do better than that. . . ."

There was no answering smile. "No, it's real, Al," she said. "They called five minutes ago. It's there!"

Beal ran to the phone and managed to get through to Chief Annis. "What the hell goes, Jim?"

Annis chuckled. "Welcome to Castle Hill, Mr. Beal. Captain Williams wants to speak to you . . ."

The captain wouldn't be there to play practical jokes. Beal knew what the word would be even before he heard it. By the time Beal got off the phone, one of his children had tuned into a TV station that was breaking into its regular programming with news of the spill. With considerable foresight, Beal grabbed a toothbrush and clean pair of skivvies before heading back to Castle Hill. By the time he arrived, his command was in a state of seeming chaos. Newspaper and TV reporters were cluttering up the circular driveway and ample lawns with their cars and satellite trucks; helicopters were dropping out of the skies; "coasties" from other stations in the group as well as Castle Hill's own reservists and Coast Guard Auxiliary members were showing up to ask how they could help. Station Castle Hill's four boats were in constant motion, buzzing back and forth between their docking cove at the foot of the hill and the *World Prodigy* to ferry people and supplies. Other boats were arriving from Point Judith, Woods Hole and Menemsha on Martha's Vineyard.

Beal himself was caught up in the frantic whirl of activity the minute he stepped inside the door. Still breathless from running up from the cove, one of his boatswains mates who had just taken a forty-one-footer around the *World Prodigy* grabbed him. Gesturing with a spread of arms, he said, "Mr. Beal, do they know on the ship that they only have *that much* freeboard? She's sinking."

Beal might have put that down to excitement if Group Commander Hamilton hadn't confronted him and said, "Al, find a place where we can beach that ship. Right now. You know the waters around here. If they aren't aware of it on the *World Prodigy,* Captain Williams certainly is. He's already contracting for two tugs to stand by to move her."

Pouring over charts with seamen who were familiar with the area, Beal came up with several contingency plans, none of them attractive. It would have to be a spot where the grounded behemoth wouldn't be broken up on a lee shore by the force of wind and wave. She would also have to rest on a soft bottom to prevent further damage. Many of the most protected coves were too small. No matter where the *World Prodigy* came to rest she would constitute an offense or threat to the public. One of the seemingly feasible plans, for instance, included First Beach, but the beach was separated only by a sand hill from the reservoir for the town water supply. It came as no surprise to Captain Williams when Beal reported that beaching the ship was possible—but only as a very last resort.

When Beal went to report his findings to the captain, he felt that the CO's office tucked away in a corner of the building was the calm eye of the storm. Only the fact that Williams had a phone in each hand—"just like in the movies"—suggested that the impression was deceptive. In physique and personality the two men could have been cast for a movie scene as well— Williams, blond, slim, soft-spoken, as "Mr. Inside" and Beal, dark-haired, husky, hearty, as "Mr. Outside." Beal was happy to learn that the captain had lucked out with his phone call in terms of having a chance at keeping the ship afloat. A tug had been spotted heading south out of Narragansett Bay with an empty barge in tow, and Williams had been able to contract for her to stand by to start off-loading the *World Prodigy.* He had also activated the Atlantic Strike Force, which was scheduled to arrive at Quonset Point, Rhode Island, around midnight in two C-130 transport planes. They would bring their powerful ADAPS pumps that were specially designed for cases such as this. Not only could they pump a very large amount of liquid in a short time, but they were hydraulically operated, which meant that they wouldn't spark and cause fire or explosion in the gases that collect at the top of oil tanks.

"Better see that the buoy tender will be over there at Quonset to meet the C-130s and get those pumps right out to the ship, Al," Captain Williams said.

"Aye, sir. You know the place is swarming with reporters who all want to see you, don't you?"

Captain Williams sighed: "Yes, I know. I don't want to keep anything from them, but there isn't much I can tell them right now. Try to make arrangements for me to meet them all at a press conference every couple of hours. A Public Affairs man is coming down from Boston to help out with that, but meanwhile try to keep them out of here. Post a guard down the hall if you have to."

"What about the VIPs? They're due to arrive in droves. Before long we'll have more chiefs than Indians around here."

"I'll have to brief them individually," Williams said. "What's the latest word on who's coming? I've already been informed that the White House wants to be kept in constant touch."

Beal reeled off the names he'd been given by the communications center: Rear Admiral Richard I. Rybacki, commander, First Coast Guard District, from Boston; Secretary of the Interior Manuel Lujan, Jr.; William K. Reilly, administrator of the Environmental Protection Administration; the Coast Guard's second in command, Vice Admiral Clyde T. Lush, Jr., from Washington; Rhode Island's Governor Edward DiPrete and Senator Claibourne Pell. In discussing anticipated arrivals, Williams and Beal realized their good fortune in being able to operate out of a commodious facility unique in the Coast Guard. Attorney Walsh had finally called back with news that representatives of the owners would be on the scene, and Williams wanted them right across the hall from him in the executive officer's office for close consultation. Public affairs experience in New York had taught Williams that it was better to have a happy press than a hostile one. Williams decided to give the reporters a large assembly room in the basement and let the TV crews edit tape on the spot in the station's garage. There were also basement offices available for the people whose roles in the drama would benefit from quiet thought. These included a contracting officer whom Williams had requested from Maintenance and Logistics Command in New York, the Atlantic Strike Force's accounting specialist and Gary Ott, of the National Oceanic and Atmospheric Administration (NOAA), who was en route from Boston to act as scientific coordinator. Ott's function would be to screen all the information and advice from the scientific community as to the environmental impact of the spill—some of it sought but much of it offered gratuitously—and relay the most pertinent facts to Captain Williams with a single voice.

"I guess we can handle them all," Beal said. "We're a lot luckier than they were in Alaska."

"You're so right—in more ways than one," Williams agreed.

Beal had personal knowledge of an important difference between this crisis and that in Alaska. His brother had been an ensign aboard the first cutter to arrive at Valdez, and the voyage had taken twenty-four hours compared to four minutes for the first Castle Hill boat to reach the *World Prodigy*. The first Coast Guard plane couldn't reach Valdez in less than two hours, whereas Air Station Cape Cod's helicopter was hovering over the Newport scene within half an hour. As a safety specialist, Williams could appreciate other differences. Oil escapes a ship's tank most rapidly immediately after it is holed; water coming in as oil spills out creates a "water bottom" that captures some oil by floating it to the top of the tank. Thus the effect of containment booms around a ship decreases by each minute lost in positioning them. The thin number two heating oil spreading toward Narragansett Bay was a very different substance from the Alaskan crude that was so thick it was described as "chocolate mousse." Although it presented its own form of environmental threat, number two oil would evaporate in hot summer sun and could be skimmed from the surface if contained in booms, whereas the glop in cold Alaskan waters had frustrated the best efforts of a specially designed Russian skimmer ship that had steamed over to offer help. But these differences were more real than apparent to the general public, and the immediate concern about the *World Prodigy* accident, running all the way up to the White House, would play a large part in the unfolding events at Newport.

If nothing else, it relieved Williams of any hesitation about committing money to the battle. Under the standing orders, he could authorize $25,000 himself; the district could authorize $50,000. Those sums were laughable in view of the fact that costs ran $1 million a day in Alaska. There was, however, a $36-million pollution fund that Williams could tap by seeking authorization on up the line, an authorization unlikely to be withheld in the climate created by Valdez. In addition, what Williams was learning from his people who were on board the *World Prodigy* and from talking to the captain and crew made it almost certain that the government would recover whatever it spent from the shipping company.

The Greek captain, Iakovos Georgoudis, was being both cooperative and contrite. He admitted that he had made "a mistake"—in fact, several mistakes. He hadn't waited for a pilot who was on the way out to meet the *World Prodigy*. Although he was on the bridge beside the helmsman and saw the buoy marking Brenton Reef half an hour before the grounding, he let his ship pass on the wrong side of the buoy. "That's *my* big question," was all he could say in explanation of an incredible error on the part of an experienced seaman who had brought his ship into Providence at least once before. The only extenuating circumstance was that he had had little sleep in the previous thirty-six hours. As it will, the grinding of rocks under the *World Prodigy*'s hull had brought the captain to his full senses, and Williams was grateful for his instant call of distress and subsequent compliance with Coast Guard directives.

In view of his previous experiences, the instant and intense reaction of Rhode Island people from the governor on down was something of a surprise to Captain Williams. Even before Williams reached Castle Hill, a citizens' watch that grew into the hundreds gathered at Brenton Point to stare in apprehension at the tanker gradually sinking within swimming distance. The governor and officials from the Department of Environmental Management were on the phone at once and soon on hand at Castle Hill, as were a flood of volunteers from the 12,000-member Save the Bay organization. They began hiring equipment and workers on their own to protect the beaches. The governor, for instance, ordered prisoners from a minimum-security institution into the fray. Much as this effort was welcome, it could have quickly become counterproductive without control and coordination. Providing this guidance to the state became Williams's responsibility from the moment of federalization, but he knew he couldn't handle it alone or at his overstressed facility. He made arrangements for the state to center its efforts at nearby Fort Adams State Park, and he made another crucial call—to an enlisted man in his command, Boatswains Mate First Class Paul Krug, who was capable of acting literally as a hands-on supervisor in all forms of environmental pollution.

On that pleasant evening, Paul Krug wasn't immediately available to his commander. Krug, whose family sheltered romantically in a lighthouse at Warwick near the head of Narragansett Bay, was out performing a duty common to fathers of young boys everywhere. He was coaching Little League. From the playing field, he saw Coast Guard choppers circling overhead and said to another father, "Must be a big search-and-rescue case going on." There was no call to Krug, an MSO man, to do anything about such a case, and he stayed on with the boys until darkness shut down play.

Arriving at the lighthouse about 9 P.M., Krug heard the phone ringing and ringing. When he got to it, an exasperated colleague in the Providence office who had taken over calling for Captain Williams said, "Where have you been? There's a hell of a spill out by Brenton Reef, and the captain wants you to report to Fort Adams State Park pronto to act as his liaison with the state environmental people."

"Just what am I supposed to do?"

"I don't know for sure. Captain's federalized the case, so I guess you'll be in charge over there."

Federalized? Krug knew that it wasn't a step that any Coast Guard officer would take unless the situation was very bad. That hadn't even been done at Valdez. While he changed into uniform, Krug turned on the TV. From the excited accounts of reporters it sounded like a major disaster in the making. If so, Captain Williams was giving him a big responsibility and an even bigger opportunity. From a personal point of view, Krug welcomed it. With more than eighteen years in the service, he was making retirement plans that included seeking a job in the private sector in pollution control. He had attended Coast Guard and EPA schools, had done time with the Atlantic Strike Force dealing with various hazards, and he had found working on pollution problems fascinating. Since no two were ever alike, solutions required ingenuity and improvisation. He headed for Fort Adams with the zest born of a challenge. If he handled this right, it would look great on his résumé.

In view of the reported size of the spill and the many miles of valuable waterfront that might be impacted, Krug's greatest concern was having enough manpower and equipment to do the job. His experience with other spills in other places wasn't reassuring. State people were always good at wringing their hands, though seldom at getting them dirty. But when Krug pulled into the large parking lot at the park headquarters, he was astonished to the point of being overawed. He had never before seen so much pollution equipment gathered in one place. There were small pickup trucks, large vac trucks (designed to suck oil into their tanks with a vacuum hose), eighteen-wheeler vac trailers and tractor trailers loaded with containment boom and sorbent (a substance like paper towel that adhered to oil and not water). Offshore there was a small armada ranging from dinghies to twenty-two-footers and military-type landing crafts to a couple of tugboats.

More daunting to Krug than the sight of all that equipment was the crew that went with it. Some 400 people were milling around waiting for orders. With no other Coast Guard personnel in sight, Krug had to take charge. It might have been easier if he had been wearing bars or stars, but he realized that to most laymen a uniform was a uniform and symbol enough of authority in times of confusion and crisis. Although Krug is a slight man who looks more like a professor or a scientist than a sailor, he is possessed of a deep, commanding voice. He began using it to sort out and summon into consultation the key people in the crowd—state supervisors and foremen for the private contractors. They had a few hours to make plans before dawn would reveal which land areas were imperiled and give them light by which to work.

There was no such lull in the offices at Station Castle Hill or out on the black waters surrounding the leaking ship. The wounded *World Prodigy* was ablaze with lights and encircled by a dozen or more small boats laying boom. A clumsy device at best, containment boom consists of floats of varying diameters linked together like sausages and supporting a curtain dangling below the surface to depths of from six inches to four or five feet. Since oil floats on or near the surface of water, a boom can theoretically capture and hold it until it can be removed by skimmers, vacuum devices or sorbents. "Theoretically" is an important adverb to use in describing booms. Waves slap oil over the top of a boom; currents drag oil under it. Blessed by calm seas, workers this night knew that deploying as much boom around the ship as possible could be a worthwhile effort.

Boom was being brought from everywhere. While the light

twelve-inch emergency boom from the Coast Guard rescue stations was being laid, word came in to Captain Williams's communications center that heavier boom was arriving aboard the C-130s out of Elizabeth City, North Carolina, bearing the Atlantic Strike Team and on the trucks of civilian contractors that were boiling down the highway from Massachusetts. At one point while it was still light it was reported that there was a stash of boom to be had at an inland fire station. Rather than search for trucks, Captain Williams ordered the Air Station Cape Cod H-3 helicopter that had been chopped to his command to pick up the boom and take it to the scene.

Lieutenant King Klosson took to the controls of the H-3 to carry out this order and became involved in one of the first of many small dramas within the main drama, this one with a special Newport twist. Although it was a sweaty business for Klosson and his crew to jackass 1,000 feet of boom through the stern hatch and coil it inside the H-3, it involved no risk while the aircraft was firmly planted on the ground with its rotors still. But during this process Klosson realized that unloading would be a very tricky business. The plan was for him to drop the boom on the water so that the men in boats could hook onto it and tow it into position. By the time he was out over the site again, Klosson's imagination had conjured up a vivid picture of the boom swinging out behind his craft like a giant tail that could tangle in the rear rotor or drag in the sea before it was freed with equally disastrous results. There was no way that he would even try it, so he swooped low to search the shoreline for a place close to the action where he could unload.

Standing out on one of those broad manicured lawns that sweep to the water's edge in Newport was a man with all the appearance of being the property's owner. As Klosson whirled over, the man made unmistakable gestures of inviting him to land. Klosson didn't need a second invitation. Within seconds he had the chopper on the ground. Within minutes citizens from surrounding homes had collected to help the helicopter crew drag the boom over rocks and shallows to a depth where the Coast Guard boat that followed Klosson could pick it up. The pace of the operation was so fast and furious that there was no time for social niceties like introductions, and soon Klosson was airborne again and headed back to Cape Cod without ever learning his obliging host's identity.

In Captain Williams's corner office at Castle Hill, there was no time for anything, including eating. Among the many local volunteers seeking to lend assistance was a pizzeria that sent a load of its product to Castle Hill. This gesture was much appreciated because, although the station's galley was working round the clock, food was in short supply. Knowing it was a favorite of his, one of Williams's men brought a slice of pizza to the captain, who was trapped at his desk. He gratefully took a bite and put it down to pick up yet another ringing phone. Uncounted hours later, he happened to notice the slice of pizza still sitting on the desk with only one bite missing, and he concluded that adrenaline was a good antidote to hunger.

Excerpts from the MSO's running "polrep"—or pollution report—offer a hint of why the captain's adrenaline was running high that night. Begin with the entry of eleven minutes after midnight on Saturday—"240011 Jun 89" in the log—which reads: "Received word that vessel boomed with eighteen-inch boom, sea barrier being placed around vessel by two Navy YP [ships berthed in Newport for Navy Officer Candidate School training].

—0021: Coast Guard 01 arrived Quonset Airport with Vice Admiral Lusk.

—0025: Coast Guard 1501 arrived from Elizabeth City with Strike Team equipment.

—0029: Coast Guard 2124 arrived Quonset Point with strike team.

—0038: Contacted Coast Guard District 1 to arrange for photos of spill area.

—0110: NOAA scientific coordinator advised he will be on scene in A.M.

—0120: On-scene coordinator's representative on board vessel reported plan to lighter off cargo, plan to off-load Nr. three center, one and two starboard tanks to raise bow. Intend to use ADAPS pumps to off-load one to four port tanks and one and two center to minimize stress on vessel.

—0146: Tug *Roger Williams* departing Newport. Tug *Towmaster* departing Fall River. ETA Brenton Tower two hours.

—0150: MSO personnel on scene report following tanks holed—Nr. four port, one and two center, six and seven starboard, deep tank forward and fore peak.

—0205: Jetline Service, Inc. advise three, possibly four, forty-two skimmers available. ETA six hours after ordering.

—0222: Vessel commenced pumping Nr. three center to *Seaboats 25* barge. Additional barges *Texaco* 80 and *Jaredth Griffith* standing by to lighter vessel.

—0440: Established 500-yard safety zone around vessel.

—0452: Coast Guard Cutter *Reliance* on scene with capabilities to refuel H-65 helo. Assuming vessel traffic control.

—0500: Barge BST thirty-nine capacity 39,000 barrels departing Chelsea, Ma. ETA 241800.

—0505: Atlantic Strike Team on scene Castle Hill.

—0615: MSO personnel on scene advised Nr. three center tank pumped for fifty minutes beginning at 0500 using vessel's system. Water found to be entering tank. Pumping discontinued. Set up ADAP system to pump over top.

—0700: On-scene coordinator conducted overflight of vessel and Narragansett Bay approaches. Sheen noted; however, minimal pockets of heavy oil sighted. Contractor crews dispatched to two locations with boom, vac trucks and personnel to conduct removal operations.

—0710: MSO personnel on scene reported that the following sites are boomed off—Bonnet Shores Beach, Wequiteaque Pond, Schofield Cove, Maxhill Marsh and Round Swamp.

—0800: On-scene coordinator conducted briefing and press conference."

By now, it was dawn on the kind of pleasant Saturday that everybody yearns for during the week—winds west-southwest at less than five knots, visibility eight nautical miles, temperature seventy-five degrees, seas calm. Those calm seas that had held throughout the night had allowed for much of the escaping oil to be contained within the ever-widening circle of booms. But enough had escaped to warrant BM1 Krug's dispatching crews and equipment from Fort Adams at first light to lay booms where it threatened to come on shore as noted in the 7:10 A.M. polrep entry. The focus of a weary, unshaven Captain Williams was still the ship, however. Reports from aboard like the one recorded at 6:15 A.M. were unsettling. Take this laconic notation: "Pumping of vsl in tanks one stbd, three ctr, and six port continue, vsl leveling out caused water bottoms to drop out of fwd tanks. Tanks burped, approx 140 gal lost out of tanks but contained within boom." Translation: When the water bottom drops out, the oil floating on top of it goes with it; when a tank burps, it shoots oil out through the vents. Off-loading a holed ship is a delicate business that requires precise calculations to maintain balance and prevent a stress that might break the hull apart. Williams had rounded up experts from the Navy and the representatives of the owner to help with these calculations, but anything could go wrong. The *World Prodigy* was turning out to be a baffling puzzle. "The ship itself was transferring liquid among the tanks and not telling us," Williams recalls. "This complicated things, because the ship would suddenly do things that the calculations didn't predict."

Despite the fair weather conditions, oil kept escaping the booms around the *World Prodigy* in sufficient amounts to reach the beaches by noon on Saturday. Hit hardest was the southern shoreline of Jamestown Island—Fort Wetherill, Hull Cove, Mackerel Cove. In consultation with Williams, Krug at Fort Adams shuttled work details with boom, vac truck and sorbents from place to place. The work force was an unusual combination of volunteers, prisoners and national guardsmen. As coasties from surrounding stations arrived, often by the busload, Krug posted them at work sites to monitor the operation and report back to him by cellular phone. Coordination was the key to any success.

The beach crews faced a hot, dirty, uphill fight. As most of the world had recently learned from watching pictures out of Alaska, the state of the art in cleaning up oil is shockingly primitive and labor intensive, which means expensive, in this electronic age. At Newport booms were deployed across the face of beaches. Oil on the surface behind the booms or escaping toward shore was snuffed up in the hoses of vac trucks where possible or soaked up by sorbents. Sorbent comes in round ten-foot lengths eight inches in diameter that can be linked into a boom to rig inside the containment boom, in hundred-foot sweep sections light enough to be towed behind a boat, and in eighteen-by-eighteen-inch pads that can be applied by hand or with any available tool such as a rake, fork or stick. All of these were put to use in the Newport battle, where the thrust of the attack was to keep the oil from reaching the shore. If it didn't evaporate in the sun, the light number two oil could contaminate the sand by sinking into it. Unless and until the ship could be securely floated and safely off-loaded, it was a finger-in-the-dike effort.

At Station Castle Hill, Saturday's surge of activity was creating madhouse conditions. As sleepless as the captain, Al Beal was alternating as hotel host, air controller, ferry boat dispatcher and station chief. Helicopters fluttered in and out with as many as eight on the lawn at one time. Beal was in constant fear of a midair collision. Although the state had prevailed upon the telephone company to install fourteen temporary lines, there wasn't much that could be done about ground-to-air communication. A man sent down from Air Station Cape Cod with a portable radio did his best, but the civilian helos bearing the media, the contractors and the VIPs didn't carry marine band frequencies. Communications with a Coast Guard fleet that had grown to a dozen craft was scarcely easier. Channels were jammed, and there was no way to recharge the cellular phones aboard ship that were being used as supplements. Beal had to fall back on a resource often tapped by the Coast Guard in crises—trust in the man or woman doing the job. "My people knew what had to be done, and they did it," he said.

One function of helicopters and boats was to ferry VIPs and media people back and forth to the *World Prodigy.* Impromptu press conferences with a governor here, a senator there and an admiral yonder were being held simultaneously—as many as six at a time—on the grounds of Station Castle Hill. Over their considerable share of the new phone lines, reporters were alerting the world to a "world class spill," based on the million-plus gallons known to have been stored in the ship's holed tanks. But anyone within sniffing distance of Newport didn't have to rely on radio or TV to know what was happening. The oil smell that Captain Williams had first detected when he stepped out of his door covered the countryside and seashore like an unseen pall on this virtually windless summer day.

For the most part schooled in the ways of grace under pressure, Newporters didn't panic. Some, like Elizabeth de Ramel, took precautions. She put her parakeet in the basement, where there was less foul air. She recalled hearing that, because of their sensitivity to gas, canaries were taken into the trenches in World War I. When a canary keeled over, the men donned their masks. Some Newporters shrugged. Helen Winslow, a member of Spouting Rock Beach Association and an organizer of an America's Cup ball, told the *New York Times:* "It may be that people play more golf than they swim." Some citizens seized the moment. A quick-witted bartender concocted a cocktail from four liqueurs, called it an "Oil Slick" and pulled in $4 a drink. Many more local people were helpful. Aside from those who dirtied themselves sopping up oil, there were those who contributed by going out of their way to do their own jobs better, such as the police and utility workers. One instance of this that Warrant Officer Beal cites is that of the bridge toll takers who let vehicles en route to the spill pass free. It was a significant act in view of the fact that the same toll takers had recently refused passage to police officers returning a criminal to Newport from another part of the state because they didn't have enough money in their pockets.

There were a few instances where the usually laudable attitude of pressing on regardless went too far. A television crew had made plans to film catamarans racing past Fort Adams on Saturday afternoon, and they calmly proceeded to set out markers for the sailboats close into shore where cleanup operations were in progress. Captain Williams managed to get hold of the producer and tell him that the area was closed. Even though they weren't filming for a live show, the producer said, "It's a free country. We've made all our arrangements, and we're going in there whether you like it or not. The next person you talk to will be our attorney."

A weary and still worried Williams snapped, "Fine. When you call him, remind him of who I am and what my powers are."

The attorney did call, and Williams explained that his powers included levying a fine of $25,000 a day on people who entered areas he declared to be closed. All the filmmakers had to do was move a mark to keep the boats away from the oil spill, he explained. The attorney got the message, and the mark was moved.

Trivial as the incident may seem, it could well have had a bearing on a much more important decision Williams made at about the same time. The owners agreed by noon Saturday to assume financial responsibility for the cleanup. But how could they possibly be on top of everything going on out there? Williams decided to retain federal supervision of the operations, which meant using federal funds and billing the company later. With an estimated $125,000 already obligated, he requested an increase in the ceiling to $200,000. The request was recognized as conservative; by 2 A.M. on Sunday morning an authorization for $250,000 came through. This response evidently emboldened Williams, who was asking for a ceiling of $2 million by 2 P.M. on Sunday.

As the hours wore away through Saturday night and into Sunday, Williams, still sleepless at his desk, was alternately dealing with good news and bad news. The good news was coming from the ship. By the steady unloading of its cargo onto smaller vessels, the *World Prodigy* was being kept on an even keel and maintaining water bottoms. Williams felt confident in releasing the standby tugs late Saturday and had his confidence confirmed by a Sunday morning report from MSO personnel on board that the *World Prodigy* had gained four feet of draft. She would surely go on floating. More good news from aboard the ship was a downgrading of the estimated leakage to 420,000 gallons.

But that was still enough oil to do a lot of environmental damage in the wrong place and under the wrong conditions, and the bad news revealed by Sunday's daylight was that the sheen of oil on the surface of the sea continued to spread. There was some hope for the already affected Newport area—light winds had shifted around to the north and might keep the slick offshore, where it could evaporate in time. But this meant that environmentally sensitive areas around Point Judith and on south to Block Island and Long Island Sound stood in danger. Skimming within the booms circling the *World Prodigy* was not capturing all the oil; indeed, the skimming had to be suspended at one point because of a breakdown of equipment and at an-

other because of a concentration of fumes so high that the
health of workers was imperiled. On shore, the messy vacuum-
ing and swabbing with sorbents went into ever higher gear as
more personnel and equipment became available. Although the
state closed beaches temporarily, nobody was giving up on saving the summer.

What with the ship steady and all the forces he could muster
in place, Williams felt able to go home for a short nap and
change of clothes some thirty-six hours after he had left his
barbecue fire unlit. He had kept going, exhilarated at being in
the thick of the kind of action for which he was trained, but he
knew that he would need some rest to deal with the problems
he would face in the long aftermath of crisis. After Williams
returned to Castle Hill, Al Beal went upstairs to one of the
bedrooms for duty personnel at the station to snatch a few hours
of sleep and get a chance to make use of his toothbrush and
clean skivvies; he wouldn't get home until Tuesday. BM1 Krug
was another very tired man as darkness fell on Sunday night. He
was in the process of shutting down the operations at Fort
Adams until dawn when the phone rang about 10 P.M. It was
Castle Hill: "Paul, Station Point Judith's been reporting a sheen
about a hundred yards off Moonstone Beach. The state's worried
about its bird sanctuary there. Got something called piping
plovers—almost extinct. Can you get 1,000 feet of sorbent boom
over there right away?"

At that point, a dog-tired Krug had a hard time equating the
fate of some birds he never knew existed with the risks and costs
of a night operation. Since he and his monitors would be
charged with verifying bills submitted to the government
through the Coast Guard, Krug was getting good at quick figur-
ing. He couldn't use amateurs since somebody might get hurt
floundering around in unfamiliar waters at night, and charges
for professionals would amount to $30,000 or so, what with
overtime. Krug was just weary enough to talk back.

"Now?" he said. "I don't want it done. We'll do it when we
have light."

"Oh, no, you won't. Orders right from the admiral . . ."

"In that case, OK."

Krug went back to work. The contractors he assigned to

Moonstone Beach managed to protect the plovers from the oil by going out in boats and anchoring boom in place with cinder blocks. In retrospect, rested, Krug felt that the admiral had been right and he had been wrong: saving Moonstone Beach was a Coast Guard duty in view of its environmental mission.

Moonstone Beach turned out to be the last crisis in the *World Prodigy* case. It was not, of course, the end of ongoing hard work for all hands. The containment area around the *World Prodigy* wouldn't be declared clean until Tuesday the twenty-seventh, and the beaches much later than that. Ironically, one of the biggest problems was disposing of the oil that was kept from having its way with the environment. Captain Williams's polrep bristles with notations about his difficulties in getting any commercial enterprise to receive and handle the barge loads of water-contaminated oil pumped from the tanks of the *World Prodigy.* On the beaches, eleven twenty-five-cubic-yard dumpsters had been placed in strategic locations to take the oil-soaked sorbents. They grew too heavy to be picked up by trucks. Krug had to call for a device called a spungee that would press the oil out of the material so that it could be sucked up by a vac truck. An estimated total of 90,000 gallons of oil was recovered from both operations.

There followed weeks and months of inquiries and court cases. The captain cooperated by pleading guilty to state and federal charges arising from his "mistake" in operating the vessel, and the company continued to agree to pay a share of costs as yet to be determined at this writing six months later. Captain Williams's bill was $3.7 million, not counting the Coast Guard's own outlay of $800,000. Was this expensive response to the *World Prodigy*'s accident justified? From his point of view, Paul Krug sees his captain's act of federalizing the operation as the key factor in averting what could have been another Valdez disaster, in saving the prized summer for both the human and wildlife of the area. "If the Coast Guard had sat back and said We'll let the owners do it, that much more oil [would have escaped] that ship," Krug said. "And [as for] the Coast Guard responding with a containment boom—if we had waited for a contractor to be called in, we're talking hours longer. A lot of that ninety thousand gallons of oil came from inside the boom around the ship. If right now a ship went aground here and I had to make first calls to a contractor, the minimum time before he'd be here is an hour and a half to two hours."

The view of Captain Williams's performance from above is equally admiring. Williams was one of three captains who were presented with commendation medals by Transportation Secretary Samuel Skinner for their work as on-scene coordinators at oil spills. Incredibly, the other two spills took place on the same weekend when a tanker ran aground in the Delaware River ten miles south of Philadelphia, releasing 300,000 gallons of heavy industrial fuel oil, and a barge loaded with heavy crude oil collided with a merchant ship in Houston Channel near Baytown, Texas, with a loss of 252,000 gallons. Williams was also one of the recipients of the 1989 Coast Guard Foundation awards. His citation read in part: "Due largely to his personal skill, leadership and dedication, the damage from this potentially disastrous environmental accident was minimal. Captain Williams's performance exemplifies the highest traditions of the U.S. Coast Guard."

Although it would seem from the Newport experience that federalizing would be the best way to handle all oil spills, the fact is that each case requires a different approach. In tackling a massive spill like the one from the *Exxon Valdez*, for instance, federal resources are totally inadequate. In June 1989 there was only $4 million available in the fund reserved for that purpose. By the spring of 1990, Exxon had paid out $2 billion and was promising to do more. Nevertheless, an officer in Captain Williams's position as predesignated on-scene coordinator does have the power to exercise the option of federalizing, and Captain Williams believes firmly that it should be used when necessary and feasible. "If we hadn't federalized this, we ought to be looking for other work," he said. "The key is fast response in an environmental thing like this. We couldn't let hours and hours go by while the attorneys tried to track down owners in Greece. Even as fast as we were, we didn't contain much of the initial spill; it was already spread out. And if that ship had just sat there going down, down, down by the bow, I suspect that the bow would have gone under. You can say that we were lucky. I don't know how it would have turned out, for instance, if we hadn't grabbed a barge that just happened to be heading down the bay for New York. We might have had to run *World Prodigy* up on a beach with screams of outrage. We were lucky with the timing and weather and all that too, but without the preparation and training we had, all the luck in the world wouldn't have helped.

"From the Coast Guard point of view, what we succeeded in doing was demonstrating a concern for the environment, demonstrating that the Coast Guard wasn't just going to let nature take its course. We did get some of the oil out of the environment, and we showed that our plans work. If Valdez hadn't already done it, our experience brought the mission back, reminded us all that the environmental mission of the Coast Guard is as vital as any of its other missions. But we didn't do this job alone. The cooperation of the state of Rhode Island was unusual, if not unique. I have never seen anything like it, and it could serve as an inspiration for other local governments. Where we failed, it was primarily a failure of technology. Booms, for example, don't really work, but there is nothing else available now or likely to be without more money and effort put into research."

Whatever other lessons are learned from the detailed reports on the *World Prodigy* case that are still being assessed, it is unlikely that anybody in the Coast Guard will ever again describe Captain Williams's command as "sleepy old Providence."

Chapter 6

The Case of the Nazi Saboteurs

As of June 1942, the most far-reaching war that the world had ever seen was far from having a predictable outcome. In control of Europe and the western reaches of Russia, the Germans and their Axis allies were moving at panzer pace across North Africa; their submarines roamed the Atlantic Ocean at will. On the other side of the globe, Japan, having overrun most of China and southeast Asia, was gaining a foothold on American territory. The front pages of the newspapers in the United States on a single day—Saturday, June 13—reflected the uncertainties of the time. Japanese landings on Attu Island in the Aleutians shared headlines with Japanese losses in the Battle of Coral Sea. A story about fighting at Sevastopol reported that the Russians were driven back at a vital point, and Field Marshal Erwin Rommel's Afrika Korps was said to be rolling north after taking over Bir Hacheim in Libya. News that a German force had also invaded the American mainland that day was nowhere to be found in the papers; the assault was known only to a handful of U.S. Coast Guardsmen on the eastern end of Long Island.

Aboard U-202, a year-old cub in the Nazi submarine wolf pack, there was a mood of swaggering confidence as she crept silently underwater toward the northeast coast of the United States.

The men of U-202 had reason to feel that any mission was possible. In their last sortie they had sunk three Allied ships; in this one, they had so far proved that the North Atlantic was a German lake by cruising 3,000 miles in fifteen days with the occasional precaution of diving at appropriate times. So good was their record that the ship's captain, Lieutenant Commander Lindner, permitted himself and his crew some liberties with regulations. He sported a beard and mustache, and all of them wore on their caps a metal model of the ship's unauthorized symbolic mascot—the porcupine. Although Lindner chafed when he had to follow orders to avoid all contact with the enemy, as in the case of a convoy outward-bound from Halifax that he let pass overhead unmolested, he was well aware of the unique and important nature of this voyage. The explosive cargo of men and material that they were carrying to American shores came right out of Admiral Wilhelm Canaris's *Abwehr,* the nation's top secret service.

There was enough time in the rather leisurely crossing for Commander Lindner to learn details of his passengers' mission that had been omitted from official orders by chatting with their lean-faced, intense, loquacious leader, George John Dasch. Dasch and his three companions—Ernest Peter Berger, Heinrich Harm Heinck and Herbert Haupt—had one thing in common: They had all spent long periods of time living and working in the United States and had somehow wound up back in the Third Reich in time for the war. Whether to escape dreary and dangerous service in the German armed forces, earn a kind of glory or get back to the United States where they had friends and relatives, they were all willing recruits for the *Abwehr's* first sabotage attempt across the Atlantic. Another four men with similar backgrounds, led by one Edward John Kerling, were heading for Florida in another submarine that had left Germany four days later. They were to meet at a designated time and place and coordinate their efforts to cripple with explosives seven aluminum factories, New York City's water supply, Niagara Falls hydroelectric plants and the Pennsylvania Railroad's famed horseshoe curve. Although none of them had been schooled in the fine art of sabotage, they had been put through a short, intensive *Abwehr* training course that would seem to guarantee their safety and success once they were ashore.

Toward the end of their voyage, nature herself appeared to bless their bold venture. Just off Nova Scotia, U-202 was wrapped in a rare summer fog so dense that she could make time and save her batteries by cruising on the surface. The fog meant that Lindner had to navigate by dead reckoning, but for a good seaman it was a small risk compared to that of being detected by the enemy. The worst that could happen would be that he might miss by a few miles the planned landing at Southampton, Long Island, an area with which Dasch was familiar, from summer excursions when he lived in the States. By 8 P.M. on June 12, Lindner calculated that he was close enough to the Long Island shore that it would be prudent to dive and stay down until the witching hour of midnight, when it would be safer to attempt a landing.

U-202 settled to the bottom at one hundred feet. As gravel rattled against her sides and bottom, the men of the sabotage group collected their equipment and positioned it near the conning tower for a quick exit. They would have to take it all with them in one load on an inflatable rubber raft as soon as the submarine surfaced. Their luggage consisted of four heavy wooden boxes filled with explosives and detonating devices, two haversacks of civilian clothes copied in Germany from ads in American magazines, two entrenching shovels, a gladstone bag in Dasch's keeping that had some $84,000 in U.S. bills sewn into its lining. When all was in readiness, Lindner gathered around him the agents and the two sailors who would row them ashore. "If you encounter anyone on the beach, overpower them, kill them. Send the bodies back with my men here and we'll feed them to the fish when we get to sea," he ordered. "I know you're against having weapons with you, Dasch, and maybe you're right. But my men will be armed with machine guns and carbines and orders to use them. We can give you covering fire as well. While you're still wearing those German naval uniforms, you should behave like men of war, not spies, and you'll be treated as such if captured. Now, please sign the ship's visitors' book before you go. It will make a fine souvenir after the war."

One of the agents took the book, drew a quick sketch of Uncle

Sam with a dagger in his back and wrote under it, "Straight to the heart."

Commander Lindner chuckled, "That's the spirit. Now for a toast." He ordered a sailor to produce a round of schnapps. When the glasses were filled and raised, he said, "To your success. *Heil Hitler!*"

Ceremonies concluded, Lindner ordered U-202 to periscope depth for a look around. He could see nothing but fog. Better to steer by the bottom. He dropped his ship down until she was on the ground again, lifted her a little and crept due north until she touched again, lifted her and moved forward once more until she touched once more. Unless his dead reckoning and the contour lines of the bottom on the chart he possessed were all wrong, he had to be about 500 yards off the beach due south of East Hampton, a few miles east of the preplanned target. Good enough. "Take her up!" he told his quartermaster.

Commander Lindner popped out of the hatch while water still streamed from U-202's flanks. He could barely see the dark shadow of the bow emerging from the darker sea ahead of him; he couldn't detect the faintest light or outline, hear the slightest sound, to indicate the presence of land. These were conditions ideal beyond hope for undercover work. When Dasch joined him on deck, Lindner asked, "What do you think of the night?"

"Christ, this is perfect," Dasch said.

The unseasonable weather having virtually eliminated the possibility that the landing would be observed, Lindner's concern shifted to his men and the raft. He instructed them to take a long tow line, which would be paid out and made fast by the submarine crew, and he gave them a flashlight for signaling and a red flare to be fired only as a last resort. The need for Lindner's precautions was evident within minutes after the raft pulled away from the ship. The landing party was swallowed up in fog so thick that they all experienced a kind of vertigo. Only when they could hear the faint swish of sea against sand could they be sure of the direction in which to row. Nerves were taut. As soon as they got in among the breaking waves of a slight surf, Dasch jumped overboard to help drag the raft up onto the beach. He sank to his armpits and had to be pulled back aboard. But he was soon out again at waist depth, and this time he did succeed in beaching his men and supplies firmly on enemy ground.

The soaking was particularly annoying to Dasch. During his last minutes aboard the sub, he had changed out of Navy uniform into the civilian clothes he would have to wear until he could find a store and buy more. Dasch's change had gone unnoticed by Lindner in the bustle of launching the raft, but not by his comrades in arms. When they brought it up on the way to the beach, Dasch explained that one of them had to be properly dressed to deal with anybody they might encounter without causing instant alarm. Sure, it was taking the risk of being nailed as a spy, but wasn't it up to a leader to take risks? That went down well enough then, but it was the first of what the others would consider strange acts by their leader. The next came almost immediately.

At first glance, the landing spot seemed as perfect as the night—nothing at all within their fog-bound range of vision but sand dunes and scrub grass. Dasch told the others to lug the cases with the explosives up into the dunes above the line of high tide and change their clothes. The sailors were supposed to wait with the raft until they could carry the haversacks with the uniforms back to the ship. The raft had taken on some water during the landing, and the sailors started to tip it to dry it out. Dasch handed the gladstone to Berger and told him to hang onto it while Dasch helped the sailors. Then out of the corner of his eye he saw a light moving in their direction along the tops of the dunes. He ran toward it.

Around 1 A.M. on Saturday, June 13, 1942, Seaman Second Class John C. Cullen left the U.S. Coast Guard Station at Amagansett, Long Island, for a routine six-mile foot patrol of the beach to the east. America was still new to a war that seemed very far away despite the big battle headlines. Unarmed, Cullen did not expect to run into anything more demanding of the Coast Guard's services than a possible boater or fisherman who had got lost in the fog. Even this was unlikely since the summer season wasn't yet in full swing, and the year-round people this far out on the island knew better than to go to sea on such a night. Cullen anticipated a duller than usual patrol with nothing whatever to look at but the sand within the small circle of his flashlight's beam.

Hair-raising surprise gripped Cullen when, alerted more by vague sounds than by sight, his eyes swept the curtains of mist and glimpsed through them three human figures. One was incongruously dressed in pants and jacket and wore a battered felt hat; the other two, in shorts or bathing suits, were standing in the water. Cullen couldn't see a boat or whatever else might be the focus of their activity. In any case, his attention was immediately captured by the fully clothed man who came charging at him through the sand. It was a spooky sight on a spooky night, and Cullen wished mightily for one of the weapons that they kept in a rack back at the station.

"Who are you?" Cullen asked the man, hoping that his voice betrayed no fear. "Are you guys fishermen? Did you get lost in the fog?"

"You might say that," the man said, between gulps of air. "How about putting out that light? I can't see you."

Cullen obliged, and the man said, "Oh, you must be Coast Guard. That right?"

"Yeah. Say, why don't you all come back to the station with me and wait until dawn? It's only a few hundred yards back that way. . . ."

"It's a thought—but no. You see, we aren't really fishermen."

Behind the man in the hat a half-naked figure carrying a bag loomed out of the mist. He said something in what sounded to Cullen like a foreign language. The man in front of Cullen snarled over his shoulder, "Shut up and get back with the rest. I'll take care of this."

"Say, what goes on here? What's in that bag?" Cullen said.

"Clams," the looming shadow said, proving that he did speak English, but the other man cut him off: "Didn't you hear me? I'll handle this."

Knowing very well that there were no clams to be found near this beach, Cullen was thoroughly confused and frightened. Although he had seen no weapons, it was clear that he was outnumbered if these men were up to no good. He was thrown even further off guard by a strange turn in the conversation.

"How old are you, young fellow?" asked the man in the hat.

"Twenty-one."

"I thought so. Just a boy. Well, I'm sure you have a mother, and I'm sure she wouldn't want to see you killed. . . ."

Cullen could hardly believe what he was hearing, and he had no idea of how to respond to such a threat. He kept silent, and the man took another surprising tack. "Look here, boy," he said, grabbing Cullen's arm. "I can't tell you what's going on just now. This is a matter for Washington."

Cullen pulled his arm free, but the man continued in a friendly, conspiratorial tone, "What's your name, boy?"

Cullen had a quick answer to that: "Frank Collins."

"Fine, Frank, and my name is George John Dasch," the man said, and then, pulling back his hat, he added, "Shine your light in my face, Frank. I want you to be able to recognize me when I have you called to Washington."

By now, Cullen had begun to think that he was dealing with a crazy, which could be more dangerous than confronting a criminal or an enemy. He wanted to run so badly that his legs twitched, but he couldn't tell whether the others had him surrounded in the fog. The only thing he'd ever heard about handling crazies was to humor them. He shone his light on the face of the man who called himself Dasch. The features were sharp, the eyes wild looking. Cullen shut the light off, but Dasch ordered him to look again "right in the eye so you'll remember me." Cullen looked again and had the feeling he might be hypnotized. Again he shut off the light and said, "I'll sure remember you, sir."

Dasch pulled his hat back down low on his forehead and said in a sane, calm tone, "Good. Now, Frank, I want you to forget all about this until you hear from me in Washington. And I want you to take this. It's not a bribe. . . ."

Fishing through his pockets, the man brought out a couple of soggy bills and thrust them at Cullen. Even in the dim light, he could see that Dasch was offering him two fifties. It was a lot of money for a young man who had been a department-store delivery boy before he enlisted. Cullen waved the money away; taking money for keeping quiet wasn't the sort of thing a Coast Guardsman would do. Dasch persisted. He reached into his pocket again and pulled out more bills.

"You're quite right. That isn't enough for an important affair like this," he said. "Here, take this. That's gotta be three hundred."

Cullen decided then that his best chance was to take the money, then see if he could get away and run back to the station for help. He put out his hand and said, "You win. . . ."

Dasch slapped the money in his palm. "Good boy, Frank," he said. "Now if you were to happen to see me in East Hampton, would you recognize me?"

"No, sir."

"You learn fast. You'll make a good sailor. You'll be hearing from me," Dasch said.

Cullen stuffed the money in his pocket and started off at a leisurely pace toward the east, and Dasch headed back toward the water. As soon as he was certain that he couldn't be seen in the fog, Cullen changed course and ran full speed toward Amagansett.

Once he got rid of Cullen, Dasch told the U-boat sailors to shove off, even though the haversacks of discarded uniforms hadn't been delivered to them. They were only too happy to comply. They were too far away to know the nature of Dasch's confrontation up there on the dunes, but his decision not to wait for the uniforms spoke of danger. Nevertheless, his words were soothing. "Tell the commander that the landings went off as planned," he said as he helped guide the raft out. The sailors jerked on the tow line to the U-202. Instantly it grew taut, and they were sucked away into the fog.

When Dasch joined his companions up in the dunes, they were uncertain and upset. Who was that fellow? Why hadn't they killed him and sent his body out to the U-boat like the commander said? "Don't worry. I took care of him," Dasch said. "He won't give us any trouble. But c'mon, start digging. We've got to bury this stuff—the uniforms too—and get out of here before the fog lifts." Weren't the uniforms supposed to go back to the boat? "I sent them away. You guys were too slow. If anybody sees that U-boat, there will be all hell to pay. Now, let's dig."

The other three had no real choice but to go along with Dasch, who was not only their appointed leader but the only one of them who knew anything about the lay of the land. He didn't share with them Commander Lindner's calculation that they were several miles away from his familiar territory. His ignorance of details in the East Hampton-Amagansett area was compounded by the fog. But when everything had been buried, Dasch led the little party confidently inland, judging direction by the receding sound of surf, as they'd done with the swelling sound in finding the beach. He blessed the fog for concealing the nearness of the Coast Guard station, as the sight of that might have caused panic among his followers. As it was, they had enough of a scare when, reaching a road, they had to duck for cover as a military truck whisked by. At that point, Dasch suggested a brief rest. While they were lying there a fog-muffled rumble shattered the stillness of the night. They knew that they were hearing the diesels of U-202. A risk-taking man by nature, Commander Lindner had evidently elected to trade noise for speed in making his getaway. To the men on shore, the sound brought a sharp realization of the fact that they had bought a one-way ticket to a place where death would await them at any wrong turning. Someone checked the time. It was four o'clock in the morning.

The thrum of the sub's engines hadn't died away before a shrill sound close at hand lifted the hair on the napes of the saboteurs' necks. A phone was ringing, but they could see no structure to house it. Fuzzy globes of light bloomed in the mist, and they could hear a man's voice answering the phone, but they couldn't make out his words. Could the call have something to do with the engine sound? Were there other invisible buildings around? Only half pretending to joke, one of the men whispered, "We're surrounded." But the blooms of light wilted, and silence returned. Dasch jumped up and led a fast march along the road and then turned inland on the first dirt road they encountered. He was hoping to run into the Montauk Highway, the major east-west artery that would lead him to Amagansett, where, according to his recollection, there was train service to New York City.

When a highway finally materialized in the mist, a disoriented

Dasch turned right. His men followed, and they marched single file to the east through the long grasses beside the road so that they could duck at the sight of any automobile lights. After they had gone a mile or so without coming to a hint of habitation, Dasch began to suspect that he was headed in the wrong direction and took the next dirt road leading off to the left. It dead-ended in a trailer camp. Dogs were barking, lights turning on. The whole place was coming awake. Any second a car might catch them in the glare of its headlights. Had he led them into a trap? Dasch elected to find a way through the trees around the camp's dark perimeter instead of going back by the road. Like the fog, this decision may have been a saving bit of luck. They literally stumbled onto railroad tracks just beyond the camp— not only the tracks themselves but the precise point where a double rail line turned into a single one. Dasch remembered that this change took place east of Amagansett. He had been heading for Montauk Point. Turning left and following the tracks, he soon led his little group triumphantly to the deserted Amagansett station.

It was 5 A.M. Saturday, and the station was locked. But Dasch was sure that there would be a train to the city in due time. It was a nervous wait for the four men as daylight and lifting fog exposed them to public view. They tried to make some use of the anxious time by straightening and brushing their rumpled, stained clothes. At 6:30, ticket agent Ira Baker unlocked the door and opened his window for business. Dasch stepped briskly up to it, learned that a train for New York would come through at 6:57, and plunked down $20.40 for four one-way tickets to Jamaica, a station just east of the city. Dasch thought they could get off there and buy real American clothes to replace the German imitations they were wearing before venturing into Manhattan and checking into a hotel. Baker evidently found nothing odd about four disheveled, unshaven men giving up on fishing and going back home for the weekend, as Dasch suggested when he said, "Fishing's pretty bad." In fact, Baker nodded in agreement.

The conductor showed no more curiosity than did the agent when he punched the tickets of four men with their noses buried in newspapers. He did wonder what they were all laughing about when one of them passed around a copy of the *New York Times,* pointing to an article on one of its interior pages. But even if they had showed it to him, the conductor would not have understood what was funny about a review of a new movie entitled *Nazi Agent* that began: "It's an old device but a good one—the substitution of identical twins—which Metro has used as the main twist in *Nazi Agent,* which came to the Rialto yesterday. And it makes for a tautly intriguing and sometimes hair-raising spy film such as one can find adequately valid in this day when spies are known to be smooth boys."

If Boatswains Mate Carl R. Jenette, on duty in the early morning hours of June 13 as petty officer in charge at the Coast Guard's Amagansett Station, was incredulous or skeptical about Seaman Cullen's breathless tale of encountering mysterious strangers in the night, he didn't let doubt get in the way of action. Immediately upon hearing Cullen's tale, he telephoned Warrant Officer Oden, commanding officer of the station, who happened to be at the nearby home of Chief Boatswain's Mate Warren Barnes. Then he summoned three other seamen, issued .30-caliber rifles to them and Cullen, belted on a .45, and headed back for the spot on the beach where Cullen's adventure had occurred.

It took only five minutes at a fast run to reach what Cullen insisted was the right place despite the fact that there was nothing and nobody to be seen. Jenette detailed Cullen and two seamen to stand guard while he and a fourth man moved cautiously through the fog in widening circles to explore the area. While they were doing this, Barnes arrived. There was a sound out somewhere on the water—a rumble. Barnes, a thirty-year veteran who had reenlisted after Pearl Harbor, recognized it as diesel engines. Through a gap in the fog, he thought he saw a low dark object about seventy feet long. He called Jenette and ordered all of the guardsmen up into the dunes and flat on their bellies for concealment and protection. They were to start firing and hold out as long as they could if there was an enemy landing.

The engine noise stopped, and about that time a guardsman arrived to summon Cullen back to the station to give a fuller report to Warrant Officer Oden. Jenette resumed searching while Barnes and some seamen stood guard. As soon as he had been debriefed by Oden, Cullen returned to the beach and joined in the seemingly fruitless search. His fellow guardsmen were beginning to hint that he was guilty of hallucinating, if not prevaricating, when the throb of diesels was heard again. This time the sound was more distinct, steadier, and it was definitely moving out and away—to the east and open ocean. A detachment of soldiers, responding to the Coast Guard's general alarm, arrived to help comb the beaches, but of far more assistance was the arrival of dawn, which begins to break about 4 A.M. at that latitude in June.

In the faint gray radiance, Barnes and Cullen, walking together, saw something at the same time—a glint of silver in the sand. Picking up the reflecting object and turning it over in his hands, Cullen absorbed its message with a feeling of awe. It was a half-empty pack of cigarettes in silver paper protruding from a box on which was stamped the name of a German manufacturer. Minutes later another guardsman found a bottle labeled *Weinbrand,* and yet another searcher came across a leather jacket that looked to be part of a foreign military uniform. Cullen had been talking to Germans, to *Nazis!* But how had they come? Why had they landed? Where had they gone? The first question was already answered to the satisfaction of an old seaman like Barnes by the sound of those engines and the fact that no enemy surface ship would dare such an approach to the U.S. coast. But more clues were needed to solve the other puzzles. Now that they knew something might be found, the men tramping the beach were filled with growing excitement as the gathering light and lifting fog made close study of the ground beneath their feet possible.

An alert guardsman named Brooks spotted a small furrow in the sand leading up from the water's edge into the dunes above high tide. It could have been made by dragging a bag or box, and they were all over it like a pack of hounds. At the end of the trail there was a misplaced wet spot in the sand. A guardsman with a stick poked through the spot and struck something solid. The group surrounding him fell to their knees and, pawing doglike into the sand, uncovered four wooden boxes bound with marlin, a tough, tarred twine, to make handles. Not far from the trove of boxes, a pair of wet swimming trunks had been dropped either carelessly or deliberately to make a marker. While the others worked on the boxes, Barnes located a second wet spot that led to the discovery of two haversacks containing German clothing, including an overseas cap sporting a metal swastika.

When they were certain that there was no more to be found, the guardsmen took the objects back to the station. There they broke open the wood of one of the boxes and came upon a tin lining. With a can opener, Barnes ripped up the tin and exposed a large number of what appeared to be pen and pencil sets. The deception of that appearance was evident when they opened another wooden box and found loose powder with an assortment of small glass tubes. What they were looking at was the ingredients for making incendiary bombs—perhaps thousands of them.

The discoveries at Amagansett Station were being relayed simultaneously to Coast Guard district headquarters in New York; they were ordered to stop opening the crates and bring all of the material there for further examination. While the boxes were being opened in the office of Captain Bayliss, the district commandant, a hissing sound came from one of them. It was a moment when heroes are made. Someone suggested completing the operation at the end of the pier, and three young officers—Lieutenant Commander J. A. Glynn and Lieutenants Junior Grade F. W. Nirschel and Sydney K. Franken— undertook the task. They transported the box gingerly but hastily to the suggested spot, finished opening it, and learned that the hissing was being caused by the contact of saltwater and TNT.

At Amagansett, there was finally time for Seaman Cullen to clear his conscience by officially transferring his "bribe" money to the Coast Guard. He hadn't even looked at the wad of bills that he handed to Petty Officer Barnes. When Barnes counted it out, the total sum turned out to be $260. Cullen had not only been insulted but shortchanged as well.

It wasn't long before the other members of the Nazi band learned, as Cullen had, that their leader could not be trusted.

In New York, according to a prearranged plan, they split up, with Dasch and Berger registering at one hotel and Heinck and Haupt at another. Times were set for them to meet casually in designated public places to exchange information and instructions. As he later claimed, Dasch had signed on for the sabotage effort as the only means of getting back into the United States during wartime. He had been quickly disillusioned and disappointed by the Germany to which he had returned in 1940; among other reasons was the fact that he hadn't been able to arrange for his American-born wife to join him. When the *Abwehr* mission came along, Dasch seized upon it as an opportunity to escape the Nazis and become an American hero at the same time by betraying his comrades and their purposes to none other than J. Edgar Hoover, head of the Federal Bureau of Investigation. Dasch selected Berger as his right-hand man because he suspected from slips during their many conversations in training that Berger was also anti-Nazi. To carry out his private plan, he would need an ally among the saboteurs, and on that same Saturday night after they arrived in New York he took the biggest risk of the whole venture by taking Berger into his confidence when they dined together.

Dasch's argument that they both would be accepted with open arms and rewarded proved convincing to Berger, but Dasch's first effort to contact the FBI with a phone call on Sunday evening to their New York office was not. Although the Coast Guard findings had by then been turned over to the FBI, they apparently hadn't filtered down to the agent fielding Dasch's call. Screening legitimate information from among the many false calls they receive every day is a challenge for police officials. This one from an excited man who claimed to have just landed from a German submarine as leader of a group of saboteurs and who wanted to see Mr. Hoover, and Mr. Hoover only, was clearly off the wall and destined for the dead file. Although he could sense the agent's disbelief, Dasch was only frustrated, not discouraged. Leaving Berger in charge of keeping the other two men in line and misinformed, he took a train to Washington, checked into the Mayflower Hotel, and on the morning of Thursday, June 18, called FBI headquarters, asking for Mr. Hoover. He didn't get through to the Chief, as Hoover was known, but by then the mystery created by the Coast Guard reports was the agency's top priority. Almost before Dasch hung up the phone, an agent appeared in his hotel room. Then and there began four full days during which Dasch talked while relays of agents and stenographers recorded one of the most amazing tales ever to come to the FBI.

A similar landing in Florida had been planned, although Dasch and the FBI did not suspect that it had actually taken place, on the night of Tuesday, June 16, on a beach near Jacksonville, Florida. Under circumstances almost identical to those on Long Island on June 13—but for encountering a patroling Coast Guard seaman—U-584 landed Edward John Kerling and his three companion saboteurs. This landing had gone unnoticed and unreported until Dasch told his story. Since Dasch's account of the Long Island affair matched that of the Coast Guard in telling detail, the FBI had to take very seriously the possibility of a Florida landing. Dasch described Kerling as a fanatical Nazi who had been active in the German American Bund, which was the association of "patriotic" Germans in the U.S., while he was in the United States. In their extensive file on that organization, the FBI found Kerling's name. One of the items about him revealed that, in an ironic coincidence, Kerling had had his own brush with the U.S. Coast Guard. But it had been a lifesaving encounter back in 1939 when Kerling's sailing yacht the *Lakal*, manned by an all-German crew hoping to get back to join in Hitler's conquests, became waterlogged and started to sink off Wilmington, North Carolina.

It turned out that the FBI files contained material on others of the saboteurs or members of their families, most of whom had been involved in pro-Nazi activities in the United States. With that information and Dasch's most priceless gift to them—a handkerchief furnished by the *Abwehr* that listed in invisible ink known Nazi sympathizers still at large in America—the FBI had no trouble in staking out the people who would be approached by members of Kerling's group. In New York, with Berger cooperating, the group that landed on Long Island was taken into custody almost immediately; by June 27, the Florida four were also in FBI hands.

There was no mention of the Coast Guard or an obscure

seaman named Cullen when the story was spread all over the nation's front pages the next morning. A single paragraph in one of the accounts is typical of the way the story was played: "Despite their training, the two gangs of four men each fell afoul of the Federal Bureau of Investigation almost immediately and the arrest of all eight was announced last evening by J. Edgar Hoover, director of the Bureau. They were in custody within a month after they had shipped on their expedition out of a submarine base on the French coast." By early July, the eight men were put on trial before a special military tribunal at President Roosevelt's orders. The trial was secret except for official releases, and a frustrated newspaperman, digging around for something to say, unearthed the Coast Guard report. It made for more headlines in the middle of July, and it created a hero in the person of young John Cullen, at a time when America was in need of heroes.

Promoted to coxswain simultaneously with the release of the story by Vice Admiral Russell R. Waesche, Coast Guard commandant, Cullen was later feted and decorated. He received the Army and Navy Union Medal of Honor, the Gold Medal of Valor of the American Legion and the Legion of Merit Medal. In presenting the last award to Cullen, who had by now risen to Boatswains Mate First Class, the New York district Coast Guard commander, Rear Admiral Stanley V. Parker, cited the young man's "coolness and cleverness." The fact that Cullen, alone and unarmed, had to demonstrate those qualities rather than the aggressiveness more commonly associated with wartime heroism led to the most important outcome of the German "invasion." After joint conferences among the services, the Coast Guard was charged with establishing a Beach Patrol Division. Within a year, there were 24,000 armed Coast Guardsmen patroling 3,700 miles of Atlantic, Gulf and Pacific coasts. No more saboteurs landed on America's beaches.

Dasch's dreams of being lionized for his act of betrayal were dashed. His life was spared, as was Berger's, but they were both given prison sentences. The other six saboteurs were executed. Shortly after the war, Dasch and Berger were deported to Germany. Although Berger disappeared from view, Dasch kept struggling to get his own story across and finally put it all into a book in 1959. With respect to actual happenings, Dasch's version differs very little from all other accounts of the event. To the extent that it can be believed, it explains why Seaman Cullen lived to tell his tale instead of being fed to the fish as Commander Lindner proposed. "A light was moving slowly down the beach! It was only a short distance away," Dasch wrote. "Berger and the other two men had gone in the other direction to higher ground, and thus couldn't see it through the thick fog. Hardly taking time to think, I left the two sailors and ran in the direction of the rays. The order to destroy anyone seen while landing burned in my mind and the last thing I wanted, now that I was safely in America, was to have some innocent American get killed."

It may have been a wide, wide war, but, as this story attests, it kept narrowing down to confrontations between human beings with human failings and motivations. Whatever else might be said about the case of the Nazi saboteurs, it demonstrated that spies are not, as the movie critic contended in that June when the war was new, "smooth boys."

Chapter 7

The Fight for the
Cape Florida Light

O N January 12, 1836, William A. Whitehead, collector of customs at Key West, Florida, wrote a letter to Stephen Pleasanton, fifth auditor of the Department of the Treasury in Washington, whose duties included supervising the nation's lighthouses. Like the Revenue Cutter Service, lighthouse-keeping was one of the federal functions under the Treasury that later would be incorporated into the Coast Guard but was then administered regionally by customs officials like Whitehead. In this letter to his superior, Whitehead said, in part:

"I regret that I have to inform you of the abandonment of the Light House at Cape Florida by the Keeper, in consequence of the deprivations and hostilities of the Indians in that vicinity. One family has been massacred and the alarm along the coast is so great that the inhabitants are all centering at this place and at Indian Key about seventy miles distant. The Keeper deemed it necessary for the safety of himself and family to leave the Cape, and intelligence has since been received that the Indians have been seen there. I have not yet received from the Keeper a report of how he left the premises. So soon as the cutter *Washington* arrives in port, now daily expected from Mobile, I shall dispatch her to the Lighthouse. Great excitement prevails here. . . ."

Great excitement may well have been an understatement for the feelings of the white population of Florida at that hour. Just two weeks before, on December 28, 1835, General Wiley Thompson and a junior officer were shot to death while walking outside the stockade of Fort King on the site of present-day Ocala. King was one of the forts ringing what was then known as the Great Swamp into which Seminole Indians who refused to move west had retreated. The next day, Major Francis Langhorne Dade, marching north at the head of two companies of soldiers from another of those bastions, Fort Brooke on the site of what is now Tampa, was slaughtered along with all but two of his men. The Indians were on the rampage; it was war.

Andrew Jackson held office in the White House. It had been General Jackson's forays into Florida in pursuit of Englishmen during the War of 1812 and later of Indians that had caused Spain to sell the territory to the United States. An Indian fighter all of his life, Jackson welcomed war against those renegades of the Creek nation who wouldn't go along with the Removal Act of 1830 and the subsequent treaties, often signed by chiefs who had been fed firewater to put them in the mood. For a generation or more, Florida Indians had caused trouble to planters in the southern states of Alabama, Georgia and Jackson's native Tennessee, particularly by offering refuge to runaway slaves. The first of the Creeks who started drifting south in the eighteenth century in advance of white settlements in the British colonies were called "Siminoli," or wanderers, by their stay-at-home relatives, and the name was changed to "Seminole" by the Spanish and British in Florida. It was a remnant of these Seminoles who retreated into the impenetrable Everglades when the rest of the Creeks went docilely west. One in particular—a chief named Osceola—is credited with starting what would be called the Second Seminole War by murdering Thompson and a Lieutenant Smith and participating in the Dade massacre.

Osceola had grounds for grievance. Some of the runaway slaves had intermarried with Seminoles. One of these was Osceola's mother-in-law. According to the U.S. slave code, a child of a slave was considered a slave. When Osceola's wife made a friendly visit to Fort King, the army seized her as a slave-by-descent. Osceola denounced the seizure and was himself thrown into irons by General Thompson. To procure his and his wife's freedom, the Indian chief promised to exert his influence on the tribe to move west. Instead, he returned to take revenge on Thompson and join other Seminoles in the action at Wahoo Swamp against Dade's forces.

One of President Jackson's first acts was to order the ships of the Revenue Cutter Service into the Navy, but apparently he had no similar authorization to militarize the personnel of the Lighthouse Service, as the immediate defection of the keeper at Cape Florida indicated. This was a serious matter. Located at the southern end of what is now Key Biscayne, Cape Florida Light was a very important beacon for coastal traffic in those days of sail. The installation consisted of a round, tapering, sixty-five-foot tower with solid brick walls five feet thick at the base. At the top was the lantern itself with an iron-railinged platform surrounding the base from which to work. A stairway of wood wound up through the tower's open interior to the lantern. A short distance from the tower there was a wooden house for the keeper's family with a detached kitchen. The buildings sat in splendid isolation on a palm-studded savannah by the sea. The keeper kept a small sloop pulled up above the tide for occasional trips to the mainland. To the Indians, the light was an eye-catching symbol of the hated white intrusion on their territory—an inviting target for attack.

Danger has not been commonly associated with lighthouse duty. Loneliness, boredom and niggardly pay were its main drawbacks. There was also a fair amount of dull work connected with keeping oil lamps cleaned and lighted. What with free housing provided, it was an occupation more likely to appeal to an unambitious family man than to the adventurous type who sought sea duty or military service. It was perfectly in character then for the Cape Florida keeper—one Mr. Dubose—to consider the possibility of an Indian attack on him and his family in that remote outpost more than he had bargained for. There is no indication that Customs Collector Whitehead disagreed with him or tried to persuade him otherwise. Instead, he concentrated on getting the light lit again by somebody with stronger motivation.

In a letter to Pleasanton, dated January 14, Whitehead wrote: "I have just received a voluntary offer from a man who I think may be trusted to go to the Cape and take charge of the Light if the Indians should not be there until Mr. Dubose may return. He is anxious to return to that quarter to ascertain if any of his property can be rescued. I have offered him the normal pay of the Keeper while he remains in charge and to reimburse him for any expense incurred in placing the Light House in a state of Defense. As I think he runs some risk of his life I would be glad to be authorized to contribute something more in the way of compensation particularly as he has suffered much in property and had all his family massacred."

Whitehead was obviously dealing with a very different sort of man—a man who had every reason to be fearful of Indians but who had evidently gained the courage of a man who has nothing more to lose. This man, named Cooley, accepted Whitehead's offer and set off for Cape Florida at once. But within a month, Cooley was disgruntled by the cumbersome machinery of federal bureaucracy, made nearly intolerable by the slow and unreliable communications between Key West and Washington. Another Whitehead letter to the fifth auditor, dated February 15, relays Cooley's sentiments and their probable consequences:

I have received intelligence from Cape Florida Light up to the tenth instant. Mr. Cooley the Temporary Keeper informed me that it will be impossible for him to continue in charge of the light if he is to be burthened with the expense of subsisting and paying five or six men which it is necessary should be with him at the light house in order to ensure his safety, and as I cannot expect to hear from you in answer to my letter of the nineteenth January for some time I am somewhat at a loss what terms to offer Mr. Cooley to induce him and his men to continue at the Light house, for I am satisfied that Mr. Dubose will not return to his duties so long as a single Indian remains in that vicinity.

When I appointed Mr. Cooley temporary keeper, I guaranteed to him the customary pay, and also, the reimbursement of such expenses as he might incur in putting the Light house in a State of defense. As he is willing to remain, provided he can feel secure in the continuance of his men—and as it is important to keep the light going—I feel disposed to modify my offer in such a way as to make it more definite and at the same time make him better satisfied with his situation. To do this, I think at present of offering him, until your views are made known, *one hundred dollars* per month for the hire of the men he has, or may have, with him, and furnish him with arms and ammunition for their defense. I shall leave my letter open until the mail closes in order that I may inform you of any change in my determination.

The Indians have not yet been at the Light house or in its immediate vicinity, but their fires, Mr. Cooley says, may be seen in different directions upon the mainland. His black boy, who he presumed had been taken off by the savages when his family was massacred has since returned to him having excaped in a boat at the time the attack was made, and states that there were about fifteen Indians in the party, and all of them well known in that quarter. Mr. Cooley has ascertained that they have made his place a second visit and taken off everything left behind them at first. They have also visited a neighboring plantation destroying the furniture of the house, etc.

I think it is highly important that the Government should send a strong land & naval force to commence its operations between Cape Florida and Cape Sable proceeding northward sweeping the Country as thoroughly as its nature will admit. The Lighthouse at the Cape can only be kept illumined by having a guard to protect the keeper*—and Government must either send out some troops for the purpose, or such an expenditure as I have alluded to must be authorized.

I am Sir Very Respectfully Yours,

W. A. Whitehead

*Mr. Cooley informs me that they keep one man constantly on guard—each one performing the duty in regular rotation.

2 o'clock P.M.—I have concluded to carry the arrangement alluded to into effect.

But for the president's personal interest, the war in Florida must have been of little moment in faraway Washington. By March 1836, there was conflict of far more consequence to consider. A group of insurgent American colonists in the Department of Texas in the Mexican state of Coahuila were slaughtered at a place called the Alamo. Meeting in Washington at the same time, a convention of Texans passed a declaration of independence and appointed Sam Houston as commander of a Texan army to wrest the colonists' lands from Mexico. As the

meeting place indicated, the United States had an interest in
this affair that didn't preclude official involvement. With all this
going on, it's not surprising that Whitehead was informed that
the government could not afford funds for Cape Florida Light
greater than those paid to keeper Dubose. Since Whitehead had
already advanced some defense money based on the proposal
in his earlier letter, he told the fifth auditor rather pleadingly,
"I presume the arrangement will receive your sanction." He
hastened to add, however, that he was advising Cooley that
there would be no more money forthcoming as a defense fund
since there no longer appeared to be any danger from Indians.
His proof of this was offered in one telling sentence: "Mr.
Dubose has made known his intention to return to the Light
House on the sixteenth instant."

Although he had apparently worked up the courage to go
back on the job himself, Dubose was not yet willing to risk his
family. He left them in Key West. Family man that he was, he
missed them, and he soon made arrangements that would allow
him to visit them regularly. Funds or no funds, he hired help—a
white man named John W. B. Thompson to act as assistant
keeper and an elderly black helper named Aaron Carter. Thus,
on July 18, Dubose felt free to leave Cape Florida for Key West.
He would bless that day for the rest of his life.

About four o'clock on the afternoon of July 23, Thompson was
walking from the dwelling at Cape Florida to the kitchen when
he saw a group of some forty Indians coming through a stand
of palms back of the kitchen. They were carrying rifles, and
Thompson didn't wait to powwow with them. He yelled to
Carter, who was close behind him, "Make for the lighthouse!
Run!" The Indians broke into a run too. Just as Thompson and
Carter reached the lighthouse, the Indians fired a volley of rifle
balls that whistled through Thompson's clothes and tore holes
in the door. But the two men managed to get through the door,
slam it shut and turn the lock. In hot pursuit, the Indians flung
their bodies against the door. It creaked and groaned but held.

The circular space at the foot of the tower was a storehouse
for the lantern's supplies and a sleeping place for Thompson
when Dubose was in residence. It was also where the arsenal—a
keg of powder, a pouch of ball and buckshot and three mus-

kets—was kept. The single window to the chamber had been boarded up and filled with stone inside as a protection against the very kind of attack that was in progress. In the dim light that filtered down from higher windows in the tower, Thompson noted that the place was a slippery mess. The Indians' shots had perforated the tin storage tanks holding 225 gallons of lantern oil, and it was seeping into his bed and all of his belongings. But he couldn't worry about that. He loaded the muskets, handed one to Carter to guard the door, and ran up the stairs to an open window, fired at the Indians, reloaded and ran up to another level and fired again, reloaded and ran to the top and fired again. Although Thompson didn't hit any Indians, they prudently retreated out of range but kept their eyes and weapons trained on the tower until darkness fell.

There was no knowing what the Indians would do, but Thompson and Carter had no choice other than to wait them out in the forlorn hope that they might become discouraged. The men inside the tower were given little time to suffer in suspense. While some of the Indians began firing at every aperture to provide a cover, others crept in and set a fire by the door. Made of yellow pine wood, the door started to burn brightly, and the flames leapt to the boarding over the window. Thompson lugged the keg of powder and a musket to the platform under the lantern. Then he and Carter started to cut away the stairs. Sparks from the flaming door ignited the spilled oil. The ground floor turned into a furnace with the tower as its flue. Thompson and Carter were forced to retreat before the heat. They gave up chopping away at the stairs, climbed to the platform, and closed the trap door behind them.

For a few merciful minutes, it seemed that they would be saved. The fire would consume the stairs, and there would be no way that the Indians could reach them. But they had reckoned without understanding how the fire would be sucked up that long, open flue. It soon ate through the trapdoor and started dancing around them inside the lantern. The heat caused the lamps and glasses to burst and fly in every direction. Thompson's clothes caught fire, and he had to tear them off. He and Carter crawled to the two-foot iron rim and railing at the outer edge of the platform. It was openwork, and they were sharply silhouetted targets for Indian marksmen. Three balls penetrated one of Thompson's feet; a fourth ball shattered the ankle on his other leg. Carter was hit, and he said, "I'm wounded." Then he fell silent, and Thompson knew that his helper was dead.

At that point Thompson considered Carter the lucky one. Thompson was being roasted alive. Death would be welcome. The keg of powder was still miraculously intact, and Thompson crawled over to it and shoved it through the flaming trapdoor. It exploded with a force that shook the whole structure. The last of the still unburnt wooden work at the top of the tower came loose and fell in a heap that seemed to smother the flames. Thompson enjoyed another instant of relief and hope, but the fallen timbers only added fuel to the fire. It rose again to lick at his body. Thompson dragged himself to the rail with every intention of jumping over instead of enduring a slow death by burning. But some instinct held him back, and within minutes the flames began to retreat. Apparently everything combustible had been consumed in that last burst. The fire fell to a heap of smoldering ash, leaving Thompson to wonder whether he wasn't being spared for an even crueler death.

Though a night breeze from the south gave him some relief, he knew it would not last long. With the rising of the hot Florida sun, his now nearly naked body would be given a different sort of baking. His feet ached intolerably, and he could feel heat within him from a rising fever. What could he possibly do but slowly fry to death? He had no food or water. Even if he weren't crippled with wounds, there would be no way that he could descend the sheer face of a brick tower, and a sixty-five-foot leap would be fatal. There was nobody he knew who might come to his rescue, and it was doubtless they would have been able to manage it in any case. He couldn't even hope that his enemy might take mercy. While he watched, the Indians looted the wooden dwelling and turned it into a burning torch. Although he couldn't see them, he could tell from the sounds they were making that they were launching the light house's sloop to transport their stolen goods. Soon he was left in dark desolation with only the soft swish of surf against sand to break the silence.

Along with its heat, the rising sun brought even to a man in

The Coast Guard's *Eagle (left)* capturing the French ship *Mehitable* and her prize, *Nancy*, in 1799 during the Quasi War with France. (COURTESY U.S. COAST GUARD ACADEMY, PHOTO BY CLAIRE WHITE-PETERSON)

Rescue swimmer Kelly Mogk, the first woman to qualify for such duty in the Coast Guard and heroine of a West Coast rescue. (PHOTO BY BRUCE A. PIT-MENTAL, USCG PUBLIC AFFAIRS)

A sister ship of CG-269 on which occurred a great tragedy of the prohibition era. (U.S. COAST GUARD PHOTO)

A 75-foot "six bitter" on the ways. Built to chase rum runners, these Coast Guard cutters were called "six bitters" because they were 75 feet long, or three times a quarter—"two bits." (U.S. COAST GUARD PHOTO)

USCGC *Cushing* escorts her prize, the cocaine laden *Zedom Sea*, into New Orleans. (PHOTO BY GENE MAESTAS, USCG PUBLIC AFFAIRS)

Admiral Paul A. Yost, then U.S. Coast Guard Commandant, tells media of biggest maritime bust in history by the *Cushing* under the command of Lt. Mark Sikorskit, left. Petty Officer Octavio Garza, background, led boarding party. (PHOTO BY GENE MAESTAS, USCG PUBLIC AFFAIRS)

Pursued by USCGC *Vashon*, drug runners beached this high speed boat on Vieques Island, off Puerto Rico, and escaped into woods, leaving 500 pounds of cocaine behind. (U.S. COAST GUARD PHOTO)

Seized cocaine-running boat with 500-pound cargo tied up alongside USCGC *Vashon* during a successful patrol out of Puerto Rico. (U.S. COAST GUARD PHOTO)

Vashon's Petty Officer Schmidt investigates cocaine found aboard beached boat on Vieques Island. (U.S. COAST GUARD PHOTO)

Cutters *Nunivak* and *Vashon*, left to right, at Patrol Boat Squadron Two's Roosevelt Roads headquarters in Puerto Rico. (PHOTO BY DORRIE SCHREINER)

Tanker *World Prodigy* surrounded by rescue boats. (PHOTO BY CHARLES KALMBACH, USCG PUBLIC AFFAIRS)

Tanker *World Prodigy* off-loading oil to barge. (PHOTO BY CHARLES KALMBACH, USCG PUBLIC AFFAIRS)

The leaking tanker *World Prodigy* surrounded by barges during oil spill operations off Newport, Rhode Island. (U.S. COAST GUARD PHOTO)

Navy and Coast Guard personnel examine spot on Long Island Beach near Amagansett where Nazi saboteurs hid explosives after landing from submarine in June, 1942. (AP/WIDE WORLD PHOTOS)

Captain Eric Williams, commanding officer of Coast Guard Marine Safety Office, Providence, Rhode Island, assessing oil damage to beach near Newport. (PHOTO BY CHARLES KALMBACH, USCG PUBLIC AFFAIRS)

Artist's rendering of Cape Florida Light, still standing, where Indians staged a bloody attack during the Second Seminole War in 1936. (DRAWING BY PAUL M. BRADLEY, JR.)

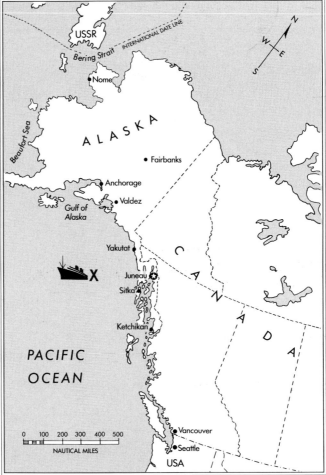

Map showing the position of the cruise ship *Prinsendam* when it caught fire.

The crippled cruise ship *Prinsen-dam* adrift in the Gulf of Alaska. (OFFICIAL U.S. COAST GUARD PHOTOGRAPH)

View of fire destruction on super-structure and bridge of *Prinsen-dam*. (U.S. COAST GUARD PHOTO)

View of the *Prinsendam* from a res-cue helicopter. (OFFICIAL U.S. COAST GUARD PHOTOGRAPH)

Jammed life boat from *Prinsendam* with rescue basket that will lift passengers one at a time to helicopter. (OFFICIAL U.S. COAST GUARD PHOTOGRAPH)

A Coast Guard HH3F helicopter hoisting a passenger from *Prinsendam* lifeboat during biggest rescue operation in history. (OFFICIAL U.S. COAST GUARD PHOTOGRAPH)

The fire damaged *Prinsendam* sinks slowly after miraculous rescue of more than 500 passengers and crewmen. (OFFICIAL U.S. COAST GUARD PHOTOGRAPH)

Survivors of the luxury line *Prinsendam* on the deck of the tanker *Williamsburg* where they had been airlifted by Coast Guard helicopters. (U.S. COAST GUARD PHOTO)

Ida Lewis, keeper of Lime Rock Lighthouse at Newport, Rhode Island rescuing two soldiers whose sailboat capsized in March 1869. Ida's brother comforts one while she pulls in the other. (COURTESY OF U.S. COAST GUARD, ARTIST JOHN WITT)

U.S. Coast Guard *Escanaba* docked at Grand Haven, Michigan (Coast Guard City).
(COURTESY TRI-CITIES HISTORICAL MUSEUM, GRAND HAVEN, MICHIGAN [COAST GUARD CITY, USA])

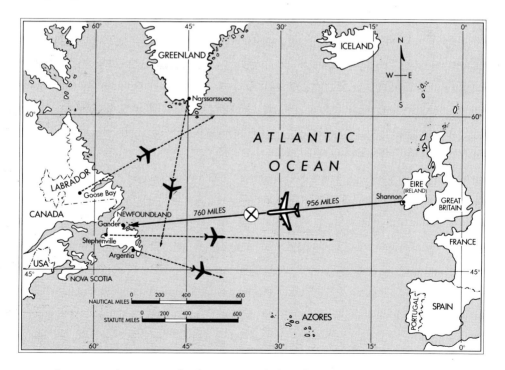

Maps shows spot where *Bermuda Sky Queen* made forced landing from which more than sixty people were rescued by USCGC *Bibb*.

Lifeboat steered by then Coast Guard Lt. jg. Mike Hall returns to cutter *Bibb* after circling *Bermuda Sky Queen* to decide upon plan of rescue operations. (AP/WIDE WORLD PHOTOS)

The "RHIB"—rigid hull inflatable boat—carried aboard Island Class cutters and used for landing and boarding parties. (PHOTO BY DORRIE SCHREINER)

Lt. Mark Rutherford, USCG, commanding officer of the *Vashon*, who initiated evacuation of St. Croix residents threatened by looters after hurricane Hugo. (PHOTO BY DORRIE SCHREINER)

Lt. jg. Mark Ogle, executive officer of USCGC *Vashon*, who led the first landing party onto the island of St. Croix after hurricane Hugo. (PHOTO BY DORRIE SCHREINER)

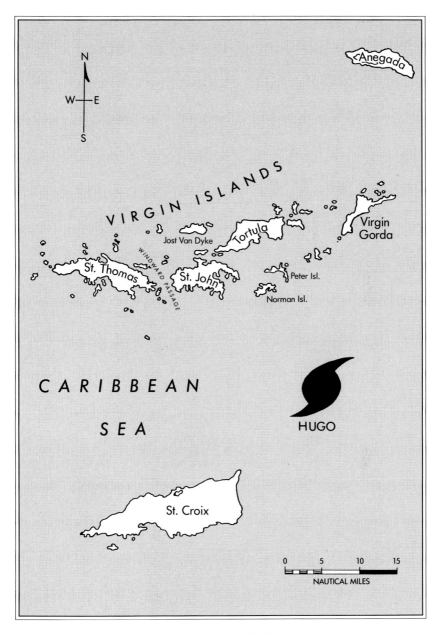

Map of U.S. Virgin Islands which were hit hard by hurricane Hugo.

The NC-4, first airplane to cross the Atlantic. (COURTESY OF THE U.S. COAST GUARD ACADEMY)

The Coast Guard's Elmer Stone, pilot of the NC-4 first, airplane to cross the Atlantic. (U.S. COAST GUARD PHOTO)

The crew of the NC-4, left to right, Eugene Rhoades, Lt. jg. Breese, Lt. jg. Walter Hinton, Lt. Elmer Stone, USCG, and A.C. Read, commanding officer and Lt. Commander U.S. Navy. (U.S. NAVY PHOTO)

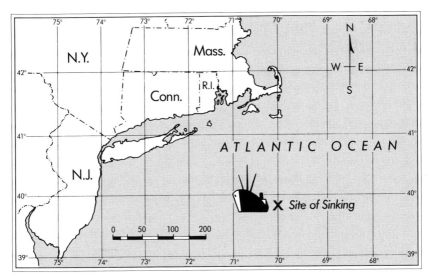

Map showing where *Lloyd Bermuda* capsized. (U.S. COAST GUARD PUBLICATION "FIRST WORD")

Helicopters on line at Air Base Cape Cod, U.S. Coast Guard. On left is CG 1472, the plane involved in the *Lloyd Bermuda* rescue. (PHOTO BY MICHAEL J. MALONEY)

Rescue swimmer Joe Rock and Flight Mechanic John Salmi poised in door of helicopter that rescued survivor of *Lloyd Bermuda* sinking in North Atlantic. (PHOTO BY MICHAEL J. MALONEY)

Visiting Dario Macias-Lopez, the *Lloyd Bermuda* seaman they rescued, in hospital are, left to right, Coast Guardsman Lt. jg. Paul Ratte, co-pilot; Randy Reed, electronics engineer; and Joe Rock, rescue swimmer. (PHOTO BY MICHAEL J. MALONEY)

Thompson's straits that hope that every new day seems to impart to human beings. There was, he reasoned, a faint chance that a ship might come in close enough to observe the lighthouse. If so, he would need a means of signaling. The only object left on the little iron platform ring was the body of Aaron Carter. It was quite literally cooked, unrecognizable as a person. But, soaked in blood, one piece of Carter's pants had not burned. That would do. Thompson tore it loose and held it in his hand while he stared out at an empty sea. Would he have strength to wave it if a ship did appear? He could only hope.

It may be just as well that Thompson knew nothing about the fact that the U.S. transport schooner *Motto* was within sight of the light when the flames from the burning buildings erupted. There was aboard a detachment of marines from the sloop of war *Concord*. Although they heard the explosion and doubted that anyone could have survived, the *Motto*'s Captain Armstrong came about and headed toward the light to see what could be done. Through the dark hours they were frustrated by a light head wind that kept them from getting closer than seven miles to the scene of action. When the wind remained unfavorable after daybreak, the *Motto* launched two rowing boats full of marines to make their way to shore. They almost ran over the lighthouse sloop, which was overturned, dismasted and abandoned by the Indians, who must have seen them coming. The derelict gave a new urgency to their mission.

On the afternoon of the twenty-fourth, Thompson saw the marines coming to the beach with the sloop in tow. Weak and miserable as he was after twenty-four hours of torture, the sight of help at hand gave him the will to hold on a little longer. Once again, though, it seemed almost as if death would have been a mercy. The seamen and marines could not devise a way of reaching him. For the remainder of that day's light, they tried various means of firing a line up to the platform. None worked. Night fell, and during the night they made a kite. With the dawn of the twenty-fifth, they tried the kite, but it proved unmanageable. Thompson fell into a state of final despair. He was now thirty-six hours into his ordeal. He was feverish and aching from his wounds, on fire with sunburn, starved and parched. The men below kept yelling encouragement to him, but he could sense their bafflement and frustration. They had come up against a problem seemingly without solution. Finally, a marine had a bright idea: he would try firing a ramrod with a tail of twine from his musket. It might act like an arrow and fly straight to the target.

By some miracle, Thompson had enough wits and strength left to catch the ramrod when it came clattering over the railing. A new surge of hope made it almost easy for him to haul up the block that they tied to the twine and hang it on the rail. With that tackle in place, the men on the ground were able to hoist two of their number up to the platform. They carried back down with them the barely living Thompson and the charred remains of Carter. The inside of the lighthouse was blackened and gutted, and the intense heat had caused cracks in its thick walls. The dwelling was a pile of ash. They buried what was left of Carter and took Thompson aboard the *Motto* to Key West.

Writing of the event on August 1, 1836, Customs Collector Whitehead told his Washington supervisor: "Thompson was brought to this place & is in a fair way to do well. Indeed his recovery is deemed certain, but it is feared he will be a cripple for life. He being a seaman by profession and only volunteering for a short time in this exposed situation, I have thought it but equitable to extend the agreed aid to sick and disabled seamen. This is the only aid I felt authorized to extend without the sanction of the department." Whitehead's hesitation to let his obviously good heart run away with his head can easily be understood through portions of a letter he wrote as late as October 11, still dealing with the funds he had advanced to Cooley for protection of the lighthouse:

"Permit me to observe that the expenditure of the Fifty Dollars took place in *January* in order to insure the *reestablishment of the Light* for the protection of the vast & increasing Commerce of the Gulf of Mexico without reference particularly to its subsequent protection. It was considered a matter of vast importance by those who know the value of the Light that it be reestablished with the least possible delay. I acted in the matter from the best motives, and I think, Sir, after this explanation the amount will no longer be considered by you as an 'improper charge.' I have therefore included it again in the account of the third quarter of the year forwarded herewith."

In other correspondence throughout the year, Whitehead couldn't refrain from reminding the fifth auditor of his many warnings as to the Indian threat and pleas for naval or military action. History has vindicated Whitehead in his bureaucratic battle, but it didn't help the mariners who had to feel their way through the dark past the Florida Reef until 1842, when the Second Seminole War died away. There are still Indians who haven't signed a treaty with the United States living in the Everglades, and Cape Florida Light, restored and heightened to ninety-five feet in 1867, has yielded its function to other lights and means of navigation. But it stands today as a tourist attraction and reminder of what has so often been required of the people who guard the nation's coasts.

Chapter 8

The *Prinsendam* Miracle

N all of the U.S. Coast Guard's two centuries of service, there has never been a Mayday! to equal the one that came clattering over the teletype in the Juneau, Alaska, Rescue Coordination Center shortly after 1 A.M. on October 4, 1980. The message read: "Passenger ship *Prinsendam* position 57-38° N., 140-25° W. Fire. Fire in engine room. Flooding engine room with CO_2. Conditions unknown. Passengers 320. Crew 190." Within minutes there were alarm bells jangling not only in Coast Guard stations all along Alaska's southern coast but also in the Alaskan Air Command at Elmendorf Air Force Base, Anchorage, and in the Canadian Forces' British Columbia headquarters. Fire at sea is the sailor's worst fear. The number of lives imperiled by this fire was staggering—and slightly understated since there were actually 324 passengers and 200 crew. The call had to be answered with maximum speed and force.

It was 1:30 A.M. when Commander Tom Morgan, executive officer of the Coast Guard's Air Station Sitka on the coast about 150 miles southwest of Juneau, was dragged out of a sound sleep by a ringing phone. The operations officer on duty at the station wasted few words: "Commander, can you fly? The *Prinsendam*'s on fire." Morgan asked no questions: "Sure. Be right over." Morgan could hear the on-duty helicopter clattering up and away as he shrugged into flight clothes and ran the 500 yards between his house and base. Sitka was a relatively small base with only two H-3 helicopters, but a complement of twenty pilots to man them around the clock. In an emergency when more than one plane was indicated, a "random" call would go out for off-duty pilots. Morgan knew that, as XO, he was first on that calling list—for him a privilege of rank since flying had been his life for sixteen years.

While his helo was being readied, Morgan was briefed in the communications center, where the emergency traffic was being monitored. The situation with respect to the fire aboard the *Prinsedam* was still ambiguous. But the ship's position was precise—170 nautical miles west of Sitka, 120 nautical miles south of the nearest settlement at Yakutat. Since Sitka was closer than any other station, theirs would be the first helicopter on the scene despite the widespread alarm. A big C-130, the service's "airborne truck" en route from the Kodiak Island Station, would be overhead but probably would be blind should they run into the tag end of typhoon Vernon, as had been predicted. Since they were 250 nautical miles from the site, Kodiak's H-3s would have to refuel at Sitka or Yakutat on the way and lose a lot of time in the process. Morgan couldn't predict the speed of response from the Air Force and the Canadians. As for surface help, Sitka's buoy tender *Woodrush* was getting under way, the Coast Guard's 378-foot cutter *Boutwell* was rounding up its crew, who were on shore leave to participate in Juneau's Centennial Celebration, and another big cutter, the *Mellon,* patroling near Vancouver to the south, was being diverted to the scene. But the *Woodrush* was slow, it would take the *Boutwell* more the ten hours to cover 300 nautical miles at top speed and the *Mellon,* 550 miles away, nearly twice that. More encouraging news was that three commercial vessels in the vicinity—the 1,000-foot supertanker *Williamsburgh,* ninety nautical miles and five hours' cruising time away, the 850-foot tanker *Sohio Intrepid* and a container freighter *Portland,* the latter two just a few more miles distant than *Williamsburgh*—had picked up the distress signals and were converging on the *Prinsendam.*

Morgan didn't have to be briefed about the *Prinsendam* herself. The 427-foot blue-and-white "pocket liner" had become a familiar sight along the Alaskan coast during the seven summers since she was built for the Holland-America Line. Although relatively small, she was luxuriously appointed with numerous bars, lounges, recreational decks and swimming pool. She was

manned by Dutch officers and a plethora of Indonesian crewmen to pamper passengers. After a season of seven-day cruises
out of Vancouver, she would take off every fall for Indonesia and
a winter round of such exotic ports as Sumatra, Bali, Java. This
"repositioning" cruise with stops in Yokohama, Shanghai, Hong
Kong and Singapore at fares ranging from $3,625 to $5,075 per
person was a favorite of people with time and money to spend.
The line could count on her being fully booked, as she was in
1980, with affluent retirees, 95 percent of whom were American.

A yachtsman by avocation, Morgan had a special affinity for
the *Prinsendam*. He had studied her with interest on the many
occasions when he was out in his motorsailor cruising the same
waters through which the liner dawdled along to give her passengers a good view of the spectacular scenery of the Inland
Passage and Glacier Bay. Painted in colors of October brilliance,
the last few days had been especially gorgeous, and Morgan had
no doubt that the passengers on the *Prinsendam* had already
concluded that the Holland-America's brochure wasn't exag-
gerating when it promised: "No matter how many cruising adventures you've thrilled to, this is the one you are likely to
remember longest." What a shock they all must be having! What
a dashing of hopes! Morgan was aware that, even if the CO_2
smothered the flames, the ship would be immobilized for several days until the engine room could be reentered safely. The
fire had to be bad for the captain to have taken such a step, and
the damage would be extensive. The cruise was effectively over.
And what if the CO_2 didn't work? It was a thought to be put out
of mind until it absolutely had to be faced. The logistics of trying
to rescue 500 mostly elderly people were daunting, and the
odds in favor of a disaster on the order of the *Titanic* were
enormous.

About the time that Commander Morgan was preparing to
take off, thoughts of the *Titanic* were also running through the
heads of the *Prinsendam* passengers, who were milling around
uncertainly on the promenade deck. They had been summoned, some from sleep and some from lingering late over
drinks and conversation in the lounges, to a place where they
could escape the smoke of what Captain Cornelius Wabeke

described as a "small fire" that was "under control." Expecting
nothing but minor inconvenience, they had arrived on deck in
a variety of dress ranging from robes pulled hastily over nothing
at all, to nightclothes, to sensible sweaters and skirts, to tuxedos
and evening gowns topped with fur coats. Even when lights
went out and accumulating smoke drove them out of the Lido
Lounge and Prinsen Bar into the fifty-degree night air, there
was a feeling of camaraderie and adventure. Although they had
picked up a bit since the smooth glass of the glorious ride past
the glaciers, the seas were still fairly calm, and the skies were
clear. Free drinks were being dispensed, the gift shop was passing out free sweaters and some bold and cold passengers were
tearing down drapes in the lounge and wrapping themselves
up. But when a group of young shipboard entertainers started
singing the Rodgers and Hammerstein medley that was part of
their show, the mood began to change. One man voiced the
growing fears of all when he said, "They were singing on the
Titanic too, before it went down."

Out ahead of Morgan in command of Sitka's other H-3 was
Lieutenant Commander Joel Thuma. Their sharing what promised to be a difficult mission was almost a coincidence, but it
seemed a strange serendipity. Mutual confidence in each
other's motives and abilities is essential to functioning in the
emergencies thrust upon the Coast Guard. In this case that
bond went back to 1957 and Traverse City, Michigan, where
Morgan, a seventeen-year-old enlistee, served on a ship commanded by Thuma's father and got to know a fifth-grader
named Joel. Now Joel was hovering near the *Prinsendam* and
radioing back a report that everything appeared to be under
control except for the fact that electrical failure made it impossible for the ship's pumps to put water on the fire. Thuma was
heading for the *Williamsburgh* about fifty miles away to pick
up some extra fire extinguishers. Could Morgan go back to Sitka
and get Warrant Officer Ken Matz, the station's fire expert, and
a portable pump?

Morgan made it to Sitka, but Thuma never reached the *Williamsburgh.* Halfway there, he received a call from Captain
Wabeke informing him that the fire was out of control and that
people were being ordered into lifeboats to abandon ship.

Thuma banked around 180 degrees to fly back and stand by to see if he could be of any help. One thing that he already knew he could do was to use his helicopter's powerful searchlight, the Nitesun, to add some much-needed illumination to what was bound to be a complicated and confusing operation.

In addition to being luxurious, the $55-million *Prinsendam* was well equipped. She was built to the highest safety standards, and she had passed a U.S. Coast Guard inspection as recently as May 1980. Among her safety features were enough small boats to accommodate the ship's capacity of passengers and crew. There were six lifeboats—two with engines rated for forty-six people each and four rated for sixty-five with a hand-operated, T-shaped lever that could turn a propeller. In addition there were two motorized, covered tenders and a dozen inflatable twenty-five-person rafts. Routine boat drill had been conducted with Dutch thoroughness the first day out, and crew and passengers, many of whom were well-seasoned voyagers, knew in theory where they were supposed to be and what they were supposed to do. What actually happened when the order "Abandon ship!" came down from the bridge may have best been described in a word by a woman who went through it—"Pandemonium!"

Inevitably, things went wrong. One tender stuck in its davits, and those assigned to it had to find other berths. While one boat was loading, a window next to it exploded in flames, and everybody in the vicinity jumped into the boat, whether it was their assigned station or not. Indonesian crew people shoved passengers aside to get into the boats first, were ordered out again by Dutch officers but scrambled over passengers once more as soon as the officers' backs were turned. Hovering alongside the six-tiered ship, Thuma couldn't be aware of all this. But he and his crew witnessed a drama of almost certain death in the making when they saw one lifeboat being lowered right on top of another already in the water. The men manning the davit falls evidently couldn't see what was below them in the dark, and the men in the helicopter couldn't directly communicate a warning. Thuma whirred in almost between the two boats while his flight chief blinked signals with the Nitesun. The strategy worked, and the descending boat remained in suspension until the coast was clear.

The first sign of a miracle in the making was that more things went right than went wrong during several dark hours when people somehow sorted themselves out into boats while dancing flames climbed higher and higher into the superstructure. An H-3's fuel is good for only six hours, and Thuma had to head to Yakutat for refueling during this process, passing Morgan, who was on his way toward the ship. By the time Morgan arrived, bearing Warrant Officer Matz and his equipment, dawn was beginning to break, and there was a flotilla of small boats, including four rafts, scattered across an increasingly choppy sea around the burning hull of the *Prinsendam.* Forty people— twenty-five crewmen and fifteen passengers—had elected to remain aboard the ship to see whether anything might be done to save her before taking to rafts they had at the ready. They were all huddled forward in the bridge area. Although the people in the boats appeared to be safe enough, their miserable condition was evident to the hovering Coast Guard crew. The confusion in loading had resulted in misdistribution; more than ninety people were jammed into the push-pull lifeboats, making it impossible to move the lever. There was a predominance of gray, white and bald heads, and a general dishabille that could result in hypothermia when the whipping tail of the typhoon caught them, if not before. Being powerless, most of the boats drifted abeam in the ocean swells, and their rolling brought on an epidemic of illness. Willy-nilly, people had to vomit or perform other natural functions where they sat or stood. But, incredibly, nobody was reported injured or in such dire straits from diabetes, heart trouble or any other life-threatening ailment as to require emergency intervention by the only helicopter in sight.

The C-130 from Kodiak, circling overhead and acting as on-scene commander, told Morgan to proceed with the tricky business of putting Matz aboard the *Prinsendam* and then finish the job of retrieving fire extinguishers from the *Williamsburgh* that Thuma had begun. "Bath of fire" may be a tired figure of speech for most people but never again for Ken Matz after that morning. He took such a bath—figuratively and literally. Although he had often faced fire during twenty-one years of special service, he had never before descended from a helicopter in a basket onto the deck of a crippled ship rearing and plunging twenty-five feet at a time in building seas. As he later told a reporter, "My insides were up around my neck." But Morgan dropped him gently on the stern by the swimming pool. While Morgan circled for another pass to deliver the fire-fighting equipment, Matz started forward along the starboard deck to enlist help from some of the *Prinsendam* crew. When he saw that he would have to go under the hull of the tender teetering from its davits, he turned, ran back around by the pool, and headed up the port side. There he had to crawl under flames shooting out across the promenade deck. But Matz made it and managed to recruit a group of officers and crewmen to return with him and field the 250-pounds-per-minute pump and extra fire hose that the helo was letting down to them.

Leaving Matz to his own devices, Morgan then headed for the *Williamsburgh.* The huge tanker was a delight to his eye. She was more like a small island than a ship. She had just taken on a million and a half barrels of Alaskan crude oil at Valdez and was southbound for Texas. The weight of her load buried the *Williamsburgh*'s full sixty-five-foot draft under water, causing her to be steady as the proverbial rock despite the seas. Forward on her long, flat deck there was a helicopter landing pad. As Morgan came in to pick up the fire extinguishers, he discovered that the *Williamsburgh* was in very able hands, but it took something of a fright to make that discovery. To save time, Morgan didn't land. He hovered and lowered his hoist. He was surprised and angry when *Williamsburgh* crewmen tied off the hoist cable to a ship stanchion. Being hooked up and unable to pull out of a situation if something happens is scary for a helicopter pilot, and Morgan yelled over his radio to the ship's master, Arthur Fertig, "Hey, don't tie me off!" Fertig replied, "Well, you've already given us a pretty good spark, and I don't want another one."

The skipper didn't have to explain. In the heat of action, Morgan hadn't been thinking about the buildup of static electricity in a helicopter. Although crude oil isn't explosive, gas accumulates in the tanks, and a spark in the wrong place could have blown the *Williamsburgh* apart. So Morgan stayed tied off and grounded until the load was attached. He wouldn't have had the same problem if he had had to land since the H-3 was equipped with a static discharge wick hanging down below the wheels that would act as a ground. But he would have to keep the possibility of electric shock in mind if they got involved in hoisting people. The trick there was to dunk the basket in the water to draw off the electricity before anyone touched it.

On the heaving deck of *Prinsendam,* Warrant Officer Matz was running into problems of his own. To reach the water, he had to rig a block and tackle arrangement to lower his portable pump over the side. Then he found that the Coast Guard's hose and fittings didn't match those on *Prinsendam* and he had to improvise a method of joining them. Once he got water flowing, he directed the crew to use it to cool down the skin of the ship. But it was too little, too late; the deck was already so hot that the tar in its seams was bubbling. After an hour and a half the pump broke away and fell into the sea, but by then nobody considered it a great loss. The fire-extinguishing equipment that Morgan had ferried over from the *Williamsburgh* was virtually useless too. The *Prinsendam* was consuming herself, and she was beginning to ship water through blown-out portholes as she rolled.

As soon as Thuma was back on the scene, Morgan headed for Yakutat to refuel and, he hoped, to be relieved by a fresh crew. The *Williamsburgh* was coming into view, and even though the weather was worsening, the prospect seemed bright for a relatively easy rescue operation. With only twenty-seven in crew, the tanker had enough space to accommodate everybody for the relatively short voyage back to Valdez. It would just be a matter of bringing the lifeboats alongside and off-loading the people. Yakutat, a village of 700 people with a small commercial airfield, was being transformed into a bustling staging area for the rescue operation. It would service all the converging helicopters and their escorting planes. The Canadians sent two Buffalo aircraft along with their CH-46s, and these established a shuttle of men and material between Sitka and Yakutat. But this activity was not yet in full swing when Morgan touched down, and there were no other airmen from Sitka on hand. There was, however, an urgent call from Joel Thuma: "Better get back out here, Tom. We're going to have to start hoisting. The weather's getting real scuzzy, and there's no way those old folks are going to make it up the side of that tanker. . . ."

"Roger. On my way as soon as we're fueled," Morgan said.

Thuma had a harder time selling his idea of hoisting people out of the boats and onto the deck of the *Williamsburgh* to the on-scene commander circling above clouds that obscured the scene and to the men behind desks at the Rescue Coordination Center in Juneau. They couldn't see what he could see, and there was sound logic in their argument: The people are safe in their lifeboats; why subject them to additional risk by hoisting? Over the radio, Thuma made his counterargument by describing the scene. The jam-packed lifeboats and life rafts had no means of locomotion and were drifting every which way. The *Williamsburgh*'s motor launch was out trying to pick up these boats, one at a time, to bring them alongside. As low as she was in the water, the *Williamsburgh*'s deck was still twenty to forty feet above the surface, depending on whether the lifeboat was in a trough or on a crest, and the only means of reaching it was by rope ladder. Elderly people who were sick, shivering with cold, tired, frightened after six hours in an open boat, were, not surprisingly, having the devil's own time making it up the ladders even with crewmen coming down to help. The unloading of a *Prinsendam* motorized lifeboat that did make it to the tanker took an hour; at that rate the job would last all night. They didn't have that kind of time. Exposure alone would take its toll in hypothermia fatalities, especially when the storm really hit. On top of that, Captain Wabeke reported that many of his passengers were on medication for life-threatening ailments. Were the risks worse in hoisting? When they arrived, Thuma and the other helos could clean those boats out by dark. What about it? The men in the C-130 were persuaded, and Thuma went to work.

In consultation with the *Williamsburgh*, Thuma arranged for the tanker's motor launch to concentrate on rescuing people from the life rafts while the helicopters would concentrate on the boats. The reasons for this division of labor were that the bigger boats provided a better platform and point of reference for hoisting and that, once emptied of people, the light rafts were likely to become airborne in the rotor wash and be a menace to the helicopters. Hovering twenty-five or thirty feet

above one of the most crowded lifeboats, Thuma and his crew
quickly established a promising procedure. A basket would be
lowered, a person would either crawl or be boosted into it, the
basket would be raised and swung aboard, another crew member would literally dump the person out, then the basket would
go down again. All of this could be done in an average time of
sixty seconds. Once the helicopter had a full load—from fifteen
to twenty people—Thuma whirred over to the *Williamsburgh,*
landed on the pad, discharged the passengers, and went back
for more.

Morgan and his crew fell into much the same rhythm when
they rejoined Thuma. As easy as it sounds in the retelling, each
individual hoist was a ticklish procedure involving the kind of
risk to life and limb that the higher command foresaw. For
starters, the pilot of an H-3, sitting in the right-hand seat with
the open door and winch handler behind him, can't see the boat
below. To make all the delicate adjustments with hands and feet
necessary to hold the plane steady above the boat, the pilot has
to follow the verbal instructions coming to him through the
headset from the flight mechanic at the hoist. Swinging down
on the cable, the empty basket can become a lethal weapon.
One woman was, in fact, knocked unconscious by the basket,
and her husband had to be sent up ahead of her to alert the
helicopter crew to her need for special handling. This hazard
was enhanced as the wind started gusting to over twenty knots.
But in other ways the rising wind was a help. In a hover over
saltwater, the rotor wash tends to recirculate the water through
the engine, and a buildup of salt can cause compressor stall and
shut down the rotor. Strong wind blows the saltwater away and
behind the aircraft, and it also provides more lift so that it take
less power and less fuel to maintain a hover. In the interests of
speed, Morgan gave up worrying about electric shock. As often
as not, rough weather and rapid handling resulted in dunking
the basket in any case, and he doubted that a shock would be
of much concern to people in the kind of distress the ones they
were hoisting exhibited.

When the basket was brought aboard the helicopter, many
survivors clung to it so tightly that the crew had to tip it over
and roll or wrestle them out. Then they would scurry to the

back of the aircraft and huddle there as far from the open door as possible. To prevent a serious imbalance of weight they had to be persuaded to move forward. "They were frightened— cold, tired, confused," Morgan recalls. "You have this big door and there the basket sits and you want them to get out and all they can see is the water down there. I could sympathize with them. Like a lot of pilots, I'm afraid of heights. I don't like to stand next to the edge of a tall building or ride up in one of those glass elevators. But piloting a plane you're strapped in and comfortable and part of your craft. I really felt sorry for them."

As more helicopters, planes and ships arrived on scene, the problems of hoisting paled in comparison to other piloting problems for Morgan. The first newcomer was the Air Force's H-3, the "Jolly Green Giant," with its mothering C-130. This was a welcome and formidable combination. Unlike the Coast Guard helos, the Jolly Green Giant could be refueled in air by the C-130, and it would presumably not have to waste time by making the three-hour refueling round-trip to Yakutat that complicated the Coast Guard effort. In addition, the Air Force helo brought flight surgeon Don Hudson and two "P.J.s"—parajumpers with specialist training in rescue and medical techniques. The first job was to put Dr. Hudson aboard the *Williamsburgh* to take over medical management of the survivors. Since the Giant's pilot had never landed on a ship at sea—or, for that matter, done much hoisting over water—Morgan talked him through these first experiences.

By the time a Canadian CH-46 helicopter put in an appearance, an aerial circus was developing. Ringmaster of the circus was the Coast Guard C-130 pilot, who couldn't see a thing from his perch above the clouds and had to rely on radio reports from the helicopters to control traffic onto and off the *Williamsburgh*. Morgan and the other pilots had to concentrate intently on the radio exchanges to avoid midair collisions. The weather and visibility were worsening to the extent that the helicopters, returning from a delivery to the *Williamsburgh*, often couldn't find a lifeboat from which they had just lifted passengers fifteen minutes earlier and would simply start picking up from whatever boat they *could* see. This circumstance would eventually lead to a harrowing climax to the unfolding drama, but it didn't seem to matter as long as the helos were finding and ferrying their quota of bodies as fast as was humanly possible. A gauge of the weather came when the freighter *Portland* tried to help Morgan by positioning herself crosswind to create a lee for a hoisting operation; she rolled so badly that she was in danger of capsizing or losing her deck cargo and had to give up the attempt.

Aboard the *Williamsburgh,* Dr. Hudson confronted a sea of misery as rough as the ocean itself. There were already some 200 survivors crowded into the cabins and passageways of the tanker's superstructure when he landed. All of them were suffering from severe motion sickness, and there were at least ten cases of dangerously low body temperature induced by hypothermia. He was afraid that somebody would die. He had an assorted corps of paramedics, including some Alaska state troopers, dropped off by arriving helicopters to help him, but Dr. Hudson realized at once that coping with the emergency could be beyond their capacity. In effect, he deputized the survivors themselves to watch each other for danger signals—changes in eye focus, pulse, breathing, color. Both Dr. Hudson and pilot Morgan noted to their surprise and encouragement that the age of the passengers seemed to be a factor in assuring survival rather than a threat to life.

There was less panic, more discipline, in the crowd as a whole than there would have been in a similar assemblage of younger people, according to Dr. Hudson. They willingly followed orders, assumed the tasks he assigned to them. "The younger people, like the Indonesian crew members, were very undisciplined. They would crawl over people to try to get in the basket first," Morgan recalls. "Also the musical people—the young entertainers—were undisciplined. They wanted to live. They were young. They wanted to fight for life. But the old people didn't. They were more resigned to what was going to happen. When you think of the people who were diabetics, had high blood pressure or heart problems, it was amazing. They seemed to have the attitude that they had led good lives; if they had to go, it was an exciting way. They underwent a tremendous amount of terror, fear, what have you, but a lot of them told us that it was really an excitement, sort of a highlight of their lives."

There were moments of excitement, if not terror, for Morgan

too. One of them came when the Canadian CH-46 developed
a mechanical problem and had to head for Yakutat. It was decided that the Air Force C-130, the most "expendable" plane
under the circumstances, should escort the crippled helicopter
in case its crew had to ditch. The big jet-prop came roaring
down through the clouds to find the Canadian. Morgan could
talk to the C-130 on the radio, but there was a great deal of
chatter and he couldn't give the oncoming plane his location
except in a vague relationship to the *Williamsburgh.* Morgan
could only sweat it out quite literally, and the result was a near
miss that still haunts him ten years later. "They came real fast
and real close, the closest I ever want anybody to be to me in
the air," he said.

Orphaned by the departure of the Air Force C-130, the Jolly
Green Giant soon got into trouble too. Its sea rescue career
began with Lifeboat Six, one of the most crowded and farthest
removed from the *Williamsburgh.* Instead of a basket, the
Giant, equipped for work over land, carried a jungle penetrator—a straight probe with three projections something like
flukes on an anchor for a person to sit on. Reasoning that the
elderly occupants of the lifeboat might have trouble handling
this device, the Air Force pilot dropped his P.J.s, Sergeants John
Cassidy and Jose Rios, to help them. It was a wise move, and in
the next hour or so, the Giant transferred forty-two people.
After a short but busy intermission to take Captain Wabeke and
the last remaining passengers and crew members off the *Prinsendam,* the Giant returned to Lifeboat Six. While the P.J.s
were trying to wrestle the hoist cable aboard, a twenty-foot
swell lifted the lifeboat and the cable tangled with the boat's
rudder. The cable snapped as the boat's weight came down on
it. The Giant was instantly out of action. Since it was also nearly
out of fuel and the C-130 was gone, the on-scene commander
directed it to land on the nearest ship, the tanker *Sohio Intrepid.* Visibility had shut down to half a mile, winds had risen
to forty-five knots, and the Giant might never have reached the
safe haven of the tanker's deck without navigational assistance
from the cutter *Boutwell,* which had recently reached the site.

Frustrating as it was for the people in Lifeboat Six, the accident that took the Jolly Green Giant out of the aerial circus

wasn't immediately threatening to the overall rescue operation. Minutes later, in fact, a partially loaded Coast Guard helicopter came by and picked up a few people from Lifeboat Six, since catch-as-catch-can was still the order of the day. The two Coast Guard helicopters from Kodiak had joined the two from Sitka. Shuttling back and forth to Yakutat, taking a full load of survivors on each trip in for fuel, and changing crews periodically, the Coast Guard helos kept doggedly at the task of hoisting until they were certain that everybody was accounted for just as dusk began to fall. Stiff but elated, Morgan finally climbed out of his right front seat in midafternoon at Yakutat, thirteen hours after he had first lifted off from base. He joined in the euphoria at the little airport as reports coming in from the ships and planes at sea gave promise that their mission had been 100 percent successful.

Trying to make sure that they had the right head count of survivors became a giant headache for Rescue Coordination Center in Juneau during the early evening hours. People were scattered everywhere. The *Boutwell* was speeding toward Sitka with eighty of them, and the *Williamsburgh* was under way for a fourteen-hour voyage to Valdez, the only port large enough to accommodate her, with another 380. Others, landed in Yakutat by refueling helicopters, were being airlifted by the Canadian Buffaloes to Sitka, where there were better facilities. Accounting was complicated by the fact that married couples and friends traveling together were split up. The first figure RCC arrived at wasn't accurate; it indicated that they had rescued more people than were listed on the *Prinsendam*'s manifest. But more was obviously better than less, and they had additional confirmation of success in that the number of boats reportedly emptied—six boats and four rafts—coincided with Captain Wabeke's report of boats launched. The effort was over, except for a decision on the fate of the smoldering, heeling hulk of the deserted *Prinsendam* that could wait until morning.

Then at 9:16 P.M. there arrived in the Juneau RCC a most disturbing message from the commander at Elmendorf Air Force base: "Where are my P.J.s?" A quick round of communication elicited information from the crew of the Jolly Green Giant aboard the *Sohio Intrepid,* bound for Valdez. The P.J.s had been left on a lifeboat with some *Prinsendam* passengers; they had a radio and flares with them. They couldn't be located among the people aboard the *Williamsburgh* or those gathering in Sitka. They might still be out there—but why, how, in what? There must have been a miscount of boats. Officers at RCC studied aerial photos that had been made of the *Prinsendam* during daylight hours. There were clearly visible davits for eight boats, and one tender still swung awkwardly from its jammed davit. The mistake was apparent. Wabeke's determination of six referred only to lifeboats, but a seventh boat—the other tender—had also been launched. So there were people in an uncounted boat, and the Coast Guard would have to look for them.

Out on Lifeboat Six a desperate fight for life was under way. The boat was riding powerless and rudderless through sleet, rain, gale-force winds and thirty-foot seas. One passenger, a sixty-seven-year-old diabetic who had left his insulin aboard the *Prinsendam,* was simply willing himself not to give in, not to die. One of the P.J.s—Sergeant Cassidy—who had spent hours in the water helping to guide the hoist penetrator to the boat, was so exhausted and full of seawater that he couldn't stop vomiting. Soaked and chilled to the bone, everyone was in the first stages of hypothermia. By the time full darkness was upon them, most of the passengers were sure they had been forgotten. The sergeants realized that saving lives had become more a matter of mind than body.

A man who had been through some sixty Alaskan rescue missions, Cassidy could speak with authority. He assured them, between bouts of vomiting, that the Air Force knew they were out there and would find a way of reaching them. Meanwhile, their job was to stay alive and alert. The sergeants rigged tarpaulins over the forward part of the boat and had the passengers crawl under them and press together to generate body heat. Protected in some measure by their wet suits, Cassidy and Rios sat out in the open to keep a watch and be ready to use their radio and flares when they could be effective. Cassidy had the presence of mind and strength to resist when panicky passengers kept urging him to fire flares into the empty night "just in case." To try to keep people's minds off the grisly present, the sergeants urged them to talk, led a sing-along that began with the only song they could think of under the circumstances: "Row, row, row your boat . . ." All the while, Cassidy and Rios kept searching the horizon with anxious eyes, wondering whether it would really be possible for anyone to find them under these weather conditions before some or all of them succumbed to hypothermia.

Once they had studied the picture of the *Prinsendam,* the RCC command in Juneau wasted no time. They ordered a C-130 from Kodiak and the *Boutwell* back out to the area around the *Prinsendam.* With the help of the *Woodrush,* the *Boutwell* raced to the last known position of Lifeboat Six and began what the Coast Guard calls an expanding square search. The procedure is to create a series of boxes around the position by making four ninety-degree turns at half-mile intervals. With lookouts posted at every vantage point and its most powerful searchlight scanning the turbulent seas, the *Boutwell* was into the second square when a flare sliced the night. This was followed by tiny flashes of light as Sergeant Cassidy caught the *Boutwell*'s searchlight in a survival mirror and reflected it back. Within minutes, the big cutter was easing alongside the small boat. It required an impressive feat of seamanship to pluck twenty half-dead people from the lifeboat with hoist and "horse collar"—a sling that fits under the armpits—in mountainous seas. But by the time Sergeant Cassidy was brought aboard the *Boutwell* at 2:30 A.M. on the morning of Sunday, October 5, 1980, every last man and woman involved in the *Prinsendam* affair had been saved.

As of this writing, the rescue of 524 persons with only a few slight injuries remains the biggest, most successful air-sea rescue in history. For Tom Morgan, a captain and commanding officer of the Coast Guard's largest installation at Governor's Island, New York, when I talked to him, it remains the "most rewarding" rescue of his thirty-two-year career. For nearly everyone who thinks about all the circumstances, the rescue most certainly fits the second Webster's definition of miracle—"an extremely outstanding or unusual event, thing or accomplishment"—if not the first—"an extraordinary event manifesting a supernatural work of God." Consider only a few what-if's: What if the *Prinsendam* had been a hundred or so miles further out at sea and beyond the range of the H-3s when fire broke out; what if she had had to launch her boats at the height of the storm instead of during the preceding lull; what if the *Williamsburgh* with her steadying load and large capacity had not been within effective range?

The fire's only victim was the *Prinsendam.* After a week of wallowing ponderously along on and off a tow line, still smoking and shipping ever more water with each roll, shadowed by the cutter *Mellon,* the once sleek liner turned on her side and slipped down into more than 8,000 feet of water. There was an exhaustive investigation by a marine court of inquiry in the Netherlands. It was determined that a rupture in an oil line had caused the fire. The court recommended mild disciplinary action against three engineering officers and the ship's chief officer for their initial handling of the situation but found no blame in Captain Wabeke's conduct. In the extensive transcript of the court's proceedings there is the following report from the Dutch Inspector of Shipping, A.P. Visser, that is all the stronger for its stiff-lipped understatement:

"Although over the course of many years a certain order has been maintained when giving the recommendations of the Head of the Shipping Inspection to this Board, it seems desirable this time to deviate from that order and to begin with expressing gratitude . . . to all who have, often under hazardous circumstances, helped to bring those on board the distressed *Prinsendam* into safety and make them as comfortable as possible. The list of names . . . numbers several pages. I will not read out that list, but I do wish to mention a few groups.

"First the U.S. Coast Guard who, only ten minutes after the first message was relayed to them, had their first helicopter airborne and, only forty-three minutes after the first message, had the cutter *Boutwell* ready to depart. The helicopters of the U.S. Coast Guard, the U.S. Air Force and the Canadian Coast Guard have played a paramount role in the rescue operations, as well as some Coast Guard cutters. Also the role of the merchant ships involved should not be forgotten. A large number of ships responded to the first call.

"The vessel actually participating in the operation, the S.S.

Williamsburgh, a large, heavy, fully laden tanker, does not at first seem to be such a good choice to act as rescue vessel, but thanks to her deck area she appeared to provide the ideal place where the helicopters were able to land large numbers of shipwrecked persons from the survival craft with comparatively little trouble. As a result of this the rescue operations took less time than they would have taken if direct transport to the shore had been necessary. The captains and crews of the helicopters and the captain and crew of the *Williamsburgh* in the first instance saw to it that the dangers to which the persons aboard *Prinsendam* were exposed were removed. In doing so, they took risks themselves, but those risks were considered and accepted with what I would like to call 'good seamanship.' "

Chapter 9

The Lady of the Light

For its issue of Saturday, July 31, 1869, *Harper's Weekly* ran a cover picture of a young woman identified only as "Miss Ida Lewis, The Heroine of Newport." Although she was no cover girl in the usual sense of the word, the young woman standing on rocky ground against a background of angry waves was strikingly handsome. Tall and soldierly, erect with straight dark brows and jutting chin, she looked capable of meeting any challenge. In comparison with other women of her time who might have found themselves on the cover of the immodestly styled "Journal of Civilization," Miss Lewis was dressed for action. No bustles or bows for her; she wore a plain dark dress with a skirt that brushed the rocks and a loosely tied homespun shawl. She could well have been one of the determined women in the news for gathering in Washington at the first National Women's Suffrage Convention earlier that year. Instead, she was being hailed for the equally unfeminine activity of making a career out of saving the lives of luckless or careless people who got in trouble at sea.

In terms of instant celebrity, today's equivalent of appearing on the cover of *Harper's Weekly* would be making appearances in the same week on the covers of *Time* and the *National Enquirer* and on the morning TV talk circuit. At the age of twenty-seven, Idawalley Zorada Lewis, a shy, taciturn New Englander, was caught in the glare of the national limelight. She never blinked. Instead of letting the kind of fame that brought a pilgrim president to her doorstep turn her head, she went right on

142

leading her hard, poorly paid life as lighthouse keeper and life-saver for another forty-two years. By so doing, Ida Lewis—unlike most celebrities who disappear quickly into the wings—has stayed firmly in the spotlight of history. Not only was hers one of the finest examples of selfless service in the 200-year annals of those who watch over America's coastlines, but she proved that women could do the job as well as men more than a century before the first female was accepted at the U.S. Coast Guard Academy or given command of a cutter.

Although the Coast Guard, as a single organization, was un-known in 1869, the experiences of the Lewis family of Newport covered the three separate federal functions that would later become its mission—sea patrol, lighthouse keeping, and lifesav-ing. For a dozen years, Captain Hosea Lewis skippered one of the vessels of the Revenue Cutter Service that was charged with apprehending smugglers and otherwise keeping order along Rhode Island's shores and harbors. When his first wife died, Captain Lewis married Idawalley Zorada Wiley, daughter of a doctor on Block Island, one of his regular ports of call. The second of their four children was given her mother's name, which she shortened to Ida. The girl inherited her father's inter-est in all things nautical. When his health began to fail, Captain Lewis was transferred to the Lighthouse Service and made keeper of a light that had been established on Lime Rock, a stony outcropping in the mouth of Newport's inner harbor that was just far enough offshore to be considered an island.

The navigational lights in those days were oil lamps, and maintaining them was an onerous chore. Filled and lit at sun-down, a lamp had to be watched through the night in case the wick was in need of trimming or the lens in need of cleaning. The flame had to be extinguished at dawn to save fuel, and the lamp polished and otherwise kept in repair during the day. It was a 365-day round-the-clock task. When Captain Lewis took it over in 1854, Lime Rock Light consisted of what has been described as "a mere sentry box" since it could be reached rather easily by rowboat from shore. After a year or so on the job, the ailing Captain Lewis apparently tired of tearing himself away from the comfort of his town house at odd times and in all weathers to row out to the light, and he decided to build a simple wooden house on the rocks and hang the light on the side of it. He moved there with his family in the summer of 1858.

Quite fortunately, as it turned out, sixteen-year-old Ida was a tomboy. Nobody recalls when it was that she learned to swim and handle a boat, but she was expert in both skills by the time the family occupied the house on the rocks. That first autumn, Ida took one chore off her father's shoulders by rowing the younger children back and forth to school. Being shallow, the stretch of water she had to contend with could kick up into a fierce chop in windy weather. Captain Lewis often feared for his daughter and her precious cargo. "Old sailor that I am, I felt I wouldn't bet a penny that they'd live," he said after seeing Ida row through one storm. "I watched them until I could bear it no longer, expecting every moment to see them swamped and the crew at the mercy of the waves, and then I turned away and said to my wife, 'Let me know if they get safe in,' for I could not endure to see them perish."

Captain Lewis need not have worried; Ida always got "safe in." Within four months after they had established a home on the rock, the whole family was in need of the kind of grit she demonstrated in her seamanship. Whatever ailed Hosea Lewis took a dramatic turn: A stroke turned him into a semi-invalid who could only sit by the stove and hobble around with a cane. In order for him to keep his job and the only family income, Ida had to join her mother in tending the light and taking care of the younger children. When it came to lifesaving, however, Ida was on her own until her younger brother Rudolph was old enough to give her an occasional hand. Although Lime Rock Light was in no sense one of the official lifesaving stations beginning to dot the Atlantic shoreline, the Lewises were the kind of seafaring people who, as Captain Lewis put it, could not bear to sit idly by and watch the sea claim a human life without trying to do something about it.

Then as now, people who found themselves in jeopardy at sea were usually the cause of their own plight. But luckily the kind of people who become lifesavers concern themselves only with human frailty rather than human fallibility. A case in point was Ida's first rescue. With nothing else to interest or amuse him, Captain Lewis kept a sharp eye on what he could see of water traffic from his stoveside rocker. One September afternoon in 1859, he was watching with a touch of nostalgia the antics of four boys in a sailboat that he recognized as one of Nick Aker's rental craft. The sun was shining, the sea was calm and the breeze was so light that the boat was hardly moving. Undoubtedly bored, the boys were cupping water from the wave beneath them and splashing each other, capering around the cockpit and deck. One of them shinned up the mast and started rocking the boat. It was then that the captain realized that the boys were inexperienced. With his weight at the top, the boy soon turned the mast into a pendulum that swung in ever longer arcs until the boat went over. Four heads bobbed to the surface, and the boys clung to the hull.

Captain Lewis called to his daughter, "Ida, have a look out there at that capsized boat. I doubt those boys can swim. Maybe you'd best row out to lend them a hand."

Ida needed no more urging. She shoved her rowboat into the water, unshipped her oars and reached the very wet and frightened boys within minutes. Ida could see that other boats were pulling out from shore too, but she rowed her survivors back to Lime Rock, where her mother gave them doses of hot molasses to ward off chill. It turned out that they were, indeed, novices and nonswimmers—students at Dr. William Leverett's private academy on Touro Street. But if foolishness brought about the accident, there was nothing foolish about the lives that were saved. Within two years, two of the boys enlisted in Company F, First Rhode Island Volunteers, one of them dying of wounds received at the Battle of Bull Run and the other serving out the Civil War. Another, Samuel C. Powell, became a physician serving Newport, and the fourth disappeared from the local scene.

Other rescues followed. Ida took them in stride. She wasn't the kind of person to brag, and neither were the survivors—for obvious reasons in most cases. One man, whose sailboat capsized in a gale and left him precariously perched on a single rock throughout a harrowing night until dawn revealed his plight to the Lewises, turned out to have stolen the boat. A soldier from Fort Adams down along the point from the lighthouse was so drunk coming back from a night in town that he kicked a hole in the bottom of his boat, causing it to sink. He was so helpless from drink and so heavy that Ida couldn't heave him into her boat despite wrenching her back in the attempt. She eventually got him ashore by tying a rope under his armpits and towing him.

Men who had enriched themselves during the Civil War and its giddy economic aftermath were already creating large estates in Newport as an escape from the demands of commerce. Three caretakers on one such estate near Lime Rock watched in fear of their jobs as a valuable sheep outran them and plunged into the water. The sheep swam away from shore, and the men grabbed a rowboat pulled up on the bank, which happened to belong to young Rudolph Lewis. The winds were high enough to create a chop that swamped the boat as they rowed after the lost sheep. Hearing their cries for help, Ida went to their rescue in her own boat. After depositing the men ashore, she rowed back to fetch the still swimming sheep and her brother's boat. It can be imagined that such survivors were nearly as grateful for Ida's silence as for her lifesaving efforts.

As it happened, it was an expression of gratitude by the garrison of Fort Adams for the rescue of two sober soldiers—one Sergeant Adams and one Private McLaughlin—that thrust Ida Lewis into the bright light of publicity. March was going out like a lion that year, and the day of the event, the twenty-ninth, was a day of record-making weather. It was cold—a blizzard with swirling snow and strong winds. Ida rather welcomed the storm. The weather gave her a good excuse to stay inside and nurse a very bad cold. With the younger children out of school, there was no reason to row to town. But Adams and McLaughlin took a very different view of the blizzard. They were in town when it started, and they shivered at the prospect of trudging through building snowdrifts all the way back to Fort Adams. An even more chilling thought, however, was what would happen to them if they were absent without leave.

A local Newport boy overheard the soldiers discussing their dilemma and saw an opportunity. "I'll row you out to the fort for a dollar," he said. "It's a lot quicker and you won't even get wet feet."

Neither Adams nor McLaughlin knew much about the sea, but they were skeptical. "In this weather?" Adams asked.

"Sure. Nothing to it. I do it all the time," the boy boasted. "I was out there checking my lobster traps this morning."

In view of the boy's confidence, a boat ride seemed the lesser of two evils to the soldiers, and they followed him down to the pier off Wellington Avenue, where his skiff was tied up. Darkness was setting in as they sailed away from the pier.

Down the coast at Lime Rock, the coming dark meant that somebody had to fill and light the lamp. Warm and comfortable on the other side of the stove from her father, Ida sat darning with her stockinged feet tucked up under her skirts. Listless and weak from the effect of her cold, she didn't argue when her mother offered to get the light going that night. But minutes after Mrs. Lewis climbed the stairs, she yelled, "Ida! Ida! A boat's capsized and men are drowning. I could see three and now I can only see two. Run, Ida, run!"

Ida uncurled herself from her seat, calling back as she headed for the door, "Where are they?"

"About due east of us a few hundred yards. I think they were heading for the fort. It was a rogue wave did it, curled right over the gunwale. I saw it. Be careful, Ida. . . ."

Ida didn't even think about finding shoes or a hat or a coat. All she did for protection was to grab a shawl she kept hanging on a peg by the door and tie it over her head. Every second counted. It was well known that a person couldn't survive more than a few minutes in water that was still winter cold. The rocks were spouting fountains of spray, and visibility through the gray mist of snow was almost nil. At the last minute, Rudolph jumped into the boat with her. Ida struck out in the general direction her mother had indicated. Fortunately, the men had enough life left in them to be calling intermittently for help, and she followed the sounds. Finally, she could see the dark lump of an overturned hull and beside it two smaller lumps of men's heads.

When she reached them, one of the men let go his hold on the hull and grabbed the gunwale of her boat amidships where she sat. The boat tilted and started taking on water. Ida had learned the hard way that she couldn't bring a heavy body over the side without her boat swamping. "To the stern!" she yelled. "Get to the back!" There was no time for argument or gentleness. When the man, half unconscious from cold, refused to release his grip, she batted his knuckles with an oar until she could pry his fingers loose. She struggled to hoist him over the squared-off stern, and he collapsed in Rudolph's arms. A little more aware, the other man was easier to handle. He was still alert enough to say, "There was a boy—the boy sailing us . . ." before he too collapsed.

With two unconscious men who might yet go into fatal shock in her boat, Ida could only spare one long and unrewarded look around for some sign of the boy. Seeing none, she rowed back to Lime Rock as fast as she could. Her brother helped her get the bodies into the house, where the whole Lewis family spent hours gradually warming and drying them. The men suffered no ill effects, and a few months later their comrades in the Fifth Regiment, U.S. Artillery, collected a purse of $218 and presented it to Ida Lewis.

How rare it was—and unfortunately still is—for the rescued to give their rescuers any thanks, let alone one as substantial as that amount of money represented in 1869. The gift was in fact reported in a local paper and rapidly soared up the news network to *Harper's Weekly.* Having pulled off quite a few other rescues with no fanfare, Ida was totally surprised by the attention. A writer who came to the lighthouse in an effort to obtain a dramatic recounting of her adventures ended up with this indelible portrait: "Ida met us at the door, as different a being from what our expectations of a possibly over-flattered and consequently spoiled girl might have led us to anticipate as may well be imagined. There was neither assumption nor affectation in her manner. She apologized simply for the everyday working garb, of plainest fashion and material, with which she was clothed, saying frankly that she was trying to help mother and 'get a little washing done.' She talked pleasantly and without constraint, but, unlike the world in general, seemed more fluent upon any theme than herself."

Ida's self-effacing silence continued throughout the presentation of other awards. The Life Saving Benevolent Association of New York came through with a silver medal and check for $100, and the General Assembly of Rhode Island adopted a resolution commending her. Even the one she most appreciated—the gift of a new rowing boat, paid for by public subscription in the town of Newport and built by Thomas D. Stoddard—couldn't move her to speech. The presentation of the boat was made at the municipal Fourth of July celebration in Newport. The words of the people who did speak give a flavor of the times and another glimpse of Ida's character from the people who knew her best.

On behalf of the donors, Francis Brinley said: "This boat has none of the glitter and pretense of the silver-oared barge of Cleopatra which floated on the Cydnus like a burnished throne, but it comes to you rich in artistic skill and freighted with the kindest wishes of the inhabitants of Newport. On behalf of the donors, and as their honored representative, I commit it to your care, knowing how well and wisely it will be used and managed by the heroine of Lime Rock, whose name and exploits will be preserved by tradition so long as any portion of the shores of Rhode Island shall be washed by the waters of Narragansett."

On behalf of Ida, Colonel Thomas Wentworth Higginson said: "Miss Lewis desires me to say that she has never made a speech in her life and does not expect to begin now. She has worked out the problem of women's rights in a different manner. She has been accustomed to assuming the right of helping her fellow men without asking any question. She receives this boat with pleasure not alone as an earnest of the good feeling of her fellow citizens but also as a means of doing a little more hereafter, if occasion should come in the same direction. Miss Lewis is grateful to you for your acknowledgement of what seemed to her a simple act of duty and she is more grateful to the Divine Providence which enabled her to do what she hopes never to have to do again."

However timid she was about speaking, Ida turned out to have a certain flair for the dramatic. Her new boat was launched at Long Wharf with a crowd of 1,000 cheering and troops from the fort firing a salute. Ida jumped nimbly into the boat, rowed skillfully through a tangle of spectator boats, paused just long enough to wave her handkerchief in appreciation and pulled for Lime Rock. But she couldn't pull away from fame. On the next Monday, two of the most glittering figures of what Mark Twain called "the gilded age"—partners Jay Gould and Jim Fisk— cashed in on her publicity by putting up funds for a boat house in which to store the new skiff. Later that year, Gould and Fisk would stand in need of whatever good works they could cite when their attempt to corner the gold market brought ruin to countless investors on "Black Friday," September 24.

The high point of that summer of recognition for Ida was undoubtedly the visit of President Grant. The old saying that "it takes one to know one" could well be applied to that meeting. No man since Washington and before Eisenhower was accorded the heroic stature by his countrymen that Ulysses S. Grant was. He was the general whose victories brought the Civil War to an end. Possessed of a great deal of courage, Grant admired this quality wherever he found it. When he read of Ida's exploits, he expressed a desire to visit her on a New England tour that summer of 1869. At forty-six the youngest man until then ever elected to the presidency, Grant was nevertheless not nimble enough to negotiate the slimy surface of Lime Rock. He slipped getting out of the boat and got both feet wet. It was a bad moment for a flustered and apologetic Ida, but Grant laughingly said, "To see Ida Lewis I'd gladly get wet up to my armpits if necessary." Grant persuaded Ida to show him around the rock and demonstrate the light. He was later heard to say that his visit to Ida Lewis was one of the most memorable events of his life.

After that, Ida was never in awe of the rich and famous, and they seemed to be comfortable with her too. Admiral George Dewey, the man who would become the hero of Manila Bay but who was then a Navy lieutenant commander and secretary of the Lighthouse Board, dropped by to have a "smoke on your half-acre rock for half an hour." General William Tecumseh Sherman, noted for his bloody march to the sea through Georgia, spent an hour on the rock because he liked the peace of the place. George Boutwell, a secretary of the treasury under Grant, sought out Ida Lewis personally to tell her that he was proud to have a woman in his department who wasn't "finicky about getting her hair wet." It was inevitable that Susan B. Anthony, the leading suffragette of the day, would want to meet a woman like Ida. More traditionally minded women also found her fascinating. "Every Mrs. Astor and every Mrs. Vanderbilt and every Mrs. Belmont called on me with whole boatloads of men and women and all talked at once and treated me as if I were a kind of real queen," she once said.

There was an unfortunate side to her sudden celebrity. Isolated and busy as she was, Ida had missed out on romance. Evidently attracted by the publicity, a man named William H. Wilson of Black Rock, Connecticut, persuaded her to marry him in 1870. The marriage didn't last long—Wilson, for reasons never understood, abandoned her. There was no divorce, but Wilson was never seen or heard of around Newport again. By the time Ida's father died in 1872, she was back at Lime Rock to help her mother, who was appointed official keeper in her husband's stead. In 1879, Mrs. Wilson was finally and officially acknowledged as keeper of Lime Rock Light. There would be more rescues and more honors—among them, membership in the American Legion of Honor, a medal from the New York Humane Society and the Massachusetts Humane Society, a lifetime pension of $30 a month from philanthropist Andrew Carnegie—in the long years to come. There would be tragedy too, in the passing of her mother, one of her brothers and a beloved sister.

Ida Lewis's last rescue took place when she was sixty-four. A woman friend who was rowing out to see Ida stood up in her boat, lost her balance and fell overboard. Ida launched her lifeboat and plucked the sodden woman out of the water, thereby achieving her twenty-third feat of lifesaving. On an October morning in 1911, sixty-nine-year-old Ida Lewis Wilson, living alone on the rock, snuffed out her light, went down to prepare breakfast and collapsed on the kitchen floor. Her younger brother Rudolph found her lying there in a coma. She never regained consciousness and died five days later. For all the fame and rewards her lifesaving sorties brought her, the constant and mundane task of light keeping was the real stuff of Ida Lewis's life. Her passing was the answer to a prayer that she had uttered when discussing the celebrated rescue of the soldiers from Fort Adams: "This lighthouse is home to me, and I hope the good Lord will take me away when I have to leave it. The light is my child, and I know when it needs me, even if I sleep."

Today, no boat is needed to reach Ida Lewis's home, which still stands on Lime Rock. A long causeway leads out to the facility, which was bought from the government by a group of

Newport residents and turned into a yacht club after World War I. The lamp Ida so lovingly tended is also there. As if intended by providence, it was found in 1933 in a store of discarded surplus from the pre-electric age at the Staten Island Depot by Dr. Horace Beck, a member of the Newport Historical Society. Ida Lewis's light still shines.

Chapter 10

The Night of the Praying Chaplains

BY the time the U.S. Coast Guard cutter *Escanaba* set sail from St. John's, Newfoundland, for Greenland on Saturday, January 30, 1943, she and the men who sailed in her were seasoned veterans in the battle with winter weather and the unseen enemy that made every passage through "torpedo junction" a feat of valor. The *Escanaba* was a clear case of design determining destiny. Built in 1932, she had a steel hull especially reinforced for ice breaking. With a home port in Grand Haven, Michigan, *Escanaba* spent tough winters plowing fishing boats and ore carriers out of the ice on the Great Lakes, and pleasant summers shepherding sailing regattas and motorboat races. When the Coast Guard was automatically incorporated into the Navy at the outbreak of World War II, the *Escanaba* was ordered to convoy duty in the iceberg- and U-boat-infested waters of the North Atlantic. The evident logic behind this order was that she was especially equipped to cope with these conditions.

Still beloved in Grand Haven, where each summer visitors in the thousands gather to salute her memory, the *Escanaba* did not let the home folks down. At a length of 165 feet, with a beam of thirty-six feet and an armament of two fifty-caliber guns, two six pounders and as many depth charges as she could hold, the *Escanaba* was considered a "light cutter," but she proved to be a heavy hitter in combat. On a single day—June 15, 1942—she

153

sank two German submarines with depth charges while guarding a convoy from Halifax to Cape Cod. Within an hour of that second kill, the *Escanaba* was involved in a desperate version of the Coast Guard's peacetime mission—the saving of lives.

The *Escanaba* had evidently cut out only two members of a German wolf pack. The torpedoes from another U-boat got through the screen and sank the cargo ship USS *Cherokee*. It was close to midnight, dark as sin, and the seas were running high. The *Escanaba* moved gingerly into the flotsam, human and material, left on the surface. No lights could be used because subs might still be lurking around. There were men swimming, men crowded onto a life raft. Volunteers from the *Escanaba* manned a Monomoy rowboat to search out swimmers. Meanwhile, the crew on the cutter tried to cope with the raft and some swimmers who came alongside. They threw out life rings on lines, but the seas swept the survivors past so fast they couldn't hold onto them. In one case, a husky *Escanaba* crewman held another one over the side by the legs so that he could grab a swimmer and pull him aboard when the ship rolled down close to the water. The maneuver saved a life, but it was too slow and dangerous. By taking the *Escanaba* windward of the raft and drifting down, they found that they could keep backing the propeller and create a relatively calm spot under the stern counter where the raft could nestle while the survivors climbed up a fire hose with a line looped around them in case they fell. In that manner, they plucked eleven men out of the water, and the Monomoy returned with an overload of another eleven. Being able to hoist the boat and its occupants aboard was sheer luck because there was a new submarine contact, forcing them to get under way at once. Risking a small boat and the men who man it wasn't a bright idea in the presence of a wolf pack. However happy they were about the lives they had saved, the *Escanaba*'s crew had the uneasy feeling as they sailed on that night that they might have found and saved more with better methods.

Especially frustrated by the experience was Lieutenant Robert H. Prause, the *Escanaba*'s executive officer. He had been in charge of the deck party trying to haul swimmers aboard, and it had been he who had suggested the human chain out of desperation as he watched a man's futile struggles to hang onto a line in the water. Impractical as it was, it proved that a strong, healthy rescuer could save a survivor suffering from shock, cold and possible injuries by literally manhandling him. But to be truly workable in a case of mass rescues, the rescuer had to be protected in order to be able to function over and over again. When they had a bit of time off in port at Bluie West One, Greenland, Lieutenant Prause turned himself into a guinea pig. Donning a rubber suit and attaching himself to the dock with a line, he jumped repeatedly into the icy water to determine how well and how long a man could work. He was satisfied with the results and sure that, given another challenge, the *Escanaba* would do a much more gratifying job.

On a trip that began some six months after the *Cherokee* affair, the *Escanaba* was patrolling the starboard beam of a three-ship convoy—two freighters, the SS *Lutz* and SS *Biscaya,* and a troop transport, the SS *Dorchester.* Conditions aboard the *Dorchester* can be imagined from the fact that, as a luxury cruise ship, she had carried 314 cabin passengers; gutted and converted for military use, she had aboard 751 passengers and a twenty-three-man Navy armed guard. Of the passengers, 524 were soldiers headed for combat. Because of the bitter cold that iced up the decks the passengers were ordered to stay below in their crowded quarters. Seasickness and boredom were pervasive from the first. A worse malady—fear—crept through the ship on Tuesday, February 2, when the Coast Guard cutter *Tampa* out ahead of the convoy detected the presence of a submarine on its sonar. The *Tampa* made a sweep around but couldn't pinpoint the U-boat's position. There was nothing to do but sail on, changing course from time to time but remaining real sitting ducks at the *Dorchester*'s ten-knot pace.

It was 1530 hours, 3:30 P.M., when the *Tampa* flashed a warning to the rest of the fleet. Master Hans Danielson of the *Dorchester* got on the public address system to pass the warning along to all hands and advise them to put on parkas and life jackets even in their bunks. He had some reassuring news as well: They were only 150 miles from Greenland. Lieutenant Junior Grade William H. Arpaia summoned his Navy gun crew to battle stations and ordered their weapons made ready for firing. Among the troops, there were four chaplains, all Army lieutenants—George Fox, a Methodist; Clark Poling, Dutch Reformed; Rabbi Alexander Goode; and Father John Washington, Roman Catholic. In charge of troop morale, they had had a busy time passing out crackers to the sick, organizing songfests for the bored and holding well-attended services. When fear started rising so did their efforts to divert the men. They used humor as much as prayer. A favorite pastime among the troops was guessing where they were ultimately going. As a presumably knowledgeable officer, Rabbi Goode was pressed to tell them, and he would reply, "What? And spoil the surprise?" Watching one of the poker games he promoted, Father Washington was asked to bless one soldier's cards. He took a look at the hand and said loud enough for the other players to hear, "What? *Me* bless a pair of measly deuces?" Hearing the men laugh at such sallies gave the chaplains hope for their ability to cope with whatever faced them in the future.

When there had been no attack by sundown, there was some relaxation of tension aboard the *Dorchester* except for those on watch. Lieutenant Arpaia had half his men stand down to get some rest, but the other half were instructed to keep a twenty-millimeter gun continuously cocked on both port and starboard sides and to fire without awaiting orders at any sign of a periscope or torpedo wake in the water. The normal seventeen-man Army lookout detail was doubled to thirty-four. Lieutenant Arpaia remained in constant consultation with Master Danielson. At one point they discussed what should be done with the codes and other confidential papers they each possessed and they decided to pack them all into the perforated metal box that Danielson had in a cabinet. As they pored over the skipper's charts together, Danielson pointed out to Arpaia that they would be crossing into an iceberg area where submarines dared not go by 2400, midnight. At that witching hour, a weary Arpaia made a last round to check out his guns and crews, and then he visited every one of the thirty-four lookouts to inform them that they should keep an eye peeled for signs of icebergs as well as submarines. The *Titanic,* he reminded them, went down as surely as if she had been torpedoed. At 2415, a few minutes into Wednesday, February 3, Arpaia retired to his cabin to try to rest.

For anyone used to sailing at night in peacetime, cruising in a wartime convoy could be a strange and eerie experience. The Christmas-tree comfort of seeing another ship's lights winking and blinking across a black and lonely expanse of ocean was not to be had. Other vessels were only ghostly electronic presences over the radio or on the radar screen; at close quarters they might loom as darker shapes against dark backgrounds. The night of February 2 and 3 through which the *Tampa,* the *Escanaba* and the U.S. Coast Guard cutter *Comanche* on the port flank herded their charges—sailing three abreast with the *Dorchester* in the middle—was a kind one for that time of year and that latitude. There was only a slight chop on a calm sea raised by a light breeze out of the northeast; with no moon, it was very dark but so clear that the smallest light was visible at a great distance. From the observation of the deck watch on the *Escanaba,* the merchant vessels were doing a good job of maintaining the prescribed "dark ship" condition that prohibited all illumination, even the dimmest of running lights. If you stared in the *Dorchester*'s direction long enough, it might be possible to catch a flash of light, instantaneous as a firefly's tail, when someone opened a door out onto a deck. Such little lapses were understandable with more than 900 people, many of them civilians, moving around the ship, and a submarine would have to cruise with telltale periscope up constantly or on the surface to catch them. But at 0100, the *Escanaba*'s officer of the deck, Ensign Henry E. Ringling, saw a streak of light, startling in its brilliance against the black night, rise above the *Dorchester,* followed by little red blobs of light bouncing about the decks and over into the water. Minutes later there was an all ships alarm from the *Comanche: "Dorchester* hit!" Almost immediately there was a message from the *Tampa,* escort commander: *"Escanaba* proceed to rescue. *Comanche* cover and assist. Searching for sub."

The *Escanaba*'s captain, Lieutenant Commander Carl U. Peterson, was on the bridge in seconds. At his order, Ringling sounded the alarm for general quarters. The sixty members of the *Escanaba*'s crew running to their stations needed no urging to make everything ready for rescue operations as quickly as possible. They had been through it and knew that wasted seconds meant wasted lives. With the blackout in full force, it would be next to impossible on the dark decks to lay a hand on anything that wasn't exactly where it was supposed to be. Sea ladders were put in position, heaving lines cut and coiled, cargo nets dropped over the side. Lieutenant Prause had trained a number of what he called "retrievers." These men climbed into rubber suits and attached themselves to the ship with lines. According to the drill, a retriever would go after any survivor who couldn't climb a ladder or haul himself up the nets, take hold of the person, signal the crew manning his line to haul them both to the cutter's side and put another line around the survivor for hoisting to the deck. The same system would be used on any rafts or boats within reach. As the *Escanaba* closed with the *Dorchester,* the men on her decks could see that the troop ship was sinking; the little red lights were hand-held flashlights of people milling around on deck or jumping into the water. It was good that they were ready.

Lieutenant Arpaia was stretched out in his bunk on the *Dorchester* and just drifting off to sleep when a dull thud and concussion shook the whole ship and startled him awake a few minutes before 0100 hours, 1 A.M. There was no loud explosion, and one of the *Dorchester*'s officers, also in his bunk, thought that they had hit an iceberg. But the damage was too severe for that. The engines stopped immediately, all lights went out, and the ship took a sharp list to starboard. On his way to the deck, Arpaia got a strong whiff of ammonia, suggesting that the refrigerator plant just above the engine room and just aft of amidships had been blown apart. The ship's whistle was sounding six blasts to signal a torpedoing on the starboard side. Arpaia had heard no firing from his own guns, and he soon discovered why. The lookouts he ran into told him that they had seen nothing and heard nothing but a slight swish before impact. Noise or no noise, the force of the explosion was greater than Arpaia, cushioned in his bunk, had realized. One of his men on the starboard gun had been bounced clear overboard. Now the list rendered all guns useless.

Arpaia found Master Danielson out on the flying bridge. He seemed stunned. He had just tried to sound another six blasts on the whistle to call for abandoning ship, but the steam gave out after two whimpers. The ship was clearly sinking, but the master didn't want to believe it. "What about the confidential papers and codes? Have you done anything with them?" Lieutenant Arpaia asked.

Danielson shook his head. "You take care of them," he said.

Arpaia ran to the master's cabin, found the metal box he had packed, ran back to the bridge and flung it overboard. All around him was pandemonium, if not panic. Both the explosion and the list had rendered nearly all of the ship's fourteen lifeboats useless. Of the six that were somehow launched, four were swamped by too many men trying to scramble into them. Life rafts were cut loose but many were simply left on deck to float free if the ship sank. Arpaia's experience suggests the state of confusion. When the gun crew he was with discovered that their assigned raft had been taken by some soldiers, Seamen Winfield McCoy and William McMinn volunteered to find another. They climbed to the top of the ship, located a doughnut raft and threw it over the high port side into the water. Arpaia dove off the ship, got into the raft and held it for the two seamen and another who was swimming nearby.

There was one small island of calm in all the chaos. The four chaplains, wearing life jackets and prepared to abandon ship, came together on the sharply canted starboard deck. When they heard the note of panic in the cursing and crying of the men around them, they began preaching calm and courage. Going overboard was obviously the only chance any of them had of staying alive, but many men froze in fear. The chaplains tried to talk them into jumping. The men in the service who never seemed to "get the word" was a standing wartime joke, but it wasn't funny that night for those who hadn't heard or who had ignored the master's instruction to wear life jackets and parkas at all times. They appeared on deck with no clothes, no life jackets. The chaplains found a locker full of jackets and passed them out or actually put them on these men. Then they did something that would be forever engraved in the memory of the *Dorchester*'s Second Engineer Grady Clark: They took off their own jackets and handed them to others. The last Clark saw of the chaplains as he swam away was a tableau of four men, arms linked, braced against the pitch of the deck, surrounded by a little knot of other men. There was no sound but that of the chaplains' voices raised in prayer.

At approximately 0120, twenty-five minutes after she had

been hit, the *Dorchester*'s stern lifted high into the air and she plunged into 1,830 fathoms of water. As the *Dorchester*'s silhouette disappeared from view, the bridge watch on the *Escanaba* was left looking into a featureless black hole. Since they couldn't run the risk of moving blindly into a sea full of survivors, if there were any, or of missing them entirely, Commander Peterson decided to risk giving a lurking U-boat an easy target. He told Ensign Ringling to fire star shells. Ringling's single, run-together sentence in the ship's logbook conveys the sense of the action: "0133 ordered to illuminate and expend twenty-one illuminating shells, ten from gun No. One and eleven from gun No. Two 0135 ceased illuminating 0143 commenced picking up survivors." What was visible in the brilliant light from those star shells wasn't recorded but can easily be imagined. The sea was covered with an inky slick of oil that had spilled from the *Dorchester*'s wound. Wriggling like worms in mud through this slop were the blackened figures of people trying to swim. Amid the inert debris were two objects that looked like boats, a few others strung with red lights were evidently rafts. When the light died away, the *Escanaba* positioned herself to windward as she had learned to do in the *Cherokee* rescue and drifted slowly into the mess with only enough power to maintain control.

From the swimmers they first encountered, it was quickly apparent that less than half an hour in the winter water had rendered most of them helpless. They couldn't climb sea ladders or cargo nets. They couldn't even catch a line with a running bowline, much less get it around themselves. It was time for the retrievers. However much they had practiced, going into oily, freezing water full of dead and half-dead men and booby-trapped with flotsam was daunting. There was hesitation at the rails. Ensign Richard Arrighi, a Coast Guard reserve officer who had trained as a retriever, mounted the gunwale, shouted, "All right, men, let's go!" and jumped. The others followed.

Early on, the *Escanaba* came upon a lifeboat with fifty-one men aboard and five more clinging to the sides. Retrievers dragged her alongside the cutter where she was made fast. One survivor fell between the lifeboat and the *Escanaba*'s steel flank. He was so slippery with oil that the men in the lifeboat couldn't pull him back aboard. Ensign Arrighi, working in the water nearby, swam over and got between the two boats. He managed to lift the survivor up and out so that a line could be put around him. At least two other retrievers, Seamen Forrest Rednour and Warren Deyampert, similarly risked their own lives. A raft drifted in under the cutter's counter. Knowing that the propeller was turning over slowly, Rednour swam in under the counter to fend off and keep the raft and its occupants from being mangled. With his help and by backing the propeller, the raft was brought into position to unload. Deyampert performed the same service for a single floating survivor threatened by the propeller.

Since it was hard to tell the living from the dead, they took aboard every floating body they could find. It was good that they did. Dr. Ralph Nix, a U.S. Public Health Service surgeon serving as ship's doctor, worked over each one of them. Only twelve out of fifty seemingly dead men failed to revive with his treatment. The rescue work went on through the next watch—0400 to 0800—which was logged by Ringling's successor as officer of the deck in another single sentence: "Under way as before on various courses and speeds, picking up survivors of *Dorchester* torpedoing." Ensign James Sullivan's entry for the next watch— 0800 to 1200, noon—is more detailed but as totally emotionless as the others: "Under way as before picking up survivors. 0920 completed picking up survivors. The following 132 men were taken on board . . ." Each name is then listed, apparently in the order that it was ascertained. It is noted that six of the dead could not then be identified. The entry concludes: "0922 under way on base course 044 degrees (p.g.c.), speed 120 R.P.M. 1000 inspected magazines and smokeless powder samples, condition dry and normal."

The *Escanaba* was soon up to full speed, zigzagging her way toward Bluie West One. The *Comanche,* arriving on the scene of the sinking half an hour after the *Escanaba,* rescued ninety-seven people. Those in the only other lifeboat were taken aboard, and Lieutenant Arpaia and his surviving companions plucked off their doughnut raft. Writing up his report a month later, Arpaia managed to convey the anguish of the experience in a very few words: "Ralph L. Taylor, seaman first class, died in our raft. We did everything we possibly could to keep him alive. We were in the raft for six hours and fifteen minutes and due to the cold water were practically unable to move at the time we were picked up. Fortunately, I had a package of morphine Syrettes in my shirt pocket, which I carried on my person all the time. After we were in the raft for about two hours McCoy was able by tearing my pocket to give himself an injection. He also gave me an injection and McMinn an injection. I believe that the effects of the morphine kept us alive and made it possible for us to resist the severity of the weather. At that time Taylor had already died. He lost his mind before dying."

The *Tampa* searched futilely for the submarine, which had not been seen by anybody on any ship either before or after the attack. Then she herded the *Lutz* and the *Biscaya* on toward Greenland. The master of the *Lutz,* unthinkingly obeying the seaman's instinct, had turned to go to the aid of the *Dorchester.* In the dark and confusion, there was a collision with the *Biscaya,* but the damage was not crippling. When the dreadful toll was taken in Greenland after the cutters arrived in port, it was determined that 661 people were missing and unreported. Of those plucked out of the water, thirteen were buried at Narsarssuak and at Ivigut, Greenland.

Disasters of this magnitude were not immediately publicized during the war. But the unusual behavior of the chaplains led to posthumous decorations for all of them in December 1944, and this was a morale-boosting story that had to be told. It was very effective, as can be judged by an editorial in the *New York Times* that said, in part: "This week General Somervell presented four Distinguished Service Crosses to the relatives of four chaplains . . . who went down with the troopship *Dorchester.* They went down because they gave their lifebelts to soldiers. . . . If in life their differing faiths separated them somewhat, in death they were united in a sublime faith and brotherhood. War the destroyer does one or two good things. . . . It teaches us the sublimity of which the human spirit is capable."

Awards were also given at a later date to the men of the *Escanaba*—the Navy and Marine Corps medal to Ensign Arrighi and seamen Rednour and Deyampert, the Legion of Merit to Commander Peterson and a letter of commendation to Lieutenant Prause. These awards were also posthumous. But, war being war, the ultimate sacrifice of the *Escanaba* people was subsumed in line-of-duty deaths occurring daily around the globe. In addition, there were military reasons for not going into detail about the fate of these men since it might have confirmed to the enemy that they had accurate knowledge of Allied ship movements.

In June 1943, only a few months after the *Dorchester* sinking, the *Escanaba* was assigned to a convoy from Narsarssuak, Greenland, to St. John's, Newfoundland. With the exception of a couple of fresh hands, the same captain and crew would be taking her out, and her old partner, the *Tampa,* would be part of an escort including the cutters *Raritan* and *Mojave,* the flagship. Their charge was a U.S. Army transport, the USAT *Fairfax.* Shortly before their intended sailing, there was a nerve-racking incident. Lord Haw Haw, the German radio propagandist with a British accent, announced that the *Fairfax* would be sunk. This scare tactic was unfortunately supported by an Army report that a submarine had been detected in Brede Fjord, in nearby Greenland.

Vessels anchored in the fjord were warned to prepare for action and asked to listen on their hydrophones for any sound of a submarine. The Coast Guard detailed the cutters *Storis* and *Algonquin* to search the fjord. When nothing was seen or heard, the convoy set sail at 2200 hours, 10 P.M., on June 10. Despite the calendar date, on the second day out the ships ran into dense fog and the kind of icy sea strewn with bergs and their small cousins, growlers, that the *Escanaba* was designed to survive. While they crept west and south around the ice field, the *Storis* and the *Algonquin* caught up to add to the strength of the convoy. They had reached 60° 50' N, 52° 00' W, shortly after dawn on June 13. At 0510 hours, 5:10 A.M., the deck watch on *Storis* saw a black cloud of smoke mingled with flame rise above *Escanaba.* At 0513, three minutes later, there was nothing at all to be seen where the cutter had been sailing but small bits of debris in the water.

The *Storis* and the *Raritan* were ordered to search for survivors. The *Raritan* found two men swimming in the sea—Boatswains Mate Melvin Baldwin and Seaman First Class Raymond O'Malley—and a lifeless body identified as that of Lieutenant Robert H. Prause. The stunned survivors had no idea of what had happened, and none of the ships in the convoy had had any submarine contacts. O'Malley, who had been standing his watch at the helm reported that a noise that sounded like bursts from a twenty-millimeter machine gun was heard in the pilothouse just before the crash of the explosion. There was, however, no firing in progress on the *Escanaba* and no other ship near enough for firing to have created such a loud noise. The theory that still prevails is that O'Malley was hearing an oncoming torpedo through the loudspeaker in the pilothouse that was connected to the hydrophone.

On August 4, 1943, the first of the continuing memorial celebrations for the *Escanaba* and the men who went down with her was held in her permanent home port of Grand Haven, Michigan. It was called Coast Guard Day, and it ended with religious services in the city park with three ministers participating and a crowd of 20,000 in attendance. The crowd has grown by ten or more times today, and the reason for this outpouring is certainly the same as that which prompted the designation of February 3 as Four Chaplains Observance Day and the building of The Chapel of Four Chaplains, an interfaith shrine, in Philadelphia. People need to know and to remember the "sublimity of which the human spirit is capable."

Chapter 11

The Last Hours of *Bermuda Sky Queen*

"YOU'RE shitting me!" was the instant response of Lieutenant Junior Grade C. S. "Mike" Hall, first lieutenant and gunnery officer of the U.S. Coast Guard cutter *George M. Bibb,* when the quartermaster shook him awake on that October morning in 1947 with the news that an aircraft was about to ditch in the Atlantic near their ship. If the language was strong, so was the provocation. Hall was shocked; he simply couldn't believe what he was hearing.

Although he was only twenty-seven, Hall had been through more unexpected happenings at sea than most mariners experience in a lifetime. As an enlisted man, he had served aboard the convoy cutter Spencer, credited with sinking three German U-boats and disabling a fourth in a French dry dock; as a commissioned officer, he had been commander of a landing craft in the Pacific. Now he was serving as a volunteer on a 327-foot cutter on weather station in the north Atlantic, one of the least desired tours of duty in the Coast Guard.

The reason for Hall's disbelief and for the average coastie's dread of weather service was the same—rough seas. Hove to in order to stay on station, a weather ship had to take whatever came along. In the fall and winter, Station Charlie on the flight line between Ireland and Newfoundland was subject to repeated gales, and by Mike Hall's 7 A.M. wakeup call on October 14, the *Bibb* had been buffeted by high winds and building seas for fifty-six hours. Moving around from west to southwest, the winds had created a cross pattern of waves three stories high converging at a thirty-degree angle with only 100 to 200 feet between crests. The *Bibb* was being tossed around like a toy in a bathtub, rising up and crashing down as if hitting a wall, rolling from side to side, shipping water bow and stern. On his way up to the bridge that morning, Hall heard the ominous, continuous clanging of the ship's bell, and he knew that it took a roll of thirty-eight degrees before the clapper would even touch the side of the bell.

Hall found Captain Paul B. Cronk already on the bridge wing, staring out over sky and sea and trying to gulp down a cup of coffee. The captain had only managed to climb into his hammock at 5 A.M. and was even more startled than Hall by the news. He had been awakened at 6:47 as soon as the *Bibb*'s radio operator received a call from British Overseas Airways plane KCC: "Station Charlie from KCC. Aircraft call KFG going to make emergency landing at sea at Station Charlie at approximately 0800 (8 A.M.)" They all knew KFG as the call letters for the big Boeing flying boat *Bermuda Sky Queen.* She had passed over and talked to them at 2:05 and again at 2:32 A.M. They had given her a fix on her position and the weather at 6,000 and 4,000 feet; she had reported that she was "well satisfied with the progress of the flight and expected no difficulty."

But the equivalent of all hell had broken loose on the emergency frequencies shortly after 5 A.M. By piecing together the fragmented messages they could pick up, the crew of the *Bibb* had a pretty good picture as 0800 approached of what had happened. After going through a stretch of blinding clouds for several hours, the *Queen* had come into clear air and had taken a celestial fix. What her crew learned was frightening. In the hours since they had over flown the *Bibb,* gale winds had cut their ground speed to fifty-nine knots. They had passed the point of no return—the point beyond which they would not have enough fuel to get back to Foynes in Ireland—but they couldn't make it to Gander in Newfoundland. Station Charlie, with the potentially lifesaving *Bibb* bobbing around down below, was only 310 miles to the east. Although young and inexperienced, the plane's twenty-six-year-old captain, Charles

Martin, decided to play it safe. He made a banking 180-degree turn and headed his forty-two-ton craft back toward the rising sun.

Martin was unable to radio his intentions to Gander. But his message was picked up by two other aircraft—a nearby freight plane and a BOAC passenger plane 300 miles to the east and heading for home. The freighter joined the *Queen* to keep watch over her, and the BOAC plane put about to help her home in on Station Charlie and pass the news to the *Bibb*. As land stations received the message and began responding, there was more alarming news: The flight of the *Queen* was no ordinary crossing. It was a charter flight with sixty-two passengers aboard, including women and children, and a crew of seven— the largest number of persons ever to be carried across the Atlantic in one airplane. A full load for a transatlantic flight in those days was, in fact, only twenty-one passengers.

As he paced the bridge wing, Captain Cronk, a sensitive man of vivid imagination, found the news that so many lives would soon be his responsibility nearly overwhelming. "In my mind's eye I saw that flying eggshell collapse as it struck the sea," he later wrote, "saw the great tail loop up and over as the plane smashed against the thirty-foot waves; saw the wings wrenched off; heard the screams of the passengers within as the sea poured in upon them. 'Oh, God, grant that I do not have to stand here helpless and see that plane open up and sink. Guide them down safely. Help me to save them.' Most of us prayed in any way we knew. Someone near me was vomiting with nervousness."

The captain's feelings were quite evidently shared by the *Bibb*'s crew. More than a hundred of them were out on deck scanning the skies. Captain Cronk ordered, "Man the rescue stations!" Men lowered scramble nets over the sides. Boat crews assembled at their posts. Swimmers put on their rubber suits with webbed fingers and toes. Loops were thrown into bowlines positioned along the decks so that they could be tossed out to people in the water. The contrast between the weather and the potentially dreadful fate facing those people in the sky heightened the drama for the men scrambling about on the *Bibb*. It was one of those bright blue and gold October mornings. The dark blue of the sea was streaked with a gleaming white lacework woven across it by the gale. Geysers of spray thrown up when the *Bibb* buried her bow were transformed into sparkling showers of diamond shards by the sun. How could anything terrible happen amid such beauty?

Standing his watch on the bridge, Lieutenant Hall was not immune to the fever of anticipation all around him, despite his experience. During the war he had often participated in the rescue of survivors from torpedoed ships but this would be different. It was one thing to see a ship blown up by enemy fire in the heat of combat and quite another to watch a plane in good working order deliberately drop into an angry sea, as if in an act of multiple suicide. It was one thing to cope with strong young men swimming in cold water and quite another to deal with women and children. No two ways about it, it would be an unholy mess. During the wait, Hall made up his mind about one thing: He would be in the thick of it. With the rugged body of a former University of Michigan football player, Hall enjoyed physical action. It was why he was still in the Coast Guard, why he was as far out at sea as possible in the service instead of behind some desk.

A long, tense hour went by before three dots appeared in the sky at 0900 and grew rapidly into the shapes of planes. Much larger than the other two, ungainly compared to the land planes with her boat-shaped hull, the *Queen* was easy to spot. Captain Cronk stepped from the bridge wing into the plotting room, got Captain Martin on the radio and tried to be calm in describing the wind's force and direction and the unfavorable sea conditions. Hearing himself, Cronk realized again that it was the worst possible surface—no sea slope between sharp crests long enough for the plane to skim and gradually settle in. Never having been through something like this, Cronk fell back on theory. He tried to sound helpful and cheerful: "How about if the ship makes a few circles at the best possible speed? I believe it will knock down the sea a bit and you can land in the center of our circle."

In a voice under remarkable control, young Martin said, "Thanks, Captain, but I think I'll just pick out a spot and set her down."

At about 1000 the *Queen* could be seen descending. It was

breath-holding time on the *Bibb.* The big plane leveled off just before touching the water. there was a roar as Martin put full power to the *Queen*'s four engines, and she rose again in a wide, sweeping circle. "Good boy, look it over," Cronk said to himself. Breathing started again in unison on the *Bibb,* but not for long. The *Queen* was coming in again. This time, throttle down and flying straight into the strong wind, the big bird hovered awkwardly a few feet above the surface like a fishing pelican and then dropped suddenly into the water just beyond the crest of a wave. Down she went into the trough, a trough so deep that she was completely out of view of the hundred eyes on the *Bibb.* The next wave broke over the *Queen,* and it was heart-stopping time on the cutter. But the plane staggered up, shouldering foam off her wings and fuselage. She appeared to be intact and floating high; sliding down the wave had prevented a smashing impact.

A somewhat breathless pilot Martin confirmed over the radio that everything seemed to be in working order and that there were no injuries. But there was no time to rejoice. On plane and ship, everybody knew that the *Queen*'s passengers had to be transferred to the *Bibb* as quickly as possible. In seas like the one that continued to roil and boil on that mercilessly bright day, the plane could spring a leak or have her wings rolled under and flip. The latter seemed inevitable to the people on the *Bibb.* The cutter had been positioned crosswind in an attempt to create some sort of lee for the landing plane, and she was rolling up to forty-five degrees on each side. Martin had tried to take advantage of this lee by landing downwind of the cutter. There would be no safe way of bringing the craft together, but Martin proposed that the *Bibb* send him a long line and take the *Queen* in tow while they worked out a plan to transfer people. Cronk agreed.

Aboard the *Bibb* the crew started hanging a six-inch line with kapok life preservers to float out to the *Queen.* Martin, who had switched off his ignition just before landing, restarted his engines and eased up toward the lee side of the ship to pick up the line. Without warning, a rogue wave picked up the plane. The ship's bulk had reduced the restraining force of the wind and the *Queen* started surfing on the wave toward the *Bibb*'s high steel side. Martin cut his engines, but it was too late. The *Queen*'s nose hit the *Bibb*'s hull with a crash as the ship rolled away. When the *Bibb* rolled back, one of the *Queen*'s engines drove a boat davit twenty-five feet above the waterline inboard; on another roll one of the plane's wingtips smashed a catwalk ten feet above the weather deck.

Ships aren't capable of instant movement. As soon as he saw the *Queen* surfing, Captain Cronk started calling for power. "Full astern!" he yelled, and yelled again and again throughout the rolling and crashing, "Full astern, damn it! Full astern!" It seemed an eternity before the screws bit into the water enough to back the *Bibb* away from the plunging plane.

Luckily, the brief collision had caused no apparent leaks in the plane's hull, and the removal of the windscreen created by the *Bibb* turned into an unexpected break for the *Queen*. The gale winds acted on its wings and control surfaces almost like the speed of flight. By making constant adjustments, the pilots could keep the *Queen* headed into wind and wave and reduce the pitching to some degree with the stabilizers. Whatever else happened, Captain Martin knew that he and his crew would have to stay alert and go on "flying" constantly. Captain Cronk had learned something useful too. Whatever else happened, he would have to keep the *Bibb* a safe distance from the plane. Beyond these conclusions, neither captain had a promising solution to their dilemma.

Although using small boats and rafts in some manner was indicated, the prospect was frightening. If the craft themselves could be kept from swamping or capsizing, getting sixty-nine people into them out of a plane rising and falling thirty feet or more like an elevator and out of them onto a rolling ship presented sixty-nine opportunities for injury or death. But something had to be tried. Both the plane and cutter had small rubber life rafts. They were rated as ten-person rafts, but this capacity was achieved only by putting three people into the raft and having the other seven stay in the water and hang onto grab lines. Since they were easy to handle and could be launched quickly, it was decided to give them a try—empty and attached to a long line. The *Queen* was first to launch a raft. The wind turned it into a kite, swooping it up off the water and spinning it at the end of the line. The *Bibb*'s small raft behaved as crazily. The cutter then launched a fifteen-man, abandon-ship raft. Although it stayed upright on the surface, it was so hard to manage in the wind and the motion was so violent that Captain Cronk decided it could be used only as a last resort. A more substantial craft was needed.

Itching for action, Lieutenant Hall offered to go as coxswain of a ten-oared Monomoy surf boat to explore ways of evacuating the plane. Hall handled the steering sweep, and he took only eight oarsmen to leave some room in case there were sick or injured passengers requiring emergency removal from the plane. He also took heaving line. The thought was that the line could be passed to the plane and attached to a person who would then be thrown into the sea and hauled aboard the boat. But just launching Hall's wooden boat without having it crush against the *Bibb*'s side was, in Captain Cronk's words, "wild work."

While Hall and his men pulled away toward the plane, the *Bibb* tried to quiet the waters by laying a surface skim of oil. This wasn't effective. It couldn't reach the *Queen*, which was blowing downwind at a rate of five knots per hour, and the *Bibb* herself was drifting through and out of the oil at three knots per hour. His inability to ameliorate sea conditions was particularly disturbing to Captain Cronk. He was acutely aware of how people were suffering aboard the pitching plane. While talking with the *Queen* on the radio, he could hear Captain Martin vomiting between sentences. Although the pilot didn't complain for himself, he did emphasize that his passengers were in similar, or worse, distress, and he didn't know how long they could take it. Under these circumstances, it was something of a blessing for Cronk that it became necessary to limit radio contact with the *Queen* to save the plane's batteries; except in emergency, communication would be conducted by bullhorn from the *Bibb* and responding light flashes from *Queen*.

Hall and his crew were finding that riding the seas in the Monomoy was a little like riding a bucking horse. Unless they got with the rhythm, they could be parted from the thwart with each downward rush and painfully slammed down again on the next rise. It took constant pulling to outpace and circle the fast-drifting plane while Hall studied it as if he had never seen one before. The *Bermuda Sky Queen* was, in fact, of a class of airplanes familiar to nearly every American. A Boeing NC 1861, she came out of the factory in Seattle in early 1941, the last of the fleet of flying boats that enabled Pan American Airways to establish the first reliable overseas commercial service. Christened *Cape Town Clipper,* NC 18612 opened the route between New York and Léopoldville, Belgian Congo, the day before Pearl Harbor. Then she vanished into secret Navy service for the duration. The rapid wartime development of aviation had demonstrated that land planes were aerodynamically more efficient and could cross the oceans as safely as the flying boats, which were sold off by the War Assets Administration at a bargain. The *Bermuda Sky Queen* was one of five picked up by American International Airways for its charter business. To get that business off the water, the company, headquartered in New York, had landed the *Queen* on the Hudson River at seventy-ninth Street, twelve days before its unanticipated rendezvous with the *Bibb.* If the idea was to attract attention, it had worked. So loud was the roar of the *Queen*'s Wright Cyclone engines on takeoff that the city's Parks Department requested that she never land on the river again.

Lieutenant Hall couldn't have cared less about the *Queen*'s history; his concern was with her structure and behavior. Jutting out about fifteen feet from each side of the plane's hull under the forward edge of the wings were miniwings called sponsons to keep the plane from tipping over in the water. To Hall they looked like lethal weapons. Rising six feet or more above the water with the roll and pitch of the plane, they would slap down so hard that they could crush a small boat or swamp it with spray. There was no safe way of coming alongside near the normal passengers' hatch in the plane's belly. There was a hatch up near the plane's nose, but it was some twenty feet above the surface at any time and lifting as high as forty feet when a wave shot the nose upward. A person could get hurt just jumping from there. As he studied the situation, Hall's instincts as a boat handler told him that it would be perilous to bring any manned or motored boat close enough to the plane to take people off directly. Quite apart from the thrashing sponsons, an approaching boat was threatened with being run down by the fast-drifting plane or surfing right into it as the *Queen* had done with the *Bibb*. Such a collision would be no contest; the boat would be demolished.

Hall tried to reach the *Bibb* on his hand-held radio to share his depressing conclusions with Captain Cronk, but he couldn't get through. They had been out circling the plane for nearly an hour, and the men at the oars were tiring. Hall reasoned that Martin would have signaled him in some way if he felt that an emergency evacuation was in order. Hall headed back to the *Bibb*. If launching the Monomoy had been wild, retrieving it was wilder still. It brought about the first of several differences between Hall and his captain. Fearing for their safety, Cronk ordered all of the men out of the boat before hauling it up on the davits. Hall hesitated. He was in the stern, where he had been manning the sweep, and he was attaching the self-releasing hook on the fall from one of the davits. The hooks were designed to let go automatically as soon as the boat was water-borne unless they were secured with the proper turns of line. Hall thought that somebody should be standing by both stern and bow falls, but the others obeyed orders and scrambled out up the nets. Cronk yelled down, "Get out of that boat, Mr. Hall. I'm ordering you out. . . ." Hall still balked. A knot of men at each davit was already straining against the falls, and the Monomoy was rising under him. Suddenly a wave lifted the boat and relieved the tension on the falls. The bow hook released; the boat hung precariously by the stern. Hall managed to scramble forward and rehook the other fall. He was carried to deck level aboard the boat.

Clearly insubordinate, Hall didn't know what to expect from his angry and agitated captain. Apparently quite conscious that the boat would have been lost had Hall obeyed him, Captain Cronk let the incident pass. He invited Hall to join him and the other officers on the ship for a conference on the bridge to decide how to proceed. Hall, the man of action, can remember feeling that the conference was interminable. Actually, Cronk was stalling for time. The best hope of all was a favorable change in the weather. One of Cronk's first acts had been to radio Washington for a twenty-four-hour forecast. The response called for a cold front to come from the northwest the next day, the fifteenth, with more gale force winds, but there would be a lull between gales within the next twenty-four hours. Cronk was hoping that the plane and its people could hold out until that lull. Nevertheless, the *Bibb* had to concoct some feasible rescue system in case time ran out.

There were few acceptable alternatives. Having people swim in fifty-degree water or hang onto rafts until they could be fished out guaranteed untold cases of hypothermia and some quite probable drownings or heart attacks from exertion, fear, shock. Hall's reconnaissance was persuasive as to the limited use of boats. Inevitably, discussion turned again to the large life rafts. Hall thought that they were the only way to go, and he supported his argument with an experience of less than a year before when he was serving on the cutter *Algonquin* out of Portland, Maine.

It had been a December day with conditions far more severe than those in which the *Bibb* now found herself. A northeaster with seventy-knot winds was raging, and a four-barge tow trying to exit the Massachusetts end of the Cape Cod Canal was losing ground and in danger of breaking up in the sharp, steep seas building up in the shallow water. When the *Algonquin* reached the scene, she didn't dare go alongside; she and the barges would have torn each other apart. But something had to be done quickly; the fourth barge with four men aboard was sinking. The *Algonquin*'s executive officer, Bob Wilson, came up with a solution: Get as close to the barge as possible, inflate a fifteen-person rubber raft, float it over to them on a line, pull them back when they got aboard. The raft would be flexible enough not to cause serious damage in collisions with either barge or cutter. They tried Wilson's plan, and it worked to save two lives before the barge sank. "Why wouldn't that work here?" Hall argued.

Captain Cronk remained doubtful after the way their rafts had behaved. But just about then, the time for discussion was ended. Captain Martin used precious battery juice to call the *Bibb* on the radio: "We're beginning to leak. The tail section's coming loose. The sponsons look as if they might break away. Everybody's sick as a dog. Isn't there some way you can get us off before dark, Captain?"

Cronk glanced at the chronometer. It was 1530 (3:30 P.M.); sundown was due at 1732. "I appreciate your plight, Captain," he said. "We're discussing ways and means right now. I'll get back to you in a few minutes."

Lacking any other suggestions, Cronk decided to go along with Hall and sent down orders to inflate the fifteen-person rafts on the fantail. But before risking that many lives on an untried tactic, he decided to propose an experiment to Captain Martin, and he got on the radio:

"Here's what we'd like to do, Captain. See if you have three able-bodied men aboard who would be willing to try riding one of your survival rafts. Maybe their weight would hold it down if they can get aboard quick enough. They ought to be men in physical condition to hold out in the water until we can pick them up if worse comes to worst. If you can do that, then what we'll do is circle you a couple of times at fifteen knots, spreading oil downwind of you. When we come around the second time we'll take station upwind. By then you ought to be in the middle of the oil and you can launch the raft in what ought to be slightly calmer seas. If the raft seems to be behaving well, cut it loose. We'll drift down on it and get the men off. If you understand what I'm saying and agree, don't waste power talking about it. Just come back on with a Roger when you have your volunteers. Over. . . ."

Within minutes, Martin signaled his agreement, and the *Bibb* went into action. There were mistakes on both craft on the first try. The cutter's circles were too wide, and she wound up too far to windward of the plane. The *Queen*'s captain inflated a raft with CO_2 compressed in a flask. When the raft seemed too soft, Captain Martin tried a second flask and the raft burst. While the *Bibb* went into fast circles so tight that she was rolling her rails under, Martin inflated another raft. This time the *Bibb* came close across the *Queen*'s bow and backed her engines full speed. The men on the *Bibb* watched anxiously as a raft was shoved from the plane's nose and three life-jacketed figures dropped into it. It was 1540 (3:40 P.M.) by the ship's clock. The raft floated like a whirling leaf, and Martin cut it loose. The people in the raft tried to use paddles to head toward the *Bibb*—a gallant but futile gesture. But, as planned, the cutter drifted down on them at three knots. With a bullhorn Captain Cronk told them not to

stand up or lean out until each of them had a bowline from the
ship tied around his body. At 3:57 P.M., they were brought
aboard the *Bibb* almost without getting their feet wet.

The men on the raft turned out to be three of nine merchant
seamen returning after delivering a tanker to England. All of
them had been willing volunteers, but Thomas R. Quinn, the
chief officer, selected Arthur Brown and Gerald Harmon to
accompany him because they were the heaviest. Their weight
would provide a test of what the raft could carry. Despite the
apparent success of the effort, these men were far from enthusiastic about it. "We were scared to death, I'll tell you," Quinn
confessed. "We really didn't think we would make it once we
were out there. I don't know whether those women and children could take it." Captain Martin wasn't enthusiastic, either.
Over the radio he reported that launching and loading the raft
had been a ticklish business. Then there was the discouraging
effect of simple mathematics. It had taken seventeen minutes
to transfer three people, and there were only ninety-three minutes until sunset. Twenty-three trips to transport sixty-nine people would take 391 minutes, or more than six hours, *if* everything went smoothly. Nevertheless, the merchant seamen's act
of courage wasn't a waste. It proved that a raft could be used
in some fashion, and the *Bibb*'s crew learned how to position
their ship and to lay down an oil slick so that it would become
effective when the ships drifted into it.

The next logical step was to try one of the fifteen-person rafts
now lying inflated on the *Bibb*'s fantail. Although the big raft
gave them more favorable odds, the Coast Guardsmen were
conscious that they had no time to waste, and the action aboard
the *Bibb* became, in Captain Cronk's recollection, "fast and
furious." In the course of this action, virtually all of Captain
Cronk's doubts and fears about using the rafts seemed justified.
The first raft snagged on something, sprung a leak and deflated.
The second's painter (the line from its bow) got caught in the
Bibb's starboard propeller and quickly wound itself around the
shaft. Launched with more success, the third and last raft
bobbed and scraped alongside with such force that it threatened to tear itself apart. This nearly unmanageable behavior
suggested that the original idea of towing a raft back and forth

between ship and plane as a shuttle was at the very least impractical. In a quick huddle of the officers on the bridge, it was
agreed to take the raft to the plane, where it would be held as
a loading platform, then drifted out on a line to a point where
one of the *Bibb*'s small boats could approach and take the passengers off for delivery to the ship.

Again, Lieutenant Hall volunteered to give this method a try,
using the ship's twenty-six-foot self-bailing motor surfboat. This
craft was a marvel of the sea—with respect to survival in water
the closest thing to a fish invented by man. Its cockpit and deck
were ringed by flotation tanks; its interior was honeycombed
with air cells and packed with buoyant material. It was self-
bailing, which meant that the hull was sealed off so that any
water that washed over onto the deck or into the cockpit flowed
out again through ports for that purpose. Should the boat capsize, the crew could stand on the keel, grab the righting lines,
lean back and rock it upright with their weight. Made of wood,
it weighed 5,800 pounds and couldn't be manhandled. It had to
be swung out on davits and dropped into the water, no easy feat
in view of the *Bibb*'s roll. Once again disaster threatened. The
surfboat's rudder shoe was knocked off when a roll of the ship
banged it against the cradle. It had to be fixed. Ducking and
dodging as the swinging hull took lethal swipes at their heads,
the ship's carpenters repaired the damage, conscious all the
while of a setting sun that was nearly touching the western
horizon.

When the surfboat was finally launched, Hall took the raft in
tow and headed for the plane. It was a ride to test both the
temper and skill of the small boat's crew. In wind and wave, the
light raft would surf madly along and threaten to ride right over
the surfboat and its occupants. In the next moment it would
hang back and drag with such force that the light towline would
snap. Hall would have to wheel around to catch and tether it
again. No heavier line could be used for fear of tearing the
fitting out of the raft's thin rubber walls. After a few time-
consuming chases, Hall gave up on towing and took the raft
alongside, where his four-man crew could help to hold the bucking monster. Back on the *Bibb*, a worried Captain Cronk,
watching the raft nearly get away from the surfboat, was consid-

erably relieved when his men reported to the bridge that they had freed the second raft from the grasp of the propeller shaft and brought it back aboard.

On the *Queen* hard choices had to be made in preparation for the arrival of the raft. Ordinarily, the rule of rescue at sea is women and children first. In this case, the all too evident risks and physical demands of the transfer process dictated a different procedure. As of that moment, nobody was injured or so acutely ill as to need the immediate medical attention available on the *Bibb*. Yet everybody was weakened by seasickness and everybody was understandably frightened. The only individuals aboard who were seemingly serene were the innocent and trusting infants. To be sure, the six merchant seamen who had lost the chance to be first insisted on being last to help with the others. As it turned out, their hardheaded strength would come in handy when a number of people froze in the hatchway at the prospect of the long, uncertain leap and had to be thrown out forcibly. The rule settled upon was that families would not be separated. A family of five and a man and wife were selected for the first try, a choice providing for two men in the party.

Hall came as close to the plane as he dared and had the crew pass the raft's painter across with a heaving line. The plane's crew hauled the raft in and tried to hold it under the nose hatch without letting it drift beneath the fuselage. The time had come. William Permet leapt first, landing in a heap. He was up quickly on his knees to grab the others. Next came the father of the family, William Bostwick, with his eighteen-month-old daughter, Sandra, in his arms. Josephine Bostwick followed, holding five-year-old Kenneth. Stewart, aged nine, was considered old enough to make the jump himself with a little coaching. When a wave lifted the raft to within a few feet of the hatch, he was told to go, but he balked. Then as it fell away he suddenly jumped and missed. The men on the raft grabbed him and pulled him aboard. A spluttering Stewart said indignantly, "I'm ruining my good suit." Catherine Permet was the last to jump for that first load. The plane's crew paid out the raft's painter and Hall maneuvered his surfboat alongside, where his crew hoisted the passengers aboard. It was 1730, two minutes before sunset.

When Hall reached the *Bibb,* he came in on the lee side and parallel to the cutter and tried to hold steady while it drifted down on him. As the boats converged, crewmen threw bowlines from *Bibb*'s deck to put around the passengers; other crewmen, soaked in cold spray, hung from the scramble nets, reaching out to grab people with their own hands. The scene so etched itself in the mind of Captain Cronk, looking down on it from the bridge wing, that he could reconstruct it in detail years later for *The Atlantic Monthly:*

"There was the boat crashing against the side as the wind pressed the ship down upon it, tossing wildly up to the rail . . . and down out of sight—and in the midst of it all a baby held aloft. Eager hands reached out for it. A woman in the boat, hysterically resisting attempts to place a line about her, screamed, 'Save my baby! Save my baby!' Then, as the baby was snatched up by those on the nets and passed on board, 'Thank God, my baby is saved!' over and over.

"So anxious was everyone to get the baby quickly on board that men got in each other's way. A burly man with a hoarse voice shouted, 'Let go, you stupid bastard! Are you trying to drown that baby?' What was funny was that he was sobbing.

"Now the women were calm and hauled on board, weak, limp, almost a dead weight, and as they were placed on their feet and felt the deck, sensed their safety, they collapsed and were carried to sick bay. A pair of bearers picked up one of the women and attempted to carry her aft, only to fetch up short on the line still fastened to her.

"The boat, the nets, the deck, had been a nightmare of shouting, tussling, weeping and cursing crewmen. Curses of excitement on their lips, but prayers in their hearts."

Including the three merchantmen, there were now ten of sixty-nine plane occupants safely aboard the *Bibb.* Cronk radioed this good news to Boston for rebroadcast since the fate of the *Queen* had already become an international concern. As darkness fell, the wind picked up, registering forty-five knots on *Bibb*'s guage. In one sense, increased wind velocity was a help. There was no time now for the *Bibb* to circle and spread oil downwind between rescue attempts, but it was discovered that the wind would carry the diesel oil down to the plane if the pump was speeded up, which spouted it into the air. Even so, waves broke through the slick and foamed into whitecaps, and Hall's next two trips, on which he ferried ten and then a dozen people, were as rough as the first. There were bruises as people jumped or were pushed from the plane, and one man cut his head. But miraculously nobody was seriously hurt and nobody was swept overboard as the operation went forward in pitch dark, relieved only by the ship's searchlight.

Although Hall's seamanship was flawless, there was no way of taking the surfboat close enough to the *Bibb* to pass people safely to the rescue crews manning the nets without having it bump and bash against the ship's steel sides. Fenders that are normally used to keep ships from being damaged by grinding against other vessels or piers were totally useless that night because of the wide and different arcs through which the two boats rolled. Wood is no match for steel in collision, and how long the surfboat could take the punishment was anybody's guess. The deck and cockpit of the boat were so constantly awash with boarding seas that it was hard to tell whether she was floating or not. Hall had to judge by feel, and by the third trip he was worried: She felt limp. Obviously losing buoyancy, she was also running low on fuel. Hall had to risk more damage by tying up alongside the *Bibb* to refuel. It was torture for men and boat. While some of the crew tried to hold the boat off from smashing the *Bibb* with main force, the others went through the dizzy dance of pouring fuel into the tanks. With almost every wave crest, the boat was thrown against her restraining line at the bow with such a jolt that the crew went sprawling into the bilge. Once he had enough fuel, Hall headed into the night to pick up the raft once more.

Quite apart from increasing concern about the condition of his boat, Hall was finding each of these trips more worrisome. The plane's faster drift rate was gradually widening the distance from the *Bibb*. The plane did not dare to drain the batteries by using lights, and she was only a faint gray ghost, appearing and disappearing as she rode the crest of waves into the far edge of the *Bibb*'s searchlight beam. The distance would put Hall out of communication with the *Bibb* except by code flashed from a signal light he kept close at his feet on the cockpit floor since his hand radio had been soaked out of commission. As he drew near enough to see the plane in detail on the fourth trip, Hall had a severe shock. There was nothing that looked like a raft bobbing near her nose. It must have broken its tether to the plane, and it would probably be loaded with people anticipating his return. Seeing a black rubber raft playing hide and seek in the waves of a sea slicked over with black oil could be impossible. But Hall cruised slowly on in the probable direction of a raft's drift and was soon able to home in on cries for help.

Reaching the raft, Hall got a second shock. It had evidently fared worse in collisions with the plane than his own boat had with the ship. Several of the flotation compartments were now flat and airless. With 16 people—one more than its capacity under ideal conditions—aboard, the raft was swamped and slowly sinking. As fast as they could be hauled or pushed, the terrified people on the raft were tumbled aboard the already foundering surfboat. Hall could sense his boat sinking, and he shouted over the confusion and panic, "Now hear me! Somebody's got to get back in that raft or we'll all sink. It'll only take a few of you and we'll keep you right alongside."

Three men volunteered, and Hall sent three of his own crew over to the raft. It was enough shift of weight that Hall thought they could make it. In the mess of humanity crowded into the surfboat, no line could be found to secure the raft, but men held it alongside by the grab lines. Hall opened the throttle to start moving upwind. There was a sickening grinding noise. Hall knew at once that a stray line from the raft was winding up in the propeller. He threw the engine into reverse. Too late. There was a clunk and clatter as the gear box came apart under the strain of the fouled line. The propeller shaft dropped away. Powerless, the boat broached. Waves poured over the side. Women screamed, and people started instinctively moving away from the flooding water. Hall thought that his boat would capsize, and he yelled, "Stop! Stay still! Keep calm!" The only hope for any of them was to maintain the balance of both boat and raft by balancing the weight of the people, and somehow he managed to get that message across even though a number of women had reached the end of their control and now gave in to hysterical weeping.

Hall couldn't blame them. They were in real peril. The *Bibb* lay inert a mile upwind, winking and blinking tauntingly as she rolled. There was no way the men on its bridge could know Hall's plight. He fumbled frantically for the signal light and asked people around him to search. But it couldn't be found in the tangle of bodies and wash of water. Being the kind of man who had to do *something* in any situation, Hall made a megaphone of his hands and bellowed, "Help! Help! Help!" into a wind that would tear the sound away almost as soon as it left his lips. Futile as his gesture might be, he thought that it would give the panicking passengers some sense of hope. In between shouts, he kept reassuring them that sooner or later the ship would come down and find them if only they would keep calm and maintain balance.

From the wing of the *Bibb*'s bridge, Captain Cronk and his engineering officer followed Hall's operation as well as they could. Through binoculars that kept misting up, they were watching a faint shadow play. About all they could be sure of was that people seemed to be moving between the boat and raft. But the engineer didn't like the looks of things. "Neither of them seem to have much freeboard, Captain," he said.

"He's got a light. If he's in trouble, wouldn't he signal?" said Cronk. Since the *Bibb* was awkward to manage with her size and windage, Cronk wasn't anxious to close in on the small boats unless it became absolutely necessary. He asked several more officers to have a look. The consensus was that, signal or no signal, Hall was in trouble. Cronk had the ship eased close enough to be heard through the bullhorn and called: "Are you all right? Acknowledge with your light."

When he heard that, Hall tried to yell back, but his answer went blowing in the wind. It didn't matter. He and everybody with him knew that at least they were not lost. Hall hoped that only he knew that retrieving them before their boats sank under them would require superb seamanship—and a lot of luck—on the part of his shipmates on the *Bibb*. Knowing the way things are likely to go during complicated rescues under adverse conditions, Hall had been resigned from the first to the probability that some lives would be lost. If his turned out to be one of them, he had already seen enough people safely across to make the sacrifice worthwhile. He didn't share these thoughts. "Hear that," he said. "They'll fish us out before you know it. Just keep calm. Don't rock the boat. You up there in the bow on the starboard side—to the right—move in a little. Try to get a feel for the balance. . . ."

By this time Hall didn't have to spell out his predicament to the watchers on the *Bibb.* If he had power, no seaman of Hall's stripe would lie crosswind in these seas. If he had light, he would signal. Cronk carefully conned the *Bibb* into a position upwind of the small boats from which he calculated that she could drift down and bring them alongside at the scramble nets just aft of the bridge. The men at the rescue nets meanwhile climbed down the nets with lines around themselves so that they could go into the water if necessary with extra lines in hand to pass around the people they would be dealing with. Everyone understood that they might have only one quick chance to pull a person aboard before *Bibb* drifted over or past the helpless, sinking craft in which they huddled. Fortunately, Cronk landed the *Bibb* right on the mark, but there was nothing more he could do as the boat and raft banged against the ship, tumbling over and around each other and spilling shrieking people into the water.

Working feverishly, the men on the nets would hang one half-limp body on a line to be hauled aboard by men above them and go after another. Before a line could be put around her, an elderly woman fell between the surfboat and the ship. Boatswains Mate Ralph Keller went in after her, injuring himself as he took the brunt of the clashing hulls. The woman was saved without harm other than trauma. Incredibly, once again nobody was lost or badly hurt. The last person to stagger aboard the *Bibb* was Lieutenant Hall, who went up to the bridge wing, saluted Captain Cronk and said, "Sir, may I have permission to take another boat and get the rest?"

Hall, who had gone into the water himself, was streaming wet. But like the men on the nets he had been too active and agitated to feel the cold. Not counting an earlier sortie in the pulling boat, Hall had been out on the water for more than two hours. But with his adrenaline up, his muscular body wasn't tired. He was resentful when Captain Cronk said, "You've had enough for a while, Mr. Hall. Go below and get into dry clothes—and stop by the sick bay for a snort to warm you up." When Hall hesitated, as he had in the boat, Cronk said, "It's an order, Mr. Hall. Get going." Hall couldn't chance disobeying twice in one day.

The surfboat and raft were in such bad shape that Cronk ordered them cut adrift to make room for other efforts. Then he called Ensign James Macdonald, who had shown some skill at handling the steering oar of a Monomoy during drills and asked him if he would be willing to recruit volunteer oarsmen and try to get the last remaining raft to the plane. Not only did Macdonald agree but his call for volunteers over the loudspeaker system started a thudding drum of running feet as men hurried to the bridge. Macdonald had to resort to a first-come, first-picked basis of choice, weeding out those who had already had a turn in the boats. Hearing the call down below, where he was drying out, Hall could only shake his head and say to himself, "Poor bastards, poor bastards . . ."

More than anyone else aboard, Hall knew the dangerous odds they were facing. He'd had the devil's own time dragging a raft down to the plane with the surfboat's motor going full blast. How could Macdonald do it with only six oars of a ten-oared boat being manned? Of course, room had to be left in the Monomoy to pick up people from the plane. Hall went back on deck to see if he could offer Macdonald any helpful advice and discovered that the others had been thinking along the same lines. The plan was to take the *Bibb* a safe half mile or so downwind of the *Queen* and launch the raft and pulling boat, spreading oil all the while. Macdonald and his rowers would simply try to hold the raft in position while the plane blew down on them. The trick would be to stay out of its way close enough to send the raft's painter to the plane with a shoulder gun. Hall still didn't like the odds. He could remember the chilling sight of those thrashing sponsons. One slip of judgment in the dark and the Monomoy would be smashed to smithereens. Still, he gave Macdonald and his crew high marks for guts, and he knew he would try it too, given the chance. It was what they were hired to do.

Launched at 2339, Macdonald's little flotilla vanished into the night more completely than Hall's had. The black raft was all but invisible, and the thin white hull of the pulling boat that flashed in the light beam only on crests was often indistinguishable from the whitecaps rolling along in the same rhythm. The plane's radio had gone dead, but Macdonald's voice would occasionally squawk out of the darkness on the hand radio: "Passing *Queen* . . . Landed painter with third shot . . . Raft secured to plane . . . Awaiting passengers . . ." There followed a long silence, then: "No sign of action on plane . . ." More silence, then: "Still no action . . . No lights . . . Nothing." Hearing this, Cronk and his officers were puzzled. The only conclusion they could reach in the absence of any contact with Martin or his men was that the twenty-two people still aboard the plane were too exhausted from fourteen hours of plunging up and down and vomiting and worrying to make the effort the transfer required. At 0045 (12:45 A.M., October 15) Captain Cronk ordered Macdonald to return to the *Bibb,* a fairly easy row downwind with no raft to tow or passengers aboard.

However logical their deduction, Captain Cronk felt obliged to make sure that there was no unimaginable problem on the *Queen.* Once Macdonald and his boat were safely aboard, Cronk took the *Bibb* in close to the plane at fifteen knots to maintain control and hailed Martin through the bullhorn. "How do you feel about spending the night on the plane?" he asked. The plane's landing lights responded with a dot-dash—"Affirmative." At another conference on the *Bibb*'s bridge, it was agreed that Martin had made a wise decision. Even if the plane sank, they had the raft, which was capable of supporting twenty-five people, fifteen aboard and ten hanging on the grab lines. The *Bibb* could drift down and pick them up in minutes. Captain Cronk sent half of his crew to their bunks and kept the other half on deck and at ready stations for instant action.

Despite only two hours' sleep the night before, there was no sleep this night for the captain. He paced the bridge, praying for dawn before disaster. His prayers were answered, and with the light at 0645 came a rise in the barometer and a drop in the wind. Large swells were still running, but conditions were much calmer than the night before. The captain's motorized gig with Lieutenant Hall in charge was launched at 0707 to transfer the remaining passengers from the plane. Hall was back at 0730 to discharge eight survivors without incident. Captain Cronk's hope that they could save everyone rose like the barometer. But the tension on his nerves increased. He was, as he acknowledged later, "taut as an E string, fearing some last-minute mishap."

That E string nearly snapped when Cronk saw Hall's gig behaving strangely, drifting away from the raft loaded with people at the plane's nose. Over the hand radio, Hall reported engine trouble and Cronk ordered Macdonald into the water in the Monomoy with only four oarsmen to leave room for passengers. The six men Macdonald picked up helped to row themselves back. Now there were fourteen safe aboard the *Bibb*, only eight more to go. While Macdonald's crew was rowing back to the plane, Cronk saw the gig, its motor running once more, headed for the raft. In his nervous state, Cronk was superstitious and feared that Hall or his boat might be jinxed. Through the bullhorn, he barked, "Keep clear there in the gig! Keep clear, Mr. Hall, and let the Monomoy in!"

When Macdonald's boat pulled alongside at 0833 and discharged six passengers, Cronk did a little jig of relief and triumph. It was all over! But he still felt testy enough to be irritated when the contentious Mr. Hall, approaching in the gig, ordered Macdonald out of the way and came alongside. Cronk had lost count. Out of the gig popped two more survivors, men who had managed to hop aboard the gig before its engine failed. Rather fittingly, the man who had brought the first load from the *Queen* to safety had also brought the last.

But Lieutenant Hall's work wasn't finished. With Captain Martin concurring, Captain Cronk decided that the *Queen* was beyond salvage. As gunnery officer, Lieutenant Hall was ordered to fire upon and sink her. All hands, including most of the passengers, watched as the big bird went up in flames and fell apart. There were lumps in many throats. The *Queen* had held together long enough to protect the lives in her keeping.

The *Queen*'s demise had turned into a national drama. Cronk's radioed reports of developments had been broadcast live across the country. The imaginative Captain Cronk knew how to keep a drama going, and his reports didn't stop as the *Bibb* steamed for Boston with its cargo of survivors. At one point, Cronk told his large audience: "We have a diaper short-age out here. We weren't able to get off the luggage. We have two babies aboard and several small children." A Coast Guard plane out of Salem, Massachusetts, responded with a drop of four dozen diapers. *Bibb* ran headfirst into the new gale that had been predicted for the night of the fifteenth and, in the midst of it, received a new distress call. A seaman aboard the Coast Guard cutter *Duane,* on her way to replace the *Bibb* at Station Charlie, was stricken with acute appendicitis. Because the *Bibb* had a surgeon aboard, the *Duane* proposed transfer-ring the seaman. Having had a belly full of heavy-weather res-cue work, Captain Cronk suggested that the cutters stay close to each other until dawn in the hope of better conditions. But if anything, they were worse. The transfer was made at first light in seas so mountainous—despite oil slicks laid down by both ships—that the *Duane* could not get her small boat back aboard. As the *Bibb* plowed onward with a recovering appendicitis victim in its sick bay, Cronk kept interest alive by radioing details of Keller's heroism in plucking a woman from between two clashing hulls and recommended a citation. By the nine-teenth, when the *Bibb*—a broom at her masthead to signify a clean sweep in rescuing everybody—arrived at Boston, interest was so intense that she was escorted into the harbor by a flotilla of boats and a flight of planes and met at the pier by a crowd headed by Acting Mayor John B. Hynes, who presented Captain Cronk with a plaque.

There were later awards, including a Legion of Merit and Gold Lifesaving Medal for Lieutenant Mike Hall. Hall never did get enough of the sea. He retired from the Coast Guard as a commander in 1964, was recalled in 1966 and retired again as a captain in 1968. Possessed of an unlimited master mariner's license, Hall then began a new career in commercial shipping, mostly on tankers, from which he retired for a third time in 1983. Despite all that came before and after, the *Queen* rescue remained a high point of Hall's long career—not because of the intensity of action, nor because of the public awards, but be-cause of what the Coast Guard officer who debriefed the *Bibb*'s crew told him privately: "Every enlisted person on the ship who was directly involved in the operation said that if it hadn't been for you, it wouldn't have succeeded." Being that instrumental in saving sixty-nine lives is a nice thing to live with for a man who had pitted himself against the sea.

Chapter 12

The Terror in Paradise

THE license plates on the automobiles in the three U.S. Virgin Islands proclaim the territory to be "American Paradise." Few of the countless millions of tourists who have visited these small islands in the Caribbean Sea east of Puerto Rico in the years since the jet plane made them easily accessible would consider this phrase promotional hyperbole. With year-round temperatures in the eighties, warm sunshine at least part of virtually every day, cooling trade winds, white beaches and mountainous hills furred with tropical growth, gin-clear waters sprouting colorful coral gardens, centuries-old buildings and ruins of Danish design, they present themselves as Edens without serpents. This last perfect touch to paradise is literally true because the mongoose, imported from India by sugar plantation owners to protect the lives of their valuable black slaves, devoured the snake. As of the fall of 1989, the only dark shadow to cross the sunny isles since the slaves revolted was a multiple murder with ugly racial overtones on the Fountain Valley golf course in St. Croix in 1972.

Largest in land mass and gentlest in contour, St. Croix is odd island out in the trio. St. Thomas, where the territory's capital, Charlotte Amalie, is situated, and St. John, site of the twenty-ninth U.S. national park, are only three miles apart across Pillsbury Sound. St. Croix lies alone in the ocean forty miles to the south. Because of a terrain more adapted to agricultural and industrial ventures and because of its relative isolation, St. Croix has had a different social and economic development than the

189

other two. For instance, the island's reasonably large enter-
prises, such as the Hess Oil refinery, have found it necessary to
import workers from Puerto Rico and other off-island places
with a predictable dilution of the native Cruzan population.
And among other distinguishing features, the very existence of
that golf course where seven whites and one black were gunned
down—the only golf course in the Virgin Islands until the early
eighties—made St. Croix an ideal place for wealthy whites from
the "continent," as the United States is called, to establish retirement or vacation homes.

One factor that makes all of the islands a paradise for tourists
is the territory's designation as a free port. In an attempt to
make viable an economy heavily dependent on tourism, the
U.S. government grants returning travelers a liberal duty-free
allowance on foreign goods. The savings are most significant on
luxury items—jewelry, cameras, electronic equipment, silver,
china, liquor and the like—and the many shops and boutiques
lining the narrow streets of Charlotte Amalie on St. Thomas and
St. Croix's Christiansted and Frederiksted glitter with delights
only wealth can command. Sleek cruise ships make weekly
rounds of the islands, disgorging swarms of shoppers. Most of
these shops as well as most of the hotels, guest houses, marinas,
charter boats, airlines and other tourist facilities are owned by
whites or Orientals who came with the capital to make the most
of paradise. Thus, even paradise is peopled with "haves" and
"have-nots" like most of the world. But the enforced intimacy
of island living makes the difference more galling to those at the
foot of the table, especially in St. Croix. As the main port with
government offices, the College of the Virgin Islands and other
territory-wide institutions, St. Thomas provides sustenance for
a substantial black middle-class community. Development on
twenty-one-mile-square St. John, where two thirds of the land
was turned into a national park with the assistance of the Rock-
efellers, has left native St. Johnians reasonably enriched by land
sales and in control of a significant portion of tourist services.
But the have/have-not line in St. Croix is a pronounced color
line.

Brief and oversimplified as it is, this description of America's
paradise is offered to establish a sense of the islands, which is

necessary to understand events that began to unfold on September 16, 1989. (I feel qualified to offer this impression by reason of many visits to all of the islands and extended stays on St. John over a period of more than thirty years. I have also made a considerable study of the region's history and sociology. Sadly, the harrowing drama in which the U.S. Coast Guard played a leading role did not shock me, as it apparently did its leading actors. It was inevitable, according to the script of history.)

The story begins fittingly with a weather report. The usual state of the weather in the islands can be judged by a ritual regularly observed by one local charter yacht's captain. Whether to startle or amuse his paying guests, he comes on deck every morning, gazes knowingly around at the bright sea and sky, claps his hands together and says, "Another shitty day in paradise!" But, as if to compensate for its serpentless condition, this Eden is periodically invaded by another dangerous physical menace—the hurricane. The meteorologist's report coming into the U.S. Coast Guard's Patrol Boat Squadron Two at the Roosevelt Roads naval base in Puerto Rico on that September Saturday warned that a hurricane named Hugo was battering the leeward islands and moving up the chain toward Puerto Rico and the continent beyond. For Lieutenant Commander Douglas B. Perkins, the squadron commander, the news had a boy-who-cried-wolf aspect. Told earlier in the season that a hurricane was headed toward his base, Commander Perkins had instituted evacuation procedures only to have the storm turn north and strike Bermuda instead. But it was not worth running even the slightest risk of exposing his boats and land facilities to a hurricane's power. The specific mission of the Coast Guard is to survive devastating weather conditions in order to help those who can't or won't.

Hunkering down to ride out the storm is not an option. Every sailor knows that the safest place in a hurricane for a seaworthy vessel is as far from land as possible, and with a lot of sea room, the Coast Guard's fast cutters could outrun the storm. There are five 110-foot cutters in the squadron—*Vashon, Monhegan, Nantucket, Nunivak* and *Ocracoke*—all named for islands. Their crews were ordered to top their tanks, say goodbye to their families and put to sea for "hurricane evasion." For the duration of that duty, they would be chopped—the Coast Guard word for transferred—to the command of either the 270-foot *Bear* or 210-foot *Dauntless,* which were both already patroling open waters in the Caribbean. Except for the fact that seas would be rough and shake them up like dice in a cup, storm evasion would be little more than a safe, sunny cruise for the men on the 110s. Their worries as they cast off lines were for the people they left behind.

The naval base at Roosevelt Roads is a sprawling installation of buildings, airfields and port facilities on the eastern end of Puerto Rico near the small town of Fajardo. Most of the structures on the base, including those for dependent housing, are built to withstand an atomic blast, not to mention the force of hurricane. Knowing this, the departing Coast Guardsmen were fairly sure that their families, installed in naval housing, would escape physical harm if they had the good sense to stick close to home. But nothing is certain in the face of nature's fury, and reports rated Hugo as a ferocious storm, picking up more force by the hour as it swept north. Even if buildings stood, the infrastructure that supported life within them—water, electricity, food distribution—would be imperiled. In addition, Patrol Boat Squadron Two's headquarters, where its communications, records, spare parts, equipment and the like were housed, was *in,* but not *of,* Roosevelt Roads. When I visited the men of the squadron, I found it symbolic that I was instructed to turn off the smooth pavement of one of the Navy's arteries onto a dirt road—the only dirt road I saw in an exploration of the whole base—to get down to the water and the squadron's ramshackle collection of temporary buildings. It was a sharp reminder that the Coast Guard, under the small umbrella of the Department of Transportation instead of the broad roof of the Department of Defense, is the chronically underfunded fifth armed service. Yet Squadron Two is stationed at Roosevelt Roads to facilitate its immediate incorporation into the Navy in case of war; the rest of the Coast Guard on the island—the Greater Antilles Section Command and the Air Station—are at San Juan and Borinquen.

Once the cutters deployed, Commander Perkins and his headquarters staff pitched in to move everything portable to higher ground and sturdier structures. It was dull, here-we-go-again duty, and they envied their seagoing comrades.

Aboard the *Vashon,* speeding around the storm and south to a rendezvous with the *Bear,* Lieutenant Junior Grade Mark Ogle, the executive officer, had one concern not shared by the rest of the crew. Young and unmarried, he and an officer from another cutter had elected to rent an apartment in Fajardo instead of staying in one of the concrete bastions provided for bachelor officers at Roosevelt Roads. Their digs were on the twenty-first floor of one of three modern high-rise buildings that soar incongruously above the rest of the low-lying old town and would be open to the wind's full blast. Neither of the roommates would be on hand to institute any damage control. As if helplessly watching a movie or TV show, Ogle could see Hugo advancing inexorably toward his home on the *Vashon*'s weather fax machine. Although they ride like bucking broncos, the 110s have all been built since 1984 and are computerized, electronic wonders. Their communications and navigation systems include Satellite Navigation, Loran C and surface radar with collision avoidance capabilities so that except in close quarters nobody even needs to mind the helm. With a little imagination, Ogle could be as aware and apprehensive of the oncoming storm as he might have been watching it from his window above Fajardo.

Through Sunday and into early morning on Monday, the eighteenth, the now considerable Coast Guard fleet—ten of the smaller cutters with those normally stationed at San Juan and St. Thomas or patroling in the area added to Squadron Two—lingered south of the storm and monitored Hugo with electronic eyes. They watched it cross over St. Croix and Puerto Rico, but they could learn nothing of the devastation it might have wrought. As if blowing out a candle, the winds created an immediate communications blackout. No electronic communication of any kind came out of the islands. But certain that their services would be in great demand, the *Bear* started leading its 110s northward at 4 A.M. on Monday. The *Dauntless* was sent to the aid of Montserrat, where 128 American medical students were in need of evacuation.

Refuelling had to be the first order of business for the 110s if they were to be capable of any extended work. Chances of obtaining fuel at St. Croix or St. Thomas, which was also brushed by Hugo, were nil, but there were good indications that parts of Puerto Rico might have been spared. Ponce, a town on the southern cost with docking and gas facilities, was a good bet, and several cutters set course for that port. But more pressing than the need for fuel for the men from Squadron Two was the need for news about their families at Roosevelt Roads. Lieutenant G. W. Dupree, skipper of the *Nantucket,* got permission from the *Bear* to reconnoiter Roosey, as the base is nicknamed. Arriving near the mouth of the harbor at 2100 hours (9 P.M.), the *Nantucket* found herself in a strange, unrecognizable place. "There were no lights at all—pitch black," Dupree recalls. "Aids to navigation had gone adrift. The water was fouled with debris. The wind was up to forty-five knots and when wind like that starts kicking up the water, the radar becomes cluttered with sea return. You can normally navigate easily with radar—see a picture of the harbor by taking occasional radar fixes. Not that night." Prudently, Dupree ordered a course change to Ponce. He had, however, come in close enough to get Roosey's port control on short range VHF radio and could pass the good news to the fleet that, although all utilities and many support structures were destroyed, the houses had stood fast. None of the loved ones were physically hurt.

Ponce was in better condition than the naval base, but the fuel trucks ordered by the cutters failed to arrive as expected during the morning of Tuesday, the nineteenth. They had to contend with nonfunctioning electric pumps and roads blocked by fallen trees. Listening to Dupree's account, the captains of the three cutters tied up there decided they could make it back to the squadron base with the help of daylight. They got under way about noon. The weather was sunny and calm, as it often is after a hurricane and just as it is always supposed to be in paradise. The beauty at sea highlighted by contrast the ugliness on shore. Roosey was even more unrecognizable by day than by night. Lieutenant Mark D. Rutherford, skipper of the *Vashon,* recalls it vividly: "There were stranded sailboats all along the shoreline. There was no movement at all because security wasn't letting people move around. It was deathly quiet. All the trees were bare of leaves. We could see the white faces of houses and buildings we hadn't known existed. It looked as though there had been a nuclear bomb that just wiped out all vegetation." Lieutenant Gary Alexander, commanding the *Ocracoke*, remembers the sickening smell—"a putrid combination of overflowing sewers and overturned mangoes."

Commander Perkins' precautions had been warranted; squadron headquarters was a sodden shambles. Getting fuel there was no easier. Although storage tanks were full, they had to be tapped by gravity—a slow process at best. The delay gave the cutters' crews a chance to check up on their families. They found them in good physical shape but having difficulties coping without light, refrigeration and water. Fortunately, the Red Cross had set up a food-dispensing station at Roosevelt Roads, and most of the families had heeded storm warnings to the extent of storing water in bathtubs and other containers, and stocking up on candles and oil lamps. Nevertheless, wives with young children like Lieutenant Rutherford's would have welcomed a husband's helping hand. It was not to be. The *Bear*, which had taken up station off St. Croix, was learning with every passing minute of that Tuesday, the nineteenth, that the largest island in paradise was turning into a kind of hell. The *Bear* radioed for the cutters of Patrol Boat Squadron Two to join her as soon as humanly possible.

Drawn to St. Croix by reports of a fire at the Hess Oil refinery, the *Bear* arrived there in early afternoon. She was still accompanied by the *Attu*, one of the 110s that had been with her during storm evacuation, normally stationed in San Juan. The fire turned out to be a false alarm, but the general devastation that the Coast Guardsmen could see through their glasses was awesome—95 percent of all the structures destroyed or badly damaged, all vegetation shredded or uprooted, power lines and antennas severed or flattened, virtually all boats of any size sunk or flung up on the beaches like shells. The first word to reach them was from a ham radio operator who reported total civil disorder—rioting, looting, shooting—in which local police and National Guard units were participating. Commander Ken Venuto, skipper of the *Bear*, sent the *Attu* with its draft of a little over seven feet, half of *Bear*'s, close to shore to pick up

what information it could. At the two major settlements, Frederiksted on the island's west end and Christiansted on the north
shore, *Attu* was able to talk to residents on the piers who confirmed the ham operator's report. In addition, oil spills were in
progress at the Hess installation near Lime Tree Bay and the
Virgin Island Water and Power Authority in Christiansted.

Commander Venuto realized as he listened to the *Attu*'s excited reports that he had run into a challenge almost unparal-
leled in the history of the service or, for that matter, of the
United States itself. It was a coincidence but nevertheless a
source of strength for Commander Venuto to recall that the
only similar situation had involved the first *Bear,* the most famous cutter in the Coast Guard's long annals. Beginning in the
mid-1880s, the *Bear* patrolled another U.S. territory—Alaska.
She recorded some forty-two voyages, averaging 16,000 miles
each, and she was often the only U.S. government presence. As
such, the job of restoring order in mining revolts and other
disorders had fallen to the vessel. It appeared to be happening
again to this newest *Bear.* There was a difference, however, in
that Commander Venuto was not alone; he was a link in an
electronic chain of command running right into the White
House. In the Coast Guard hierarchy, the *Bear,* berthed in
Portsmouth, Virginia, reports to the Seventh Coast Guard District in Miami, which reports to the Atlantic Area Command in
New York, which reports to the commandant in Washington,
who is linked to the commander-in-chief through the secretary
of transportation. By reason of her location during Hugo, *Bear,*
in the person of Commander Venuto, was designated on-scene
tactical control and by reason of the crippled communications
in Puerto Rico she also assumed radio guard for the commander,
Greater Antilles Section. In fact, while she cruised around St.
Croix assessing damage, *Bear* constituted the only direct communication channel between the stricken islands and the U.S.
mainland.

Human nature being what it is, a certain amount of confusion,
lawlessness and chaos occurs whenever the normal order of
things is disrupted, whether by man or nature. Commander
Venuto could simply be dealing with that sort of anticipated
reaction to Hugo or he could have run into a far more ominous

situation. In either case, caution was indicated in order not to make matters worse. More information was essential for making the right decisions. The decision, in consultation with higher command, was to limit action to "showing the flag" in the waters around the island while trying to get more hard facts. Accordingly, the *Bear* directed the 110s steaming over from Roosey at full speed through the night of the nineteenth to patrol different sectors—*Nantucket* to Frederiksted, *Ocracoke* to Christiansted, *Vashon* and *Nunivak* off the south coast. By dawn on Wednesday, anyone on St. Croix with eyes to see would know that the Coast Guard was present in force.

But what could they—should they—do? Mixed signals were coming from the islands. Despite what the *Bear* and the *Attu* had learned, Governor Alexander Farrelly was issuing soothing statements from his office on St. Thomas to the effect that all was under control on St. Croix, that reports of lawlessness were coming from hysterical tourists, that no federal intervention was needed. Use of federal force in defiance of local authority is a very delicate matter, one to be decided at the highest levels of government. In the course of a conference call with Miami and New York in the very early hours of Wednesday, Captain Paul M. Blayney, commander of the Greater Antilles Section, was directed to fly to St. Thomas and obtain firsthand the governor's assessment of security on St. Croix—just that and nothing more. At first light, Captain Blayney took off in a Dolphin helicopter to carry out his mission.

Meanwhile, the *Nantucket* was getting a very different story. She arrived in Frederiksted harbor about midnight Tuesday. The sky was alight with a column of fire rising from the center of town. The *Nantucket*'s crew could hear sporadic gunshots and shouting. Lieutenant Dupree was under orders from *Bear* not to land but to stay on patrol off Frederiksted and try to pick up information. If possible, he was to bring Lieutenant Gina Jacobson, a marine safety officer and the only Coast Guard person permanently stationed on St. Croix, aboard the *Nantucket*. Every hour throughout the night, Dupree tried to reach Jacobsen on her radio frequency without success. At 0630 hours, he ordered his executive officer, Lieutenant Junior Grade Glen Gebele, and a complement of seamen to take the ship's RHIB—

rigid hull-inflatable boat powered by an outboard—and ride along the beach close enough to talk to anybody who appeared. Dupree conned the *Nantucket* as close to the storm-damaged pier as he dared for the same purpose.

Technically, he was obeying orders by not actually landing. Even without orders, Dupree would have hesitated to put a party ashore at that point. There were only sixteen men on the *Nantucket.* They could go armed with M-16s, shotguns and nine-millimeter barettas, but if there was true civil disorder, as the sounds and sights of the night indicated, they had too few people and too little fire power, and could create more havoc than calm. Dupree's strategy worked. People were attracted to the beach and pier. From Gebele's radioed reports of what he was learning by talking to them, Dupree was quickly concluding that his worst fears were true. There had been no law and order on the island for three days. Although there were two uniformed policemen close enough for Gebele to hail, they were doing nothing. They were two of only twenty policemen out of a force of one hundred on the island who had reported for duty, and they had no idea of any recovery plans. Set free when the hurricane threatened to bring the jail down upon them, some 200 criminals, including murderers, were roaming the island. The National Guard turnout was worse than that of the police. Just 119 members of a 900-man unit were milling about the airport miles from either town. The fire *Nantucket* saw in the night was the total devastation of a restaurant torched by looters in revenge after they had been driven away at gunpoint.

Incredibly, the official line was the same as the governor's on St. Thomas. Anthon Christian, a police commissioner, was brought aboard the *Nantucket.* "No problem," he told Lieutenant Dupree. "There was a little looting in the beginning, but it is dying down." Dupree pressed, "What about the fire last night?" The commissioner exchanged glances with an assistant he had brought along and then asked, "What fire?" Either this man was way out of touch or deliberately playing dumb, a knee-jerk reaction of Cruzans ever since the murders. "Have you been in touch with the governor or the National Guard commander?" Dupree wanted to know. "No, sir, no need," Christian said. Dupree gave up, sent his guests back to shore and got on the radio to the *Bear* to deliver a full report, which he ended by saying, "There's apparently no law and order at all. We've got to get outside force in here ASAP." The only good news he could offer was that Lt. Jacobson had spotted the cutter and turned up on the pier in uniform; she was whisked aboard the *Nantucket* over her protests that she would be deserting her duties, which had to do with the kind of oil spills in progress.

On his rounds, Captain Blayney was quickly forming the same impression Dupree had. He arrived at Governor Farrelly's mansion in Charlotte Amalie just in time to ride back to Harry Truman Airport in the governor's limousine. Farrelly was unwilling to make any decision until he personally assessed conditions on St. Croix, and he planned to fly there for that purpose. Having gained no useful knowledge to pass up the line during his ride, Captain Blayney decided to take his chopper over to St. Croix too. He dropped into a scene of bedlam. No commercial planes had been flying, and several hundred people, mostly tourists, were camped out in the waiting rooms and on the tarmac in hopes of getting off the island. They were terrified. "You didn't need any other reports of what was happening after looking into the eyes of those people," Captain Blayney said. "When you see families trembling and huddled together, you can tell that there's more than storm trauma. I had already seen storm trauma in San Juan and St. Thomas, where I sat down with stricken families in what was left of their homes. In St. Croix there was fear in their eyes—a palpable difference." The only reassuring note was that Blayney ran into an FBI agent from San Juan, also over to learn what was happening, and discovered that a small contingent of U.S. marshals had been brought to St. Croix to try to round up the criminals released from jail. The captain got back into his helicopter and whirred out to the landing pad on *Bear;* he now felt the need to get on the nearest radio and relay his personal observations to the states.

The *Vashon* reached St. Croix at dawn on Wednesday, the twentieth, and took up station, as ordered, off the southwest tip of the island. In this area a shallow shelf of reef extends some five miles out, and the *Vashon*'s skipper, Lieutenant Rutherford, felt frustrated and useless. He was too far away even to show the flag effectively. When he heard the *Nantucket* radioing the need for outside force to the *Bear,* Rutherford suggested to *Bear* that he take *Vashon* into Frederiksted to join the *Nantucket.* "They were so busy handling the entire recovery operation as on-scene tactical control that they would have gone for almost any reasonable suggestion," said Executive Officer Ogle, who was handling communications. "They just said, 'Sure, go ahead.' " Rutherford lost no time in conning the *Vashon* around the point and into Frederiksted harbor. *Nantucket* was anchored close to the pier at the north end of town, and Rutherford dropped anchor to the south of her about 700 yards offshore. From there, the *Vashon*'s crew could see looting in progress at a beachfront hotel.

Not long after the *Vashon* had her hook dug into the bottom, the bobbing heads of swimmers appeared alongside. Brought aboard, the swimmers turned out to be two young men, tourists from Washington. They were panting from the exertion of their swim and the urgency of the message they were bringing. Not only was there no law and order at all, but there were scores of people whose lives had been openly and directly threatened gathered together for mutual protection at various places in Frederiksted. Nearly everybody on the island, good or bad, was bearing some sort of weapon. Liquor stores having been widely looted, many people were also drunk. The young men told the astonished Coast Guard a tale of days and nights of sheer terror.

Peter Grant, a free-lance photographer, had gone down to St. Croix for a swimming vacation with a friend, Blair Gordon. They stayed at the King Frederick, the beach hotel near where the *Vashon* moored. Spending most of their time snorkeling and diving over reefs aswarm with multicolored tropical fish, they had what Grant called a "fantastic week." It was so like the advertised paradise that they canceled plans to stay in Puerto Rico on the weekend of the sixteenth and seventeenth to enjoy a few more days of it. They were in great physical shape; they had made new friends. The only less-than-idyllic experiences they had involved racial tension.

"There is extreme racial tension on the island, but it doesn't make the brochures," Grant said. "We were not in the upper-crust part of town. It was a real low-budget, get-away-from-the-twentieth-century vacation. So you go to the grittier grocery stores, and they would bag everybody else's groceries and not yours. You had to lock up jeeps at night or they would be stolen. Things like that. It wasn't terribly frightening, and you could deal with it—until after the storm. I can't blame the people. Land is overvalued, and the natives can't buy. People come in and take over the island and what do you expect. The impression we were given was that the storm was like the people's sign to take their island back. There was nobody to control them, and they were taking it back."

Because of danger to the hotel from rising water in the storm, Grant and Gordon were evacuated along with other guests and offered refuge in a house up the hill. When Hugo hit and the house blew apart, they went into town the next morning with a restaurant owner who had been staying with them to check on his place and distribute food before it spoiled. They had heard rumors of looting, so they went armed with machetes and sticks. Looting was, indeed, going on everywhere they looked. Apparently it had begun innocently enough with people forcing their way into boarded-up stores for essential food and supplies to repair damaged homes. But it soon turned into a criminal carnival. Windows were smashed and whole families trooped in and out of stores helping themselves; one small boy hung his belt with expensive watches like shrunken heads of the envied rich. Jeeps and trucks careened through the streets with refrigerators, TV sets, mattresses and couches taken from vandalized hotels, stores and homes. In the lots of auto rental establishments, people were stripping the cars and jeeps for parts; a shopping center looked like "the Saturday before Christmas—except that nobody was paying for anything," according to one of Grant's companions. The only uniformed men in sight were joining in the spree. The young men from Washington retreated with others from the King Frederick to a cottage colony called Sea Park a few blocks above the hotel.

There were twenty-seven people sheltering at Sea Park, and they were distributed around some five bungalows. They went out only in groups and only down to the beach to wash or in search of food. They lived on rationed food and water; Grant, for one, lost eight pounds in three days. The looting and noise grew worse, especially at night. By Tuesday night, the people at Sea Park, like the crew of *Vashon,* were hearing shots, wild shouts and drums and seeing the flames from the restaurant that had been giving them food. They were also hearing the soothing voices of radio announcers on St. Thomas saying that, although everything was destroyed on St. Croix, the islanders and tourists were working together in a heroic effort to survive. Was this the message reaching the outside authorities, the fellows out there on the Coast Guard cutters who seemed to be doing nothing? It would have been funny if it hadn't been so frightening and frustrating. A businessman coming out from town with news of an ever-worsening situation told them that he had painted "Send troops!" on the roof of his store to attract the attention of overflying aircraft, but to no avail.

When Wednesday dawned, a food party from Sea Park returned with the most frightening report of all. Terrorists had delivered a message to forty people, most of them tourists, who were holed up in a place in town called Liberty Hall, that they would be firebombed that night. With one building already destroyed by a firebomb, it couldn't be considered an idle threat. "We held a meeting at Sea Park," Grant said. "The two women who ran the place said that they didn't know whether we would survive the night. We voted as a group to stay together. Then the manager said that she had a gun with three bullets. It was about the size of a pillbox. I said 'If they are making firebombs, we have gasoline and glass bottles and can certainly make our own.' I couldn't believe I was hearing myself say this. I couldn't believe what was going on. Here we had survived a hurricane and were talking about not being able to survive the night. So Blair and I took the two women who were running things aside and said, 'We're going to try to swim out to the Coast Guard.' They said we couldn't do it because there were sharks out there and the currents were bad. We said, 'We don't have much choice. It's either fight tonight or swim out there today.' "

Finally persuaded, the women wrote down a list of names and addresses of the people in jeopardy, tucked it into a plastic capsule and hung it around Gordon's neck. If he made it to the cutter, loved ones back in the States would at least know that their relatives had survived the storm no matter what else happened. In order to avoid the mayhem and, if possible, make the swim undetected, Grant and Gordon had to enter the water where they would have a long diagonal course to the *Vashon,* the closer cutter. They wore fins to help them, but it was a scary struggle for Grant, who had injured a shoulder in the storm. In better shape, Gordon tried to buck up his friend by clowning around—pretending to dive and look for sharks, joking that it might be the Croatian Coast Guard out there. But it remained grim going for Grant, who repeated over and over to himself, "You survived all this and now you're going to drown? Just start moving. Just start swimming." Few people have been happier to land in the hands of the U.S. Coast Guard.

After a quick debriefing of the young men, Lieutenant Rutherford immediately radioed their story to the *Bear.* It came into radio central in the bowels of the *Bear* while Captain Blayney and Commander Venuto were still giving their assessments of the situation to Seventh District in Miami. Venuto had sent an armed landing party ashore in Christiansted and had been receiving hand radio reports from them that there were people requesting evacuation. But the *Vashon* weighed in with the first credible account of an actual threat to life. It was passed up the line as far as the White House chief of staff. A response was forthcoming within an hour, but it was a baffler to the Coast Guard. They were ordered to evacuate "all Americans," an impossibility since everyone on the island except for a few foreign tourists was an American citizen. But, as members of an emergency organization in which the person on the spot is often required to interpret orders loosely to act immediately and effectively, the officers on *Bear* didn't wait for an amendment to the order that eventually arrived before instructing the *Vashon* to get together with the *Nantucket* and rescue the people in Frederiksted who feared for their lives.

With respect to how to accomplish the feat, the cutter officers were on their own. Quelling civil disorder wasn't in any of the courses at the Coast Guard Academy. "They only teach general leadership," according to Lieutenant Bryon Ing, skipper of the *Nunivak.* "That's the ability to think, make a decision, act on it. Hopefully, the same thought process will work for search and rescue, disaster relief, law enforcement." Rutherford and Ogle, in radio consultation with Dupree, decided to use the RHIBs from both cutters and a squad of four men from each boat, led by the executive officers—Ogle and Gebele. They would leave two men with each boat to handle and protect it, and the officers and the other four men would form a landing party. It was a pitiful force to send into a population that was apparently up in arms, and they would have to rely more on the symbolism of their uniforms and weapons than on whatever fire power they could muster. They made sure that they would stand out. They went dressed in informal blue uniforms and Coast Guard "baseball caps"; their chests and backs were covered with bulletproof vests and reddish orange life jackets. They wore side arms and carried M-16s and shotguns. They put a vest and jacket on Peter Grant too, and took him along as a guide. The plan was to evacuate people by RHIB as quickly and with as little fuss as possible. They would try to avoid confrontation with rioters and looters and under all circumstances avoid shooting unless forced to return fire in self-protection. For any armed person with contempt for authority, the Coast Guardsmen would make marvelous targets.

The landing party's first unpleasant discovery was that there was a three-foot ground swell, and Hugo had left no sand beach on which to land. There was nothing but coral, which could shatter a propeller or tear a hole in a hull. They had to jump overboard in water up to the armpits and wade ashore, and they knew in advance that they would have a hard time getting the evacuees aboard the RHIBs. They waded ashore right at the abandoned King Frederick Hotel. Two families with trucks were busy loading them with sofas and mattresses and paid no attention to the invading guardsmen. Grant led them right past the looters and on up to Sea Park. The people gathered there were even more fearful than when Grant had left them. Theirs was the only place with a well, and they knew it was only a matter of time before they would be overrun by people wanting water. "OK," Ogle told them, "we'll take you out. But you only have five minutes to pack up. Just grab essentials—money, IDs, medicine." Nobody lingered. While two guardsmen stayed at Sea Park, another two escorted the people to the beach, where younger members of the group helped older ones wade out and scramble into the boats.

During this operation, a man approached Ogle and told him that there was a group of people nearby who also wanted to leave the island. Among them was a couple in their eighties; the husband had suffered a recent heart attack and had been badly lacerated by flying glass in the hurricane. Weighing their need against that of many more people holed up in Liberty Hall and under open threat, Ogle had to tell the man that they would come back for him and his friends if they could. A woman departing with the Sea Park group tossed the keys of several rental cars to Ogle and Gebele and said, "Take your pick. If you can use them, be my guest." It seemed an ideal way of moving inconspicuously through the unruly crowds to reach Liberty Hall, but Grant had returned to the *Vashon* with his companions and they had no idea of how to find the place, especially with roads blocked off by storm debris. An elderly couple, home owners who had no intention of abandoning all they owned, overheard them talking and offered to lead them in their own car. It turned out to be a lucky break since the trip was like threading a maze with only one possible route.

Only a few blocks from the pier, Liberty Hall had by then become a rallying point for both tourists and residents who were upset and uncertain about what to do or where to go. The nearly one hundred people gathered there greeted the arrival of the Coast Guardsmen with cheers. Even though many of them did not want to leave the island, they viewed the men in blue as the first sign in days that the island had not been completely abandoned to lawlessness. Somebody offered the use of a pickup truck to take people who wanted to be evacuated down to the pier. The lieutenants radioed their cutters to send the RHIBs over to the pier, and the guardsmen took turns escorting the truck—one walking on each side brandishing an M-16. There was palpable hostility radiating from the crowds that reluctantly gave way. There were curses and taunts—"Why you need those guns, mon? You scared?"

Poignant scenes at Liberty Hall stuck in Lieutenant Gebele's mind. Men, determined to stay and defend their property, were parting with weeping wives and children. Gebele saw one man standing off to the side next to a Chevy Blazer packed high with personal belongings on which a dog sat guardian. The man was so visibly shaken that Gebele approached him and asked, "Do you live here? Do you have any place to go?" The man waved at his vehicle, "This is all I have left, all I have left. I had a restaurant with a big food freezer and when they came looking for food my watchman exchanged fire with them. So they burned my place down last night with a Molotov cocktail. Now they hate me for not giving them food, and they'll kill me. I don't know what to do." Gebele expressed sympathy but had to say, "We can take you but not your Blazer or your dog." The man wrung his hands and said, "But it's all I have left," and then another man who knew him came up and led him away, promising a safe haven in the hills.

With forty or so people from Liberty Hall finally transferred to the pier, Lieutenants Ogle and Gebele and their enlisted men decided to go back for the old people near Sea Park. Everything seemed to be secure at the pier. Seaman Brandon Spies from the *Vashon* and Boatswains Mate Second Class David Lukasik from the *Nantucket* had been posted on the shore end of the pier to permit passage only to those people who wanted to be ferried out to the cutters. The boat handlers were having trouble enough without playing to a crowd. They were squeezing ten people a trip into the small RHIBs. With the swells threatening to throw the boats against the jagged ends of the battered pier, one seaman would try to hold the boat off while the evacuees jumped into it. Fortunately, most had fled without luggage, but Machinery Technician First Class Mark Ruble of *Vashon* was nearly crippled when an excited woman threw a hundred-pound suitcase on his back. This particular woman might be excused because she had been startled into evasive action, as was everybody else on the pier, by the loud crack of rifle shot.

For Spies and Lukasik it was a spine-tingling moment. The shot couldn't have been more than a few hundred yards away. It came from behind a building, and they could hear people yelling: "A Coast Guardsman's been shot! . . . He's dead! . . ." They had just seen Lieutenant Ogle leading the shore party off in that direction to get back to their rental cars, and they could believe that anything might happen. Almost everybody in sight had a gun in hand—some for protection, some for assault, with no way of telling the difference. There was even a fourteen-year-old boy holding a .38, and his father told Lukasik, "Look at this—my son's got a thirty-eight. Can you believe it? You tell people up in the States what's going on here." When a woman tried to bring a boy holding a toy gun out onto the pier to board one of the RHIBs, Lukasik teased the boy into giving his mother his "weapon" to hide in her purse because he was afraid that somebody would think it was real. Almost more nervous-making for Spies and Lukasik than all the guns was the impression that everybody was drunk. "You could just smell rum in the air," they said.

Spies and Lukasik ran around the corner of the building sheltering them from the shooting. A vivid scene etched itself in Lukasik's mind. A man in white shirt and gray pants holding a shotgun peered down over the balcony railing of a two-story building. A body lay in the street with about twenty people milling around it. A man ran up to Lukasik and said, "That's the store owner up there. He shot a looter. He's dying." The words were wrapped in rum, and the man was armed, as were most of the rest of the people. "You gotta do something," the man was saying. "You gotta do something." When they saw that the dying man wasn't one of theirs, the Coast Guardsmen started backing away. It seemed to infuriate the crowd. They turned ugly, cursing and calling for action. "You can't leave us now, mon," somebody called. "Sun going down, and that's when the shit hit the fan here."

But Lieutenant Dupree, in touch from the *Nantucket* by radio, ordered a quick withdrawal. They weren't possessed of enough force to become involved with looting and shooting, and the coming of sundown meant the need to complete the evacuation mission as rapidly as possible. If nothing else, the shooting helped in that regard. Once they got to the pier, many people, especially wives and children being sent away by fearful husbands, had last-minute second thoughts about leaving paradise. Mark Ruble can recall feeling angry and frustrated as a group of women stood casually chatting on the pier while he was sweating to keep his boat from dashing itself to pieces.

When he called, "Let's get in the boat, let's get in the boat," they kept saying, "Not yet, not yet," until they heard the shot. Their quick reaction almost made the pain of being hit with the suitcase worthwhile.

The original landing party, on their way down to rescue the man with the heart attack, heard the shot too. They had been told that things got rough with the coming of dark, and the shot was clear warning that they had to move fast. The people were waiting for them, bags packed, in a condominium. As at Liberty Hall, not everybody wanted to go. An elderly lady armed with a BB gun decided to stick it out. Checking another apartment, Boatswains Mate First Class Mike Hudson from the *Vashon* got his worst fright of the day. A snarling German shepherd came at him, and Hudson leveled his M-16 with intent to kill. But the owner grabbed her dog in time, and she elected to stay. Minutes later Hudson, hidden in a tree, found himself for the first time that day aiming his gun at a human being.

Because there were so many looters in town, Ogle and Gebele didn't think it would be safe to try to take the ten people who wanted to be evacuated back to the pier. And because their own landing had been so difficult and they had the old couple to consider, they looked for a better spot further south on the beach. If they could find one, they could get some help from the *Nunivak,* just anchoring south of *Vashon* and launching a RHIB. Gebele jumped into one of the rental cars, gunned it in low gear through sand, leaped out to move boulders out of the way, kept going somehow until he located a promising spot. Then he drove back for the people. Men were running down the beach from town toward them, and there was no way of guessing their intent. Hudson and a seaman from the *Nantucket* kept the runners covered while the officers piled the evacuees into two cars and drove to the place Gebele had selected. There they abandoned the cars, motors still running, and started guiding the people out to the boat from the *Nunivak.*

It was still too rough and treacherous to beach a boat, but by pulling the engine up and going overboard to hold her head to the waves the crew was able to get within fifty feet of shore. The evacuees did what they could to help. The eighty-year-old with heart trouble picked up his bags and started into the water, saying, "Do you want me to carry these?" Gebele said, "Drop them and let us get you aboard. We don't want you stressing out on us." Gebele carried the man's wife out and lifted her into the boat. "Quite a lift," he recalls, "with all that armour on. When I got her up, I went under water." But the old man didn't stress out, and Hudson and his mate were able to put up their guns when the runners veered off into the brush at the last moment. Evacuation Frederiksted had been completed before dark and without a shot fired or a person harmed by the Coast Guard rescuers.

During these same hours, the *Bear* and the *Ocracoke* had also been evacuating people from Christiansted but under less trying circumstances. Not that there was anything that could be called law and order. At one point the men of *Ocracoke* saw a running gunfight, the outcome of which they never knew. "It was Wild West," as one of them said, and those tempting shops full of jewelry and rare antiques were stripped, according to Lieutenant Alexander. Armed guards had to be furnished for the members of the Coast Guard's Atlantic Strike Team that arrived to help handle the oil spills—an operation as successful as the evacuation.

With a size and supplies more suited to caring for refugees, the *Bear* directed the cutters at Frederiksted to sail around and transfer their people—seventy-seven in all. Leaving *Nunivak* to show the flag in Frederiksted, *Nantucket* and *Vashon* complied, and by the wee hours of September 21 *Bear* was en route to St. Thomas with 139 grateful men, women and children. Many were the verbal and written expressions of thanks from these people. But a letter written by Albert Morris of Portland, Oregon, to Congressman Enrique de la Garza of Texas seems to speak for them all. Morris wrote in part:

"I was a victim of Hurricane Hugo when it struck St. Croix, Virgin Islands. While the forces of nature were severe enough, they will never have the lasting impression that the looting, setting of fires and the physical threats to life by the local natives will have for years to come. I personally was almost stabbed by a local native, who was recognized by two residents as a local drug dealer. This occurred immediately after the hurricane while I was assisting in removing computers and other office equipment from our hotel, for relocation to the Sea Park Motel, for security and to prevent complete loss. Certain members of our group were verbally abused by natives and also observed them looting stores, hotels, etc., accompanied by local policemen. The fact was, there was complete lawlessness, and life-threatening lack of security and safety. Crew members from the U.S.C.G.C. *Vashon* came up to the Sea Park Motel on the afternoon of September 20, armed with machine guns, and gave us five minutes to leave and escorted us in lifeboats out to the *Vashon*. That night we were taken to the U.S.C.G.C. *Bear*, which took us to St. Thomas. Following necessary approvals, they took us via an HC-130 C.G. cargo plane to Borinquen Airbase in Puerto Rico and then to Miami, arriving approximately 3 A.M. on Sept. twenty-second. While we had to leave most of our luggage and personal possessions, we were happy to be alive and away from St. Croix. Were it not for the Coast Guard and their assistance, there is doubt that I would be alive today."

Indeed, he and his companions might not have lasted the night at Sea Park, which was later found to have been destroyed. Throughout the night there was continued shooting and another fire in Frederiksted. It wasn't until some time during the day of September twenty-first that members of the Eighty-second Airborne Division sent down by the president began to restore law and order in that part of paradise. For the men of Patrol Boat Squadron Two, the days after the evacuation were anything but days of rest. They were, however, able to return to the kinds of missions for which they were equipped by training and experience, such as transporting patients from a powerless St. Croix hospital to St. Thomas, checking out reports of people lost at sea and searching suspicious vessels for drugs. It would be a long while before a semblance of the old order would be restored to their base at Roosey. The buildings were such a damp mess that a seaman had to be detailed to make a daily patrol to cut back the mushrooms sprouting out of the rotten wood in the flooring.

For the *Vashon*'s executive officer, Lieutenant Junior Grade Mark Ogle, there was a particularly difficult homecoming. His three-bedroom apartment in the modern Fajardo high rise had been turned into a one-bedroom apartment by the winds that knocked down the walls. He and his roommate had to lug what was left of their personal gear down twenty-one flights of stairs. But in view of what he had been through on St. Croix, it didn't seem to matter all that much. He had learned that he and the men he served with could do well what had to be done under circumstances in which an error could be literally fatal. It was a lesson worth the cost.

There are also lessons to be learned from this experience about boasting of paradise. But they are beyond the scope of a book about the Coast Guard and its missions. Nevertheless, the final words of Albert Morris's letter linger in the mind: "We frequently are informed through the media of pseudo-terrorist activities in other countries, but certainly not in America. I believe that it will be years before the trauma and impact of this unfortunate disaster are forgotten, if ever, and complete emotional and economic recovery is resumed."

Chapter 13

The First Flight Across the Atlantic

I F it took iron men to sail wooden ships, the same could be said of flying planes for the first twenty years or so after man took to the air. For very good reasons, early airplanes were called "crates" or "kites" with a kind of wry affection. They consisted of wooden frames covered with fabric. On these frail structures were mounted heavy gasoline engines of the tractor (propeller in front to exert pulling force) or pusher (propeller in rear to push) type or, in some cases, both. With no hydraulic help, rudders, elevators and ailerons were managed by the pilot's muscle power. Like seamen, fliers in open cockpits were exposed to the elements. The pilot's instrument panel was only a little more complicated than the mariner's binnacle—compass, clock, oil and water meters, altimeter, inclinometer, tachometer. More often than not, the pilot's most reliable guide to his plane's attitude and performance was his "seat-of-the-pants" feeling. Small wonder that the men who made pioneering flights were heroes in their time comparable to the astronauts of today.

One of these iron men of early flight was Elmer Fowler Stone. A short, rugged, fearless and, as it turned out, farsighted graduate of the United States Coast Guard Academy at New London, Connecticut, Stone saw the possibilities of putting the airplane to use in his salty, seagoing service as early as 1915, just twelve years after the Wright brothers' first historic flight. Then a lieu-

212

tenant, Stone and a fellow lieutenant, Norman Hall, prevailed upon their commanding officer to let them investigate the capabilities of the Curtiss F flying boat at the Curtiss Flying School in Newport News, Virginia. The promise in their report was so great that the Coast Guard assigned Stone and five other officers to learn how to fly at the Naval Aviation School at Pensacola, Florida, in April 1916, and sent Hall to a Curtiss factory to study aeronautical engineering. When World War I broke out, the Coast Guard automatically became part of the Navy, and Elmer Stone became the Navy's chief test pilot in the development of seaplanes. It was the best of training for a feat that would earn Elmer Stone a place beside—and a little ahead of—Charles Augustus Lindbergh in the pantheon of pilots.

A logical aim of the Navy's aircraft development program was to arrive at a plane that could counteract Germany's most powerful weapon—the U-boat. What was wanted was a plane with the range and cargo capacity to scout and bomb submarines, ideally a seaplane that could cross the Atlantic under its own power and do away with all the delays and difficulties of delivery. In 1911, Glenn Curtiss had made the first plane that could take off from, and land on, water, and in 1914 he produced a multiengined craft called *America* that was supposed to be capable of an Atlantic crossing. That capability was never tested because of the start of war in Europe. When America entered the war in 1917, Curtiss and Naval engineers were put together to design a large flying craft to be known as N(avy) C(urtiss). The first of these—NC-1—went into production in January 1918, at the Curtiss plant in Garden City, Long Island, and was flown successfully on October 4, 1918. She was still making test flights along the East Coast when the armistice was signed on November 11.

Although the NC-1 was no longer needed for combat, its very existence constituted a challenge. It was the most advanced and largest airplane of its day. It had a wing span of 126 feet and an overall length of seventy feet. It was a biplane with three tractor-type twelve-cylinder Liberty engines installed between the wings. The engines could develop approximately 1,200 horsepower, which was enough to lift the plane's loaded weight of 24,000 pounds off the water. The wings and tail assemblage were a filigree of fine light woods such as cedar, mahogany, spruce and ash with a skin of linen cloth; the hull section was a boat made of wooden ribs and stringers and sheathed in mahogany. Fuel was stored inside the hull, and there were three open cockpits atop the hull—one in the nose for the commander, who also acted as navigator, another just forward of the engines with dual controls for pilot and copilot and a third aft for mechanics and radioman. It was no beauty. In fact, it was so ungainly and unorthodox in the eyes of most aviation "experts" of the day that it was called the "flying wooden shoe," among other things. But it was supposed to be able to cross the Atlantic, and the Navy decided not to let peace get in the way of proving that it could.

There was a flying fever in those days. Under the demands of war, aviation had developed to the point where its potential uses for commerce and pleasure were obvious and exciting to the general public. Flying circuses, featuring converted wartime planes and pilots, became a popular form of entertainment, and prizes were posted for races and records to take the place of military incentives. One of the largest of the prizes soon after the armistice was the London *Daily Mail's* promised $50,-000 award to the first ship to cross the Atlantic by air. While civilian competitors laid plans to try for the prize as soon as weather permitted in the spring of 1919, the Navy decided to beat them all to the mark with its NC. It wouldn't be appropriate for the U.S. Navy to dignify what amounted to a sporting event by becoming an official entry, but the existence of a race was a powerful stimulus. Nor could the Navy afford to take any but the most reasonable risks since its crews would be serving under orders rather than as private adventurers. The crossing would be a full-blown Navy project. The four NCs on order from Curtiss should be completed and all used on the same flight; a fleet of destroyers would be stationed across the ocean as a navigational chain to insure safety and success. It was nevertheless a crazy gamble. Winning would bring no prize; losing would certainly bring enormous embarrassment to the Navy and, by extension, to the nation.

In those days of hands-on flying, selection of crew may have been even more vital to the pioneering mission than design and construction of the craft. Performance could depend as much on guts as skill. For instance, engine trouble could be anticipated on a flight of long duration, but it could also be repaired in the air in many instances by a mechanic who was willing to attach a safety line and walk the wings. Even though Coast Guard personnel were supposed to revert to their peacetime positions in the Treasury Department, it was inevitable that the Navy would want to "borrow" the Coast Guard's top test pilot— Elmer Stone—for the transatlantic venture. It's sure that Stone was happy to stay. Not only had war disrupted plans to start a Coast Guard flying service but at that time a return to the Treasury Department meant a reduction in pay for Coast Guardsmen.

It's an amusing reminder of the unevenness of human progress that the most modern aircraft of that time was disassembled in Garden City and moved by horse and wagon twenty-two miles to the Rockaway Naval Air Station to be reassembled and tuned up for a flight of several thousand miles across the ocean. Provided with two tractor/pusher engines in tandem between the wings outboard of the hull, a second NC, called NC-2T (for tandem), was able to lift 28,000 pounds. Since the pusher propeller was designed to function most efficiently in the slipstream of the tractor propeller, it occurred to the engineers that an unmanageable control problem would be created should one of the tractor engines fail and make it impossible for the pusher to develop full thrust. Thus, to provide an equivalent four-engine thrust, a tractor/pusher tandem was tried in the middle above the hull on NC-3 with two tractor engines in the outboard positions. With this configuration, NC-3 could take off with as much weight as NC-2T, and the same configuration was used on a converted NC-1 and a newly built NC-4. While NC-2T was in a hangar at Rockaway undergoing a similar conversion in late March 1919, NC-1 was moored out on Jamaica Bay. An unpredicted storm hit on the afternoon of March 27, causing the plane to drag her anchor and crash into a marine railway. The plane's upper and lower port wing panels were smashed. With an early May deadline for departure, NC-2T had to be eliminated from the fleet and cannibalized for parts to repair NC-1.

This episode was only the first of many difficulties, some

amounting to disasters, that befell the pioneers in their rush to prepare for the transatlantic flight. Coast Guard Lieutenant Stone, appointed first pilot of NC-4, displayed his mettle in the next. At 2 A.M. on the morning of May 4—the day appointed for takeoff—Chief Mechanics Mate Rasmus Christensen, engineer of NC-1, was fueling his plane in the hangar when the electric motor pumping fuel from the drums caught fire. Christensen yanked the hose from the plane, but some gasoline was spilled in the process. This too caught fire and set alight the starboard wing panels of NC-1 and the tail section of NC-4. Undoubtedly too charged up at the day's prospects to sleep, Stone was also in the hangar studying the plane he would fly. He grabbed a fire extinguisher and along with Christensen put out the flames. But the damage had been done. Fortunately, the wing panels and tail section of NC-2T were still intact and could be transferred to replace those on the burned ships, but it would take at least a day. Commander J. H. Towers, USN, commander of Seaplane Division I and also captain of NC-3, rescheduled takeoff for May 6.

Then came a real tragedy that demonstrated the general quality of the men of Seaplane Division I as nothing else could have done. When the engines on NC-1 were being revved up for a test, CMM Edward H. Howard, engineer of the NC-4, somehow got a hand caught in the whirring propeller. It took his hand clear off. But Howard walked himself 300 yards to the base infirmary, walked back after he had been bandaged up, found Commander Towers and said, "I'll be all right, sir. I just hope there's bad weather for a couple of weeks and I'll make the trip with you." Of course, Towers had to turn him down and replace him with CMM Eugene S. Rhoads. Still, the spirit of the injured man inspired them all.

The weather did stay bad for another couple of days. When at last the planes took off from Rockaway at 1000 hours (10 A.M.) on May 8, 1919, the crew of NC-4 in addition to Stone and Rhoads consisted of Lieutenant Commander Albert C. Read, USN, captain/navigator; Lieutenant Junior Grade Walter Hinton, USN, copilot; Ensign Herbert C. Rodd, USN, radio officer; and Lieutenant James L. Breese, USN, engineer. The first leg of the course was a 540-nautical-mile run to Halifax, Nova Scotia.

NC-1 and NC-3 reached Halifax without incident at approximately 1900 hours (7 P.M.), averaging sixty nautical miles an hour ground speed. Not so NC-4. She seemed suddenly heir to all the problems that had been plaguing the enterprise.

Just off Cape Cod, NC-4 lost oil pressure in the pusher engine of the tandem, and it had to be shut down. Immediately losing speed, NC-4 also lost sight of the other two planes. Within half an hour the tractor engine on the tandem threw a connecting rod. This couldn't be repaired in the air or anywhere else. The two outboard engines did not have enough power to keep the heavily loaded plane aloft. As she gradually lost altitude, Ensign Rodd tried to radio Commander Towers in NC-3 to inform him of their plight. Unfortunately the windmill generator powering the radio depended on the propeller wash of the now-defunct forward engine; the plane's airspeed itself wasn't sufficient to generate the power the radio needed. They would have to go down unreported. The one redeeming factor in the situation was that they were only eighty miles from the Naval Air Station at Chatham, Massachusetts; they might be able to get there if Stone could land them safely on the water. Stone's skill honed in his test-pilot work combined with relatively favorable sea conditions resulted in a smooth landing. Using the two engines, they turned the plane into a boat and cruised at up to ten knots toward Chatham, where they arrived at daybreak on May 9.

Despite this turn of events, the men of NC-4 did not consider themselves out of the race. Given even a little bit of luck, there was a real possibility of catching up with the other planes. The second scheduled leg of the flight was 460 nautical miles from Halifax to Trepassey Bay in Newfoundland, the staging area for the ocean hop to the Azores some 1,200 miles away. The precise timing of all of these flights depended upon weather and mechanics, either of which could delay the front-runners. But another bad break awaited the NC-4 in Chatham.

It turned out that the only Liberty engine available to replace the forward engine of the tandem had only 300 horsepower instead of 400. There was, however, a 400-hp model in Trepassey, and they decided to take a chance on the one in Chatham getting them there. It took a few hours to install the new engine, but it took six anxious, nerve-racking days of inactivity to wait out bad weather before they could take off again at 0916 hours on May 14. Even so, it would be possible now for NC-4 to catch up by flying straight through to Trepassey because the weather had delayed the others as well.

Once in the air, Commander Read faced one of the toughest decisions of the flight: Should they risk a night landing at Trepassey or spend the night at Halifax? The decision was made more difficult by the intense interest in Washington. Soon after leaving Chatham, Read received a radio message from the assistant secretary of the Navy, Franklin Delano Roosevelt: "What is your position? All keenly interested in your progress. Good luck.—Roosevelt." Read's response was: "Roosevelt, Washington—Thank you for good wishes. NC-4 is twenty miles southwest of Seal Island making eighty-five miles per hour." But, since NC-1 and NC-3 were reporting plans to take advantage of the improving weather by leaving Trepassey for the Azores late on the fifteenth, there was a fair chance of being cautious and still joining them. Read ordered his pilots to take her down at Halifax.

The next day a bit of serendipity finally attended the so far luckless passage of the NC-4. The other two ships were out taxiing for their ocean-crossing takeoff as NC-4 landed on Trepassey Bay. Loaded with every last drop of fuel that the tanks would take, neither NC-1 nor NC-3 could get off the water. The spectacle of the stranded sister ships was a source of wicked pleasure to those aboard NC-4. Their engineer, Lieutenant Breese, was evidently the only man in Seaplane Division I who understood the problem immediately. The fuel gauges on the NCs had been calibrated with the planes on land, but when they were afloat the tanks were canted slightly down with the result that there would be approximately 200 pounds additional fuel if the tanks were topped off on water. By the time that Breese's analysis was passed around, Commander Towers elected to reschedule departure for the sixteenth. To insure a daylight arrival in the Azores, an evening takeoff would once again be necessary, which meant that NC-4's crew had plenty of time to install and test the new 400-hp engine awaiting them at Trepassey.

May 16, 1919, was a day of bright sunshine and high hopes at

Trepassey Bay, Newfoundland. There was a festive atmosphere as virtually the entire population of the small community found vantage points around the bay to observe the event. Anchored offshore were destroyers USS *Prairie* and USS *Aroostook,* their rails lined with seamen and newspaper correspondents. Anticipating frigid air flowing through their open cockpits, the plane crews shrugged into heavy flight suits over their naval uniforms, slipped woolen socks and fur-lined boots over their silk socks, and donned fur-lined hoods. At 5:32 P.M., Eastern Summer Time, with the sun still shining brightly, Commander Towers signaled a start by firing up the engines on NC-3. With, in effect, the world watching, they were going to try for a formation takeoff.

Aboard NC-4, as the plane roared down the bay, pilots Stone and Hinton put their joint muscle power behind an effort to lift the aircraft off the water. Nothing happened. "What's wrong?" Stone asked Engineer Breese on the intercom. "Gotta be too much weight," Breese said. "Let me try throwing a couple of cans of oil we probably don't need overboard." Amazingly, getting rid of that little bit of weight worked. NC-4 rose slowly into the air. But the other two ships stuck to the water as if glued. Read ordered Stone to circle and land while Breese once more advised the others about the weight problem. It was a most unhappy turn of events for Lieutenant Junior Grade Braxton Rhodes, one of the engineers aboard Towers's lead plane, NC-3; *he* was determined to constitute the excess weight, so he was left behind. With the weight problem solved, all three ships were finally airborne a few minutes after six P.M. They came around to a southeast heading and leveled off 600 feet above the water to face the oncoming night.

However adventurous in some respects, the flight of Seaplane Division I was not likely to be a lonely one. Stationed at fifty-mile intervals along the projected course from Newfoundland to the Azores were twenty-five U.S. Navy destroyers. Not only would they serve as points of radio contact by which the captain/navigators of the planes could check their course, but they would fire rockets and make smoke to give the pilots a visual reference when they passed over. Although the ships would seem to represent a secure safety chain below the fliers, fifty

miles constituted a wide span of ocean if anything went wrong
in between destroyers. But nothing did go wrong before the
planes were swallowed up by the dark. Then the lights failed to
function on NC-3, the lead plane. Commander Towers ordered
the other planes to open up the formation to avoid collision. But,
the night being clear, NC-3's blackout was a minor mishap. The
planes droned on so steadily that the flight threatened to
become boring.

Excerpts from the Navy's Washington log of radio reports
from both planes and ships tell the ongoing story. . . .

May 16, 1919:

"Planes passed Station No. 2 at 2335 Greenwich mean time
(7:35 P.M. Washington time)."

May 17, 1919:

"Planes passed Station Ship No. 3. NC-1 passed at 2403 GMT,
last plane passed at 0015 GMT."
"All seaplanes passed Station No. 6 at 0205 GMT."
"NC-4 passed Station Ship No. 11 at 0550 GMT."
"NC-3 passed Station 13 at 0623 GMT."
"Seaplane NC-4 passed Station Ship No. 14 at 0606."
"NC-4 passed Station No. 18 at 0945 GMT."
"NC-4 reported sighted land at 1135 GMT."
"Latest information received: NC-4 passed Station 22 at 1210
GMT.
"NC-1 passed Station 18. NC-3 off course somewhere between
Station 17 and Station 18."

The terse entries in the log only hint at the kind of trouble the
little fleet of planes began encountering about 1000 GMT on the
morning of May 17. They ran into a rainstorm that soon thick-
ened to the point of zero visibility. At exactly the same time, the
intercom system on NC-4 went dead. The noise from the four
thundering Liberty engines was so great that it was virtually
impossible to communicate between cockpits by voice. Commander Read in his forward perch signaled back to Stone to
climb. At 3,200 feet, they broke out into the sunshine. But when
his calculations told him that they were approaching the next

destroyer, Read instructed Stone by improvised sign language to take the plane down for visual contact. Descending through the dense fog bank, they all experienced vertigo. The compass started to spin crazily. They were perplexed and disoriented until Read saw through a slight break in the overcast that NC-4's left wing was pointed directly at the ground. They were falling in a spin.

It was a harrowing sight. The plane's designers had warned them that it would be very difficult to keep these planes from stalling in rough air or at a reduced speed and that it might be next to impossible to pull them out of a resulting spin. A pilot himself, Read felt helpless and afraid. Frantically, he shouted and waved at Stone. He couldn't tell at once whether his dread message was getting through. Whether it did or not, Read knew that not even test pilot Stone had had experience with pulling an aircraft of this size and weight out of a spin. A difficult feat in clear weather with the guidance of a visual horizon, coming out of a spin in this kind of fog was a matter of feel and fumble. It was time for prayer.

Stone's keen instincts and practiced seat-of-the-pants responses came into full play as he realized what was happening. With Hinton helping to provide the muscle power, he wrestled with the controls until he could simply feel that NC-4 was once again riding straight and level. Getting Read's nodding assent, Stone took the plane once more above the clouds. They would forget about visual contact unless and until the weather broke or their navigational calculations put them over the islands. But when another break in the clouds gave Read a glimpse of what should be the Island of Flores according to the charts, he decided that it was necessary to risk descending once more. This time they broke out into gray skies that provided clear horizontal visibility at 200 feet. Although land was in sight, they were quite conscious that the flight was far from over. Their destination in the Azores, Ponta Delgada, lay 250 miles to the east. Beyond that, there would be another 800 miles to Lisbon, Portugal, before it could be said that they had spanned the space from continent to continent and still another 775 miles to Plymouth, England, where the first Atlantic flight was meant to end in the port from which the Pilgrim fathers set sail for America.

The fog that threw a fright into the crew of NC-4 would prove nearly fatal for the other airships. Uncertain of their whereabouts, both NC-1 and NC-3 decided to set down on the water until they could get a good fix. NC-1 was, in fact, quite close to NC-4, only about forty miles northeast of Flores when she came in for an unanticipated landing. The storm that had brought the rain and fog had kicked up the seas, and NC-1 was smothered by a ten-foot wave. Wing struts and tail beams shattered under the weight of water. The wings began to fill, and the fabric had to be slashed to drain them. The impact opened seams in the hull, which began leaking too fast for the bilge pumps to keep pace. All hands began bailing. All hands, including the skipper, were soon desperately seasick. For an agonizing three hours, the crew of NC-1 had to face the distinct possibility of death at sea. Lost, sick, slowly but surely sinking, they nevertheless kept bailing. Their only hope was to hang on until the weather cleared. If their calculations weren't completely off, out there in the fog there was a U.S. destroyer.

The worst moment of the flight for the crew of NC-1 came when the dim shape of a ship loomed in the mist, and the flare pistol that the skipper tried to fire to attract attention fizzled in the damp. What they couldn't know then was that they had been sighted from the bridge of the Greek steamer *Ionia* through one of those occasional rips in the curtain of fog. She was in the act of searching for them, but it would take hours more until the two vessels made connection shortly after dark. The *Ionia* sent a boat to pick the men off NC-1, which seemed to float easier without their weight. Not long after that, the USS *Harding* took them aboard and also took the NC-1 under tow while the *Ionia* continued her own voyage.

By then, the American fleet converging on the Azores had learned that NC-3, skippered by the division's commander, Towers, had disappeared without a trace. NC-3 had had only a little better luck than NC-1 with its landing in the rough seas. The impact buckled the engine struts and loosened the flying wires. Although the hull leaked, it was possible to keep ahead of the water with pumps and bailing. They were afraid to use the engines for fear they would shake loose and tear the aircraft apart. They could raise nobody on the radio. They could hope, as had the men of NC-1, to be found during a search in clearing weather, but it might take some time since Towers had estimated his position as considerably south of the course when he landed in the hope of getting a fix. The only mitigating factor in their situation was that NC-3, drifting nose to wind, was being blown toward Ponta Delgada.

When that second round of fog closed in, Read in NC-4 decided, as he had en route to Halifax, to be cautious. If he missed Ponta Delgada in the fog, there would not be enough fuel left in his tanks to do any extensive searching. But Horta on the Island of Fayal, where the USS *Columbia* was supposed to be standing by, was a hundred miles closer. At 1323 GMT, May 17, NC-4 glided in for a safe landing in the Horta harbor. They were given an exultant greeting aboard the *Columbia,* but exultation soon gave way to anxious concern over the fates of NC-1 and NC-3. The bad news notwithstanding, nobody thought of keeping NC-4 out of the air. It was both a military mission and a race, and the fittest would have to carry on to the finish. There was further news that sounded a note of urgency. Two British pilots, Hawker and Grieve, who took off from Newfoundland for Ireland on the eighteenth had managed to stay aloft for 1,100 miles before they crash-landed at sea and were rescued by a steamer. Another pair, Alcock and Brown, were standing by to leave Newfoundland as soon as the weather cleared. Also awaiting better weather in Horta, the crew of NC-4 fretted away a stretch of time, which again is documented with immediacy in excerpts from the Navy's Washington log. . . .

May 17, 1919:

> At 7:07 P.M., Washington time, the Navy Department received this message from Admiral Jackson on the *Melville* at Ponta Delgada: "Received at 1540 GMT from NC-1, 'I S W, S O S, landing now, NC-1, we want bearings. Lost in fog about position twenty.' This is latest information. Following destroyers are searching: *Phillip, Waters, Harding, Dent.*"
> At 8:46 P.M. Washington time, the Navy department reported this message from the *Columbia* at Horta: "Last news of NC-3 at 0915 GMT when she asked for compass signals near Station No. Eighteen. Destroyers now search for both planes. De-

stroyer *Harding* in position latitude thirty-nine degrees fifty minutes, on course 289, speed twenty-two knots, reports hearing NC-1 signals at 1027 GMT. Signals getting stronger as approaching."

At 10:55 P.M., the Navy department received this cable gram from the *Columbia* at Horta: "USS *Harding* reports crew of NC-1 safe on board steamship *Ionia*. Plane was being towed, but towline parted. Latitude thirty-nine degrees forty minutes, longitude thirty degrees twenty-four minutes."

May 18, 1919:

Received at 8:45 A.M. from Admiral Jackson at Ponta Delgada: "Following received from MC-4: "Weather conditions unfavorable. Will not attempt flight this morning."

Received at 3:55 P.M. from Admiral Jackson at Ponta Delgada: "Following received from USS *Harding:* "Report plane NC-1 broken, lower planes badly damaged. Pontoon missing. Boat floating high. No serious damage apparently. *Fairfax* will tow to Horta as soon as practicable, depending on state of sea."

Received at 4:17 P.M. from Admiral Jackson at Ponta Delgada: "All available destroyers joining scouting line north from Corvo, scouting to westward. *Columbia* directing scout line. *Texas* and *Florida* have been ordered to join search for NC-3."

May 19, 1919:

Received 1:35 P.M. from Admiral Jackson: "NC-4 will leave for Ponta Delgada as soon as weather is suitable. At present heavy squalls and rain prevailing. It is doubtful if NC-4 can start today."

Received at 2:20 P.M. from Admiral Jackson: "NC-3 sighted on water seven miles from Ponta Delgada under own power."

Received at the Navy Department at 7:17 P.M. from Commander J. H. Towers, USN, at Ponta Delgada, for delivery to Mrs. Towers, wife of the Commander of the transatlantic flight squadron: "Mrs. Towers, 1715 Nineteenth Street. Safe and well—Jack."

May 20, 1919:

Received at 4:27 A.M.: "NC-4 in Horta in good condition, weather bound. Will proceed to Ponta Delgada at earliest moment; will dispatch as soon thereafter as she is refueled and weather permits. All stations for fourth leg are covered by destroyers. NC-3 arrived at Ponta Delgada 1750 GMT. She sailed 205 miles after landing at 1330 GMT on the seventeenth, southwest of Pico; most remarkable exhibition of pluck, skill and seamanship. Impossible to use NC-3 for fourth leg: center engine struts badly damaged and boat leaking, personnel O.K."

Received at 11:17 A.M.: "NC-4 arrived at Ponta Delgada 1424 GMT."

Received at 4 P.M.: "NC-1 sank at sea. . . ."

As usual, spare "cablese" only hints at the unfolding human drama. The fifty-two-hour voyage of the NC-3 was a proud sea saga on its own. The crew took turns steering to keep the craft's head into the wind so that she wouldn't broach in seas running as high as thirty feet. To assist in this process, they improvised "sea anchors" from canvas buckets trailed on long lines. When the left wingtip broke off under the weight of a wave, crewmen took turns crawling out on the right wing to prevent the left wing from dipping under and filling. They subsisted on spare rations of radiator water, salt-soaked sandwiches and chocolate. On a radio that could receive but not transmit, they learned of the NC-1's similar fate, of the NC-4's continuing success, and— unhappily—of the fruitless search for them that was being conducted west and north instead of south of the designated course.

A temptation devised by the devil was presented to the crew of NC-3 when Pico, a 7,000-foot volcanic mountain, materialized out of the haze to the southeast of them. Navigator/captain Towers used it to confirm his calculation that they were only forty-five miles from Fayal. Should they try for land they could actually see? They had two hours' fuel left in the tanks, and it was probable that the damaged engine struts would hold up that long. What wasn't probable was that they could cover forty-five miles in two hours, bucking the heavy seas and westerly winds. With nearly incredible fortitude, they passed by land in sight and sentenced themselves to another twenty-four hours of drifting backward in the direction of land they only hoped to find closer to their path.

In the light of this gamble, NC-3's show of bravado once they drifted within sight of the Ponta Delgada breakwater is understandable. The USS *Harding* came charging out to rescue them, but they waved her off; they would come in under their own power. Just before they reached the breakwater the right float came off. Commander Towers still rejected assistance. Men climbed out on both wings and kept moving back and forth to maintain the plane's balance. The two outboard engines were started. Although NC-3 shook like a wet dog from the vibration of the loose engines, the pilots were able to maneuver her into the harbor and onto a mooring amid cheers, whistles, sirens, guns from assembled boats and crowds on shore. It was deservedly a heroes' welcome, but NC-3's flying days were over.

From then on, it was as if Seaplane Division I had outflown its bad luck. Going on alone, NC-4 arrived without incident in Lisbon on May 27 and in Plymouth on May 31 to become the first plane to fly the Atlantic. It was recorded as a flight of 3,936 nautical miles or 4,520 statute miles accomplished in a flying time of fifty-two hours and thirty-one minutes. At the time, it was held to be miraculous. "In the days of Columbus, it took seventy-one days for his caravels to cross from Palos to the Bahamas. The NC-4 went from Rockaway to Plymouth, more than twice the distance covered by Columbus, in less than seventy-one hours," crowed a contemporary publication. The crew was decorated by the king of England in London and sent to Paris to receive the personal congratulations of President Woodrow Wilson, who was attending the Peace Conference at Versailles. But for them, the most moving welcome was a quiet one in Plymouth where, alongside their families, stood Mechanics Mate Ed Howard, his one good hand raised in a victory salute.

"A happy nation or a successful flight has no history," journalist Walter Duranty wrote of the NC-4's venture when she landed in Lisbon. His words were prophetic in the sense that the Lone Eagle's solo flight across the Atlantic eight years later eclipsed NC-4's in the public mind down to the day of this writing. But Lindbergh himself tried to keep the record straight when he said: "I had a better chance of reaching Europe in *Spirit of St. Louis* than the NC flying boats had of reaching the

Azores. I had a more reliable type of engine, improved instruments and a continent instead of an island for a target. It was skill, determination and a hard-working crew that carried NC-4 to the completion of the first transatlantic flight."

Pilot Stone eventually returned to the Coast Guard and was instrumental in developing its air arm, which now plays a vital role in virtually all of its missions. Stone, who died in 1936, is fittingly designated Coast Guard Aviator Number One and is the only Coast Guardsman enshrined in the Naval Aviation Museum in Pensacola, Florida. Although she may have looked like a crate or kite or flying wooden shoe, NC-4 was obviously made of sturdy stuff since ten years later she crossed the Atlantic again from New York State to England, a longer route, in two days, seven hours and thirty-three minutes of flying time. She too was enshrined at Pensacola.

Chapter 14

The Will to Live

THE alarm came out of the wildest night of the year along America's northeast coast. Toward sundown of a moist and balmy Wednesday three days after Christmas 1988, a cold front boomed in from the west-northwest on winds gusting up to eighty miles an hour. So sudden and severe was the change in weather that Tom Grant of the National Weather Service in New York's Rockefeller Center called it "a little bit crazy." The temperature dropped fourteen degrees in thirty minutes from a near record high of fifty-nine in New York. There was rain, thunder, lightning. Homes blacked out as uprooted trees crashed through power lines on Long Island and the Connecticut shore. Manhattan police closed five blocks of Eighth Avenue after pedestrians were hit by debris blowing off rooftops. At the main terminal of Baltimore-Washington International Airport, wind smashed through huge plate-glass windows and ripped off a section of roof; in Philadelphia two people were crushed to death when wind dropped the concrete cornice of a factory building on their parked cars. It was no night to be at sea.

By 7 P.M. the storm was at its height and driving solid sheets of rain across the dunes and scrub pines of Cape Cod when the auto-alarm sounded in the U.S. Coast Guard station at Woods Hole. Later recorded accurately at ten minutes after seven— 1910 hours in nautical terms—the fifty-second alarm was followed by a male voice coming out of the night on the radio's distress band. The accent was American, the tone tense:

"All stations. All stations. Motor vessel *Lloyd Bermuda,* motor vessel *Lloyd Bermuda* in distress thirty-eight degrees north latitude seventy degrees west longitude. Request assistance from any possible source. . . ."

"*Lloyd Bermuda,* this is U.S. Coast Guard Woods Hole Massachusetts Group. What is your exact position and also nature of distress? Over."

"The nature of distress is we have lost deck cargo, we have taken on water, we are awash, we are sinking thirty-eight degrees north latitude seventy degrees west longitude. That's very close position. Over."

"This is Coast Guard Woods Hole Group. Roger. How many people on board and do you have small boats? Over."

"Eleven people on board. Eleven people on board. Over."

"Confirm eleven people on board. Over."

"Roger. Eleven people, one, one. Over."

"This is Woods Hole Group. Roger. Sir, are you preparing to abandon ship or are you fighting the flooding? Over."

"We are preparing to abandon ship but have extremely high seas. We have twenty-five-to-thirty-foot seas and . . . ah . . . fifty-to-sixty-mile-an-hour winds. So we have great difficulty. Over."

"This is Coast Guard Woods Hole Group. Do you have life rafts rigged at this time? If so, what color, what color? Over."

"Life rafts . . . ah . . . white, white. Over."

"This is Group Woods Hole. Roger. Do you have survival suits for all eleven people? . . ."

"We have life jackets. We do not have survival suits."

"This is Coast Guard Woods Hole Group. Roger. Sir, how soon before you'll be abandoning? Over."

"I don't know. We just have to wait. We have to wait and see. Real soon, real soon. Over."

"This is Coast Guard Woods Hole Group. Is there a canopy on the life rafts? Also how many life rafts are there? Over."

"There are two. I'm abandoning ship, I'm abandoning ship. Over."

"Roger. This is Coast Guard Woods Hole. Can you key your mike, key your mike? . . . You're fading out . . . Try to key your mike, key your mike somehow . . . Over . . ."

No answer. Four minutes had elapsed since the first alarm

sounded. The operator at Woods Hole knew at once that it was a search-and-rescue case beyond the group's capacity and called the round-the-clock Rescue Coordination Center of the Coast Guard's First District headquarters in Boston on the SARTEL, the search-and-rescue communications line. While it was still 1914 hours, RCC contacted Lieutenant Junior Grade Alberto "P.V." Perez-Vergera, a pilot who was taking his turn as duty coordinator at Air Station Cape Cod, on the SARTEL, and said: "Cargo ship sinking with eleven persons on board at thirty-eight degrees north, seventy degrees west. Launch aircraft."

Perez-Vergera immediately hit the "whoopee" that blared its alarm into every nook and cranny of the air station's headquarters building. In the controlled, clear monotone cultivated by men accustomed to crises, the lieutenant said over the intercom loudspeakers: "Ready H-3 on line. Ready H-25 on line. Cargo vessel sinking thirty-eight degrees north, seventy degrees west. Ready H-3 on line. Ready H-25 on line. Cargo vessel sinking thirty-eight degrees north, seventy degrees west." It was after dinner, and the ready crews of both the H-3, a large Sikorsky HH-3F helicopter, and the H-25, an HU-25 executive Falcon jet modified for Coast Guard purposes, were trying to relax in preparation for whatever they might get in the way of sleep that night. Lieutenant Commander Kevin Marshall and Lieutenant Junior Grade Paul Ratte, pilot and copilot of the H-3, were at their desks trying to clean up the paperwork that always seemed to accumulate when they were off flying. *Well, some other time,* Ratte thought as he pushed the papers away and headed for the operations center.

It was Ratte's preassigned function to be briefed by Perez-Vergera on the job ahead while Marshall ran to the line to check out the aircraft—in this case CG 1472. Ratte knew from the coordinates and the request for the H-25 that they would be heading a long way out to sea. It was SOP—standard operating procedure—for the jet to accompany the helicopter, the workhorse of search and rescue, on any mission more than a hundred miles offshore. The jet acts as eyes and ears for the helo. With its speed, the jet can reach the data base ahead of the helo and usually drop markers to spot the trouble; with its altitude, the jet can stay above the weather and have clearer communications over longer distances than the helo. And in the event of an accident to the helo, the jet is on hand to drop rescue aids and summon help.

Perez-Vergera had little more to offer Ratte in the way of hard information. Apparently some deck cargo had gone overboard, causing the *Lloyd Bermuda* to capsize. The eleven people aboard were supposedly getting off onto white life rafts, but it wasn't certain since the radio had gone dead. The *Lloyd Bermuda*'s position would be at the outer edge of the H-3's range, which meant taking off with maximum fuel. Since most search-and-rescue flights are much shorter, the tanks are kept at half full to make the ship easier to fly and give it as much weight-bearing capacity as possible during the rescue. There's a standard computer program for takeoff data based on ambient conditions—temperature, humidity, pressure and the like—and on normal fuel weight. But full tanks would change the configuration. Rather than try to work out the changes in the cockpit by hand, Ratte took some time in the operations center to run the program through the computer. What with the weather— an 800-foot ceiling, thirty-five knots of wind blowing out of the north, a driving rain—and the fact that maximum fuel weight would be unforgiving of any mistakes on takeoff, there would be enough other things to do on board. "At maximum gross weight, the aircraft flies sloppy, and your margin for error is less," Ratte said. "Even though the H-3 is a two-engined aircraft, if you lose an engine on takeoff you won't be able to continue flying. You have to make a controlled landing—hopefully controlled—on whatever is in front of you."

While Ratte was running his program, crewmen were wheeling both aircraft out of the bright, warm hangar to the wet, windy runway. It was a soaking, all-hands job since the station was running on minimum staff for the Christmas holidays. Ratte was first aboard to switch on the electrical system and start warming up the navigational gear, a must in a twenty-year-old machine like CG 1472. The crew—Petty Officers Randy Reed, AE3, the electronics engineer; John Salmi, AD3, the flight mechanic; and Joe Rock, ASM2, the rescue swimmer—soon followed, strapping themselves into seats in the dark, wire-festooned cavern behind the pilots. As air commander, Marshall had to spend minutes more out in the rain while he walked around and eyeballed his aircraft to make sure that everything was secure for takeoff.

Marshall finally buckled himself into the vacant right-hand seat and looked out of a windshield awash. A bleak place at best, Air Station Cape Cod in Otis, Massachusetts, consists of an airstrip and a knot of functional, slab-sided buildings in a far corner of the vast reaches of Otis National Guard Air Base. There was no glow from human habitation against the clouds that blacked out the stars, but there were flashes of unseasonal lightning that struck a ghostly sheen from the fuselage of the H-25, CG 2103, that was taxing for takeoff in front of them.

"I've seen better nights," Marshall said. "Well, let's go."

Marshall dropped his eyes from the unfriendly night to the reassuring array of lights and dials on the instrument panels. He and Ratte were running through the routine checklist when suddenly they were in trouble. An important part of the AFCS (automatic flight control system) by which their altitude when engulfed by clouds was determined—the port gyro—would not align. Flying with a malfunction like that under this night's conditions could be suicidal. It takes three minutes to run through the sequence of the system's "fast erect" procedure. The pilots had to wait out four sequences—twelve precious minutes—before the gyro was properly aligned. Finally satisfied, Marshall poured on the power and lifted his weight-clumsy bird into the sky, anxious to make up the time lost to the delay. Normally, the crew would have been off the ground within fifteen to twenty-five minutes.

Takeoff time was officially clocked at 1953 hours—7:53 P.M.— of December 28, 1988, thirty-nine minutes after the whoopee first sounded. The log would record: "LCDR MARSHALL ABN FM CGAS CAPE COD WITH NITE SUN [a million-candle-power searchlight] AND RESCUE SWIMMER. DELAY DUE TO REFUELING AND GYRO MALFUNCTION."

When she headed out to sea from Port Elizabeth, New Jersey, on December 27, nobody aboard M/V *Lloyd Bermuda* expected anything but tedium for the next several days. Carrying sixty-nine containers, some of which were stowed on the long open deck stretching from the bow to the deckhouse aft, the sixteen-year-old freighter was making her routine weekly run to Bermuda. The schedule had allowed James Grose, the American captain, to spend Christmas at home, but for the crew, mostly family men from the Philippines, Peru, Guatemala, Honduras and Indonesia, it had been a bleak holiday season livened only by a Christmas Eve party at the Seaman's Church Institute Center in Newark. At least they could look forward to enjoying a bit of sun on the island before the ship turned around again.

The weather worsened continually as they churned along a southeasterly course toward Bermuda, and Captain Grose kept reducing power and speed. By Wednesday afternoon the wind was salting the rain with spume whipped off the tops of seas as high as a three-story house. The captain took the *Lloyd Bermuda* off course to head into the blasts coming from the north and ordered her engines throttled down to 230 rpm's. At that rate, she was barely making five knots. Nobody wanted to brave the weather, but bosun Dario Macias-Lopez, one of the Honduran seamen, stepped out on the boat deck after the evening meal to have a look at the containers on the main deck just below him. He was thinking about going forward to inspect the lashings. With the vessel rolling and pitching in the seas, it would be a perilous passage. Dario hesitated, hugging the deckhouse for what shelter it afforded and discussing the matter with some other crewmen who had joined him. He was just about to go when a solid wall of water rose above the port bow and fell in a foaming, hissing mass around the containers. The ship staggered up again and the water drained away, leaving an empty space where four containers had been lashed down on the port side of the deck. Losing this weight caused the ship to list sharply to starboard. Dario and the others ran into the deckhouse to get their life jackets.

On the bridge, Captain Grose immediately sounded the general alarm and got on the radio distress band to call, "Mayday! Mayday!" Although he hadn't yet noticed the ship's list, Asmi Anwar, the Indonesian chief engineer, knew that they had run into serious trouble when the alarm pierced the quiet of his cabin, where he had gone to rest after dinner. He grabbed his life jacket and headed for the bridge. Captain Grose ordered Anwar to start pumping ballast water from the starboard tanks to balance the loss of weight. Anwar ran down to the engine room. With the two crewmen on duty there, Anwar managed to get the ballast pump going, but the list to starboard kept increasing at an alarming rate. Anwar ordered the others to get out of the engine room through the stern door opening onto the main deck. He headed for another door on the port side. That door was jammed. When Anwar turned to follow the others, there was water washing through the stern door and flooding the engine room.

With his life jacket on, Dario Macias-Lopez ran back to the boat deck on the port side. The ship was now listing so badly to starboard that he knew there would be no chance to launch the lifeboat or life raft on that side. Other crewmen were already there, and they all began working at the ties holding down the raft. They had to stop so that the raft wouldn't drop on a crew-man clawing his way up the slanted deck beneath it. While they watched in horror, the crewman slid off into the sea and an untended line wound its way around Macias-Lopez's torso and leg like a snake. The others were trying to help Macias-Lopez free himself when the ship slid under the water, dragging him with it on the line. In the engine room Anwar was engulfed in the fast-rising water, swirled around in the sudden dark and banged against jutting pipes and engine fittings.

As a good bosun should, Macias-Lopez carried a knife, and he managed to saw through the line binding him to the ship before he lost his breath. He popped to the surface like a cork. Evi-dently having crashed through the glass ventilating skylight of the engine room by the force of the rising water, Anwar also found himself bobbing on the swells in his life jacket. His ship had vanished. There was nothing around him but wind and wet and a vast loneliness. Beneath him he could hear the eerie thump, thump, thump of the still-turning propeller as the *Lloyd Bermuda* plunged 1,200 feet to the bottom of the Atlantic Ocean.

Once aloft, Commander Marshall swung CG 1472 to a south-easterly heading and gave the helo full throttle. The plane's normal cruising speed is 120 knots; its maximum speed—or "red line"—142 knots. But with the weight of maximum fuel, CG 1472 could never attain maximum speed. She was aided on her way this night, however, by the wind, which picked up to fifty knots over open ocean and, being out of the north, was on her stern quarter. To be sure that they were making the most of power and wind, the pilots pushed the old helo until she started to shudder and then backed off slightly on the throttle. Not only the lives of those in peril on the sea but their own lives depended upon getting there as soon as humanly and mechanically possible.

From the moment of takeoff, CG 1472's crew would be struggling with the intractable figures of an equation involving time, distance, wind velocity and fuel consumption. The data base lay 215 miles ahead of them, just short of the advertised 300-mile radius of the HH3F helicopter. This meant that they would have just thirty or forty minutes of searching and hovering time on the scene—and only if they didn't have winds on the nose when they returned. For the most part the clouds they were punching through went clear down to the surface of the water. What glimpses they got of the sea through infrequent holes revealed towering, whitecapped waves. Given these conditions, they weren't looking at much time to find any object at all— even the disabled hull of a ship if she hadn't already sunk—let alone to winch eleven people to safety in their helicopter. To gain time, Marshall asked Ratte to find another airfield along the coast within range and out of the wind blowing off Cape Cod.

As he started to work on this problem, Ratte made a disturbing discovery. Because the craft was seldom, if ever, called upon to work so far offshore, her chart pack contained no chart showing the data base in relation to the shoreline. The best Ratte could do was to close his eyes and try to visualize the relationships based on the coordinates and the charted airfields along the coast. He came up with Suffolk County National Guard Base on Long Island and asked Avionicsman Randy Reed, who was perched behind him fiddling with the dials of his radio, to try to contact Suffolk. But Reed was having his own problems.

"I can't get anything, Lieutenant," he said.

"What do you mean?"

"We're in some kind of fluky meteorological situation that's playing hell with the radio. I can hardly hear Boston now, and with CG 2103 gone . . ."

Reed didn't have to finish the sentence to give them all the sinking sensation that they were alone out there in the night. A few minutes earlier Lieutenant Ansley in the jet had radioed that he was returning to base to switch to the other jet because of mechanical problems. Now they had arrived at precisely the moment for which jet cover had been intended. Although Boston had advised that a C-130, the Coast Guard's big Lockheed cargo plane, was en route from Elizabeth City, North Carolina, and that the cutter *Tamaroa* was being diverted from her patrol station off Cape Cod, the plane wouldn't be on the scene much before they were, and the cutter would have to crawl her way through the night because of the heavy seas.

"Keep trying, Randy," Ratte said.

"I am trying, damn it. . . ."

The frustration tinged with fear in Reed's voice was shared by all hands. The isolation and uncertainty of what lay ahead weighed heaviest on swimmer Joe Rock. Out of the action and hunched over in the gloomy stern of the helo, Rock had nothing to do but think—and pray. One of the first coasties to go through the Navy's survival swimming training in Pensacola, Florida, twenty-four-year-old Joe Rock had been on duty as an aviation survivalman for three years but had never yet been required to go into the water on an actual rescue case. Commander Marshall was virtually promising him that he wouldn't have to swim on a night like this, either, but there was no way of knowing for sure until they reached the site. In view of the lack of information as to what actually happened to the *Lloyd Bermuda,* it only made good sense for Rock to squeeze into his dry suit—just in case. After wrestling with his feelings for a while, Rock gained a measure of peace. "I said a prayer, and reconciled myself to the fact that whatever happened next would be in the hands of the man upstairs," he said.

But there could be no peace for the pilots, who were in danger of arriving at a point of no return with every minute and mile that they rode the tailwind out to sea. After an agonizing hour, frustration turned to anger. "We were irate with not getting the answers we needed," Ratte said. "We wanted to reach somebody on shore who had his feet dry and could think a little, who could pull out a chart and look at it and pick some options for us and call these places and find out the weather." They never did find that somebody on shore, but as they found themselves on the edge of despair, the voice of a man who was literally upstairs came booming into Reed's ear. The C-130 had arrived. Ratte cut in with his mike: "C-130, our plan is to go back to Suffolk because of the headwinds. What do you think?" Whether his feet were dry or not, the C-130's navigator had his head above the weather and apparently the right charts in front of him. He came back almost immediately. "Yeah, we concur with Suffolk."

With communications established and a decision made on their destination, the crew of CG 1472 could concentrate on their mission. It was comforting too to learn that Ansley was once again outbound in CG 2111 and that Air Station Cape Cod's other H-3 was also en route, manned by a crew recalled from their holiday slumbers. But, as they approached the data base, Marshall and Ratte still had little to go on for their search. From its position aloft, the C-130 had spotted nothing; neither had the two merchant vessels—M/V *Eagle* and M/V *Medallion*—that were steaming into the area in response to *Lloyd Bermuda*'s SOS. Before he started looking for anything, Marshall's responsibility for the safety of his aircraft and crew forced him to deal with that intractable fuel equation. "Whenever we go offshore, we always think ahead and decide what we call our Bingo fuel stage is—the stage when we have to leave," he said. "We figure out how many miles it is, how the wind will affect us. We throw in a factor of maybe fifteen minutes of extra, which we call 'the extra fifteen minutes for Mama.' It's not a guess. It's a calculated number, but everyone has a different factor they throw in for safety." Marshall and Ratte came up with a time on the scene of about forty-five minutes, and Marshall dropped the helicopter through the clouds until they broke out at 500 feet.

At that level, they were close enough to see the whitecaps—an unwelcome sight to Joe Rock, who joined the other crew members at a window to add two more eyes to the search. It was also probable that anybody in the sea could now see them, and they turned on all the lights. One of these was the powerful Nitesun. It could illuminate any object on which it was focused as brightly as daylight, but it created only a small dot on an immense dark sea for search purposes. They also had radar, which they tuned for a metallic return. In a capsize, the *Lloyd Bermuda* might be lying on her side or turned bottom up, and the lightless hull would show up on the radar screen. But the radar proved to be counterproductive. The one contact that they chased was a waste of extremely precious time; it turned out to be one of the merchant vessels standing by. The clock ticked mercilously on. They were below their Bingo point and using up Mama's time when somebody aboard thought that he spotted a light source. They had to have a look—a look that revealed nothing beneath them but wild waves.

"We've got to go," Marshall said. "Give me a course for Suffolk, Paul."

What should have been a moment of relief from tension was instead a moment of shock. They had been too busy circling and hovering and staring at the sea to pay much attention to the weather. Squaring away for Suffolk was like hitting a solid wall in the dark. The weather was as crazy out where they were as it had been in New York. An almost instant shift brought the wind around from the north into the west and increased its velocity from forty to sixty miles an hour. Lighter after consuming more than half of its fuel, CG 1472 was showing 140 knots airspeed with throttles wide open, but she was making only seventy-five miles an hour over the ground. Ratte punched the figures into the navigator and came up with a frightening result: They had a three-hour and forty-five minute flight through the impenetrable weather to Suffolk, the nearest airport, and three hours of fuel in the tanks. The two pilots looked at each other and asked each other aloud, "How do we do this?"

"Maybe we swim," Marshall said grimly. "What are the options, Paul—if any? Let's at least get out of this wind some. How about Montauk?"

Still off the charts, Ratte did a run-through of the coastal configuration in his head. Montauk would be too far, wind or no wind. So would Block Island. But Nantucket? Checking out the coordinates of Nantucket, he estimated that it would only be ten or fifteen miles further than Suffolk and with the better weather in that area, it was possible. "For crying out loud, let's turn to Nantucket," he said.

When Marshall brought the plane around to the new heading, ground speed picked up to ninety miles an hour. Ratte radioed the C-130 navigator to check his figures. Back came the not-too-encouraging reply, "I guess Nantucket's OK, but you're going to make it there on fumes, buddy."

"How about dropping down and checking the winds for us?" Ratte asked.

"Roger."

In the CG 1472 they were maintaining their usual cruising altitude of about 1,000 feet, and they didn't want to waste gas climbing. As if descending an invisible staircase, the C-130 leveled off every 1,000 feet and took a reading of the wind with its computers. At 6,000 feet the wind was due west, which meant that it would be on the beam or a little abaft the beam on a course to Nantucket. Marshall climbed, eased off on the throttle to an economical cruising speed and took his first easy breath in half an hour.

Being out of foreseeable danger didn't make the two-hour cruise to Nantucket a happy one for the men aboard CG 1472. Adrenaline always flows freely in anticipation of dangerous action, and there's a physical letdown when no action occurs. Psychologically, it is dispiriting to well-trained and highly motivated people when they find it impossible to carry out an assignment, and the psychological impact is greater by an immeasurable factor when failure means loss of human life. Their spirits on this occasion weren't much lifted by the fact that the front behind the wind change was dissipating the clouds and allowing Reed to monitor the radio traffic between the planes and ships back on the scene. Nobody was having any more luck than they had had. The helicopter that followed them out was already headed back to Air Station Cape Cod empty-handed. Having monitored the exchange between CG 1472 and the C-130, they had left enough gas to return to Cape Cod because their craft was due for maintenance and would be unflyable after they landed.

The island of Nantucket, a faintly darker presence in a dark sea, loomed ahead when Randy Reed's excited voice broke into everyone's thoughts: "Hey, the on-scene aircraft have got something. . . . The Falcon spotted it, and they're going down to drop a marker, but they're about out of gas and have to head for home. . . . The C-130's dropping down for a look. . . . They've got it too. They think it's a life raft with eight people, and they're trying to give the *Eagle* the position. . . ."

Marshall broke in, "Well, men, what do we do? The other H-3 is out of business. The *Eagle* may get to them, but you know it can be hell to pay to get people aboard a ship with seas like this. If we can get gas on Nantucket, we could go back. What do you say?"

A minute's silence and then another voice: "It's what we're here for, isn't it?"

"Right. Anybody too tired? How about you, Joe? I still don't think we ought to put you down there. If they're in a raft, they're probably in good enough shape to get themselves into a basket."

Rock, who had just about decided that the man upstairs wasn't going to put him to the test that night, summoned up the will to say, "I'm OK."

"Good. Paul, see if you can get hold of P. V. and have him wake somebody up on that sleepy island to bring us some gas. . . ."

At midnight on a mid-winter's night, the airport on Nantucket, a summer place, cannot be called lively. In fact, the frugal New England caretakers turn out the lights before they go home. But in a faint wash of natural light from a sliver of moon peeping through the scattering clouds, the crew of the CG 1472 could pick out the landing strip from the surrounding countryside. They knew too that the field was equipped with pilot-controlled lighting that works something like remote-control garage doors. The incoming plane dials in the right frequency, clicks the mike and—presto!—runway lights come on. The system worked beautifully for CG 1472. By the time the big blades above them stopped turning, they could see a pickup truck tearing down the field. It was the gas man, and in a few minutes more he had his tank truck beside them pumping another load of maximum fuel into CG 1472.

Discussing the possibility of saving eight lives as they stood on the deserted tarmac, the crew found themselves pumped full of adrenaline again. Far from being tired after five and a half hours of tense flying, they were raring to go. But once in the air, where Reed could monitor the on-scene action on the radio, they got another dose of disappointment. The *Eagle* had found what the planes had spotted. Instead of a life raft, it was a cluster of life jackets with three men clinging to them. As Marshall had presumed, getting them aboard had had what looked like tragic consequences. The *Eagle* crew had thrown ropes to the men and pulled them up the steep sides of the ship. Chief Engineer Asmi Anwar and Seaman Jorge Montoya made it. Cook Mario Suchite was pulled out of his life jacket, lost his grip on the rope and fell back into the sea. He was last seen disappearing below the surface. Miracles do happen, and Suchite could still be out there, and then there were eight more people who could still be alive. But for the men in CG 1472 the news meant that they were heading out for another search with the same time restrictions and a high probability of an equally frustrating result instead of heading for a certain rescue.

To Joe Rock, a qualified medical emergency technician as well as a swimmer, there was material in that news for pondering during the seemingly endless flight. The men who did manage to get aboard *Eagle* were reported to be in fair condition despite some four hours in the water. Indeed, they were on their feet on deck and helping to scan the seas for their comrades. By rights, they should have been suffering from severe hypothermia. People weren't supposed to survive more than two and a half hours in the forty-three-degree temperatures of the Atlantic waters. But, counting the man who fell off his rope, three people had lasted four hours. But why? Was it possible that the data base could be in the Gulf Stream, where the water could be as much as ten degrees warmer? If so, their chances of finding others alive nearly eight hours after the sinking improved immensely. Rock raised the question with the pilots, who were presumed to know something about the Gulf Stream since they were both graduates of the Coast Guard Academy at New London, Connecticut. Without the chart for the data base, they couldn't be sure, but they agreed that Rock's hunch was a good one. It was a thought that cheered everybody, but Marshall said, "We're still not going to let *you* swim in it if we can help it, Joe."

At 290320—3:20 A.M. on December 29—the CG 1472 was back on the scene and starting its search. Through the radio came a voice from the *Medallion* beneath them: "We've got something. A dark object off our stern—too far away to identify." Marshall swooped down over the *Medallion* at seventy-five feet. In the bright shaft from the Nitesun the object revealed itself to be only an empty pallet of lumber. But it was part of a lot of debris spread all around—a hot area. Randy Reed stopped fiddling with the radio to move the Nitesun around outside his window. Reed was noted for his sharp eyes, so Ratte froze the Loran with an instant reflex action when he heard a voice behind him: "Got something at eight o'clock." As Marshall wheeled around to go back to the spot the Loran recorded, Reed said that he thought he had glimpsed the reflective tape used on life jackets. This time Marshall came to a hover. Both Reed and Ratte saw a man in street clothes tied to some boards. His hand rose to shield his eyes from the blinding Nitesun. He was alive!

From the looks of the man, they knew that he couldn't get into a sling or basket himself. "OK, Joe, I guess it's into the water," Marshall said. But the command was unnecessary. What had to be done was like a single thought in the minds of all five men. Even before getting the word, Rock, who was already in his dry suit, put on his flippers, mask and snorkel. Although normally the helicopter hovers low enough for the swimmer to jump free, it is SOP at night or in waters full of debris to send the swimmer down on the hoist. As another night precaution, chem sticks like the ones kids use on Halloween are tied to the swimmer's suit; they glow phosphorescent green for twelve hours. Rock stepped up to the door that flight mechanic John Salmi had slid open and began shrugging himself into the horse-collar harness. Having said his prayers, his only thought as he looked down at the figure sliding up and down the waves on his makeshift raft was: *How am I ever going to get him up here?*

Salmi, firmly secured by his safety belt as he hung out the door to assess the job on his hands, was happy not to be in his friend

Joe's flippers. The seas were still running twenty to twenty-five feet and the wind still blowing at forty-five to fifty knots. But the conditions would give him nearly as much trouble as they would Joe, and he was facing an equally tough test in his own way. At twenty-three, Salmi had just completed his syllabus at the air station to become a full-fledged flight mechanic; this would be the first time he had performed by himself. On any gauge his adrenaline would measure as high as Joe's, but he would have to keep his feelings under tight control. Because of the nature of the beast, they were flying, Salmi became the key man in the whole operation from the minute they spotted a survivor.

Positioning a hovering helicopter for rescue work is a tricky business. The plane does not stand still. In the moving air, it's like a boat in a swirling current. With a practiced coordination of hands and feet comparable to that of an organist playing a Bach fugue, the pilot has to make constant adjustments to power, rudder, rotor pitch. Difficult enough in calm daylight with visible reference points, the job of staying over the target on a windy night with a vertigo-inducing blend of sea and sky can prove next to impossible. Even if the pilot can hold his craft into the wind as steady as a church, the whitecapped waves marching under him give him the feeling that he's moving in the opposite direction. From where he sits on the right-hand seat of the cockpit, the pilot can never eyeball the target during the action. The open door from which the winch cable is suspended is on the left side amidships, and the pilot has no choice but to respond blindly to the voice instructions of the flight mechanic, who wears the mike of a hot line on his chest. An important part of the training that Salmi had just completed was to learn how to keep talking to the pilot in that clear crisis monotone no matter how exciting or disastrous the action taking place before the mechanic's eyes might be.

Although conditions couldn't have been worse for hovering in most respects, Marshall did have a form of reference this night in the lights of the *Eagle* and *Medallion* hove to about a mile upwind. Working by the book, he would have dropped two tungsten flares that burn with a bright orange flame to leeward and windward of the target to help judge his drift. But mindful of the need for speed this night, he dropped only one upwind before backing down into position. He was busy with another problem—altitude. Even though Rock would be winched down and the survivor winched up, they could be dangerously whipped around by the wind during a passage of seventy-five feet. Somehow he had to get closer without risking a hit from a rogue wave rising out of those rough seas. Ratte has a vivid recollection of the process: "We go down lower to the water. We have two altimeters. One is barometric for flying in the air traffic control system because everybody can twist to the same setting in reference to barometric pressure. The other is radar bouncing a signal off the surface, and we use that. The needle is looking like the oil gauge on an engine that is about to fail because the seas are coming up so that one minute we are at twenty-five feet and the next at fifty or sixty in the trough. Kevin is constantly making power changes, trying to average it out, trying to keep some rhythm with the waves."

Meanwhile, Salmi's voice—calm in these initial stages—is droning in Marshall's ears: "Forward and right forty ... Forward and right ten ... Hold ... Hold ... Left a little ... Down a little ... Up a little ... Launch!" Rock is on his way down. It's three minutes after the survivor was first sighted. With good timing, Salmi dropped his friend in a trough about twenty-five feet from the man on the boards. Randy Reed kept the Nitesun beam focused on the survivor to guide the swimmer. There were tiny arcs of phosphorescent green as Rock flailed his way toward the light.

Joe Rock's first reaction to feeling the cold water slap his face was a sense of being alone, utterly alone, despite the machine hanging precariously in the air above him. He was not only immersed in water but encased in a dome of noise made by the wind and the clatter of the chopper. Communicating with the crew of CG 1472 other than by the prearranged hand signal for the hoist was out of the question. Even if he could use it with all this noise, the difficulties of digging out the emergency radio tucked away in his clothing were too great to contemplate. He had to accept being alone, on his own, responsible for every action and decision. "It hit me in an instant," he recalls, "that this is what it's all about."

There was no question as to what to do at once—get to the survivor. Rock started swimming. In those waves the process was like clawing his way up a mountainside. Every so often he would glimpse the man on the boards. He looked like a tortured figure on a cross. Rock had the illusion that the figure was always receding. Only when they were in the same trough and he could see the man's face was he sure that he would make it. Closing in, Rock wondered if the movement Reed and Ratte claimed to have seen from the plane wasn't a delusion of wishful thinking. The man showed no signs of life.

During the swim, Rock had decided to go by the book, and the book said to establish contact. "Hi, fellow, I'm here to help you," he yelled into the wind. "In a couple of minutes we'll have you up in that helo."

No response, none at all. No sign that the man heard him or was even aware of the brilliant lights and loud clatter of the plane. Hands on now, Rock could tell that the man was alive—but barely. He was breathing but not shivering with the cold—a sure sign of the last stages of hypothermia. The sopping pants and shirt and raincoat he wore would long since have lost any warming effect. What life he had left was evidently flowing into his hands, tightly gripping the stack of fifteen-foot two-by-fours to which he had tied himself. Rock marveled at the man's ingenuity and clear intention to stay alive. If he could manage it, it would be worth every effort to save a person with such a will to live.

Rock wasted no time trying to untie the firm, wet knots. He used his knife to cut the straps. In the process he lost a glove and exposed his hand, but he was too totally engaged to feel the cold. The man didn't float free; showing no other evidence of consciousness, he held his grip. Rock kept talking—"It's OK, fella . . . Let go . . . I'm here . . ."—while he tried to pull the hands away. He couldn't call for the rescue basket until the man was well separated from the wood.

A time-consuming struggle ensued. It was like some terrible child's game. The man's strength was incredible. Tiring himself, Rock had to use both of his hands to pry one of the victim's hands off the wood. As soon as that hand came free, the man would grab the wood with the other. Although Rock had a suspicion that the man didn't understand English—whether he could hear Rock or not over the commotion around them—he tried reasoning and pleading: "Please, let go. Please. You have to let go so we can get you up into the plane. Please let go of that wood. . . ."

No use. Ever-conscious that they were running out of hover time, Rock finally got angry. "Listen, fella, if you don't let go we're both going to die out here. Damn it all, let go!" he shouted. Rock thought of hitting the man. But then he decided to use his anger and desperation to make one last all out effort to pull those hands loose. It worked! He kicked the lumber away and started towing the man's free body into the waves as he'd been trained to do in survival school. He signaled Salmi to send down the basket

As Rock was aware from occasional glances aloft, the men in CG 1472 weren't having an easy time of it either. The *Eagle*, drifting down ever-closer, was creating some lee from the fierce winds, but the helicopter was doing a nervous dance. Salmi would have the devil's own time with the basket. *Pray that his training works as well as mine has so far*, Rock thought.

The tension inside the helicopter was such that it embedded itself in the memories of the pilots. The adrenaline quite evidently rises again when they speak of it. Marshall, a classically handsome man with an air of studied calm, lets the words tumble out when he reaches this part of the story: "We had to time the waves and put the basket down near enough for Joe to grab it. The pilot can't see anything that's going on beneath him. Every once in a while I'd see Joe float out with his buddy there. Then we would start moving in, and I would lose sight of him. I would keep an eye on the waves and try to hold it steady for Salmi. He would be talking continuously, conning me: 'Right, right forward, back, back . . .' Every time we put the basket down, the high waves would pick it up and throw it away from Joe. When the basket would pop out of the water it would start swinging wildly. Salmi would have to bring it halfway up and get it under control again. We had to do this about ten times. While we were doing it I looked out forward and saw a glint in the water. I told Paul, 'There's something ahead of us; see if you can make out what it is. . . .' "

Ratte, who offsets the youthfulness of his round-cheeked face with a trim mustache, lets even more remembered excitement flow through his voice and words: "Here's where things get interesting. While Salmi starts conning us over to the survivor, the *Eagle* sees us in a hover and starts coming over in a kind of friendly gesture of help. Honestly, we'd rather not be disturbed at this point. I look up every now and then and just have in the back of my mind that he's getting closer. Kevin probably doesn't look. He's busy listening to John, and John is going back to rudiments. In the training syllabus, the mechanic has to get the pilot directly over target—kind of like putting the toothpick in the coke bottle. The swimmer is not supposed to have to swim at all. John's trying to do that. Kevin is doing the best he can but he's kind of all over the place.

"Normally the copilot is very quiet. But I start interjecting things mainly to calm John down, like, 'OK, you can do this thing.' I am probably using relatively colorful terms. I say, 'Hey, let's toss the training bullshit out the window. Do whatever you have to do. If you have to put the basket in the water and drag it to him, do it.'

"I imagine I'm frustrating John, trying to tell him how to do his job. But my adrenaline is pumping just slightly less than his. He eventually gets the basket in the water and Joe grabs it and puts the survivor in and John hauls it up. The survivor is so stiff that he's put another death grip on the basket. In addition, his limbs are cold and his knees bent in the basket. John's mike is still hot and he's reporting this: 'We can't get him out of the basket. . . .' I keep interjecting things I hope are helpful: 'Forget the basket. Let's get Joe back. Just send down the hook. . . .'" While the hook is going down I see in the searchlight bounding around up front what Kevin had seen—a spot of light and a guy in the water."

Those last minutes down in the water that may have looked from above as if Rock had just "put the survivor in" the basket had a very different look from the surface, as Rock recalls. "The wind blew the tops off the waves and into our faces. It was difficult for me to breathe even with my mask and snorkel. It was like getting thrown into the rinse cycle of a washing machine. As the helo moved in, John put the basket in the water ten feet from the crest of a large wave. I turned with the man and swam for it. I had almost reached the basket when the wave fell and the basket swung wildly away from me. After several attempts, and primarily John's expert hoist control, I was able to get the man into the basket. As I signaled for John to raise the basket, a gust of wind caught the helo and blew it away from us. I felt the basket leave the water. I covered the man with my body for fear he would fall out. We were brought to an abrupt halt as a large wave crashed into us. Somehow, the helo crew managed to get the man on board. Next John lowered me the rescue hook and I went up on my harness. Once on board the 1472, Randy and I fought to pry the survivor out of the basket. John and Commander Marshall had spotted a second survivor. John asked me if I was OK and could I go down again. I remember saying, 'Just one more, right?' I was pretty tired, but I figured nothing could be as bad as the first one. I was wrong."

Going down again, Rock was too focused on the victim below to be aware of the problem that would turn this attempt into a kind of nightmare. Not so the pilots. The *Eagle* was blowing down on them, and she was lying crosswind. "I realize I'm starting to see the whites of the eyes of a guy on the *Eagle*," Ratte says. "The pilothouse of a 400-foot ship is as high as we are. It is starting to fill the window. I get on the radio and start polite for the first couple of calls to the *Eagle:* 'You've got to get out of the way. . . .' Down in the water, Rock soon becomes conscious of the *Eagle*'s looming presence. He had found a man who was naked except for his life jacket. The man was floating face down with a bad head wound and showing no signs of life. It was easier to get him into the basket, but Rock had the strange feeling that he was working on stage. He could see people hanging over the rails of *Eagle* and watching him in the glare of the Nitesun. When the basket had gone up and Rock was waiting for his own hoist, he noticed that the helicopter was bobbing and jerking and then backing away. He knew that they had reached the critical point in hover time. Could they be leaving him there for *Eagle* to retrieve? It wouldn't be like them. He trusted everyone up there in CG 1472. They were friends, a team. But he knew that the mission came first, and he couldn't know what they might be facing in the cockpit. It was a very bad time for a very tired man.

Marshall was fighting severe downdrafts created by the wind swooping over the towering superstructure of the *Eagle*. "It was like the microbursts in a thunderstorm," he remembers. "When you have a high wind down, you just don't have enough power. At one time we were pulling with all the power we had and even more than we were supposed to use to stay airborne, and we were still settling into the water. I thought we were going to touch down. I was calmly—well, not so calmly—yelling at Paul, 'Get that boat out of here!' " Realizing himself what was happening, Paul was no longer polite in his transmissions to the *Eagle*: "Get the hell out. Come ahead full and get out of our way!" Suddenly there was a burst of smoke from *Eagle*'s stack and she slid off the screen of their windshield. Marshall moved back into position, and Joe Rock was fished out of the water for the last time that night.

With Rock aboard, CG 1472 squared away on course for Cape Cod, which they could reach safely this time, barring accident. It was a time of easing tension for the pilots, but not for Joe Rock. As EMT, he had to take charge of treating the men he had saved. Still breathing, the first survivor, whose identification showed that he was bosun Dario Macias-Lopez, was in hypothermic shock. Rock estimated his temperature at eighty-eight degrees. The only way to save him would be slow warming. Rock and Reed stripped him of his wet clothes and put him into a thermal recovery capsule—a sheepskin-lined sleeping bag. The heat of another body would have to be added to the bag, and Reed volunteered to undress to his skivvies and climb in with Macias-Lopez. Rock then turned his attention to the second, unidentifiable man, though he knew it would be futile. Blood from his head wound formed a pool where he had been stretched out in the front of the helo's cargo cabin, and he had no pulse or breathing. Not wanting Dario to see the sight of a dead comrade if he regained consciousness, Rock covered the body with a blanket, and then he moved the bag with Marcia-Lopez and Reed to the rear of the plane. There were just two more things Rock could do for Macias-Lopez. One was to help him keep a grip on consciousness through the last sense known to go—hearing. Rock urged Reed to sing and talk to Macias-Lopez constantly. After he got on the intercom and told Commander Marshall that there wasn't a minute to waste in getting Macias-Lopez to a hospital, Rock did the only other thing within his power—he prayed.

Trusting Rock's judgment, Marshall decided to land at Falmouth Hospital. It could save half an hour of ambulance time. After all they had been through, it would have been unthinkable to anyone aboard CG 1472 not to take this last small risk to make sure their mission ended in the saving of a life. But, as in almost every other instance that night, the risk turned out to be greater than anticipated. Approaching Falmouth, they discovered that their searchlights—the Nitesun and built-in nose light—were no longer working. They had only their hover lights to illuminate the pad by the hospital. But Marshall stuck with his decision.

"A thing like that throws a little fear into you," he said. "I had been there before and knew that there weren't any power lines, but there was some construction going on, and I didn't know whether there were cranes or what they might have put up. But the winds were down to thirty-five, so it wasn't so bouncy. We had plenty of power, so I was confident if we saw something we could get out of it. Still, we took special care because we had been flying for almost twelve hours and were all very tired. You aren't as picky with yourself when you're tired; you start accepting things that shouldn't happen. I told the crew that if anybody saw anything he didn't like we would just pull out."

Nobody saw anything. The log tells it all: "290605—CG 1472 ON DECK FALMOUTH HOSPITAL TRANSFERRING SURVIVORS." Dario Macias-Lopez had a temperature of ninety-four degrees on admission to the hospital; his will to live was clearly pulling him through. But that would not have been enough without the good fortune of landing in what did turn out to be the Gulf Stream and without the determination of the men of CG 1472. The other man they found was pronounced dead on arrival. Macias-Lopez and the two men pulled aboard *Eagle* were the only survivors out of *Lloyd Bermuda*'s eleven-man crew.

It says a great deal about the high value that civilized men put on human life that nobody, least of all the men of CG 1472, ever questioned the risks, costs and labors involved. Admiral Paul A. Yost, commandant of the Coast Guard, pinned the Distinguished Flying Cross on Marshall and Rock and the Air Medal on Ratte, Reed and Salmi. Although most rescues end for the Coast Guard with the delivery of half-dead survivors to some hospital, this one had a warmer conclusion when Ratte, Reed and Rock visited a recovering Dario Macias-Lopez. He had no memory of details after cutting himself loose from the sinking ship, and he didn't recognize the strangers ushered into his room until they spoke. When he heard the sound of Reed's voice—the voice that had talked and sung him to safety—Macias-Lopez rushed to Reed and expressed the thanks he couldn't speak in English with a tight Latin embrace.

Sources

Introduction

—*The Oxford History of the American People*, by Samuel Eliot Morison, Oxford University Press, New York, 1965.

—*Early History of the United States Revenue Marine Service* 1789-1849, by Horatio Davis Smith, Naval Historical Foundation, 1932.

—*Stamford Advocate*, May 24, 1990.

—Press releases for Nomination for Secretary's "Way-To-Go" Award from office of Vice Admiral Clyde T. Lusk, Jr., vice commandant, U.S. Coast Guard.

—Press release and citation for Medal of Honor, Douglas Munro, Naval Historical Center, Department of the Navy.

—Interview with Seaman Brandon Spies, USCG.

—*Coast Guard: 200 Years of Service*, Overview, 1989–1990.

Chapter One

—*Our Naval War With France*, by Gardner W. Allen, Archon Books, 1967.

—*George Washington's Coast Guard*, by Irving H. King, Naval Institute Press, 1978.

—*The Coast Guard Under Sail*, The U.S. Revenue Cutter Service, 1789-1865, by Irving H. King, Naval Institute Press, 1989.

—Naval Documents related to the Quasi-war between the United States and France, prepared by the Office of Naval Records and Library Navy Department, under the supervision of Captain Dudley W. Knox, U.S. Navy (ret.), 1936.

—*The Oxford History of the American People*, by Samuel Eliot Morison, Oxford University Press, New York, 1965.

Chapter Two

—Interviews with Lieutenant Commander William Peterson, USCG; Lieutenant Junior Grade William L. Harper, USCG; Aviation Survivalman Third Class Kelly Mogk, USCG.

—Press releases, Thirteenth Coast Guard District, Seattle, Washington.

—*Commandant's Bulletin*, U.S. Coast Guard.

Chapter Three

—*Guardians of the Sea, History of the United States Coast Guard, 1915 to the Present,* by Robert Erwin Johnson, Naval Institute Press, 1987.

—*Always Ready, The Story of the United States Coast Guard,* by Kensil Bell, Dodd, Mead & Company, New York, 1944.

—*Patrol Board 999,* by Harold Waters and Aubrey Wisberg, Chilton Company, Philadelphia-New York, 1959.

—*Rum Row,* by Robert Carse, Rinehart & Company, Inc., New York, 1959.

—*Encounter With the Gulf Stream Pirate,* by Frank Lehman, 1979, files of Public Affairs Office, U.S. Coast Guard, Washington.

—*Rum War, The U.S. Coast Guard and Prohibition,* by Donald L. Canney, Coast Guard Bicentennial Series.

—"The Day the Coast Guard Hanged a Man," *Coastline,* February, 1985.

Chapter Four

—*The Times-Picayune,* New Orleans, October 5, 1989; April 14, 1990.

—Interviews with Lieutenant Mark Sikorski, USCG; MK2 Octavio Garza, USCG; BM1 Jack Musgrave, USCG; Lieutenant Junior Grade Tom Meyers, USCG.

—Press release USCG *Vashon,* December 1989.

—*Mobile Press Register,* Mobile, Alabama, October 7, 1989.

Chapter Five

—Interview with Captain Eric J. Williams, III, USCG; Chief Warrant Officer Fourth Class Al Beal, USCG; Boatswains Mate First Class Paul Krug, USCG; Lieutenant King Klosson, USCG.

—*The New York Times,* June 25, 26, 1989.

—"Close Call! The Narragansett Bay Oil Spill," by Carole Jaworski, *Nor'easter,* Fall 1989.

Chapter Six

—*The New York Times,* June 13, 28, 29, 30, July 16, November 10, 1942; August 20, 1943.

—*They Came to Kill,* by Eugene Rachlis, Random House, New York, 1961.

—*None More Courageous,* by Stewart H. Holbrook, The Macmillan Company, New York, 1942.

—*Eight Spies Against America,* by George J. Dasch, Robert M. McBride Company, New York, 1959.

—*Hitler's Spies and Saboteurs,* by Charles Wighton and Gunter Peis, Henry Holt and Company, New York, 1958.

Chapter Seven

—*Historically Famous Lighthouses,* CG-232, U.S. Coast Guard.
—Letters from collector of customs, Key West, Florida, to Treasury Department, Washington, 1836, National Archives.
—*Always Ready, The Story of the United States Coast Guard,* by Kensil Bell, Dodd, Mead & Company, New York, 1944.
—*Keepers of the Lights,* by Hans Christian Adamson, Greenberg: Publisher, New York 1955.

Chapter Eight

—*The New York Times,* October 5, 7, 1980.
—Interviews with Captain Tom Morgan, USCG; Commander Joel Thuma, USCG.
—"*Prinsendam* Fire," by Josh Eppinger, *Popular Mechanics,* April 1981.
—"Last Cruise of the *Prinsendam,*" by Joseph Blank, *Reader's Digest,* November 1983.

Chapter Nine

—*The Light Houses of New England,* by Edward Rowe Snow, Dodd, Mead, & Company, New York, 1945, 1973.
—*Harper's Weekly,* July 31, 1869.
—"Ida Lewis, Keeper of Lime Rock Lighthouse and the Rescue of Two Men on 4 February 1881," by Dennis L. Noble, *Historical Paintings Project,* U.S. Coast Guard.
—*The Coast Guard Along the North Atlantic Coast,* by Dr. Dennis Noble and PA3 Kenneth Arbogast, a Bicentennial publication by the *Commandant's Bulletin,* December 1988.
—"Fifty Years at Lime Rock," *Cobblestone,* June 1981.
—Documents on file in the library, Newport Historical Society, Newport, Rhode Island.

Chapter Ten

—"The Rescue of the Dorchester Survivors by the USCG *Escanaba,*" by Donald L. Canney, *Historical Paintings Project,* U.S. Coast Guard.
—"Legend of the Four Chaplains," by Lawrence Elliott, *The Reader's Digest,* June 1989.
—Report on activities of the USCG *Escanaba,* prepared by Statistical Division, U.S. Coast Guard, 1943.
—Report of Lieutenant Junior Grade William H. Arpaia, USNR, to vice chief of naval operations on "U.S.A.T.—Sinking of," dated March 9, 1943.
—Ship's Logbook, U.S. Coast Guard Cutter *Escanaba,* February 1943.
—"Summary of Statements by Survivors SS *Dorchester,* Passenger-Cargo Ves-

sel, 5654 G.T., Merchants-Miner Transportation Co., operated by AGWI Lines, Inc., Chartered to Army Transport Service," memorandum for file, Navy Department, Office of the Chief of Naval Operations, March 1, 1943.
—*The New York Times,* December 3, 20, 21, 25, 1944.

Chapter Eleven

—*The New York Times,* October 15, 16, 17, 19, 20, 1947.
—Interview with C.S. "Mike" Hall, Captain, USCG, ret.
—*"Bermuda Sky Queen* Rescue, 14–15 October 1947," by Robert Erwin Johnson, *Historical Paintings Project,* U.S. Coast Guard.
—"The Rescue on Station Charlie," by Captain Paul B. Cronk, *Atlantic Monthly,* September 1950.
—*Guardians of the Seas, History of the United States Coast Guard, 1915 to Present,* by Robert Erwin Johnson, Naval Institute Press, 1987.

Chapter Twelve

—Interviews with Lieutenant Commander Douglas B. Perkins, USCG: Lieutenant Junior Grade Mark Ogle, USCG; Lieutenant G. W. Dupree, USCG; Lieutenant Gary Alexander, USCG; Commander Ken Venuto, USCG; Captain Paul M. Blayney, USCG; Lieutenant Junior Grade Glen Gebele, USCG; Lieutenant Mark Rutherford, USCG; Peter Grant, free-lance photographer; Lieutenant Bryon Ing, USCG; MKl Mark Ruble, USCG; Seaman Brandon Spies, USCG; BM2 David Lukasik, USCG; BM1 Mike Hudson, USCG.
—*Newsweek,* Oct. 2, 1989.
—*Time,* Oct. 2, 1989.
—*Coastline,* Seventh Coast Guard District, October 1989.
—Letter from Albert Morris of Portland, Oregon, to Congressman Enrique de la Garza.
—*Sitrep One Hurricane Relief/Civil Unrest Frederiksted St. Croix,* USCG *Nantucket* to USCG *Bear.*
—USCG *Vashon* Patrol Report 09-89, 16–29 September 1989.

Chapter Thirteen

—*A History of Coast Guard Aviation* by Dr. Robert L. Scheina, *Commandant's Bulletin* 21-86, October 10.
—"The First Transatlantic Flight," by Capt. Frank A. Erickson, Ret., '31, *The Bulletin,* U.S. Coast Guard Academy Alumni Association, May/June 1977.
—*The Wave of Long Island,* May, 1986.
—"The Flight Across the Atlantic," Department of Education, Curtiss Aeroplane and Motor Corporation, New York, 1919.
—Interview with Paul Johnson, curator of museum, U.S. Coast Guard Academy.
—*Air Search and Rescue: 63 Years of Aerial Lifesaving, A Pictorial History 1915–1978,* Department of Transportation, U.S. Coast Guard.

Chapter Fourteen

—*The New York Times,* December 29, 30, 1988.

—"Heroes," by J.A. Fishman, *Motor Boat & Sailing,* March 1989.

—Documents relative to the *Lloyd Bermuda* sinking from the Marine Safety Office, U.S. Coast Guard, Providence, Rhode Island.

—*The Cape Cod Times,* December 30, 1988; January 1, 1989.

—Unpublished manuscript by Joe Rock, ASM2, U.S. Coast Guard.

—Interviews with Lieutenant Commander Kevin Marshall, USCG; Lieutenant Junior Grade Paul Ratte, USCG; ASM2 Joe Rock, USCG.

—*Commandant's Bulletin,* U.S. Coast Guard, 1989.

Index

259